RETURN TO ME

Books by Lynn Austin

All She Ever Wanted

All Things New

Eve's Daughters

Hidden Places

Pilgrimage

A Proper Pursuit

Though Waters Roar

Until We Reach Home

While We're Far Apart

Wings of Refuge

A Woman's Place

Wonderland Creek

Refiners Fire

Candle in the Darkness

Fire by Night

A Light to My Path

Chronicles of the Kings

Gods & Kings

Song of Redemption

The Strength of His Hand

Faith of My Fathers

Among the Gods

The Restoration Chronicles

Return to Me

The Restoration Chronicles • Book I

RETURN TO ME

LYNN AUSTIN

BethanyHouse
a division of Baker Publishing Group
Minneapolis, Minnesota

Published by Bethany House Publishers
11400 Hampshire Avenue South
Bloomington, Minnesota 55438
www.bethanyhouse.com

Bethany House Publishers is a division of
Baker Publishing Group, Grand Rapids, Michigan

Printed in the United States of America

Library of Congress Cataloging-in-Publication Data
Austin, Lynn, N.
Return to me / Lynn Austin.
p. cm. — (The Restoration Chronicles; 1)
Summary: "After years in exile, Iddo and his grandson Zechariah follow God's leading home to Jerusalem, where they struggle to rebuild their lives and God's temple—bringing to life the biblical books of Ezra and Nehemiah"—Provided by publisher.
ISBN 978-0-7642-1150-8 (cloth : alk. paper)
ISBN 978-0-7642-0898-0 (pbk.)
1. Bible. Old Testament—Fiction. 2. Exile—Fiction. 3. Obedience—Fiction. 4. Jerusalem—Fiction. 5. Babylon (Extinct city)—Fiction. I. Title.
PS3551.U839 R48 2013
813'.54—dc23 2013023290

Cover design by Jennifer Parker
Photography by Mike Habermann Photography, LLC

13 14 15 16 17 18 19 7 6 5 4 3 2 1

To my husband, Ken

and to my children:

Joshua, Vanessa, Benjamin, Maya, and Snir

"Return to me," declares the Lord Almighty,

"and I will return to you."

Zechariah 1:3

October 539 BC

A boom of thunder woke Daniel from a deep sleep. He lay in the darkness, disoriented, waiting for a flash of lightning to illuminate his room. The thunder rumbled again—but it wasn't thunder, it was pounding. Who would pound on his door in the middle of the night?

"Coming," he called as the noise continued. "I'm coming." He climbed from bed, his movements slow at age eighty-two, and wrapped his outer robe around his shoulders like a blanket. The stone floor felt cold beneath his bare feet as he groped his way in the dark. He opened the door to a blaze of blinding torchlight. "Yes? Who is it?" he asked, shielding his eyes.

"You're needed at the palace, my lord."

Daniel squinted at the bright light. Two men in blood-red tunics. The king's servants. He wondered if he was still dreaming. On another night years ago, King Nebuchadnezzar had also sent servants to bring him to the palace in the dark of night. The king had suffered a nightmare and would have executed Daniel and all the other wise men if the Almighty One hadn't shown Daniel the dream and its meaning. He had been a much younger man, back then. Nebuchadnezzar's grandson summoned him now.

Daniel rubbed his eyes, struggling to shake off his sleepiness. "The palace? Why? What's wrong?"

"King Belshazzar and the queen mother have called for you. They're waiting at the royal palace, my lord." The urgency in the servant's tone convinced Daniel this was no dream.

"Very well. I'll need a moment."

"Please hurry, my lord."

It was useless to ask why he was being summoned. The servants likely didn't know the reason, and besides, a summons from the palace couldn't be ignored. Daniel smoothed his sleep-rumpled hair, changed into his robes, and fastened his sandals as quickly as his age allowed. The king's servants walked briskly as they led him through the maze of streets and courtyards and hallways to the palace. Daniel had grown into manhood here in Babylon. He had served three generations of pagan Babylonian kings. Nothing these monarchs did should have surprised him, but his stomach churned with dread just the same.

The journey ended at the palace banquet hall. When the towering doors swung open, Daniel saw King Belshazzar and hundreds of guests gathered for one of the young king's lavish parties. The remains of the extravagant meal lay abandoned on all of the tables along with empty wine vessels and pitchers of strong drink. The party seemed to have halted in mid-motion as if frozen in time. Instead of drunken laughter and merriment, the guests spoke in hushed voices that rustled through the room like dead leaves. As Daniel entered, even the whispering stopped. The air stank of wine and sweat—and fear.

He glanced around as the servants urged him forward. The court musicians stood like statues, their instruments silent in their limp hands. He could tell by the guests' bleary eyes and sprawling postures that many of them were drunk, yet their expressions were unusually somber. Everyone seemed shaken, as if the earth had quaked, halting the revelry in mid-stride. Daniel saw them watching as he walked forward between the tables, approaching the royal dais where King Belshazzar and the queen mother awaited him. Gold and silver serving dishes glittered in the torchlight on the head table, and when Daniel recognized the designs on some of them he nearly lost his balance. These treasures had come from the temple, God's holy temple in Jerusalem. Like the Jewish people themselves, these sacred vessels had been torn from their rightful places to be demeaned and abused by pagan people who worshipped idols. The blasphemy of their use at the king's orgy shocked him. *"How long, O, Lord? Will you forget me forever? . . . How long will my enemy triumph over me?"*

Royal magi and enchanters in dark robes hovered around the king like a flock of crows, watching Daniel approach. Again, he remembered the night that King Nebuchadnezzar had called for all of his wise men and wondered if he was Belshazzar's last resort. Typically, these Babylonian rulers sought Daniel's advice only in a crisis. Otherwise, they preferred that he stay far away and not remind them of the Sovereign God of Israel and His laws.

Daniel halted in front of the king but didn't bow down. Belshazzar appeared ill, his face a sickly gray. His voice quavered when he spoke. "A-are you Daniel, one of the exiles my forefathers brought from Judah?"

"I am."

"I'm told that the spirit of the gods is in you." He glanced at the queen mother as if for confirmation. "They say that you have insight, intelligence, and outstanding wisdom."

Daniel didn't reply. Flattery from a man who displayed no common sense or self-control, much less reverence for God, meant nothing to him.

"I want you to look at this." The king pointed to the wall behind him. Daniel took another step closer and saw markings on it, as if streaks of light shone down on the wall from a source high above. But there was no window, no source of light. Daniel stepped onto the dais and skirted around the king's banquet table as he tried to discern what the markings were. They appeared to be letters and words, writing of some sort.

"I summoned my wise men and enchanters," Belshazzar said, gesturing to the men. "I asked them to read this writing and tell me what it meant, but they couldn't do it."

Daniel silently prayed for wisdom as he examined the wall up close, running his fingers over the rough plaster. "Where did these markings come from, Your Majesty? Who wrote them?"

When the king didn't reply, Daniel turned around to ask him again and saw terror in Belshazzar's eyes. He couldn't seem to speak. One of the men seated beside him said, "The fingers of a human hand appeared and wrote on the plaster of the wall."

Belshazzar nodded, swallowing, and finally found his voice. "It-it's true. I sat right here and watched as a . . . a hand . . . out of nowhere . . . wrote the words that you see."

Had it been a hallucination, the result of too much wine? A lifetime of strong drink led men to delirium. Daniel had heard of men who preferred death to the horrid beasts of their drunken imaginations. But everyone in the banquet hall stared at the writing, too. It couldn't be a mass hallucination. Besides, Daniel saw the writing, as well.

He turned to study the wall, reading the words out loud: "*Mene, mene, tekel, parsin.*" They were three weights, three units of money. Again, he silently asked the Almighty One to show him the meaning.

"Now, I have heard," the king began, his voice shrill with fright. He cleared his throat to start again. "I've heard that you're able to give interpretations and solve difficult problems. If you can read this writing and tell me . . . tell us . . . what it means, you'll be clothed in purple and . . . and have a gold chain placed around your neck . . . and I'll make you the third highest ruler in the kingdom."

The third highest ruler. An honor indeed. Babylon's reigning monarch, King Nabonidas, had gone away for the winter months, leaving his son Belshazzar in charge as second-in-command. But Daniel wanted no part in this corrupt kingdom. He simply wanted to return home to his bed.

It was becoming very clear to him what the writing on the wall meant. He had spent more than sixty-five years as a captive in this nation and had served on the king's advisory council most of that time. But for the past few years, he had watched the Babylonian empire slowly disintegrate before his eyes. King Nebuchadnezzar's dream had foretold that this day would come and Babylon would fall. The statue's golden head would be replaced by a chest and arms of silver. Daniel's own dream of four great beasts had confirmed that the Babylonian kingdom would not last. But the demise had come much sooner than Daniel had imagined. He wondered what Babylon's downfall would mean for him and his fellow Jews, languishing in exile.

"Well? Can you tell us what the writing means?" the king asked.

"You may keep your gifts for yourself and give your rewards to someone else—"

"But I demand to know the meaning of the writing! How dare you refuse me?"

"Let me finish," Daniel said, holding up his hand. "While I don't want or need your rewards, nevertheless I will read the writing and tell you what it means." He waited until the murmuring stopped and a hush fell over the room. He would speak for God, declaring the truth, and whatever happened after that . . . his life was in God's hands, as it always had been.

"O king, the Most High God gave your forefather Nebuchadnezzar sovereignty and greatness and splendor. All nations and men of every language dreaded and feared him. Those who the king wanted to put to death, he put to death. Those he wanted to spare, he spared; those he wanted to promote he promoted. But when his heart became arrogant and hardened with pride, God deposed him from his royal throne and stripped him of his glory. He was driven away from people and given the mind of an animal. He ate grass like cattle and his body was drenched with the dew of heaven until he acknowledged that the Most High God is sovereign over the kingdoms of men."

Belshazzar gestured impatiently. "I've heard my grandfather's story. Get on with it. I want to know about the writing."

Daniel drew a breath, exhaling slowly to steady himself as he prepared to confront the king with God's judgment. "But you his heir, O Belshazzar, have not humbled yourself, though you admit that you knew about Nebuchadnezzar. Instead, you've set yourself up against the Lord of heaven. These are God's holy vessels," he said, gesturing to the banquet table. "They were consecrated for use in His temple, yet you brought them here so that you and your nobles, your wives and your concubines, could drink wine from them. You praise gods of silver and gold, which cannot see or hear or understand. But you don't honor the God who holds your life in His hand. Therefore, God has sent the hand that wrote that inscription."

The young king stared at him, waiting. Daniel could see that even after this dramatic reminder, Belshazzar's heart overflowed with fear, not repentance.

"This is what these words mean," Daniel said, his voice gathering strength. "*Mene*: God has numbered the days of your reign and brought it to an end."

Murmurs chased around the room. The drunken king lowered his head to his chest for just a moment, then lifted his chin again, defiant.

"*Tekel*," Daniel continued. "You have been weighed on the scales and found wanting." The king's wise men seemed appalled that Daniel would speak so bluntly. He didn't care. "*Peres*: Your kingdom is divided and given to the Medes and Persians."

Loud voices reverberated all over the room. Nervous laughter. Outrage. Daniel turned away from the writing, preparing to leave.

"Wait!" the king commanded.

Daniel halted. What now? He tried to draw a deep breath but couldn't.

"Clothe him in purple. Place my gold chain around his neck. Tomorrow Daniel shall sit at my right hand, the third highest ruler."

Daniel's shoulders sagged in relief. He shook his head in disgust. He didn't want the honor, but Belshazzar seemed determined to follow through on his promise. It took Daniel thirty minutes to free himself from the ongoing drama and return to his bedroom. The sun still hadn't risen, but Daniel thought he heard sounds of turmoil in the city streets below the palace. Had word of the startling events at the banquet hall spread so quickly?

Daniel didn't concern himself with such things. God had made it clear tonight that the kingdom of Babylon was finished, Belshazzar and his father, Nabonidas, were doomed. What their downfall would mean for Daniel's own life or for his people, he couldn't guess. Ever since the Babylonians had taken him captive in Jerusalem as a young man, his life had been in God's hands—the same hand that had written on the wall tonight. And so it would always be. No matter what came next, Daniel rested safely in the grip of his Sovereign God.

Part I

Babylon

By the rivers of Babylon we sat and wept
when we remembered Zion. . . .
If I forget you, O Jerusalem,
may my right hand forget its skill.
May my tongue cling to the roof of my mouth
if I do not remember you,
if I do not consider Jerusalem my highest joy.

Psalm 137:1, 5–6

CHAPTER 1

Iddo awoke from the dream, gasping. The nightmare had nearly devoured him. He heard his wife's soothing voice, felt her hand resting on his chest as if trying to calm his pounding heart. "Shh . . . It was just a dream, Iddo. Just a dream . . ."

But it wasn't a dream, at least not the kind that other people had when they slept, seeing visions that made no sense in the light of day. In Iddo's dreams he relived memories, powerful memories, as real as on the day he'd lived them as a child. The images and sounds and horrors had imprinted on his soul the way a stylus presses into soft clay. The kiln of suffering had hardened them, and they could never be erased.

He drew a shaky breath, wiping his hand across his face, scrubbing tears from his eyes. "I'm sorry, Dinah," he whispered. "I'm sorry . . ."

"Are you all right?" she asked. "I'll make you something warm to drink."

He rested his hand on her arm, stopping her. "No, stay in bed. Why should we both be awake?" Iddo rose from their mat, groping in the dark for his robe. He wouldn't be able to sleep now.

During the daytime he could control the images that circled the edges of his consciousness like jackals by looking up at the cloud-swept sky or studying the perfection of his infant grandson's tiny fingers. But at night, when darkness hid the Creator's beauty, the images and sounds closed in on Iddo, scratching and clawing, refusing to be silenced. Once they pounced they would strip him of everything he had accomplished, ripping at the man he now was, reducing him to the ten-year-old child he had been when Jerusalem fell—helpless, terrified, naked, and shivering before his enemies. Forty-seven years had passed since he'd lived the real nightmare, and Iddo had spent those years here in Babylon. He had a wife, children, grandchildren—all born here. Yet the atrocities he'd seen in Jerusalem remained as vivid as the world he saw every morning. The nightmare never faded, never blurred.

He waited for his heart to slow, his breathing to ease, then shuffled to the door, opening and closing it soundlessly so he wouldn't disturb his household. Outside in his dark courtyard, he traced the familiar silhouette of the mud brick houses in his neighborhood, the spiky date palms growing along the nearby canal. He lifted his chin to watch stars disappear, then reappear behind the playful night clouds. "'When I consider your heavens,'" he whispered, "'the work of your fingers, the moon and the stars, which you have set in place, what is man that you are mindful of him?'" The psalms of King David were another weapon he used to keep the jackals of fear away.

The terror that had destroyed Jerusalem was the Almighty One's punishment. All of the prophets had said so. God no longer dwelled with His people because they'd been unfaithful to Him. His temple was destroyed, His people scattered among the nations, living among pagan gods. Iddo's only hope, his family's only hope, lay in studying God's Law, filling his heart and mind with the Torah, obeying every word of it every day of his life. If he sought the God of his fathers with all his strength, maybe the Holy One would show mercy and return to His people again.

Iddo shivered in the cool fall air, waiting for the nighttime peace to still his soul. But instead of the deep silence that he craved, he heard remnants of sounds from his nightmare: a low rumble like hundreds of marching feet, faraway screams and cries—or were they only the cries of birds? Iddo had spent many nights awake, but the sounds from his dreams had never lingered this way. Was he imagining things? He climbed the outdoor steps to his flat rooftop and looked out at the city. Lights danced in the distance like summer lightning—only it couldn't be lightning. The star-filled sky stretched from horizon to horizon in the flat landscape, the night clouds mere wisps.

A sudden movement in the street below caught his attention, and he squinted down at the shadows. His neighbor, Mattaniah, stood with his hands on his hips gazing toward the center of Babylon. Beside him stood another neighbor, Joel, who was a descendant of temple priests like Iddo. Could they hear the sounds, too?

Iddo hurried downstairs and out through the courtyard gate to the street. The two men turned at the sound of Iddo's footsteps. "Did the noise wake you, too?" Mattaniah asked.

"What is it? What's going on?"

"We don't know," Joel said. "The Babylonians are holding a festival of some sort for one of their pagan gods tonight, but my son Reuben thought it sounded more like soldiers marching."

"Yes . . . I thought so, too," Iddo said.

"We were wondering if the armies of the Medes and Persians had attacked the city," Mattaniah said.

Joel shook his head. "They'll never succeed. Babylon's gates are heavily fortified and the city walls are twenty feet thick. They're impregnable!" But Iddo remembered Jerusalem's toppled walls and shuddered. "My son went to have a look," Joel continued. "We're waiting for him to come back."

Iddo stood with his neighbors, listening to the distant sounds, talking quietly as they waited for Reuben to return. By the time the young man finally jogged home, flushed and breathless, an arc of pink light brightened the eastern horizon. "You won't believe it, Abba! I walked all the way to the plaza by the Ishtar Gate, and the streets are filled with soldiers all around the southern palace. Thousands of them!"

"Babylonian soldiers?" Iddo asked.

"No, sir. They weren't like any Babylonian soldiers I've ever seen."

"Then it is an invasion!" Mattaniah said.

"It can't be. How would the enemy get past our walls?" Joel asked.

"I think I know how," Reuben said. "I followed the river on the way home and the water was only this deep . . ." He gestured to the middle of his thigh. "The soldiers could have waded into the city beneath the walls, using the riverbed for a highway—like that story in the Torah when the waters parted for our people, remember?"

An invasion. Iddo turned without a word and hurried back to his walled courtyard, closing the wooden gate behind him, leaning against it. He must be dreaming. He hadn't awakened from his nightmare after all. Any moment now Dinah would shake him, and he would wake up. He closed his eyes as he slowly drew a breath, then opened them again. He was still in his courtyard, still aware of the distant rumble of marching feet.

If this wasn't a dream, then for the second time in Iddo's life enemy soldiers had invaded the city where he lived. His nightmare had become a reality once again. He took a few stumbling steps toward the house, stopped, and turned in a useless circle, like an animal trapped in a pit. He had to flee, had to escape with his wife, his family. Maybe it wasn't too late. Maybe they could wade out of the city and hide in the marshes beyond the walls. Maybe the Almighty One had parted the waters just for them, so they could escape. He took two steps forward and stopped again.

The Almighty One.

Would He help them? Iddo needed to pray, to ask for His wisdom and protection before fleeing. He climbed the stairs to the rooftop—barely able to manage them on trembling legs—and fell prostrate, facing west toward Jerusalem. "Blessed art thou, O Lord our God, King of the Universe—" He stopped. His father and grandfather had lain prostrate in the temple courtyard in Jerusalem with all the other priests, praying day and night for help and protection and salvation. Their prayers had gone unanswered.

"Blessed art thou, O Lord our God . . ." Iddo began again. Maybe something would be different this time, and the Almighty would hear His people's pleas for mercy. Iddo and the others had obeyed everything the prophets said: *"Marry and have sons and daughters. Seek the peace and prosperity of the city to which I have carried you into exile."* Iddo had done that. He and the other priests had not only tried to obey every letter of the Law, but they had constructed a fence of protective laws around the Torah to make sure no one even came close to breaking one of God's commandments. They honored the Sabbath day as best they could, even when their captors denied them a day of rest. They gathered for prayer three times a day as the three Patriarchs had done, and—

Iddo lifted his head. Why was he praying all alone? The other men must be awake by now. He would go to morning prayers, gather with the others, and decide together what to do. His household was stirring when he went downstairs to fetch his prayer shawl and phylacteries. Dinah knelt in front of the hearth with a fistful of straw, blowing on the coals to start the fire. His daughter, Rachel—lovely, vulnerable Rachel—hummed as she folded the bedding. Iddo heard murmuring in the other rooms, as well, the rooms he had added onto his house for his sons Berekiah and Hoshea and their wives and families. His newest grandson was crying to be fed, and his helpless wail sent shivers through Iddo as he remembered the children in Jerusalem who had been too hungry to cry. Would it be the same in this invasion? The suffering, the starvation?

"I'm going to morning prayers," he told Dinah.

She looked up at him in surprise. "So early? You never go this early."

"I need to talk with the others. Something has happened, and I'm not sure—"

"What do you mean? What happened?" She rose to her feet, studying him with dark, worried eyes. Her long hair still hung loose and uncovered, and Iddo resisted the urge to gather the soft weight of her curls in his hands. Not a single strand of silver marred Dinah's dark hair, while his own hair and beard had turned completely white ten years ago, when he was still in his forties. "Are you all right, Iddo?" she asked.

He looked away. "Joel's son came home this morning with . . . with some news. I need to talk with the others to understand what it means."

"What news?"

He couldn't say it out loud, couldn't speak of an enemy invasion. "Just make sure you and the other women stay here. The children, too. Don't let anyone leave our courtyard until I come back. Don't go to the marketplace or the well or the ovens—"

"Iddo, you're scaring me!"

"Don't worry," he told her. Useless words. If what Reuben said was true, they had every reason to worry. He turned to go, hesitating in the doorway for just a moment, wondering if he should ask his sons to come with him. But no, Berekiah and Hoshea rarely went to morning prayers—why should today be any different? "I won't be long," he told Dinah. He had no idea if it was true.

The *Beit Knesset*, or house of assembly, was nearly full when Iddo arrived. It didn't take long to learn that the rumor was true: Foreign soldiers had invaded Babylon. One of Israel's elders—a member of The Great Assembly—had traveled all the way from the other side of the city with the news. "The Persians and Medes diverted the water of the Euphrates into a canal north of the city," he told them. "Their armies waited south of the city until the water was shallow enough to wade through and then entered beneath the walls in the middle of night."

The room went silent for the space of a heartbeat, two heartbeats. "How could this happen?" someone finally asked. "How could Babylon's king and his army be taken by surprise? Didn't they post watchmen? Didn't they see?"

"The Almighty One's hand is in this," the elder replied. "He promised that one day the Babylonian empire would fall, and last night it happened. The Babylonians were holding a festival to their idols and didn't even realize that the Medes and Persians were inside their walls until it was too late. King Belshazzar is dead. Thousands of his noblemen have been executed. Darius the Mede has taken over his kingdom."

Iddo sank onto one of the benches that lined the room's perimeter as everyone began talking at once, flooding the room with panicked questions.

"Will these Medes and Persians slaughter and pillage like the Babylonians did?"

"How can we protect our families?"

"Should we flee the city?"

"How can this be happening to us a second time?"

They were the same questions that Iddo lacked the strength to ask. The elder held up his hands for silence. "Listen . . . please . . . We're waiting to hear what Daniel the Righteous One and Judah's princes have to say, but in the meantime you should all return home. The Babylonians are staying inside their houses today, and so should we. If the city is still quiet by the time of evening prayers, we'll gather here once again. Maybe we'll have more news by then."

As Iddo prepared to leave, a single question filled his thoughts: How could he protect his family? The truth was, he couldn't. While younger men hurried home to barricade their doors, preparing to protect the people they loved with kitchen knives and clubs, men like Iddo who remembered Jerusalem knew they couldn't save themselves.

Dinah had the morning meal ready when he returned. His sons and daughters-in-law and grandchildren had gathered in the large, central room of their house. "What's going on, Abba?" Berekiah asked. "Mama said you looked worried—and that you told us all to stay inside."

The room grew quiet as Iddo explained what little he knew about the invasion. Even his young grandchildren grew very still. "What will this mean for us?" his son Hoshea asked when Iddo finished.

"No one knows. But one of the elders from the Great Assembly promised to return with more news when we gather for evening prayers. We'll find out then. In the meantime, we must all stay inside like the Babylonians are doing." He looked at Dinah, and the fear he saw in her eyes made him reach for her hand. He was her protector, the patriarch of their family, and it grieved him to know that he couldn't keep her from harm.

"Can't we go to the well for water?" his daughter asked.

"No, Rachel. Nor to the market or the ovens."

"But—what will we do?"

"We'll stay here at home. Like we do on the Sabbath."

"But what if we run out of water?"

"We can manage until sundown, Rachel." His words came out sharper than he intended, but her question brought back memories of the long siege of Jerusalem, when the city had run out of food as well as water. He remembered his mouth being as dry as sand and the unending ache in his stomach. He remembered the vermin he had eaten to try to fill it, the brackish water that hadn't quenched his thirst. "We'll spend the day praying for mercy," he said, looking at his sons. "I'll be up on the roof if you'd like to join me there." He laid down his uneaten bread and went outside to climb the stairs.

Iddo's neighborhood and the distant city looked eerily still from the rooftop. The low rumbling of marching footsteps had finally ceased, and as he knelt on the sun-warmed tiles, he couldn't decide if the silence was a good sign or a bad one. On an ordinary day, he and his sons would have begun work by now, Iddo laboring as a scribe, tallying business accounts for the Babylonians, handling their correspondence, keeping track of their shipments and trading ventures spread throughout the empire. His two sons had formed a trading partnership of their own that had made steady profits—until now. Who knew what would happen now? But Iddo and his sons, like their forefathers, were born to be priests of the one true God. If they lived in Jerusalem instead of in exile, they would be offering sacrifices at His temple, just as Iddo's father and grandfather had done, all the way back to Israel's first priest, Aaron. Iddo remembered Jerusalem's temple, remembered watching the sacrifices as a boy, inhaling the aroma of roasting meat, listening to the Levite choirs and the trumpets. Now the holy temple was gone.

But Iddo was still a priest. As soon as he'd reached adulthood here in Babylon, he had begun his apprenticeship with the older priests who had been exiled with him, learning the regulations, trusting that one day the temple would be rebuilt as the prophet Ezekiel had promised. "It's a waste of time, Abba," both of his sons had said when they'd reached the age of apprenticeship. "Why learn dead rituals for a dead religion?" Were they right? Were the faith of their father Abraham and the laws given to

Moses mere relics of the past, as dead as the corpses that had filled Jerusalem's streets?

The city of Babylon remained quiet the entire day. None of Iddo's fears of death and destruction had materialized—yet. "Come with me to the house of assembly to pray," he told his sons that evening. "I want you beside me to hear whatever news there might be. Then we can decide together what to do."

"Shouldn't we wait a few more days until the dust has settled before going out?" Berekiah asked. "We don't know what our new captors will be like and—"

"No. You should set an example of faith for your children." Iddo gestured to Berekiah's oldest boy, Zechariah, who was nearly twelve years old and Iddo's favorite. He had fetched his father's prayer shawl for him and stood with it in his hands, watching them, listening. "We need to pray. Don't you realize how serious our situation is?" Iddo asked.

"Of course I do. And I am thinking of my children. What if our new Persian overlords misinterpret our gathering and think we're planning a rebellion?"

"I'm willing to take that chance. Come on, it's time to go."

"May I come, too?" Zechariah asked. Before Iddo could reply, Dinah gripped their grandson from behind and pulled him close. "No, Zaki. Stay here. We don't know if it's safe yet."

The knowledge that he couldn't make his family feel safe fanned Iddo's anger into flames. He would fight this enemy of fear, replacing it with faith. The Holy One was with them, not their enemies. He reached for Zechariah's hand. "Yes, you may come with us. The Almighty One will keep us safe." He hoped it was true.

No one spoke as Iddo and his sons and grandson walked to the house of assembly. Hundreds of men had already jammed into the room and a tremor of excitement rippled through the gathering. "What's going on?" he asked one of his fellow priests. "What did I miss?"

"It's *Rebbe* Daniel," the priest whispered. "He's alive! He survived the invasion and came all the way from the king's palace to pray with us."

Iddo's uneasiness melted in relief. Rebbe Daniel the Righteous One was highly revered in Babylon, not only among the Jewish community, but among the Babylonians and their leaders, as well. If the Medes and Persians had let him live, then there was hope for Iddo and his fellow Jews. Iddo had only seen this legendary man twice before, and he was overjoyed to see him now, glad that his sons and grandson would hear what he had to say. The room fell quiet as the elderly man stepped onto the *bimah* to speak.

"We have nothing to fear from our new rulers," Daniel said. "Darius the Mede has asked me to serve him as I served the Babylonians."

"We're safe, then?" someone asked.

"Yes. We're all safe."

Iddo closed his eyes as the news sent murmurs of relief rippling through the hall.

"There's more," Daniel continued. "I have been praying and studying the prophets' words for some time now, and the Holy One has shown me that the years of our captivity are nearing an end. He spoke through the prophet Jeremiah, saying that we would serve the king of Babylon for seventy years, and when those seventy years were fulfilled, He would punish the Babylonians. This invasion by the Medes and Persians is the beginning of that punishment. More than three thousand of our captors have been executed, including the king and his noblemen. Our exile is coming to an end. We will soon return home to Jerusalem."

A shout went up from the gathered men. Iddo laid his hand on Zechariah's shoulder to steady himself. Home. To Jerusalem. He longed to shout praises along with the other men, but the news had stolen his breath. He was afraid to believe it, afraid to put his faith in something as impossible as returning to Jerusalem. And even if it did turn out to be true, could he bear to return to the ghost-filled ruins he had left behind as a child?

"Our captivity began when King Nebuchadnezzar brought King Jehoiakim here to Babylon in bronze shackles," Daniel continued. "I was part of that first group of exiles sixty-seven years ago. That means our seventy years of captivity are nearly over. We need to pray today and every day that the Holy One will now have mercy on us and restore us to the land He promised our father Abraham. That's what I've come here to do with all of you tonight—to pray."

"Did our new captors say that we could return?" someone asked.

"Not yet—but God promised that we would. We've endured punishment for a time, but the Holy One promised to take us back, to restore our fellowship with Him, to continue His plan to redeem all mankind through our people."

As Rebbe Daniel prepared to pray, Iddo turned with the other men to face the *Aron Ha Kodesh,* where the sacred Torah scrolls were kept. Daniel prayed aloud, lifting his hands to heaven, and the faith and conviction in the man's voice sent shivers through Iddo.

"O Lord, the great and awesome God, who keeps His covenant of love with all who love Him and obey His commands, we have sinned and done wrong. We have been wicked and have rebelled. All this disaster has come upon us, just as it was written in the Law of Moses. But now, O Lord our God, who brought your people out of Egypt with a mighty hand, hear our prayers and in keeping with your mercy, forgive us! Look with favor on your desolate sanctuary. We don't make requests of you because we are righteous, but because of your great mercy. O Lord, listen! O Lord, forgive! For your sake, O my God, don't delay because your city and your people bear your name."

The prayers went late into the evening, and by the time they ended, Iddo's legs could barely carry him home. But his worry had vanished as if lifted from his shoulders to ascend with his prayers. "See, Zechariah? The worst is over now," he said as they entered the gate to their courtyard. "But we must do as Rebbe Daniel told us and continue to pray. The Almighty has promised that if His people humble themselves and pray, then He will forgive our sin and heal our land. We will return to Jerusalem and—"

Berekiah took Iddo's arm, stopping him before he entered the house. "Abba. You don't really believe that we'll return to Jerusalem, do you?" he asked quietly.

"Of course I do! You heard what Rebbe Daniel said. The Almighty One has promised through His prophets that we will." Iddo looked down at his young grandson, eager to reassure him, but the boy's father nudged him toward the door.

"Go inside, Zechariah. Your grandfather and I will be there in a moment." Hoshea also waited behind, and Iddo saw his sons exchange worried looks.

"Listen, Abba. It's crazy to believe that we'll be allowed to return," Hoshea said. "Slaves never go free, and exiles never return to their native lands."

"The slaves went free under Moses," Iddo said. "It must have seemed just as impossible back then, too."

"And who will dare approach this new 'pharaoh' and demand that our captors set us free?" Berekiah asked.

"Maybe the Almighty One will send Rebbe Daniel to—"

"To do what? Can he perform miracles like Moses did? Will God send plagues and darkness to convince this army of conquerors to free us? You don't really believe all those tales, do you?"

Iddo couldn't reply. What had seemed so believable as he'd prayed in the house of assembly seemed absurd as he faced his sons' doubts.

"Abba, you of all people should know that prayer isn't a magic formula. The Holy One doesn't do our bidding. If He did, we would still be living in Jerusalem and offering sacrifices at the temple, not living here in Babylon."

"But the Holy One must bring us home," Iddo said. "If our people remain here, our faith will become extinct. I see it happening little by little every day. How can we survive if we stay here, surrounded by pagan people and their wicked practices? We'll become just like them."

"But our faith hasn't been extinguished, Abba, it has endured—even here."

"Then why don't you practice it? You hardly ever come with me to pray or to study the Torah."

"There's a difference between ritual and belief," Berekiah said. "Just because I don't pray three times a day with the other men doesn't mean I don't believe."

"But now that our leaders have asked us to come together and pray for our freedom, are you going to join us? Do you believe the Holy One's promises?"

When Berekiah didn't reply, Hoshea answered for both of them. "We think our leaders are wrong to raise everyone's hopes when the truth is that we'll never be allowed to return. It won't happen."

"Enough! I won't listen to another word!" Iddo yanked his arm free and climbed the stairs to the roof alone, to pray.

He knew it was his fault that his sons didn't believe. When they were boys, Iddo's own faith had been too weak to support the weight of their doubts and questions. Now they were grown men, more concerned with the world in front of their eyes than with the unseen world of faith and prayer.

But Iddo would teach his grandson Zechariah to believe. He would do everything right from now on. Maybe then the Almighty One would hear their prayers and end His people's exile.

Chapter 2

Dinah pulled the last round of bread from the fire and set it out to cool beside the others. The crusts had baked to a dark golden brown, filling the room with their mouth-watering aroma. "What else?" she asked, glancing around. "Is everything ready? Shabbat is nearly here." The sun dropped below the flat horizon much too soon on these short winter days and Dinah, her daughter, Rachel, and two daughters-in-law, Sarah and Naomi, needed to finish preparing all of the food before it did. "Are the lentils ready?" she asked.

"Yes, Mama."

"And you'll make sure everything else is prepared, Rachel? Before your father comes home from prayers?"

"I will, Mama."

"Good." She looked around again and saw a haze of smoke from the hearth lingering in the room. They usually prepared meals outside in the courtyard, but the rainy winter day had driven them inside. Dinah propped the door open to chase the last of the smoke away. When she was satisfied that everything was ready, she fetched the extra pot of food from the warming shelf beside the hearth. "I'm taking this next door to Miriam's family. I'll be right back. Close the door if it gets too cold in here."

"Why don't you invite them to eat here with us?" Naomi asked, shifting her infant son to her other shoulder.

"I did invite them, but Mattaniah said no. He thinks the noise and activity is too much for Miriam." Dinah had to admit that her household was very lively with her extended family all living and eating together. But Dinah loved every minute of her busy life. At age fifty-four, her arms were full, her heart content.

She dashed from the house and hurried next door through the spitting rain, the pot of warm food swaddled in cloths. "I brought something for your Sabbath meal," she said when Miriam's daughter, Yael, opened the door. "How is your mother feeling today?"

"The same," Yael said with a shrug. She was ten years old and had barely known her mother to be well. But in recent months, the sharp decline in Miriam's health worried Dinah. "Come in," Yael said, opening the door wider. "Mama will be happy to see you."

"I can't stay long. Shabbat begins soon. I'll just set this by the fire to keep it warm until dinnertime." But the fire on the hearth had gone out, leaving the room as cold and damp as a cave. Dinah set down the food and bent to add fuel and rekindle the embers. "Is your father home?" she asked, hearing the murmur of voices in the next room.

"Not yet. Parthia is here to read Mama's fortune. She promised to read mine, too. Want her to do yours?"

"I don't think so, Yael. I can't stay long."

"But this new seer is always right. She told Abba that he would prosper, and the very next day someone hired him to build a storehouse."

Dinah blew on the coals until the straw caught fire, uncomfortable with Yael's news. She knew that Miriam's husband had paid for a string of Babylonian healers and astrologers, seeking signs and omens, desperate for a cure for his wife. But now Yael was becoming fascinated with the hocus-pocus, as well.

When the fire was blazing, Dinah stood, wiping soot and straw from her hands on a piece of sacking. She studied Yael's bright, eager face and saw a lovely child beneath her nearly wild exterior, a girl who was certain to grow into a beautiful woman. She needed a mother's guiding hand to prepare her for womanhood, but Miriam was too ill for the task. Yael often roamed the neighborhood by herself and played near the canal with Dinah's grandson, Zechariah. What would become of her if Miriam died? "Maybe I will peek in and see how your mother is doing," Dinah said. She couldn't resist brushing Yael's dark, untamed hair from her eyes, but the girl squirmed away from her.

"I have to fetch Mama some water. You go ahead. I'll be right there."

Dinah parted the curtain that divided the two rooms and found Miriam propped up on her sleeping mat, her thin face as pale as the plastered wall behind her. A dark-robed Babylonian woman with soot-black hair and skin like burnished pottery perched on a stool in front of her. Layers of necklaces and amulets hung around the woman's neck, and she wore an elaborate golden headpiece that dangled onto her forehead. Loops of shining bracelets encircled her dark wrists, jingling and tinkling as she ground spices together in a bowl on her lap. Strewn in front of her was an array of pots, filled with odd-looking leaves and roots. A plume of incense curled from one of the pots, making Dinah cough when it caught in her throat.

"Dinah, come in," Miriam said when she saw her. "This is Parthia, my new seer." The woman glanced up at Dinah without a word before resuming her task.

"I can only stay a moment. The sun is going to set soon. I brought some stew for your Sabbath meal."

"Dear Dinah. You're always so good to us."

"How are you feeling?"

"Much better. Parthia brought good news today. She said my stars are moving into a favorable position for healing."

Dinah couldn't reply. She stepped aside as Yael crowded into the room juggling three cups of water in her small, nail-bitten hands. She gave one to Dinah, one to her mother, and kept the third for herself. Dinah took a dutiful sip, even though she hadn't asked for a drink.

"I want to repay you for all of your help, Dinah," Miriam said. "Is there something you'd like to ask the seer while she's here?"

Dinah took another sip of water, stalling for time. She longed to ask if Rebbe Daniel's promise of a return to Jerusalem would really come true. Her husband had talked of nothing else since the evening after the invasion, and she feared Iddo's heart would break if it didn't happen. But she couldn't imagine the catastrophic changes in her own life if it did occur. "Thank you . . . but no," Dinah finally replied. "Iddo got angry with me when I asked your last astrologer for signs."

"But why? What was the harm in seeking guidance to choose Rachel's wedding day? Doesn't he want your daughter to begin her married life under the most favorable stars?"

"Yes, of course, but . . . but Iddo says . . ." He had called it Babylonian nonsense and told Dinah she should pray for the Almighty One's blessing on Rachel instead of dabbling in pagan astrology. He had forbidden her to have any more to do with their neighbors' sorcery.

"Iddo doesn't need to know, does he?" Miriam asked with a smile. "Give Parthia your cup."

Dinah handed it to her without thinking and a moment later the seer tossed a pinch of powder from her bowl into the water. Her bracelets jingled as she swirled the contents around, muttering unintelligible words. Then the clinking stopped as she stared into the cup, studying the mixture, waiting for the water to settle.

"I see a great tearing in your life," the seer began. "Something very precious to you will be ripped away and—"

"Stop!" Dinah snatched the cup from her, spilling some of the contents onto the stone floor. "I don't want to hear any more!"

"Why not?" Miriam asked. "Don't you want to be prepared for the future?"

"I know my future will hold sorrow; everyone's does. We can never be prepared for it." Dinah thought of the suffering her parents had endured, and what Iddo had endured as a child. If they had known what was coming, could they have prepared for it? In fact they *had* known the future—Israel's prophets had warned them of the coming judgment—yet everyone had suffered just the same. "It doesn't help to know," Dinah finally said, "because we'll only worry about it ahead of time. I'll face whatever comes when it comes."

"Read mine next," Yael said, holding out her cup to the seer.

The woman glanced at Dinah with contempt in her eyes, then rose from her stool. "Not here, little one. Come. I brought the charts that I promised so you can learn how to read the stars." She carried the water and her bowl of powder to the front room with Yael scurrying behind her.

"I'm sorry," Dinah said. "I didn't mean to spoil anything."

"It doesn't matter. Mattaniah pays her well." Miriam sank back against the cushions again. The life that had animated her a moment ago seemed to escape from her the way a lump of bread dough sinks after being punched, releasing the air. "I can understand why you don't need to know your future, Dinah. Your life is already so wonderful. But if you suffered from my ill health, you'd want to know what to expect."

"But that seer can't possibly know for certain what will

happen, can she? Why waste the good days of your life worrying about something that may never come to pass?"

"If I'm going to die, I want to make preparations for my family."

Dinah crouched in front of her friend and took her hand. "Miriam, none of us knows if we'll live to see tomorrow. Why not live each day with hope?"

"But she does give me hope. She was right about the Persian invasion, you know. She said that Babylon would undergo a great upheaval, and she was right. She saw it in the stars."

Was there a difference, Dinah wondered, between this Babylonian woman with her stars and swirling water and Israel's prophets, who also claimed to see the future? Why would Iddo listen to one and not the other?

"Mattaniah told me what Daniel the Righteous One said," Miriam continued. "How our people may return to Jerusalem soon. So I asked the seer about his prophecy, and she said—"

"Wait! Don't tell me!" Dinah stood, dropping Miriam's hand. "I don't want to know."

"Are you sure?" A thin smile brightened Miriam's face.

Dinah hesitated for just a moment before saying, "I'm sure. Listen, I should go. See how dark it's getting already? *Shabbat shalom*, Miriam." She bent to kiss her friend on both cheeks.

"Shabbat shalom. And thank you again for the food."

Dinah hurried home to wash and change her clothes for the Sabbath. Her sons' wives had scrubbed their children—four boys and three girls—and gotten them ready while Rachel rolled out the rug where they would eat, placing the bread and wine at the head where Iddo would sit. Dinah had just finished lighting the Sabbath lights and reciting the blessing when her sons arrived home from work and Iddo returned from prayers in the house of assembly.

"May we soon be celebrating Shabbat in Jerusalem," Iddo

said as he kissed Dinah in greeting. She helped him out of his damp outer cloak and hung it on a peg near the hearth.

"Do you truly believe that we'll be returning?" she asked, thinking of Miriam's seer.

"Of course. We're praying for the Almighty One to work a miracle so we can go home."

But she *was* home. *This* was her home, the place where she had been born. Even if the Almighty One did work a miracle to bring about a second exodus, why would her husband want to return to the place of his nightmares? Their home was here in Babylon, not the desolate, ruined city of Jerusalem filled with skeletons and ghosts, a thousand impossible miles away.

"Is everything ready?" Iddo asked. "Call the children. Let's wash and eat."

Dinah watched with contentment as the men performed the ritual hand-washing and the children scrambled into their places on the rug.

Thirty-six years ago, two very different suitors had asked Dinah's father for her hand. Joel had been handsome and assertive, already a community leader at a young age. He had been born in Babylon, as she had been. But Dinah had been drawn to Iddo by his gentle nature, his uncompromising adherence to his religion. When he had awakened, screaming from a nightmare on the first night they shared a bed, his vulnerability had made her love him all the more. She longed to protect him, to help chase away his demons. But even on their happiest days, sadness always hovered over Iddo. He was like a mouse cowering in the shadows, waiting for the hawk to dive down and snatch him away. She slowly had discovered that the things she loved the most about him—his gentleness, his rigid legalism—were symptoms of a deep, unbearable grief, the same haunted grief she'd witnessed in her parents and in other Jews from the generation of the exile. As the years passed, what Dinah had grown to love the most about her husband was his ability to move forward in spite of that grief.

As Iddo blessed the bread and broke it, blessed the wine and poured it, the fierceness of her love for him gripped Dinah like a fist. She watched him pass around bowls of stew and lentils, olives and roasted grain, and saw a man who was old before his time. Would the Holy One tear Iddo away from her? Is that what Parthia had seen? If death was going to rip Iddo from Dinah's arms, she didn't want to know.

She began to relax after her busy day of cooking as the leisurely meal unwound, enjoying the food and the traditions, laughing and eating and singing with the others. But her deepest satisfaction came not from the rituals but from her family.

"May we soon return to Jerusalem!" Iddo said, raising his cup of wine. Dinah lifted her cup along with everyone else, but Iddo's words had created a tension in the room that he didn't seem to notice. "I can faintly recall celebrating Shabbat in Jerusalem when I was very young," he continued. "But those memories were overshadowed by the years when Jerusalem was under siege."

The room fell quiet. Iddo never spoke of those memories, and it must have surprised everyone that he did now. "We were starving near the end. There was nothing to eat for many, many days. And now . . ." His voice trailed off as he stared down at the table.

Dinah reached for his hand. "Now we've been richly blessed with abundant food," she said.

He looked up at her, puzzled, and pulled his hand free. "Now we will return to the Promised Land," he corrected.

"I hope you're right, Abba," Berekiah said, "but I worry that you may be disappointed. The world isn't the same place it was when you were a boy. The nation of Judah no longer exists."

"They wanted to cut us off from our land and our faith and

our traditions," Iddo said, "hoping we would mingle with the pagans and disappear!"

Dinah had never seen him this way at dinner before, his face flushed, his quiet voice raised. "Hasn't the Holy One been with us here, Iddo?" she asked. "What difference does it make which patch of land we live on?"

"It makes a huge difference!" He turned to their grandson, Zechariah. "Do you remember what we studied the other day about God's four promises?"

"Yes, Saba." The boy smiled as if pleased to be included in the adult conversation. He was such a bright boy, a gifted boy, yet still sweet and tender at age eleven. Since the day he was born he'd been able to make Iddo smile, bringing a light to his eyes each time he toddled into the room, helping him forget the grief that haunted him. Even if Dinah didn't have a million other reasons to love her firstborn grandchild, she would love Zechariah for that reason alone.

"He promised to give us the land," Zechariah replied, holding up one finger. "He promised that we would be as numerous as the stars in the heavens. . . ." He held up a second finger.

"It must be a pretty cloudy sky," his Uncle Hoshea muttered, "if we're the only stars that are left."

"He promised that through us all the nations of the earth would be blessed. . . ."

"All of the nations hate us," Hoshea said, speaking louder this time. "It's impossible to see how we have blessed anyone."

"Hoshea, please," Dinah murmured.

"But it's true, Mama. The only way we're a blessing to the Babylonians is as their slaves and servants."

"Tell us the fourth promise, Zaki," Dinah said.

"He promised to live among us and be our God."

"Yes! We were created to live with God," Iddo said. "And His dwelling place on earth is His temple in Jerusalem. That's why it's so important for us to return and to rebuild it. Without it, our sins will continue to separate us from Him."

"Does it have to be in Jerusalem?" Hoshea asked.

"Of course it does! Do you think He would dwell among us here, alongside pagan idols and pagan temples?"

Dinah's grandbaby fussed in his mother's arms as if sensing the unsettled atmosphere. Shabbat dinner was never this loud, with raised voices and arguments. Dinah stood and took the child from his mother. "Let me see if I can soothe him," she said. She left the room without looking back and carried the baby outside to the courtyard, gently rocking him in her arms.

The rain had stopped but the winter night was cool, and she held her grandson close to keep him warm. She brushed her cheek against his smooth, soft skin as she tried to soothe him and quiet her own worried heart. A handful of stars peeked between the clouds, and she thought again of God's promise to Abraham to make his family as numerous as the stars. But why couldn't the promise of many descendants come true here? Dinah was content with her life. Why couldn't Iddo be content, as well?

"Something very precious to you will be ripped away . . ."

Dinah gripped her grandchild tighter, humming a lullaby to push away the seer's words. Little by little, the baby stopped fussing and her own soul quieted, as well. When he was asleep, she carried him inside and tucked him into bed. But before she had time to rejoin the others who were still sitting together after the meal, a man from their community arrived at the door.

"Forgive me for disturbing your Sabbath meal," he said, "but it's time. My wife, Keziah, asked me to fetch the midwives."

"Yes, of course," Dinah said. "Babies don't wait until Shabbat is over, do they? Especially third babies. Let me get my shawl, and I'll come with you."

Dinah loved being a midwife, bringing new babies into

the world. She loved working side-by-side with her cousin Shoshanna, who was also a midwife, even when it meant that her meals were interrupted. She told her family where she was going and hurried down the street to fetch Shoshanna.

Keziah's baby was larger than the first two had been, and though the labor went smoothly, she had a difficult time delivering. Dinah soothed her as she struggled through hours of pain and endless contractions. "I can't do this anymore!" Keziah moaned.

"Think of the future," Dinah coached. "Think of holding your precious child in your arms. A brand-new life."

"I can't!"

"Yes, you can, Keziah. Find the strength inside yourself." After a hard struggle, Keziah's first son was finally born. She was exhausted but joyful as she held him close, and the look on Keziah's face brought tears to Dinah's eyes. The miracle of birth always moved her.

Long after midnight Dinah and Shoshanna returned to their homes. Dinah tried not to awaken Iddo as she crawled into bed beside him, but he was already awake. "I'm sorry if we upset you at dinner," he said as he held her, warming her after the chilly walk home.

"I hate it when you argue with each other."

"But do you agree with our sons, Dinah? Do you think they're right and that the prophets are all wrong?"

"I don't know. . . . What do I know of such things?" She closed her eyes, wanting to sleep, not talk. Why spoil the contentment she felt after the miracle of her night's work?

"Dinah, it's important to me to know how you feel about it. Do you agree with our sons?"

She sighed and rolled over onto her back, knowing Iddo wouldn't let the matter rest until she answered him. "Berekiah and Hoshea were only asking you to look around and see what you have now, here in this place, instead of longing for the past or trying to see into the future."

"But God always keeps His promises. He said as long as the sun and moon remain, Israel will remain. And what do you see shining in the sky every morning?"

"The sun—but it rises above Babylon, too, not just Jerusalem." Iddo gave an exasperated huff in reply. "I was born here, Iddo. This is the only home I've ever known. I've been happy here all my life with our family and my work. I've never experienced what you did or known your grief. . . . I just wish . . ."

"What? What do you wish?"

"I wish Rebbe Daniel and the other prophets had never offered you this hope. What if they're wrong and this turns out to be another loss in your life?"

"They won't be wrong."

Dinah brushed her fingers through his white hair, trailed them down his soft white beard. "Then from now on I will pray that the prophets are right. Now please, Iddo. Let's go to sleep." She closed her eyes again and nestled in his arms. But as she tried to sleep, Dinah still feared that if his hopes didn't come to pass, the disappointment would kill him.

"I see a great tearing in your life . . ." A shudder passed through Dinah. She wished with all her heart that she had never allowed the Babylonian woman to gaze into her cup.

Chapter 3

Zechariah sat hunched against the morning cold as he ate breakfast with his father and grandfather. Kindling a fire was forbidden on the Sabbath, and the air in the unheated room sent a chill through him. He felt his father watching him and looked up. "Come to work with me this morning, Zaki. I want you to see—"

"On Shabbat?" his grandfather interrupted. "It's bad enough that you choose to work on the Sabbath, but why ask your son to desecrate it?"

"It just occurred to me that he will turn twelve soon. He'll be an adult and his Torah studies will be finished. It's time he learned the trading business from Hoshea and me."

"And what if he prefers to come to the house of assembly with me?"

Zechariah stared at the floor as the argument bounced back and forth. He loved both men, but sometimes he felt as though his father was gripping one of his arms and his grandfather the other, yanking him in opposite directions, tearing him in two. He hated being trapped in the middle, but if they asked his opinion, he would rather go with Abba. Working alongside his father would be a welcome change from praying all morning—even though he hated to disappoint his grandfather.

"He's my son," Abba finally said. "It's my decision. We'll be back in time for afternoon prayers." He stood, motioning to Zechariah. "You ready?"

Zechariah tried to mask his excitement as he rose to his feet to fetch his outer robe and sandals. He couldn't meet his grandfather's gaze as Saba gathered his prayer shawl and phylacteries, then shuffled out the door to walk to the house of assembly alone.

Abba strode briskly as they left their Jewish neighborhood, but Zechariah slowed his steps to gaze all around as they walked through Babylon's strange, exotic streets. He rarely glimpsed this alien world except from the rooftop of his home. "What's that building?" he asked as they passed a magnificent pillared structure.

"That's the temple of Ishtar, one of Babylon's gods."

"Was the temple in Jerusalem like that?"

"I don't know. I never saw it. You'll have to ask Saba."

Two men were ascending the temple stairs wearing the most beautiful white robes Zechariah had ever seen, embroidered with purple and gold. "Who are those men?" he asked.

"Priests, I suppose. I don't really know much about Babylonian religion. They have at least a dozen temples to their pagan gods here in this city, not counting the great *ziggurat*."

Zaki stopped to stare until the men disappeared inside, then hurried to catch up with his father. "Saba says we'll wear white robes like that when we're priests, someday."

"You and I will never be priests, in spite of what your grandfather thinks."

"Why not?"

"Because there's no longer a temple in Jerusalem. It's gone. Destroyed."

"But Rebbe Daniel said—"

"The prophets are all dreamers, son. It's much wiser to place your hope in things you can see right in front of you. Then you won't be disappointed. That's why your uncle and I are working so hard to build this business for you and your brothers. You know I love your grandfather, but we can't all live in a dream world like he does."

"Is it true what you said this morning? That I'll get to go to work with you after my birthday instead of studying the Torah?"

"Well . . . maybe you should continue to study it some of the time. But my business will be yours someday, so it's time you learned how to run it with me." They reached a squat, low-roofed building near the canal a few minutes later and went inside through a rear door. After passing Babylon's towering buildings, Zechariah was disappointed in his father's gloomy office. The walls inside the one-room structure were lined with shelves and stuffed with even more scrolls and clay tablets than at the yeshiva Zaki attended. Abba showed him the worktable where he and Uncle Hoshea sat all day, buying and selling goods throughout the empire, keeping track of debts and sales. The work seemed no different or more exciting to Zechariah than sitting in the yeshiva all day, studying Torah scrolls.

Abba led the way to the front of the building and opened a door that overlooked the canal. "This is our slowest season of the year," he said. "The ships from Armenia won't begin to arrive until the trading season resumes in the spring."

"Ships like that one?" Zechariah asked, pointing to a tall-masted vessel similar to the ones he saw on the canal near their house.

"Some of them are. But the ones that come from Armenia are round and made from willow staves and animal skins. They sail downriver from Armenia with goods to sell—and carrying a donkey or two. Since the river can only be navigated in one direction, the traders sell their goods, dismantle their boats, and then load the staves and skins on their donkeys for the return trip. It's interesting to watch."

"I wish I could travel someplace new."

Abba rested his hand on Zaki's head for a moment. "Maybe you and I will have that chance someday. Listen, I have to go over my accounts now. Go ahead and explore while I work."

For the next two hours, Zechariah wandered along the edge of the canal outside his father's building, watching the flurry of activity on the waterfront and in the other shops and warehouses. He loved listening to the slurping, splashing sounds that the water made against the dock and dreaming of faraway places. But even though he wasn't doing any forbidden work, Zaki still felt guilty for not going to the house of assembly with Saba and the others on this Sabbath morning. When he finally turned to retrace his steps, he heard music in the distance and the persistent thumping of drums. He raced back to his father's office. "What's that music, Abba? Do you hear it?"

Abba had been hunched over his worktable, but he sat up straight, cocking his head to listen. "I don't know what that is. . . . But give me a minute to finish this, and we'll go see."

A short time later Abba closed the building, and they hurried up the street together, following the sound. "It's a royal procession," a stranger told Abba when he asked. "You'll get the best view from the top of the wall."

Abba found the nearest stairway leading to the top of Babylon's massive walls, and they puffed their way to the top. Zechariah had never been up this high in his life. The walls were as wide as The Processional Way, Babylon's main street, and wide enough for teams of horses and chariots to race each other. Tiny Persian soldiers in bright blue tunics swarmed in the street below like busy insects as they cleared a path for the procession. The music grew louder and louder, the drums banging and thumping in time with Zaki's heart. An escort of musicians paraded past first, followed by four magnificent white horses pulling a golden chariot. The man riding in the chariot wore a long, purple robe trimmed with gold, and the people lining the street bowed down to him as he passed. "Is that the new Persian king?" Zechariah whispered.

"Yes, I suppose it is. It's a good thing we're watching from up here. We only bow down to the Almighty One."

The dazzling parade slowly moved past—soldiers on horseback, noblemen in chariots, and golden images of Babylon's gods on wheeled carts, glittering in the bright sunshine. Zaki had never seen anything like this before, but Abba assured him that kings and emperors always traveled in such splendor wherever they went. "Did King David and King Solomon travel that way, too?" he asked.

"Maybe . . . That was a long time ago, son."

As Zechariah gazed out over Babylon, the city looked beautiful to him, the buildings and temples decorated with glazed bricks of blue and red and gold. His Jewish neighborhood of tightly clustered square buildings was dull in comparison, the color of mud. He made a slow turn, taking it all in, and couldn't imagine living anywhere else but Babylon. At last they descended the stairs again and headed home.

"Abba, are we really going to move back to Jerusalem like Saba said last night?"

He shook his head. "No king would ever let his slaves go free. Has anything changed since the Persians arrived?"

"No." Zaki's life had continued the same as always, with school and chores and prayers in the house of assembly. Today was the first hint that something new may be coming, and he was excited about it, even if his father's workplace had been a disappointment.

They went to prayers together, as Abba had promised.

Afterward, Zechariah walked home with his grandfather, trying to make amends. "There's a little time to study the Torah before we eat," Saba said. "Shall we go up to the roof?"

Zechariah stifled a sigh. There would be no escaping to play with his neighbor, Yael. She was his best friend, and even though she was a girl, she behaved more like a boy, exploring the canal with him whenever they had free time. He couldn't wait to tell her about all the things he'd seen today with his father. But Saba had already opened the gate to their courtyard and was heading toward the stairs to the roof. Zechariah glanced at the distant palm trees near the water's edge one last time before racing up the stairs ahead of him. He enjoyed learning with Saba—as long as the lessons didn't take forever.

From the rooftop he saw the Euphrates River gliding through the middle of the city like a thick brown snake. He could see the top of the ziggurat in the city's center, a long distance away from his Jewish neighborhood. He would love to climb that mountain of bricks someday and see what the view was like from such a glorious height.

"What are you looking at?" Saba asked when he reached the top of the stairs.

"I like the way the sun is shining on the ziggurat. Doesn't it look beautiful?"

Saba turned his back on the view without replying.

"Saba, I've been wondering: How can seventy years of exile have passed already? You aren't seventy years old, and you remember being brought here."

"Our captivity began before I was born, son. Groups of our people were forced into exile three different times in a little more than twenty years. I don't remember the first two invasions, but when Judah's last king rebelled against the Babylonians, their armies demolished everything and brought me here."

Zechariah sank down on the rug beside his grandfather, hoping he would tell him more. Saba never talked about the past or the things he remembered. But he'd offered a few hints at dinner last night, and Zechariah longed to hear more. "How old were you then? My age?"

"I was ten when the Babylonians broke through the walls and destroyed the temple. Now you and I will be among those who are blessed to return and rebuild it."

Zechariah felt pulled in two directions again. Babylon was his home, Jerusalem a distant place he knew only from the Torah. He celebrated the story of the exodus from slavery in Egypt at Passover every year, but it had always seemed like a myth to him, no different from the exaggerated stories that the Babylonians told about their gods, Marduk and Ishtar and Enlil. He thought of the temple and the priests he'd seen today and asked, "Do you remember the sacrifices at the temple?"

"Only vaguely. I was just a boy, too small to see over the heads of the taller men. I remember my mother lifting me up once, so I could see my father in his white robes, but I was too young to understand what the sacrifices were all about."

"Did the soldiers really destroy everything?"

Saba nodded, closing his eyes. "We tasted ash in our mouths for days and days. The charred land was empty, and when the wind blew, the ash went down our throats and into our eyes. The stench of death was everywhere. You couldn't escape it." Saba's voice had grown very soft. "You can't imagine our fear to find ourselves in enemy hands. They stripped us and forced us to march, and we were so terrified. . . ." He fell silent, shaking his head as he stared down at his lap. Zechariah knew about Saba's nightmares. He'd heard him screaming in the night.

"It must have taken a long time to walk here," Zechariah said after a moment.

"Yes, but we had no choice. The soldiers forced us to keep going no matter how tired we were—for miles and miles, across mountains and deserts. . . . Many people died along the way, especially the old ones and the little children who were already weak from starvation. People had to carry their loved ones' bodies until nightfall because the soldiers wouldn't let them stop to bury them, and we couldn't leave them for scavengers to feed on. So we buried them at night, with nothing to mark their graves and no chance to grieve or to pray before falling asleep and waking at dawn to march another day." He stopped again as his voice choked with emotion.

Zechariah was sorry for making his grandfather sad. He searched for something to say to cheer him but couldn't think of anything. At last Saba cleared his throat. "And now, if it pleases God, we will go back the way we came," he said. "The Almighty One will provide a new exodus from slavery and we'll return home, just as He promised through His prophets."

Zaki thought of how Abba had called the prophets a bunch of dreamers. He and Saba couldn't both be right.

When Zechariah heard voices in the street below, he stood to peer over the parapet. Yael was entering her courtyard with a Babylonian woman, draped in golden jewelry. He wanted to wave, but Yael didn't look up and he didn't dare call out to her. Saba stood and came to peer over the wall beside him. "What is that woman of wickedness doing in our neighborhood? And on the Sabbath, no less!"

"Yael's mother is sick, and she's the woman who's been reading her future in the stars. Yael says the stars and planets control our destiny and that—"

"Nonsense! The Almighty One created the heavenly bodies so we could keep track of the times and seasons. Why would He allow something as distant and impersonal as a star to decide our fate? Yael's father knows that pagan sorcery is forbidden. The Torah says a woman of wickedness like her should be stoned to death."

Zechariah couldn't imagine such a horrible death, pummeled with rocks and stones until you died.

"Promise me you won't go near that woman," Saba said.

"I promise."

"Come, let's begin." Saba turned his back on Yael's house, and they sat down in a patch of sunshine to study together.

"Will you help me practice my Torah portion, Saba? I want to read it perfectly on the day of my bar mitzvah. I want you to be proud of me."

"I already am proud of you."

They worked until it was time to eat, and Zechariah made good progress in studying the passage of Hebrew Scripture. When the meal was ready and they left the rooftop, Zechariah lagged behind so he could dash over to Yael's house and see if she wanted to go exploring after the meal.

He halted before reaching Yael's gate. The Babylonian woman stood with her back to him while Yael knelt beside the threshold. They were digging a hole—something that was forbidden on the Sabbath. Zechariah remembered his grandfather's story of how they had buried their dead loved ones along the road into exile and wondered if Yael's mother was going to die.

When Yael looked up and saw him, she motioned to him. He shook his head, remembering his promise. She hurried over, brushing dirt off her hands. "Come on, Zaki. Want to help us?"

"What are you doing?"

"The seer brought a clay demon and we're burying it under our threshold to keep the evil spirits away until Mama gets better. The stars say she will recover if nothing interferes."

"Do you really believe all that stuff? I mean, it seems . . . stupid."

Yael planted her hands on her hips, challenging him. "What if your mother was sick? What would you do?" For all her bravery, tears shone in her eyes.

"I don't know. I guess I'd try anything." He didn't want to imagine losing his mother, even though Safta Dinah and his aunts would take care of him. Yael had no one. He thought again of how Saba had lost his entire family. Why did the Holy One let things like that happen?

"Want to see the demon before we bury it?" Yael asked.

"I can't. I promised Saba that I wouldn't go near . . . her." He tilted his head toward the Babylonian woman.

"Parthia? Why not? . . . Hey, you know what Parthia said? She said I have the gift of divination. She's teaching me to tell the future like she does."

"The future?" He took a small step backwards. Saba said Parthia should be stoned to death.

"She says I can earn money telling fortunes and help pay for Mama's potions and things. It costs a lot of money for seers, you know. Here—give me your hand, and I'll tell you what I learned so far." She grabbed Zechariah's hand before he could stop her and turned it palm-side up. "This is your lifeline. . . . Hey, yours is really long! And this is your love line. See all these little lines branching off of it? You're going to have a harem full of wives."

"I am not," he said, snatching back his hand. Yael laughed at him. But she had such a happy, carefree laugh that he couldn't help smiling.

Then her laughter died away and she said, "I'm afraid to look at Mama's lifeline."

Zechariah felt sorry for her. They had lived side by side since they were born, yet Yael's life was so much harder than his was. He couldn't imagine his friend telling fortunes like the Babylonians, working to earn a few pennies, even though everyone Zechariah knew longed to see the future.

"Come back, Yael," the woman called, beckoning to her. "The hole is big enough. We must finish this."

"Are you sure you don't want to see the demon before we bury it?" Yael asked.

"No thanks. I have to eat. You want to go down to the canal with me afterward?"

"Sure. See you later, Zaki."

He hurried inside and quickly washed his hands before sitting down with his family. As he listened to his grandfather recite the blessings and break the bread and pour the wine, he wondered why his father didn't believe in tying on phylacteries every morning or resting on the Sabbath like Saba did. Were Saba's beliefs as useless as Babylonian sorcery? How was Zechariah supposed to tell the difference between superstition and faith? He felt pulled in opposite directions again, as if he sat in an oxcart with an animal tied to each end. The direction Saba pulled seemed right—but so did Abba's way. Zechariah loved both men, but how was he supposed to choose?

He remembered what Rebbe Daniel the Righteous One had said in the house of assembly and suddenly decided that if the Holy One made a way for them to return to Jerusalem, it would be a sign that the stories in the Torah were all true. If not, then Abba must be right, and the prophets were all dreamers. But it would break his grandfather's heart if Rebbe Daniel was wrong.

Chapter 4

Yael knelt beside her mother's pallet and gently shook her shoulder. "Mama . . . Mama, please wake up." She felt bones beneath her mother's pale skin where flesh and muscle should be. Mama hadn't eaten in days. All she did was sleep. A tremor of fear shivered through Yael as she shook her again. "Please wake up and eat something, Mama. You can't get well if you don't eat."

At last Mama stirred and opened her eyes. They looked huge and dark in her thin face. "Yael . . . ?"

"I brought you some food. You need to eat so you'll get well." Mama couldn't die, she couldn't! The clay demon Parthia had buried last week was supposed to chase the evil spirit of sickness far away. Parthia had promised it would work. But Mama gazed up at Yael as if too weak to move.

"Where's your father?"

"At work." Yael lifted the bowl of food and held it near her mother's face so she could smell it. "Zaki's grandmother brought us some food. You should eat it while it's still warm."

"Dinah? . . . Is Dinah here?"

"No, she didn't want to wake you. Shall I help you sit up?"

"Go get Dinah. Ask her to come here."

"Why? I can help you."

"I know . . . just go get her, please."

Yael set the bowl of food on the floor and hurried next door, wishing she didn't feel so afraid. She found Dinah sitting outside in the courtyard with her family, enjoying the sunshine. "Mama is asking for you," she told her. "Can you come right away?"

"Of course." Dinah stood and passed the baby she'd been rocking to his mother. "How is your mother feeling today?"

"I—I don't know." Yael saw her friend Zechariah sitting with the others and said, "You come, too, Zaki." He made Yael feel brave when she went exploring with him, and she needed courage right now. She didn't want anyone to know how scared she really was.

She led the way home and then into her mother's room and saw Dinah's shock as she knelt beside the pallet. "Oh, Miriam . . . I'm here now," she said, taking Mama's hand. "What do you need, dear one? I want to help you."

Mama's voice sounded whisper soft, as if she was breathing out each word. "Dinah . . . promise me you'll take care of my Yael when I'm gone . . . treat her as if she's your very own daughter. . . ."

Yael collapsed to her knees beside her. "Mama, no! Don't talk that way!" Was she getting ready to die?

Mama didn't seem to hear her as she gripped Dinah's hand, gazing up at her. "I should be teaching Yael things . . . but I can't. . . . Promise me you'll teach her, Dinah."

"Of course, Miriam. But . . . but you'll be able to take care of Yael yourself when you're better."

Mama shook her head. "Help her find a worthy husband. . . . Promise you'll do that for me."

"Of course. But you must get well, dear one."

"Take Yael home with you. She'll be your daughter from now on."

"Mama, no! You won't die! The stars all say you'll be healed."

Mama released Dinah's hand and groped for Yael's. "They're wrong. I don't want to leave you, my sweet Yael, but I'm just so tired. I can't fight this sickness any longer."

Yael buried her head on the bed, weeping as she clung to her mother.

"Shh . . . shh . . . I'm not afraid," Mama soothed, stroking her hair. Her touch felt as soft as a breeze. "Dying is as easy as closing my eyes and falling asleep."

"Please don't leave me, Mama! Please!"

"I would stay if I could . . . but I can't hang on any longer, Yael. I'm sorry . . ."

"Zaki, go home and get your father," Yael heard Dinah saying behind her. "Tell him to find Mattaniah and bring him here right away."

The next several hours were like something from a nightmare. Abba arrived home and everyone gathered around Mama's bed, sitting with her and weeping as they said good-bye. Night fell and Mama slept, but even though Yael was exhausted, she couldn't rest. She lay curled beside her mother, listening as she drew one ragged breath after another. Eventually her breathing slowed. Then stopped.

"Mama!" Yael screamed.

"She's gone," Mattaniah said. "She's gone."

Yael flung herself into her father's arms, weeping angry tears. "Why didn't you do something? Why didn't you save her? You let her die!"

"I tried everything, Yael, every omen and potion and ritual I could find. There was nothing more I could do. I'm grieving as much as you are." She had never seen Abba cry, but he was weeping now as he held her tightly.

"What are we going to do without her?" she asked, her voice muffled against his chest.

"I don't know . . . I don't know . . ."

"How could she go away and leave us?"

"She didn't want to, Yael. She would have stayed if she could."

Mama was dead. Gone forever. Yael sat in a daze for the next few hours as the house filled with people who came to mourn with them. Dinah and her cousin Shoshanna washed Mama and anointed her with spices. The potent scent filled the room and clawed at Yael's throat. She looked at her mother's beautiful face one last time before they wrapped her in a clean shroud.

Yael clung to Abba's arm, unable to watch as they buried Mama, unable to think of her mother's soft, warm body lying in the ground the way they had buried the clay demon. She wanted to dig up the clay figurine and smash it to pieces. It hadn't done any good. Nothing had done any good.

As they walked home from the graveyard, the mourners' wailing cries seemed to echo in Yael's ears even though they walked in silence now. She realized that the cries were coming from a place deep in her heart. People tried to comfort her, but their words made her feel worse. "She suffered for so long," everyone kept saying. "You didn't want her to keep suffering, did you?" As if wanting her mother to live made her a terrible person.

The women brought food, but Yael couldn't eat. She stood in her family's courtyard, wishing everyone would go away and leave her alone. As she stared out through the open gate at a group of departing visitors, there stood Parthia, looking all around at the mourners in surprise. Rage boiled inside Yael, spilling out as she ran toward the seer. "This is all your fault!" she cried, shoving Parthia backwards. "You said Mama would get better, but she died! She died!" Yael was angry enough to claw out the seer's eyes, but Zechariah's grandfather raced up behind her and caught Yael before she could strike Parthia again. He gripped Yael so tightly she couldn't break free as he pulled her back inside the courtyard.

"Go away!" Iddo shouted at Parthia. "Go away and don't ever come back! You don't belong here!" He lifted Yael in his arms and carried her the last few yards to the house. "I know . . . I know," he soothed. "I know how you're suffering."

It was true. Zaki said his grandfather had lost both of his parents when he was Yael's age. She let Iddo hold her until the flames of her anger and grief had cooled, then wiggled out of his arms and went inside the house to hide.

The day seemed one hundred years long, but at last all the mourners left. Yael went outside again and stood with her arms wrapped around her father's waist as he said good-bye to Zaki's family, who were the last ones to leave.

"I'm so sorry, my friend," Iddo said, resting his hand on Abba's shoulder. "I understand your grief. But soon you'll leave all these sorrows and memories behind when we go home to Jerusalem."

"Why should I go there?" Abba asked. Yael heard the bitterness in his voice and knew he shared her anger. "I don't believe any of that stuff. Religion didn't do my wife any good."

"You mean those spells and Babylonian superstitions? That isn't true religion, Mattaniah."

"What's the difference? Aren't they all just myths and tales? The Red Sea parting? Miracles? Bah! Why would God take my wife? My child's mother?"

"I don't know, Mattaniah. I'm sorry. There's no easy answer, so I won't insult you by offering one."

Yael slid out of her father's arms. How could anyone expect them to leave their home? Mama was buried here in Babylon. They couldn't leave her here all alone. Yael hurried across the courtyard and ran out through her gate, not sure where she was going. She heard Zaki calling behind her, "Yael, wait! Where are you going?"

She ignored him and kept running, but he quickly caught up

with her. "Stop following me!" she said, shoving him with her elbow. When he stayed right beside her, she halted suddenly, turning on him. "What do you want, Zechariah?"

"I want to come with you."

"Why?"

"So you won't be all alone."

"But I want to be alone. I don't want to talk to you or anyone else."

"That's fine," he said with a shrug. "We don't have to talk."

He kept pace with her as they started walking again, heading toward the canal. Yael didn't say so out loud, but the farther they walked, the more relieved she was that Zechariah had come along. She would have been afraid by herself, especially when she saw a gang of Babylonian boys fishing along the canal. Zaki steered her to a clump of palm trees and scrub bushes farther upstream, and they sat down together in the shade. Birds wheeled overhead, calling to each other as barges and single-mast vessels floated down the canal. How could the world keep going the same as before, as if nothing had happened? It didn't seem fair.

"What happens to people after they die?" Yael asked after a while.

"The Torah says their body stays here in the ground but their spirit keeps on living in a different place."

"Where? Where does it go?"

"No one knows for sure. The Torah doesn't tell us about the afterlife because we're supposed to pay attention to how we live now, so that we'll be ready for eternal life."

"Do you believe that? About our spirits not dying?"

"My grandfather explained it this way: the Holy One told Adam and Eve that if they ate from the forbidden tree they would die. Well, they ate anyway, but they didn't drop dead as if the fruit was poison. They kept on living but in a different place, not in *Gan* Eden. This teaches us that death isn't the end. Our spirit keeps on living, but in a different place."

"So I'll see Mama again?"

He nodded. "And she won't be sick anymore."

Yael began to cry, and Zechariah wrapped his arms around her, letting her lean on him. They sat side by side for a long time until the warm sunshine and gently lapping water made Yael feel sleepy. She stood, leaning on her friend's shoulder as she struggled to her feet. "Let's go home," she said.

They were nearly there when Parthia suddenly stepped out of the shadows and into Yael's path. "I'm so sorry about your mother, little one. She was a very brave woman."

"You were wrong!" Yael lunged at her, fists tightened as she tried to strike her. "You said Mama would get better, and she didn't!"

Parthia was too quick for her this time. She caught Yael's wrists in her hands and held them tightly. "I'm sorry but the spirit of unbelief was too strong, and it hindered my efforts. It came from there," she said, indicating Zaki's house next door with a tilt of her head. "I did everything I could, but it wasn't enough. I told your mother that the spirits of unbelief were too strong here among the Jews, but she wouldn't leave and come with me."

"I didn't want her to die!"

"I know, little one. I know."

Yael finally stopped struggling, and Parthia pulled her into her arms, holding her tightly. The seer smelled wonderful, like incense and sweet perfume. And she was so beautiful with her burnished skin and fine linen robes and golden jewelry. Yael clung to her, weeping, longing to hang on to a part of her mother and what she had believed.

"You are a young woman of great faith, Yael. And you have been given the gift of deep spiritual insight. I have been waiting for all of the mourners to leave so I could talk to your father. I want to ask him to let you come and live with me. I'll teach you everything I know, everything your mother believed. You'll be like a daughter to me—"

"You need to leave here right now!" Zaki's grandmother interrupted. Yael released her hold on Parthia and looked up to see Dinah hurrying toward them, shaking her finger. Zaki was by her side. He must have gone home to get her.

"Quick, I have something for you," Parthia said. She slipped a necklace over Yael's head, letting it drop beneath her clothing. "It's the moonstone amulet I promised you. Wear it for protection. And take these star charts I made for you." She pushed a bag stuffed with scrolls beneath Yael's arm, pulling her outer robe over them to conceal them.

"You need to go back where you belong," Dinah said, "and don't come around here again. Yael, your mother asked me to take care of you, remember? I promised her that I would and—"

"The child is strong enough to decide for herself," Parthia interrupted. "It should be Yael's choice." Her bracelets jingled as she rested her hand on Yael's head. "What would you like to do, little one? You are welcome to come home and live with me."

"She isn't yours," Dinah said, pushing Parthia's hand away. "Yael is Jewish. She belongs with us. That's what your mother wanted, remember, Yael?"

Yes, she remembered. But Dinah and her God might be the reason why Parthia's spells hadn't worked. Should she leave and go live with Parthia, following Mama's beliefs?

The two women were watching her, waging a silent tug-of-war. Yael didn't know what to say. Parthia broke the silence first. "Don't worry, little one. I will talk to your father another time and explain to him about the gift of insight that you've been given. Such a gift could earn him a great deal of money." She turned and walked away.

Yael didn't care about money. She didn't want either woman to take care of her, she wanted her mother back. She ran into her house and threw down the scrolls, then collapsed on Mama's bed, crying as if she would never stop.

Chapter 5

Iddo hated walking through these pagan sections of Babylon, but there was no way to avoid them. He kept his head lowered, staring at his feet to avoid glimpsing the forbidden images and idols, wishing he could move faster through the crowded streets. The Babylonians decorated their important buildings, temples, and even the city walls with images. Iddo had asked his neighbor Mattaniah to walk with him, not certain he could find his way through the sprawling city by himself.

"Any idea why the Men of the Great Assembly called this meeting?" Mattaniah asked.

"You know as much as I do—something about a proclamation from the Persian king that concerns us."

Five months had passed since the Medes and Persians had invaded Babylon, and so far Iddo's life had continued the same as always. In his experience, important news usually meant bad news, so the mysterious proclamation was a greater source of worry for him than the idolatrous sights. Iddo had entertained the fleeting fantasy that he and his fellow Jews were assembling for an audience with King Cyrus so they could tell this new pharaoh to let their people go the way Moses once had. But in truth, Iddo's sons had eroded his certainty these past few months by insisting that the prophets were foolish dreamers and that their people would never be allowed to go home.

"You haven't come to prayers lately," Iddo said. "We've missed you."

"I've been very busy at work," Mattaniah replied. "We have a commission to build a new storehouse by the river."

"So you will return when the work is finished?"

"I don't know, Iddo. What good are prayers?"

"How will our people continue in the faith if young men like you and my sons keep drifting away?"

"I have to work to pay my bills and feed my daughter."

Iddo decided to let the matter go. Dinah said he nagged too much and was too hard on people who weren't as committed to their faith as he was. Iddo walked on in silence beside Mattaniah until they finally reached the southern palace, once home to Babylon's kings and now to their new Persian overlords. Other Jewish leaders and elders were already gathering in the huge paved square in front of the palace, and he and Mattaniah found a place to stand beside their neighbor, Joel. Iddo knew it was foolish, but he always felt uneasy around Joel, the man who had also asked for Dinah's hand in marriage years ago. Of course Dinah hadn't chosen Joel—but Iddo wondered if she ever regretted her choice, especially when her cousin Shoshanna had married him instead.

"Did we miss anything?" Iddo asked him.

"Not yet. But that's Daniel the Righteous One, isn't it? Standing up there at the top of the stairs?"

Iddo shaded his eyes. "Yes. And those men with him are Judah's royal princes. I've only seen them a handful of times at important occasions, so I forget their faces. But who can forget those embroidered robes?"

"Well, this must be a very important meeting if they're here," Joel said.

Maybe Iddo's fantasies would come true after all. Maybe Judah's princes and elders really would demand their nation's freedom. "The older, gray-bearded man is Sheshbazzar, son of King Jehoiachin," Iddo told the others. "The younger one is his nephew Zerubbabel, son of Shealtiel and grandson of King Jehoiachin."

"I didn't know Judah still had a royal family," Mattaniah said. "I thought the Babylonians executed them."

"Not all of them," Iddo said. "The Holy One promised King David that he would always have an heir, and the Holy One doesn't lie. Rebbe Daniel is also descended from the royal family."

At last Daniel stepped forward and raised his hands for silence. "This is a day of great news for our people," he began, "the day that the Holy One promised us. It's only right that Prince Sheshbazzar be the one to read the royal announcement from our Persian sovereign, King Cyrus."

Iddo tensed with anticipation as Sheshbazzar unrolled the scroll he held and began to read. "Hear the words of Cyrus, king of the Persians and the Medes and of all the earth: 'The Lord, the God of heaven has given me all the kingdoms of the earth and he has appointed me to build a temple for him at Jerusalem in Judah. . . . '"

Iddo gripped Mattaniah's arm. "What did he say?"

"'Anyone of his people among you—may his God be with him, and let him go up to Jerusalem in Judah and rebuild the temple of the Lord, the God of Israel, the God who is in Jerusalem.'"

Iddo gave a cry of joy as shouts and exclamations rang through the crowd.

"' . . . And the people of any place where survivors may now be living are to provide him with silver and gold, with goods and livestock, and with freewill offerings for the temple of God in Jerusalem.'" Sheshbazzar looked out over the crowd as he rolled up the scroll again. "Rejoice, people of God! King Cyrus is allowing us to go home to Jerusalem! We're going to rebuild God's temple!"

There was a long moment of silence as the men stared at each other in disbelief. Then everyone began talking at once. "Can this really be true?" Mattaniah asked.

"I don't believe it," Joel said. "There must be a catch—some stipulation or requirements or . . . something."

"It's a miracle!" Iddo breathed. He had prayed for this, hoped for it, but even though he'd just heard the news with his own ears, he could scarcely believe it.

"King Cyrus has reversed the policies of the Assyrians and Babylonians," Sheshbazzar shouted above the astonished murmuring. "He is allowing all of the captured nations to return to their homelands and worship their gods—including us."

"We're going home," Iddo said. "We're going home!"

"The prophet Isaiah predicted this day nearly two hundred years ago," Rebbe Daniel said, stepping forward to stand beside Sheshbazzar, "and he even singled out King Cyrus by name, saying, 'He is my shepherd and will accomplish all that I please; he will say of Jerusalem, "Let it be rebuilt," and of the temple, "Let its foundations be laid."' And now it has happened. This is the mighty hand of God!"

Iddo could no longer see the platform through his tears. All around him men were hugging each other, laughing, weeping like children, unable to stop their tears. "Take this joyous news home to your families," Sheshbazzar said above the noise, "and celebrate the goodness of God. This is truly a day of rejoicing."

Iddo longed to run all the way home, shouting the good news to anyone who would listen. But he was so moved, so shaken by what he'd heard that he stumbled along in a daze, instead. "I'm glad you came with me, Mattaniah, because my family won't believe me when I tell them. They'll think I'm making it up."

"I'm not sure I believe it myself."

"Just think! Our brethren will gather from all of the places where we've been exiled, creating an exodus as great as the first one. There must be a million of us by now with our children and grandchildren, scattered throughout the empire. We'll need carts and wagons—"

"Do you really believe everyone will return?"

"Of course! Why wouldn't they?"

Mattaniah hesitated, frowning as he looked at Iddo. "Well . . . because it will mean giving up everything we've worked for here. It's not as if we've been slaving to make bricks without straw for pharaoh all these years. Many of our fellow Jews have prospered and become rich. They would have to start all over again in a land that's been desolate all these years."

"But who wouldn't be willing to sacrifice everything they have now for their children's future?"

"For some of us, the future is here," Mattaniah replied. "Like the Jew whose storehouse I'm building. He has a very comfortable life here and so do his sons."

"But didn't you hear what the proclamation said? We're not only going home, we're rebuilding the temple. God will dwell with us again. Think of it!" Iddo thought he might burst from joy as he envisioned serving as a priest with his sons. "When we celebrate Passover in a few weeks, Mattaniah, won't it be glorious to remember that first exodus now that the Almighty One has provided us with the miracle of a second one? Who would have ever believed it?"

"Yes . . . Who would have ever believed it?"

The evening meal was waiting for Iddo when he arrived home. His sons and their wives milled around the courtyard in the fading evening light, waiting to hear the reason for the gathering of elders. He saw their worried faces and could no longer hold back his tears, too overcome with joy to speak.

Dinah hurried over to him. "What is it, Iddo? What happened? What's wrong?"

"These are tears of joy, Dinah. The Persian king has set us free."

His sons quickly gathered around him, too. "What, Abba? What did the king say?"

Iddo wiped his eyes. "The Persian king announced that he is allowing our people to return home to Jerusalem and rebuild the temple."

"I don't believe it."

"It's true. We're going home after seventy years, just as the prophets said we would."

Iddo's son gripped his arm. "Are you certain you aren't mistaken?"

"Ask Mattaniah and Joel. They heard it, too. Didn't I tell you we would return home to our land?"

"This is unbelievable," Berekiah said.

"Our leaders won't waste any time. As soon as they can make the arrangements, we're leaving Babylon for good." His family didn't seem to share his joy. They looked stunned, incredulous. Maybe they needed time for the news to sink in.

"Come, Dinah. Open a skin of wine," Iddo said. "This is a night to rejoice and celebrate and praise the Almighty One for this incredible miracle."

A spontaneous celebration broke out that evening as everyone in the community gathered in the square by the house of assembly. Musicians brought out their instruments and Iddo and the other men danced and whirled in joyous circles, clapping and singing and praising God. He couldn't remember ever being this happy in his life. *"Give thanks to the Lord for He is good,"* he sang along with the others. *"His love endures forever."*

Dinah's cousin Shoshanna led a circle of dancing women, singing the song of their ancestress, Miriam: *"I will sing to the Lord, for he is highly exalted. The horse and its rider he has hurled into the sea."*

Iddo was nearly exhausted by the time the celebration ended and people drifted home, but he still felt too restless to settle down for the night. He was bursting with joy and with thoughts of the Almighty One, and who better to share them with than his grandson. "Come with me, Zechariah," he said, steering him away from the rest of his family. "I want to show you something."

"Where are you going this time of night?" Dinah fussed. "It's late." But her worry couldn't destroy Iddo's good mood. He felt giddy with joy, not wine.

"We won't be long. Go on home with the others." He led his grandson in the opposite direction, down the narrow lanes through the maze of houses.

"Where are we going, Saba?"

"I thought we would walk to the canal where you like to play."

Zechariah halted like a guilty man, forced to return to the scene of his crime. Iddo laughed out loud. "You thought I didn't know where you ran off to on Sabbath afternoons with your friend Yael?"

"Are you mad at me, Saba?"

"No, son. I'm not mad. Who can blame a young boy for preferring activity over study now and then? Come on, show me where you go."

Zechariah still looked unsure and a little worried, but he led Iddo through the dark streets where very few of the drab, mud brick homes still had lamplight shining from their windows.

"What do you think of the announcement, Zechariah?"

"Everything the prophets said came true, Saba!"

Iddo heard the wonder and awe in his grandson's voice, and

laughed. "Yes, of course! Our God is real and His word to us is real."

"Abba said that kings never let their slaves go free, but King Cyrus did! He really did, just like Pharaoh! The Torah is all true, Saba!" Iddo pulled the boy close for a hug.

They reached the wide, shimmering void of the canal a few minutes later and halted near the bank, listening to the gentle sighing of the water. Fishing boats rocked on the waves, their tall masts swaying. The air was cooler by the water, and a cluster of palm trees swished softly in the breeze. Best of all, the sky seemed to open up above their heads.

"Look up, Zaki. See all those stars? Do you remember how the Holy One created those stars and the palm trees and the birds? What does the Torah teach us?"

"It doesn't say how. God just said, 'Let there be light' and—"

"And there was light! Exactly! The Almighty One *spoke* creation into being with His words. That's why I brought you here, to talk about the importance of words. Today King Cyrus gave us a proclamation—words on a piece of paper—and do you see the power that those few words have? They will move us from Babylon to Jerusalem, from people with nothing to people with a homeland. Those words will move stones into place to build a temple for our God. Powerful words, yes?"

"Very powerful!" Zaki's dark eyes glistened in the moonlight.

"Do you know why God is allowing us to return? Because of His grace and love. He will forgive us and dwell among us again."

They gazed at the water, and it was so still that Iddo could see the moon's reflection on the shimmering surface. When Zechariah shivered and crossed his arms against the nighttime chill, Iddo turned and motioned for them to start walking back.

"We're made in the Holy One's image, so our words also have power. You tell someone they're ugly or that they're a fool, and if you repeat it often enough, you might create ugliness or foolishness in that person. You praise them for their goodness or kindness, and your words just might create even more kindness in that person. We must be careful to speak words of life."

A few minutes later they reached the gate to their house. Iddo thought of his sons, how convinced they had been that the prophets' words weren't true, convinced that their people would never return from captivity. He wondered if their words of unbelief would now have power over them. Perhaps they hadn't wanted the prophecies to be true because they didn't want to return. And as unimaginable as it was to Iddo, he wondered if his sons would fulfill their own words of unbelief and refuse to walk through the door that the Holy One had so miraculously opened.

Chapter 6

Dinah lifted her water jar onto her head and made her way to the community well. Time was passing much too quickly. Ever since King Cyrus made his proclamation, the weeks had raced by like fire through straw. On the surface, her life continued the same as always as she cared for her home and her family. But an undercurrent of change crackled beneath each day, slowly growing into an inferno that threatened to consume the life she knew and loved. Dread of the future robbed Dinah of the present, as if she knew the precise hour of her death and watched time speed toward that date.

Her friends and neighbors already stood laughing and gossiping around the well when she arrived. "Dinah! We've been waiting for you," her cousin Shoshanna said. "We want to hear all about your plans for returning to Jerusalem. Aren't you excited?"

Dinah lowered the rope and bucket into the well shaft, as careful with her task as with putting her feelings into words. The other women looked up to her, respected her, but the truth was, Dinah didn't want to leave Babylon. Every day she searched for a way to talk Iddo out of going. But she didn't dare admit in public that she disagreed with her husband. "Iddo is doing all the planning," she said as she drew the bucket to the surface again. "He said the journey would take at least three months. I can't imagine such a long, exhausting trip, can you? It seems impossible."

"I think it's exciting," Shoshanna said. "Joel wasn't sure he wanted to go at first, but I convinced him that we should."

"Shoshanna! Why?"

"Because this is the most important thing we could ever do. If we don't obey the Almighty One and rebuild our temple, we'll be separated from Him forever."

Dinah stared at her cousin. They had worked side by side as midwives for twenty years. How could they feel so differently? Dinah quickly finished filling her jar as Shoshanna explained to the others how Joel and Iddo had produced their genealogies to prove their ancestry as priests. The women seemed interested, but Dinah simply wanted to hurry home before Shoshanna asked more questions.

Iddo assumed that their entire family would leave Babylon together, but Dinah knew that her sons didn't want to go. What would she do if the unthinkable happened and her family split in two, some staying here, others moving to Jerusalem? The uncertainty weighed on Dinah's heart and interrupted her sleep. *"I see a great tearing in your life,"* the seer had told her. As each day passed, she tried to cling to everything she treasured, but it became more and more impossible, as if precious jewels were slipping through her fingers, lost forever.

At dinner that night Iddo turned to their sons and asked, "How many carts will you need for your families? How many oxen and donkeys? The elders have asked all of the family heads to provide them with an estimate."

Their sons exchanged looks. Berekiah finally replied for both of them. "Abba, we've . . . um . . . we've decided to wait here in Babylon."

"What?" Iddo spoke the word with quiet disbelief, not anger.

"We won't be leaving when the first group departs next month."

"I don't understand."

"Our children are too small to travel such a great distance. Maybe when they're a little older . . ."

"And Naomi and I have the baby to consider," Hoshea added. "He's too small to travel that far."

Iddo's face turned as hard and white as marble as he gazed at his sons. "You can't stay here in Babylon. The Almighty One has made a way for us to return, so we must obey Him."

"I understand, Abba. But this isn't a good time. Hoshea and I have decided to come later."

Dinah waited for her husband's response. He had gone very still, his face showing no emotion at all. Please, God, maybe he would see the wisdom in staying here as well. As the terrible silence lengthened, she dared to say, "Maybe we should all wait and go together, Iddo."

"No, no, no!" His voice grew louder with each word. "God worked a miracle for us, and you're going to refuse it? There will always be one more reason to wait, one more excuse. The Almighty One lost patience with our forefathers, and He will lose patience with us if we ignore His command."

"But this is a bad time, Abba—"

"And when will it ever be a good time? Surely there were women with babies during the first exodus. And many small children, too."

"It was a difficult decision to make," Berekiah said, "but Hoshea and I both believe it's the right one for us."

Iddo closed his eyes as if he could shut out the reality of what their sons had just told him. When he opened them again, he leaned toward both men as if to convey the seriousness of what he was about to say. "Come with me. Now! All of you!" He swept his arm to include the entire family, then rose to his feet and motioned toward the door.

"All of us?" Dinah asked as she stood and went to him. "What about dinner? And . . . and the children?"

"Dinner can wait. Bring all of the children. I want everyone to see what I'm going to show you."

Had Iddo lost his mind? They left their half-eaten meal and followed him out of their house, carrying their little ones. A few minutes later, they were walking through Babylon's darkening streets. Dinah had lived in this city all her life, but she'd never been where her husband was now leading her. She pressed close to the others in a tight little group, as if the dangers she had long been warned against lurked beyond every corner. "Where are you taking us, Iddo?" she asked. He didn't reply.

At last he halted and gestured to an enormous stone building in front of them. "This is a temple to one of Babylon's idols," he said breathlessly. "An obscene place where worshipers serve their goddess by sleeping with strangers. Young girls sit on display here like produce in the marketplace, waiting to be chosen by men they've never met before. They turn the sacred act intended by God for marriage into a vulgar, degrading ritual of blasphemy!"

"Abba, don't—" Berekiah began, but Iddo interrupted him.

"I can't imagine letting my daughters come to a place like this, can you? And these pagans have the nerve to call their orgies worship. When mankind stopped worshiping the one true God, *this* is where it led them!" Dinah looked away from where Iddo was pointing, shivering in the cool evening air.

"Listen to me," Iddo continued. "All of you were born in Babylon. You all grew up here where sights like these now seem like everyday things to you. But more and more young women from our community are being enticed by Babylonian men. More and more of our sons are being attracted to Babylonian women. In another generation or two, *this* is where our sons and daughters and grandchildren will be coming to worship. And they'll think nothing of it!"

Before any of them could reply, Iddo turned and strode away, leading them deeper into the city, farther from home. Dinah gripped her grandson Zechariah's hand, heartsick with dread and sorrow at what Iddo was forcing them to see. She heard the din of murmuring voices in the distance and a few minutes later, Iddo halted again. Dozens of diseased and disabled people sat in the city square, huddled on rugs and beneath makeshift hovels. The murmuring was the sound of their voices, pleading with the passing crowds.

"They're calling out their symptoms," Iddo said, "hoping that some stranger will share news of a potion or an amulet or a curse that will bring a cure. Their sorcery is evil, their superstition useless, but our own neighbors, Miriam and Mattaniah, turned to such omens and sorcery for a cure. You were all influenced by such things. Don't tell me you weren't impressed, Hoshea, when one of Miriam's seers correctly predicted that your last child would be a son. And you, Dinah—didn't you want to ask an astrologer to seek the best day for our Rachel's wedding?"

Dinah stared at her feet, ashamed to remember that the seer had made another prediction for her. "This is how idolatry begins," Iddo said. "With simple curiosity. Before long, we grow accustomed to seeking signs and omens, and they no longer seem like abominations. The idols seem worthy of our worship. The pagans believe they can manipulate their false gods and bribe them to do their bidding. But the Holy One cannot be bribed. Instead we bend our wills to match His. The Torah instructs us to remain separate, to be holy."

He walked on—for miles, it seemed to Dinah—leading them at last to the base of the great ziggurat at the very center of

Babylon. "This!" he shouted. "This is what's at stake! Worship of the one true God will be lost forever, swallowed up by this counterfeit religion, this tower of man's own creation, unless we obey our God! He opened a way for us to leave all of this and to return to Jerusalem and to Him. He provided the means for us to rebuild His temple. We dare not disobey. I've seen the wrath of God. I've experienced it. And I don't ever want to see it or experience it again!"

A crowd of curious Babylonians gathered around as Iddo pleaded with his family. Unlike Dinah's quiet neighborhood that grew more deserted after dark, Babylon was coming to life as night fell, like a living beast awakening from its afternoon slumber. "Please, Iddo. Let's go home," she begged.

He gazed at his family for a long moment, then turned and led them back the way they had come. Dinah breathed a sigh of relief when they reached their own familiar streets at last, but Iddo paused again in front of the house of assembly. "My children, listen to me, please. We've been studying the scroll of the prophet Jeremiah. He was right about everything—the fall of Jerusalem, the fate of our kings, our exile. And he was right about our seventy years of captivity, too. But please, please, listen to me. Jeremiah also said, 'Flee from Babylon! Run for your lives! Do not be destroyed because of her sins. It is time for the Lord's vengeance; he will pay her what she deserves.' Don't be fooled by the bloodless invasion by the Persians. God is going to punish Babylon's wickedness, and if you live here, if you're part of this city, you'll be punished, too. Please don't refuse His grace."

At last they reached home and went inside to finish their ruined meal. Dinah saw the deep pain in Iddo's eyes as he pleaded with them one last time. "The only thing that matters is doing God's work. The only thing. If you turn your back on His light, you'll worship the darkness."

Chapter 7

"Zechariah? Are you coming to afternoon prayers with me?" Saba asked.

Zechariah shook his head, staring at the ground beside their gate. He knew that if he looked up he would see disappointment in Saba's eyes. His grandparents were leaving for Jerusalem soon, and Zechariah was running out of time to spend with Saba, but he was too restless to sit in the house of assembly and pray. In fact, he longed to burst through the courtyard gate and keep on running and never stop.

He was so confused. Rebbe Daniel's prayers had been answered, the prophets' predictions had come true—which meant that Saba had been right about the Holy One and all of His miracles, and Abba had been wrong. Yet in spite of his grandfather's impassioned pleas, in spite of the things he had shown Zechariah and his family in the streets of Babylon that sobering night, Zaki's father and all of his aunts and uncles had decided to stay in Babylon.

Zechariah waited until Saba was out of sight. Then, knowing that everyone would assume he had gone with his grandfather, he slipped through the gate and ran across the lane to his friend Yael's house. He found her kneeling alone in her cramped courtyard, stirring the lifeless coals in the hearth as if expecting flames to magically appear. She heard him come in and looked up. "I hope you came to help me start this fire because I'm not having any luck with it."

"I came to ask if you wanted to go down to the canal with me."

A spark of life returned to her eyes, and Zechariah could tell by the way she scrambled to her feet, brushing the soot from her hands, that it probably didn't matter to her where they went. "Sure. Let's go."

They walked side by side to the edge of the canal, the familiar fishy scent growing stronger, the air cooler as it fanned through the tall palm trees. Zechariah lost track of time as they explored all their usual places, poking sticks into holes, watching fishermen mend their nets, running up and down the shoreline. When they finally ran out of energy, they sank down in their usual spot to watch a crane pick its way along the opposite shore. Zechariah scooped up a handful of pebbles to toss into the water, offering some to Yael, but she shook her head. He felt sorry for her. She was still so sad, still grieving for her mother.

"Shouldn't you be studying or praying or something?" she asked after several minutes had passed.

"Probably. My birthday is soon and—"

"Your birthday is in the month of Iyyar? Then you were born under the sign of the ram."

He glanced at her, uneasy to hear her talking about pagan things, especially after his grandfather's speech. "I should be getting ready for my bar mitzvah but—"

"Why aren't you?"

"I just don't feel like it," he said with a shrug. "It's supposed to be a happy occasion, but I don't see how it can be happy when everyone in my house is arguing with each other."

"What about?" She sat with her legs tented, her arms wrapped around them, her chin resting on her knees as she listened.

"The same thing everyone else is arguing about—going back to Jerusalem. And my family is putting me in the middle of their tug-of-war. My grandfather keeps begging my father, telling him that he has to return to Jerusalem for *my* sake. As if the future of the entire priesthood depends on me. My father refuses, and they've been pulling on me, back and forth—and I'm tired of it."

"At least the fighting will end in a few more weeks. Once your grandfather leaves, what's there to argue about?"

Zechariah stared at her for a moment, surprised to realize that it was true. But instead of constant fighting, there would be silence . . . and a hole in Zechariah's life that no one but Saba could ever fill.

"Do you wish you were going, Zaki?" she asked.

He threw another stone into the water. "I wish my whole family was going." He couldn't shake his lingering fear that Abba was making a mistake. That they would all face the Holy One's wrath if they remained behind. "I hear that you and your father are going," he said. "Are you excited?"

Yael suddenly sat up straight, folding her thin, limber legs beneath her to sit cross-legged. "If I tell you a secret, will you promise not to tell anyone? No one else in the whole world knows about it. But you have to promise, first."

He had just confided in Yael, so he understood her need to share. But he wasn't sure that he wanted the added weight of a secret on his shoulders.

"Promise?" she asked again, poking his arm.

"I promise," he finally said.

"I'm not going to Jerusalem." Her voice dropped to a whisper. "I'm staying here."

"Staying? . . . Did your father change his mind? His name is on the list, and his genealogy as a Levite was approved and—"

"Abba is going but I'm not. I'm going to live with Parthia."

Zechariah stared at her to see if she was joking, but he could tell by her crossed arms and jutting chin that she wasn't. "You mean . . . that Babylonian woman? The sorceress? Why?"

"Because if I leave here, I'll lose all my memories of Mama. This is where she lived, where I remember her. She's buried here. And I know you'll hate me for saying this, but I don't want to go where they worship your God. He let my mother die."

"That's not true—"

"Besides, I heard your grandfather telling Abba that no one will be allowed to consult the stars or seek omens in Jerusalem, and my mother believed in all of those things. I want to worship the moon goddess like she did."

Zechariah fought the urge to grip his friend's thin shouders and shake some sense into her. The moon goddess? Omens? All the things that Saba said would happen to them if they remained in Babylon were already happening to Yael. She was his friend, and he cared about her—and he didn't want to lose her to idols.

"Your father agreed to this? He's letting you stay here?"

"No, of course not. I'm going to run away. Parthia already said I could live with her."

"Yael, you can't do that! My grandmother is going to take care of you, remember? I was there when your mother asked her to. It's what she wanted."

"Mama didn't know that your grandmother was leaving Babylon. She never would have wanted me to leave. No, I've made up my mind to run away and live with Parthia—but you can't tell anyone, Zaki. You promised."

He felt desperate to stop her, but he didn't know what to do or what to say to change her mind. "Yael, none of that stuff Parthia taught you is true. She can't see the future any more than the rest of us can."

"Doesn't your God have people who can tell the future? Your

grandfather said one of them predicted that we'd go back to Jerusalem."

"That's different."

"How do you know?"

"Because . . . because there's only one God, and none of the other gods are real."

"How do you know they aren't real?"

"I've been studying the Torah for my bar mitzvah and learning about the real God, the God of our ancestors. Our people are supposed to worship Him alone. We say it every morning when we pray—'Hear, O Israel: The Lord our God, the Lord is one.'"

"Girls don't pray, Zaki. Besides, I don't care about the stupid Torah." She lifted her chin even higher.

Her words and attitude shocked him. Zechariah's father may not pray all the time like Saba did, but he still believed in Israel's God. How could he convince Yael to believe? "Listen, you and your family are from the tribe of Levi and mine are priests. Our families were chosen to serve in the Almighty One's temple—"

"Then why is your father staying here instead of going back?"

"I don't know . . . but . . . but you're my best friend, Yael, and I'll miss you when you and your father move to Jerusalem, but that's what I think you should do. I can't explain it, but I get a terrible feeling inside when I think of you running away to live with that wicked woman."

"She's nice to me."

"Isn't my grandmother nice to you, too?" Yael gave an indifferent shrug. "Please don't do this, Yael. If you really want to stay here in Babylon then come live with me. I'm sure my mother and father won't mind. You can be my sister from now on. But please don't live with that Babylonian woman."

"Abba will never let me stay behind with your family. The only way I can stay is if I run away. But you can't tell anyone, Zaki." She poked his arm again, harder this time. "You promised!"

He felt trapped. He couldn't break a promise, but he couldn't let his friend run away to live with that wicked woman, either.

Yael stood, brushing sand off her clothes, and started walking back home without him. Zechariah hurried to catch up. "Listen, I can help you talk to your father about staying here and living with me and my parents."

"Your parents won't let me learn about the stars and worship the moon goddess." She broke into a run, sprinting the rest of the way home, leaving Zechariah behind.

"Do what you want, then," he shouted behind her, kicking at stones. "I don't care." But he did care. He slouched through the gate into his courtyard, weighed down with worry, and nearly collided with his grandmother.

"Where have you been, Zaki? We've been looking all over for you."

"I went for a walk with Yael."

"Well, go up to the rooftop right now. Your father and grandfather are waiting to talk with you."

"Am I in trouble?"

She shook her head. He saw tears in her eyes. "No, Zaki. You're not in trouble."

He took his time climbing the steps, afraid to face them. They were talking quietly when he arrived, but they stopped when they saw him and waited for him to sit down on the rug beside them. Zechariah saw his father's jaw tighten and his hands squeeze into fists as he waited for Saba to speak.

"Just so I'm clear, Berekiah," his grandfather began, "you said you plan to return to Jerusalem at a later time—just not with this first group?"

"I have small children to consider."

"So if you *are* coming at a later time, why not let Zechariah come with Dinah and me now?"

Zechariah's stomach plummeted as if he'd fallen down a deep

well. Go with Saba on the long journey to Jerusalem? Without his mother and father? He couldn't speak. Abba appeared stunned as well, as he groped for words. "He . . . he's my oldest son. My firstborn. He belongs here with me. His mother and I would grieve if he moved so far away from us."

"Exactly! And that's how your mother and I feel at the thought of being separated from you—our firstborn son."

"I know, I know, but—"

"And if you're coming soon," Saba continued, "you'll only have a short time to miss Zechariah. Let him be among the first to return, to be part of this new exodus. You'll be reunited with him when you come with the rest of your family, no?"

Zechariah's father groaned. He stared down at the rug, holding his head in his hands. "I know what you're trying to do, Abba, and I don't want to argue about this anymore. I'm tired of arguing." He lifted his head again as he rose to his feet. "Come on, Zaki." Zechariah stood and was about to walk away with Abba when Saba stopped them.

"Why not let Zechariah decide for himself if he wants to stay or go? He'll be an adult in one week, a Son of the Commandments. He'll be responsible for following God himself from now on, so a decision as important as this one should be his to make."

Abba reached for Zechariah and pulled him close as if he'd been about to fall off the roof and it was up to Abba to save him. "Don't put my son in the middle of this. He can't make a decision as difficult as this one."

"Why not? I allowed you to decide important matters once you became of age, remember? You decided you didn't want to come to prayers with me anymore. I tried to change your mind, but you said it was your decision to make, not mine, and so—"

"Stop it," Abba pleaded. "Just stop!"

Zechariah longed to run back to the canal and hide until all of this was over, but Abba clung to him.

"No, I won't stop," Saba said. "Is what we're telling Zechariah about his bar mitzvah true or isn't it? If he's truly of age and responsible for following God on his own, then he should be allowed to decide for himself whether he wants to return to Jerusalem or stay here in Babylon."

Abba looked down at Zechariah, ran his hand over his head, stroking his hair. Then he looked at Saba again. "Listen, I understand how hard it must be for you and Mama to leave all of us behind, I truly do. But—"

"Don't change the subject. Your son is old enough to decide for himself. Do you want him to resent you when he's older because you made this decision for him? That's the choice I had to face, you know. If I forced you and your brother to come to prayers with me every day, you would have seethed with resentment."

Zechariah watched his father's face as he struggled to reply. Then he saw defeat in Abba's eyes before he closed them and lifted his hands in surrender. "You win," he said. "Zechariah is old enough to decide if he wants to stay or go." He gave Zechariah a gentle shove toward his grandfather and walked away from both of them, hurrying down the stairs. Zechariah started to follow, but his grandfather stopped him.

"Wait, Zechariah. Listen to me." Zechariah's stomach twisted as he looked at his grandfather. "You have a calling to be a man of God. To serve as His priest. Your father and your uncle do, too. Your life will be without meaning if you don't follow that calling. Do you understand that?"

"Yes, Saba." The knowledge terrified him. The God who had worked a miracle at Passover, who was working the miracle of a second exodus, was calling Zechariah to serve Him.

"You must choose for yourself," his grandfather continued. "And you mustn't let either your father or me sway you. Do you understand?"

He couldn't reply. How did adults make up their minds? How did Saba decide it was right to go and Abba that it was right to stay? And even if Zechariah did choose, how would he know if he was making the right choice or a mistake, as Saba insisted that Abba was doing? He thought of Yael and her fortune-tellers, searching the stars, seeking omens to glimpse the future, and for a moment Zechariah thought he understood why people went to seers and used sorcery.

"I don't know how to decide," he finally said.

"Ask God for guidance. From now until the day we leave, every morning when you pray, every time you go to the house of assembly with me, ask the Holy One to show you what He wants you to do. Then listen for His voice."

"Will I hear Him talking to me?"

"He has many ways to answer us besides a voice that we can hear. Sometimes the answers come in dreams, but most often the answers we seek are found in His Word."

It seemed impossible to Zechariah. His parents and grandparents had been deciding for him all his life. He nodded to Saba and went downstairs, wondering how he could ever make such an important decision.

Chapter 8

Zechariah sat cross-legged beside his study partner in the house of assembly, staring at the scroll as his partner read aloud from Genesis. Zaki heard none of it. They were supposed to be studying this weekly portion from the Torah so they could discuss it with the rebbe later today—and the rebbe was notorious for asking difficult questions. Zechariah had to be prepared. Yet he couldn't seem to concentrate. The buzz of droning voices sounded like a beehive. He looked up at the room full of yeshiva students with their faces bent over their scrolls in concentration and saw only the tops of their heads, covered by the dark circles of their *kippahs*.

He watched an older boy stroke his chin and the stubble of his newly grown beard. A younger boy played with the fringe on the corner of his garment, twirling the tassels around his finger. All of the students seemed intent on their work. None of these students, he guessed, wrestled with a decision as impossible as the one he wrestled with.

"Zechariah . . . Zechariah!" His study partner elbowed him in the ribs. How long had he been calling his name?

"Huh? . . . Sorry . . ."

"What's wrong with you today? You were a long way from here—and not even pretending to listen to this Torah passage."

"Sorry," he said again. "I haven't slept all week. I keep having these weird dreams."

"What kind of dreams?"

They were nothing like Saba's nightmares, but they still alarmed and confused Zechariah. "I don't know . . . galloping horses and Torah scrolls that fly through the air like birds. Last night I dreamed about workmen measuring the foundations of Jerusalem as they got ready to build." And one dream that he didn't want to share had been about Yael. She was lost, and he'd searched everywhere for her only to discover that the Babylonian sorceress had hidden her inside a large storage basket. He awoke from these dreams drenched with sweat, wondering what they meant. If God had sent them as signs or as an answer to his dilemma, Zechariah had no idea how to interpret them.

"Well, we'd better finish studying this passage, or the rebbe will give us both nightmares. He always seems to know when we aren't prepared."

Zechariah bent over the scroll again, forcing himself to concentrate. Every morning and evening when he'd gone to the house of assembly to pray with his grandfather, Zechariah asked the Holy One whether he should stay in Babylon or go to Jerusalem. Nothing ever happened. No voice called down to him from the clouds, no answer leapt off the page of the Torah, no burning bushes appeared. And every day as the time of departure drew closer, Zechariah felt more and more pressure to choose.

This was too hard, he decided as he looked around at the other students again. How could he concentrate on his studies? Tomorrow was his bar mitzvah. He would go up to read the Torah for the first time, and from that day forward he would be considered a man in the Almighty One's sight. He would have to make difficult decisions like this for the rest of his life. Was it always going to be this hard?

Somehow, Zechariah got through the rest of his studies that morning. Thankfully, the rebbe called on every student but him that afternoon, as if aware that Zechariah's mind was elsewhere on the day before his bar mitzvah.

"So, Zechariah. Have you decided what you will do?" his grandfather asked as they walked home from prayers later that evening. It was the first time that Saba had mentioned the decision since telling him he had a choice a week ago. Abba hadn't asked him about it either, but Zechariah had caught his parents gazing at him as they ate together as if he were a stranger.

"No," he told his grandfather. "My heart says to stay here with my parents."

"You are a man now, not a child."

"Even so . . ." Zechariah's eyes filled with tears at the thought of never feeling his mother's arms around him again or seeing Abba smile at him in pride. "How will I know for sure if the Holy One is speaking to me?"

"His answer will be unmistakable. In the meantime, you can't trust your emotions if you want to do what God is telling you to do."

They walked side by side in silence the rest of the way, but Saba stopped when they reached home, pausing just outside the gate to their courtyard. "Tomorrow will be a joyful occasion for all of us as we celebrate with you. But you must be careful not to let your parents or me or anyone else pressure you into choosing what they want you to do. It must be what the Holy One tells you to do."

Zechariah barely slept, tossing on his mat all night. He walked to the house of assembly with his family the next morning with the new prayer shawl they had given him draped around his shoulders. Abba hired musicians with flutes and cymbals and drums to accompany his procession, making music as their neighbors and friends walked with Zaki, clapping and singing. As they crowded inside the house of assembly, Zechariah suddenly felt nervous about reading the Torah for the first time, even though he had practiced and practiced. Everyone in his family, everyone in his community, would be listening.

The leader began with prayer, and while Zechariah waited to be called up to read, he prayed, just as he'd prayed every day, asking the Holy One to show him if he should go to Jerusalem or stay in Babylon with his family. God still didn't answer him.

At last the moment came. It was time for Zechariah to read. His heart beat faster as he stepped onto the bimah. He watched in a daze as the leader carefully removed the scroll from the ark and laid it out before him, opening it to today's passage. Zechariah drew a breath and exhaled slowly to calm himself. He looked down at the page, focusing on the tiny Hebrew letters. Then he cleared his throat to read from the first book of the Torah.

"'The Lord had said to Abram, "Leave your country, your people and your father's household, and . . ."'" Zechariah paused, hearing the words as if for the first time. He had read this Hebrew passage over and over during the past few months as he'd practiced it. But his daily language was Aramaic, and he had been so intent on learning to read and pronounce the unfamiliar Hebrew words that he hadn't paid any attention to the meaning of them. Now God's words to Abraham seemed to pierce him like an arrow.

Leave your father's household.

He swallowed and drew a breath to continue. "'"And go to the land I will show you. . . ."'" The room shrank until it seemed as though all of the other people had vanished. A bright light, shining like a hundred torches, illuminated the page. It was so bright it made his eyes hurt. He put the pointer under the words to keep from losing his place.

"'"I will make you into a great nation and I will bless you; I will make your name great, and you will be a blessing. . . ."'"

Could this be the answer Zechariah had prayed for? *Leave your father's household.* The assigned Torah portion for this day had been scheduled long before Zechariah was born, long before King Cyrus gave his proclamation to return to the Promised Land. Zechariah cleared his throat again.

"'So Abram left, as the Lord had told him. . . .'" As Zechariah continued to read the passage, every word, every letter shimmered on the page like sunlight rippling on the waves of the canal. This was much more than a trick of lighting or the slant of the glowing sun, because along with the light, Zechariah also sensed a Presence beside him, surrounding him, loving him. He knew without knowing how that it was the Presence of the Almighty One. And Zechariah never wanted Him to leave his side.

Somehow he kept reading. The golden warmth that filled the page and surrounded Zechariah seemed to consume him, filling him with joy. This was what it was like to be in the presence of God, the God of his ancestors. This was the Presence that had once filled the temple. And the Holy One was speaking to him—to *him*! God was calling him to leave Babylon and follow Him.

Zechariah must return to the Promised Land. And to God.

He closed the Torah scroll and looked up. Everyone in the room was looking at him, smiling at him. He should feel proud of the job he had done. He had read perfectly. But God's presence had vanished along with the light, and now he felt terrified.

Saba hugged him tightly after the service, and Zechariah could tell he was proud. "That was perfect, son. Perfect." The musicians played their joyful music again as Zechariah walked home for the celebration. But he wondered if the day really had begun or if he was still in bed, still dreaming. When his mother took his face in her hands and kissed both of his cheeks, he nearly changed his mind. How could he ever bear to kiss her good-bye? How could the Holy One expect him to? He thought of Abraham and Sarah and remembered that they had left their families behind, too.

Everyone gathered to eat the feast that his mother and grandmother had prepared, but Zechariah wandered away from the food-laden table without an appetite. He stood looking through the gate, wishing he could gallop far away on one of the horses from his dreams and never tell anyone about what had happened when he'd read from the Torah. After a few moments, he felt a hand on his shoulder.

"What's wrong?" Abba asked. "You did very well. You read every word perfectly. Why aren't you celebrating?"

What could he say? How could he describe what he had experienced in the assembly hall that morning? It would be like trying to describe a dream, and they always slipped through your grasp when you tried to put them into words.

"Zechariah, what's the matter?" Abba asked again. He lifted Zechariah's chin until he was looking up into his father's eyes.

"Saba told me to pray and ask the Holy One whether He wanted me to stay here with you and Mama or go to Jerusalem. So I did that. I've been praying and praying every day and . . ." He was afraid to say the words out loud, afraid they would sound silly. But he was even more afraid of their permanence.

"Tell me, son."

"The Holy One said, 'Leave your father's household—'"

"Wait . . . You mean the Torah passage you just read?"

Zechariah nodded. "I think . . . I think the Holy One wants me to go to Jerusalem. To the land He promised to Abraham's offspring—to us." He saw emotion twist his father's face, as if he was fighting tears. Abba gave his shoulder a hard squeeze and hurried away.

Zechariah shivered at the enormity of what had happened this morning. The God of Abraham and Moses had spoken to him through the words of the Torah. Those sacred scrolls weren't mere stories of the dusty past for old men to read, but the living Word of God. The Almighty One was real, and He was inviting Zechariah to walk with Him in faith the way Abraham had, the way Moses had.

He closed his eyes for a moment, longing to pray for strength, for guidance, longing to feel God's presence again, but he didn't know how to pray to the Almighty One outside of the house of assembly. He opened his eyes again and gazed around at the gathered crowd, eating, laughing, balancing plates of food in their hands. Some of them would be going to Jerusalem. Others had decided to stay here. He thought of Yael and realized that now, more than ever, he had to convince her not to run away with Parthia and be a seer and adopt Babylonian ways. He wanted her to go with him and follow God. They would go together.

Zechariah wove his way through the courtyard, dodging around all of the adults, searching for her. He found Yael sitting with his younger sisters and cousins, eating the sweet treats that Safta had made, giggling with them. She was just a child, he realized, like he had been yesterday. Today he was an adult, and he felt responsible for her. He reached for her hand and pulled her to her feet. "Come with me, Yael. I have to tell you something."

"Don't eat all the treats while I'm gone," she called back to the others. Zechariah led her through the crowd and out through the open gate, stopping on the other side. "Why so serious, Zaki? What's wrong?"

"The Holy One spoke to me, and now I know that He's real and that all of the stupid Babylonian gods are false. The Almighty One is . . ." How could he describe the certainty he had experienced for those few brief moments, the sense of radiant awe and joy he'd felt in His presence?

Yael was gazing back at the celebration, not at him, shifting her feet impatiently. "Is that all you wanted to tell me?"

"Did you hear the passage I read from the Torah?"

"I guess so, but what does that have to do with anything?"

"I asked God for a sign, whether He wanted me to go to Jerusalem with you and the others or stay here in Babylon."

"A sign?"

"Yes . . . You know how your father hired the seer and asked her to look at the stars so they would guide him? Well, I asked God to give me a sign—He can do that, you know, without using sorcery or the stars. And He answered me! He answered me through the words of the Torah, just like Saba said He would."

"Why are you telling me this?"

"Because I'm going to Jerusalem, Yael, and you have to come with us. You and I belong with our own people, not here in Babylon. We'll go together!"

She took a small step back, and he could see that his enthusiasm hadn't convinced her. "But my mother is buried here."

"So? That's no reason to stay."

"You'll never understand." She turned to go, but he grabbed her arm again.

"Maybe we can bring her bones with us. The Torah says that Moses carried Joseph's bones back to the Promised Land so that he could be buried there."

"Do you think Abba will do that?"

"I don't know, but you belong with the living, Yael, not with the dead. And not with the Babylonians. You have to come with us."

"Is your whole family going now? Did your father change his mind, too?"

"No. He's still staying here." Zechariah felt a new wave of misgiving. "But I've decided to go with my grandparents. And with you."

"I told you, I'm not going. I'm staying here."

She was just a slender little thing, the arm he was holding so thin he could almost encircle it with his fingers. He should let her go and be done with her. Why should he care what she did? Why did he feel the weight of her secret like a heavy stone that he had to drag everywhere with him? "Yael, your mother isn't here anymore. Her spirit doesn't live inside her body anymore—"

"Stop it! . . . Let go of me! I don't want to listen to you!"

"There's no reason for you to stay here. Please come with us, Yael. It will be the best adventure we've ever had in our lives."

She finally yanked her arm free and glared at him, her arms folded across her chest, her mouth stubbornly closed.

His mother called to him from the other side of the gate, "Come on, Zechariah, you're missing the feast. And you're the one we're honoring today."

"You'd better go," she said, tilting her head toward the party. "They're waiting for you."

"Are you coming with me, Yael?" He meant to Jerusalem, but she simply shrugged in reply. "Yael, please!"

"I never should have told you my secret," she said.

He sighed and left her standing alone outside the gate, knowing she was right, wishing that she never had told him.

Chapter 9

Tomorrow. They were leaving Babylon tomorrow. How had the day crept up on Dinah so quickly? She wasn't ready. She would never be ready. But Iddo assured her that he had packed everything they needed for their new life. It was time to go.

Dinah's quiet Jewish community had become nearly unrecognizable, the market squares and homes overflowing as exiles from throughout the empire assembled to begin the long journey to Jerusalem. Thousands of horses and mules, camels and donkeys jammed the lanes and alleyways. But as she lay in bed, trying in vain to fall asleep, it seemed that all of the pieces of her life had been tossed haphazardly into a sack, shaken together, then dumped out again. And now, against her will, others had sifted through those pieces, deciding which ones she would be allowed to keep and which ones had to be thrown away.

Iddo lay awake beside her, neither one of them able to sleep. "What are you thinking about, Dinah?" he whispered. She couldn't reply. He sat up on one elbow to look down at her in the dark. "I wish you could have been with me yesterday to see all that gold and silver! I saw the temple treasures, Dinah, can you imagine? The Persian treasurer counted out every single item to

Prince Sheshbazzar, more than five thousand articles—so much gold that it didn't look real! The Persians are sending soldiers with us tomorrow to keep the caravan safe."

Tomorrow. The word felt like a kick in the stomach. The journey that had once been a distant worry would begin tomorrow. Staying or leaving, it was probably too late for anyone to change his mind.

Iddo lay down again. "I was very disappointed when they announced the final tally of how many people are going, though. Only a little more than forty-two thousand. Can you believe that? It should be ten times that number. Hundreds of thousands of us were exiled, Dinah—including the northern tribes, who the Assyrians carried off. They're free to return home from exile, too, but not a single one of them is going."

"That still seems like a lot of people to travel in one caravan."

"We won't all leave at the same time. We've divided them into smaller caravans, leaving a day apart from each other. You and I will be in the first one, along with the temple treasures. Even so, I just don't understand why we are so few people. . . . But I can hardly lecture the others when our own sons aren't coming."

Dinah turned over, facing away from him. The hours seemed to pass slowly and quickly at the same time as the moon made its way across the sky. Iddo rose long before Dinah did, but it was still dark outside, the stars shining in the heavens, when he came to tell her that it was time to go. She tied on her sandals and combed her hair, pinning it up beneath a scarf.

"The caravan is assembling over on the main street," Iddo said. "I've loaded all of our things, but look around and make sure we didn't forget anything."

Dinah heard his voice, but his words meant nothing to her. "What did you say, Iddo?"

He rested his hand on her shoulder, his eyes filled with pity.

"This day will be the hardest one. I promise you that it will get better from now on."

Dinah's family roused from their beds to say good-bye, standing bleary and teary-eyed in the predawn darkness. When she finally had to let go and walk out of her loved ones' embraces, it was worse than a death. People didn't choose to die, but she and Iddo could have chosen to stay. For the hundredth time she remembered the seer's words: *"I see a great tearing in your life. . . ."*

She reached for Zechariah's hand. But his father grabbed him one last time and held him so tightly that Dinah wondered if he would ever let go. She hadn't seen Berekiah weep since he was a boy, but he was weeping now.

"Don't do that to the boy," Iddo said. "He asked for God's guidance, and the Almighty One answered."

"Why is it so impossible to follow God?" Berekiah asked bitterly.

"It's hard," Iddo said. "That's why so few people do it. But it's not impossible."

Berekiah finally released his son. "You'll come later, right, Abba?" Zechariah asked tearfully.

"When we can, son. As soon as we can."

Dinah had to believe he was telling the truth, or she never could have found the strength to leave her family behind. She took Zechariah's hand, gripping it tightly in her own, and turned away. They followed Iddo through the streets, jammed with Jewish families dragging their children and possessions to the waiting caravan. The sounds of heart-wrenching sobs and lingering good-byes filled the morning air. The crowd jostled her. She had to look down to watch her footing on the dark, uneven road, her tears still blinding her, and when she finally wiped them away and looked up, Iddo stood waiting beside the two-wheeled cart that held all their possessions. A lifetime of memories crammed into a wagon that a single mule would pull—a mule that would plow land when they arrived. Iddo helped Dinah and their grandson climb onto the seat he'd made for them. He would walk in front of them, leading the mule.

The stars were beginning to fade, the sky in the east turning light when the cart finally lurched forward and began to move. The procession filled the road from one side to the other, and Dinah couldn't see the beginning or the end of it. They had traveled a very short distance and were still inside the city walls when she saw their neighbor, Mattaniah, running toward them against the flow of the caravan, weaving in and out between wagons and animals and people. He halted beside Iddo to ask breathlessly, "Is Yael with you?"

"No, I haven't seen her all morning. Have you, Dinah?"

She shook her head.

Mattaniah swayed as if his knees threatened to buckle. "She's missing, Iddo! I can't find her anywhere!" Iddo pulled the cart over to the side, motioning to the others to go around them. "I woke Yael up this morning, and we carried everything to our cart and loaded it. She said she was going to sleep in the back of it, but when I looked beneath the blanket just now, she was gone!"

Too late, Dinah remembered her promise to Miriam to take care of Yael as if she were her very own daughter. She had been too engulfed in her own grief to do what Miriam had asked.

"I thought she might be riding with you," Mattaniah continued, "but if she isn't here . . . Have you seen her, Zaki?"

Dinah saw the unmistakable look of guilt on Zechariah's face. He wouldn't meet anyone's gaze as he shrank back from Mattaniah as if wanting to hide. "Zaki? Do you know where Yael is?" Dinah asked.

"I-I promised not to tell. I can't break my promise."

"Well, I can't leave her behind!" Mattaniah shouted. "Don't you understand that? She's my daughter!"

"Tell us, son. Please," Iddo said.

"But I gave my word, Saba. How can I break my word?"

"A promise may be broken if it's a matter of life and death. Yael is just a child. She can't survive here without her father. You have to tell us what you know." But Zechariah bent forward and buried his head in his arms, sobbing. Mattaniah seemed about to leap onto the cart and shake the truth out of him, when Dinah suddenly remembered something.

"Wait! Don't torture the boy. I think I might know where Yael is. After Miriam died, I overheard that Babylonian woman telling Yael that she could live with her. She was enticing her to become a sorceress even before Miriam died."

"You're right," Mattaniah said. "She had the nerve to come to my home and ask to take Yael with her. Of course I refused but—"

"Do you know where she lives?" Iddo asked.

"In the Babylonian part of town, near the temple of Marduk."

"I'll go with you." Iddo handed the reins to Dinah. "Wait here. And we'd better ask some of the other men to come with us, Mattaniah. We may have to threaten her if she's hiding Yael."

"What if Yael isn't there?" Mattaniah asked. "Then what am I going to do?"

Zaki lifted his head and wiped his eyes. "Saba? I-I just remembered a dream I had about Yael. I dreamt that the wicked woman was hiding her in a big storage basket."

"Thank you, son." He and Mattaniah hurried away, racing back toward the city.

"What a terrible way to begin a journey," Dinah murmured.

"Yael won't like being carried away from here against her will."

"I know, Zaki. But sometimes we have no choice." Dinah wondered how many other people in this dreary caravan—wives and children too young to decide for themselves—were making this journey against their will.

Zechariah lowered his head again. "Yael's going to hate me," he said with a moan. "She's going to think I told on her."

"We'll make it very clear to her that you didn't. Besides, that woman has no right to steal one of our children away like that."

There was nothing to do now but sit and wait, watching as carts and wagons and camels and pedestrians streamed past. Dinah wondered if she and Iddo would have to stay behind in Babylon after all, and join a later caravan. But as the sun rose higher in the sky, Iddo and Mattaniah finally returned. Yael was in her father's arms, weeping inconsolably.

"Let me take her," Dinah said, reaching for her. "Yael can ride with us for a little while." They would console each other.

"It's a good thing Zechariah told us about the basket," Mattaniah said as he handed his daughter up to Dinah. "That's exactly where we found her, hiding in an empty storage basket." He thanked them again and jogged ahead to where he had tethered his own cart.

Yael gave Zaki a malevolent look as she settled onto Dinah's lap. "You broke your promise!"

"I didn't tell them your secret, I swear! I never told anyone!"

"He's telling the truth," Dinah said as the cart lurched forward again. "I was the one who guessed where you were. Zechariah didn't tell."

The steady stream of traffic hadn't stopped flowing while they'd waited, and Iddo quickly rejoined the river of vehicles moving out of Babylon. Before long, Dinah saw the massive city gates ahead, guarded by armed soldiers, the enemy who had kept her people inside all their lives, reminding them that they were slaves. She was about to pass through those gates for the first time in her life. Her people had been set free. Under any other circumstances, Dinah would have rejoiced.

She held tightly to Yael, who had cried herself to sleep in her arms. The caravan stretched in front of them and behind them on the vast plain as far as Dinah could see, enveloped in a cloud of dust like the glory cloud that had accompanied Moses and her ancestors. As the miles rolled past, she wondered if Iddo would grow tired of walking. But no, he stood taller than she had ever seen him, his back no longer bent as if carrying a heavy load. His face shone with sweat and with tears of joy in the sunlight. She closed her eyes, unsure in that moment if she loved him or hated him.

Chapter 10

I'm tired of riding, Abba," Yael called to her father. "May I please get down and walk?" The cart's monotonous bumping and swaying, the endless rumble of the wheels along the dusty road bored her. A choking cloud of grit hovered over the caravan like fog.

"I suppose so." He slowed the cart so she could scramble down to walk beside him. "But be careful, Yael. And stay close."

Yael would never admit it to anyone, but one month into the journey she was glad that her father had found her and forced her to come along. At first the open countryside that surrounded and dwarfed her had terrified Yael. She had clutched the moonstone amulet Parthia had given her, wishing the seer could have read her stars one last time and given her a glimpse of her future before Abba had snatched her away. But little by little as the days and nights passed, Yael had found comfort and hope in looking up at the familiar stars each night and watching the moon goddess' steady waxing and waning. Parthia had taught her well, and Yael knew that once she was able to study her star charts again, she would find advice and direction for the future on her own.

It didn't take long before Yael grew tired of trudging along at the caravan's dreary pace. She walked faster and faster through the weeds along the side of the road until she was far ahead of her father. She heard Zaki calling to her above the rumble of hooves and wheels and finally stopped to wait for him. He straggled up beside her, puffing for breath. "Your father said not to run off like that. You're going to get lost."

"How can I get lost?" she asked, spreading her arms. "You can see forever! I would stand out like a flea on a bald dog." She wished she could run through the green fields and wade through the canals on the north side of the road, exploring all the way down to the Euphrates, washing her dusty feet in the wide, murky water. The river was nearly always in sight, sometimes tantalizingly close to the road, sometimes shying away again to disappear for a while like a serpent slithering into the grass. So far, the caravan road had followed the winding Euphrates like a shadow, staying just beyond the broad swath of green farmland and date groves along the river's banks. But on the other side of the road, away from the river, the flat landscape looked desolate and lifeless.

"Let's walk together," Zechariah said, tugging her arm.

Yael wiggled out of his grasp and stayed right where she was. "No. You're no fun anymore." She watched as their two carts rumbled past and continued down the road, side-by-side as if competing in a slow-moving chariot race.

"Come on. We don't want to fall behind," Zaki pleaded.

"I know, I know! 'It's important to keep up. No dawdling or lagging behind,'" she said, imitating the nagging voice of their caravan driver. She stubbornly waited until the two carts had nearly vanished in the dust cloud then raced to catch up, reaching them before Zaki did.

"Stop running off," Abba scolded. "If you don't stay where I can see you, I'll make you ride in the cart again."

They heard shouts ahead and the irritated bray of camels.

The flow of vehicles slowed and began squeezing to the right side of the road. "Another caravan must be coming," Zaki said. "We have to get out of the way." He was right. And now their entire procession of people and carts would have to move aside to make room for the string of camels and donkeys approaching from the other direction, their drivers bellowing at their laden beasts. The delay would slow their own progress.

"Get in the cart," Abba said.

"Why? I promise I'll stay close from now on and—" But her father picked her up and set her on top of their load before she could finish.

"These traders would love to carry away a beautiful young girl like you and sell you to some rich man for his harem."

They had to move aside again to let three more caravans pass before the day ended. By the time they camped for the night, the sun had already set and the sky was growing dark, the air cool. No matter how hot the sun shone during the day, the desert air turned surprisingly cold at night.

Yael helped Safta Dinah fetch water and kindle a fire to prepare their evening meal. Abba said their leaders carefully planned each day's journey to allow them to reach a caravan stop with a source of water by nightfall. But some delays couldn't be helped, and as time passed, the group had divided into three smaller ones, a day or two apart from each other. So far, Yael and her father were still in the leading group along with Zechariah and his grandparents. They camped with each other and ate together every night, and she had begun calling Zaki's grandmother "Safta," the same as he did. Dinah had seemed pleased.

While Yael helped prepare the meal, Zechariah helped the men set up the shelters where they would sleep. Little more than a roof over their heads, the tents needed to be simple so the men could take them down quickly each morning and pack them away. The wind tried to blow out the fire as Yael and Dinah cooked, and it carried particles of dirt that blew into their food no matter how carefully they tried to shield it. They had to shake grit out of their clothes every night.

After their meal of flatbread and lentils and dates, they all sat around the fire, weary from the long day of traveling. Their neighbors from back home, Shoshanna and Joel, had camped alongside them, and they all talked together as they watched the embers die. "Our father Abraham began with a journey like this into the unknown," Zaki's grandfather said, "traveling in the desert, camping beneath the stars." He had become more talkative as they'd traveled, as if weariness and discouragement couldn't touch him.

"And his wife Sarah went everywhere with him," Shoshanna added. She reached for her husband's hand like a new bride. Safta's jolly cousin didn't seem to get sad or to miss home the way Safta did.

"Zechariah, do you know why the Almighty One chooses to take us through the desert?" Iddo asked. Zaki shook his head, enthralled with his grandfather's stories. This was exactly what Yael had meant when she'd told him he wasn't fun anymore. "It's because He wants to use the desert to strip us of our self-sufficiency," Iddo continued, "so we'll learn to trust Him and lean on Him."

"Is He going to feed us with manna?" Zaki asked. "Like in the Passover story?"

"He doesn't need to send manna this time," Iddo replied. "He already provided everything we need through our fellow Jews, the ones who aren't making the journey with us. The Persian king ordered them to pay our way."

Yael stood, feeling restless. She was tired of sitting still and didn't want to hear stories about the God who had let her mother die. But Abba grabbed her hand to stop her before she could take two steps. "Where are you going?"

"Just over there. I want to get away from the campfire so I can see the stars."

"No, Yael. You can't leave the caravan for any reason. You could easily get turned around in this trackless waste and die of thirst."

"Besides," Iddo added, "there's nothing out there except the bones of people who wouldn't listen."

Yael exhaled. "I know you think I'll run away again, but I won't. I promise. I'll just be standing right over there."

"I'll go with her." Zechariah stood and walked a few yards away from the others, motioning for Yael to follow. Abba released her and she hurried away, stopping beside Zechariah a short distance from the smoke and firelight. The sky was blacker out here than on any night in Babylon, the stars more numerous, more brilliant. Shining across the middle of the sky was a milky swath, like clouds, that Parthia said was a thick band of stars, all gathered together in a luminous ring. Yael searched the sky for the constellation of the twins and smiled to herself when she found it. She wished she could peek at the sky charts that Parthia had given her, but she didn't dare. They would have to remain hidden in her bag for now.

"Please don't be mad at me anymore," Zechariah said. "Can't we be friends again?"

"You can't keep a secret. Abba said you told him where to look."

"No, I didn't! The only thing I told him was that you might be hiding in a storage basket."

"How did you know that's where I'd be?"

"I had a dream. I know that sounds weird, but it's true. I dreamt I saw Parthia hiding you in a storage basket."

Yael stopped gazing at the stars to look at him in surprise. "You have dreams that foretell the future?" There had always been something . . . different . . . about her friend, different from the other boys in their neighborhood. Sometimes when they played together they could almost read each other's thoughts and know what the other would say before they spoke.

"I have a lot of strange dreams," he said with a shy, little shrug, "but that's the only one that ever came true."

"The gods speak to people in dreams, you know."

"Don't say *gods*, Yael. There's only one God. You need to forget all that pagan stuff from Babylon." She ignored him and looked up at the stars again. "So, can we be friends?" he asked again.

She planted her hands on her hips and gave him a stern look. "Will you promise not to tell my secrets this time?"

"Yes, I promise."

"All right. . . . In that case, I'll tell you another one of my secrets to see if you can be trusted."

"I can."

She moved closer to him and lowered her voice. "I know how to see the future in the stars. Parthia taught me. She told me I had a true gift for it."

"Why do you need to know the future?"

"Because everything in my life keeps changing—first my mother died, now my father is taking me hundreds of miles away from home. The future is like a huge, deep hole in the road up ahead, and I want to see it before it comes so I don't fall in and get swallowed up. I want to be sure there's a way to get across it to the other side. The stars can tell me all that."

"We're supposed to trust the Almighty One, Yael." She heard disapproval in his voice and knew he was frowning at her. "Abraham didn't know what was ahead of him, either, but he had faith—"

"That's the God of *your* father and grandfather. My mother believed in the moon goddess. You follow your family's beliefs, and I'll follow mine."

"Yael, your father is a Levite. You worship the same God I do. The only God."

"No, I don't—and that's another secret you can't tell." She turned away from him to walk back to the campsite.

"Yael, wait . . . Listen!"

"Don't forget," she called over her shoulder to him. "It's a secret."

Part II

Promised Land

When the Lord brought back the captives to Zion,

we were like men who dreamed.

Our mouths were filled with laughter,

our tongues with songs of joy. . . .

The Lord has done great things for us,

and we are filled with joy.

Psalm 126:1–3

Chapter 11

Zechariah stood behind the loaded cart and pushed as his grandfather prodded their mule up the hill. The hard work tired him, but they were nearly there, nearly to Jerusalem. Last night their caravan had camped outside the village of Bethel, agonizingly close to their goal. Zechariah had barely slept as he'd waited to make the final climb up to the city, starting just after dawn. "I never knew the Promised Land was so mountainous," he said, straining as he pushed. "It's so different from Babylon."

"It's beautiful, isn't it?" Saba asked. "I forgot just how beautiful after living in a flat, featureless land for nearly fifty years. We're almost home . . . at last."

For most of their journey, the view of endless wilderness had barely changed from day to day. Pale sand and dark rock. Lifeless. Colorless. Then they'd reached the snow-capped peaks of the Mount Hermon range and the countryside had turned greener. They had traveled through Galilee, past the shimmering lake that nestled among the hills, and Zechariah thrilled to know he was following in Abraham's footsteps, retracing the path that the patriarch had taken when he entered the Promised

Land for the first time. Like Abraham, he had obeyed God and left his father and mother to make this journey.

The cart finally reached the crest of the hill, and Saba halted by the side of the road for their first glimpse of Jerusalem. Yael and Safta stood beside them. But instead of a city, Zechariah saw a wasteland. Desolate piles of rocks and rubble, overgrown with weeds and bushes. No signs of life. "Are you sure this is the right place, Saba? Maybe Jerusalem is on the other side of that hill over there."

"No, son. That's Jerusalem down there—what's left of it."

"It doesn't even look like a city," Yael said. "Where are all the palaces and temples and big buildings like they had in Babylon?"

As Zaki shaded his eyes to study the view in front of him, he began to see traces of crumbled walls beneath the vegetation, gates and towers and charred buildings where the city had once stood. How would they ever clear out all that growth and move all those stones? Where would they begin? The task seemed overwhelming. His grandfather wiped away tears, and Zechariah wondered if they were tears of joy or sorrow. Maybe both. Beneath all the debris lay the bones of Saba's family and thousands of other people who had been massacred.

"Oh, Iddo," Safta groaned. "It will take a lifetime to rebuild all of that. How can we possibly do it with so few people?"

Saba cleared his throat. "That rubble shows us the consequences of our disobedience. It should serve as a warning to us not to fail again."

"Where was the Almighty One's temple?" Zaki asked.

Iddo pointed to an enormous pile of toppled building stones on a distant hill above the other ruins. For a moment he seemed too moved to speak. "Up there," he finally said. "It used to be right up there on Mount Moriah. And that's where we'll rebuild it."

The caravan had continued flowing past them all this time,

and the first vehicles in their group had already reached the ruins below. The collection of carts and people and livestock that had seemed so numerous along the caravan road looked tiny and insignificant against the expanse of destruction. Zechariah wondered if Safta was right, that it would take his entire lifetime to rebuild all of this.

Saba gave the reins a tug, and the cart began to move again, joining the others as they headed down the winding path into the city. "Where did you live, Saba?" Zechariah asked as they started downhill. "Are we going to rebuild the same house that you lived in before?"

"My family's home was in Anathoth, not Jerusalem—a couple of miles from here. But we took refuge inside the walls when the Babylonian army surrounded the city. See that hill, closest to us? Can you make out the circle of walls around it? That's the *Mishneh*, or Second Quarter, built during the time of King Hezekiah."

Zechariah looked where Saba was pointing and saw the faint outline of city walls. But huge sections of them, along with the gates, had been toppled. Rubble lay strewn everywhere, swallowed up by a sea of weeds and scrub brush and tangled vines.

"Hezekiah had to expand Jerusalem," Saba continued, "because so many refugees fled here to escape the Assyrians. The old city couldn't hold them all. God performed a miracle to rescue the king and his people from their enemies."

Zechariah looked up at him. "If the Almighty One could rescue Jerusalem in King Hezekiah's time, why couldn't He rescue it from the Babylonians, too?"

"Because we no longer deserved His mercy. By then our sins were too great, in part because of the long, evil reign of King Manasseh. See that valley south of the city? That's the Valley of Hinnom where Manasseh—"

"Don't say it, Iddo." Safta interrupted. "It's too horrible."

He nodded and didn't finish. But Zechariah knew from his studies that people used to sacrifice their children to Molech in that valley.

"The blood of those innocent children contributed to Jerusalem's destruction and our peoples' exile," Saba said.

The main road and city streets were so overgrown with vegetation and choked with rubble that it took the rest of the afternoon to reach the narrow Kidron Valley east of the City of David. "Our leaders have decided to camp here for now," Saba told them, "beside the Kidron Brook."

Zechariah helped pitch their tent and make camp. At dinner, he poked at his food, weary from the effort of scrambling over debris and the hard work of pushing the cart up and down Jerusalem's many slopes. But his disappointment outweighed the weariness he felt. Jerusalem no longer resembled the beautiful city that the psalmists had described. Restoring it would be challenging enough if Zaki were a grown man and an experienced builder, but he was neither. Why had the Almighty One commanded him to come here? What could he possibly do in the face of such overwhelming desolation?

He was about to say good-night to the others and try to go to sleep when he heard a single flute playing a slow, haunting melody. He listened for a moment, and the sound began to grow as other instruments joined in—more flutes, finger cymbals, drums. The tempo gradually quickened, and he heard clapping and then voices, singing a familiar song of hope and joy: *"Those who trust in the Lord are like Mount Zion, which cannot be shaken."* His family used to sing it at Passover and weddings.

"It's a celebration," Saba said. He smiled for the first time all day. "Let's join them." He led the way, with Safta, Zechariah, Yael, and Mattaniah following behind. Zaki's pulse began to beat in rhythm with the joyful music as they joined in the singing.

"As the mountains surround Jerusalem, so the Lord surrounds his people, both now and forevermore."

Before long, it seemed as though everyone in the caravan was dancing and singing in spontaneous celebration. *"I rejoiced with those who said to me, 'Let us go to the house of the Lord.' Our feet are standing in your gates, O Jerusalem."* It was true. He had sung the words of this psalm all his life, and now he was standing here, in Jerusalem. Zechariah's weariness and discouragement vanished as he danced and celebrated with his grandfather and the others until late into the night.

It was barely dawn when Saba shook him awake. "Get up, Zaki. Get dressed. There's a mob of local men coming." Zechariah tossed back the covers and scrambled to his feet, his heart pounding. While he dressed and put on his sandals, Saba roused Joel and Mattaniah. They hurried to the edge of the camp, joined by hundreds of other men from their caravan, halting near the Kidron Brook. On the other side of the narrow stream a mob of Samaritan men, several hundred strong, marched steadily toward them. Many of them carried swords. Others had bows and arrows. Some carried farm implements such as scythes and hoes and winnowing forks.

"What do they want, Saba?" he whispered. It surprised him that his grandfather had asked him to come at all, considering the danger. Maybe his grandfather no longer saw him as a boy but as one of the men.

"I imagine they've come to see what we're doing here."

"Are they Jews, like us?"

"Some of them might be. The Babylonians left the very poorest of our people behind during the exile and carried away all our leaders and craftsmen and priests. But most of those men are probably descendants of exiles from other countries who were forced to settle here the same way we were forced to go to Babylon."

Zechariah watched as Prince Sheshbazzar walked forward to speak with the mob's leader—a fearsome-looking man with a sword strapped to his side. The white-bearded prince would be no match for him. "We've come in peace," Sheshbazzar called out, holding up his hands.

"Who are you?" the leader asked. "What are you doing on our land?"

"I'm Sheshbazzar, a descendant of King David and of Judah's last king, Jehoiachin. We're all sons of Abraham, returning from exile in Babylon to reclaim our ancestral land. This is our destination—the city of Jerusalem and the land of Judah."

The mob began to shout and jeer in protest, and when their leader settled them down again he said, "This is *our* land, not yours! We've lived on it and tended it for three generations. You have no right to settle here. Take your caravan of intruders and move someplace else." There were shouts of agreement from the mob and more sword-waving, but Sheshbazzar continued to speak calmly to them.

"King Cyrus, the Persian monarch, authorized us to return and rebuild the temple of our God. I'm certain that the governor of your Trans-Euphrates Province received a copy of this proclamation from Persia. He will verify that what we're saying is true."

"We'll send envoys to him immediately, but in the meantime, take your caravan off our land and camp someplace else. This land belongs to us. If you try to occupy it or do any rebuilding, we will interpret it as an act of war."

Zechariah's pulse raced as he listened. *An act of war?* The Holy One needed to strike this enemy dead the way He once killed the Egyptians under Moses.

"Listen, we don't want any trouble," Sheshbazzar continued. "But Jerusalem has been deserted all these years, so it will make no difference to you if we settle there—and that's what we intend to do."

"You have no right!"

"When you contact the governor, you'll see that we have every right. We've been commanded by God and by the king to rebuild the Holy One's temple, and that's our most important task. There will be many of us settling here in Jerusalem in the days to come. Others from our caravan will return to the villages where their forefathers lived, to reclaim their ancestral land. They must start plowing and planting before the fall rains begin."

"They may reclaim *nothing* until we've received word that what you're saying is true!" the leader shouted, and the mob behind him responded with such a terrifying cry, waving their swords and scythes above their heads, that Zaki was certain they would surge forward and attack.

"We will not take any of your land," Sheshbazzar shouted above the noise. "Only what's rightfully ours. But we cannot wait to begin building. We must obey our God, not your threats." The angry response reached an insane pitch as the prince turned his back on the men and walked away with the elders. Zechariah wanted to run—he and Saba were unarmed! The Samaritans could easily wade across the shallow creek.

"Let's go eat our breakfast," Saba said, turning his back, as well.

"But, Saba—"

"The Almighty One is on our side. Do you believe that, Zaki?"

He didn't reply. Any faith Zechariah possessed came secondhand from stories in the Torah, not real life. He glanced over his shoulder at the shouting mob as he followed his grandfather and Mattaniah back to their tents.

"So the opposition has started already," Mattaniah said as they walked. "I wondered if it would. Do you think we should be worried? Will we have to fight them?"

"The Samaritans will find out soon enough that our claims are legitimate. In the meantime we can trust God."

"I was hoping that the local people would be friendly," Mattaniah said, "so we could work alongside them."

Saba shook his head. "We would be wise to keep our distance from them and trust no one." He halted before they reached their tent. "Let's not talk about this with the women and worry them unnecessarily."

"But our families are very vulnerable living in tents in this unprotected valley," Mattaniah said. "And the Persian guards will be heading back to Babylon soon. We'd better start building homes higher up on the ridge right away."

"The temple must come first. The very first thing that God commanded our ancestors to do after leaving Egypt was to build His sanctuary. The people camped below Mount Sinai in tents until it was finished. Building His sanctuary must be our top priority, too."

Zechariah hurried through breakfast and his morning prayers, looking over his shoulder, expecting the Samaritans to attack any minute. When they didn't, he worried that they might come at night, while everyone slept. Then, for the second time that morning, Saba surprised him when he invited him to survey the temple mount with him and the chief priests.

As usual, Saba walked too slowly. Zechariah raced up the ramp that led into Jerusalem ahead of his grandfather, then stopped to wait for him near the top. He could see the caravan sprawled out, without protection, in the valley below, and he also noticed the scattered Samaritan settlements dotting the Kidron Valley and perched on the slopes of the Mount of Olives. Workers resembled tiny ants as they tended their vines and groves on the terraced hillsides. The olives would be ready to harvest soon, the dates and figs in another month. The sight of those Samaritan villages made Zechariah uneasy.

The men had been so angry this morning, insisting that this was their land.

Saba soon caught up with him, and they continued to climb until they reached a pile of ruins below the temple mount, swarming with men and even a handful of Persian soldiers. "Why all the activity around here?" Saba asked the others. "What's going on?"

"This is where the palace once stood," the high priest replied. "Sheshbazzar and Zerubbabel were looking through the rubble and found an underground storehouse. We've decided to use it as a treasury to store the temple vessels and other supplies. Can you come back and help us, Iddo? We'll need you to record the transfer of all the silver and gold from the Persian guards."

"Yes, of course I will."

Saba and the other chief priests assembled outside the palace, then made their way to the stairs that led to the top of the mount. The ascent was harder than Zechariah had anticipated, the steps broken and slanted and clogged with stones, but he arrived on top at last, winded from the steep climb. On the wide, flat plateau that had once been the threshing floor of Aranau the Jebusite before it became the temple mount, barely a square foot of land could be found that wasn't covered with debris and weeds. The tumbled building stones were too huge to climb over, so Saba and the other men could only walk forward a short distance. Scrub trees and scraggly cedars and thorn bushes grew among the rocks.

"This can't be right," Saba said. "How could the temple mount have trees growing on it? I don't remember seeing trees."

"Nearly fifty years have passed since the temple was destroyed," his friend Joel reminded him. "Fifty years is plenty of time for saplings to sprout between the ruptured paving stones and grow into trees."

Zechariah tugged his grandfather's sleeve to get his attention.

"Saba, isn't this the place where Abraham offered to sacrifice Isaac before there was a temple?"

"Yes. That's right."

"Well, there must have been trees when Abraham was here. And bushes, too. Didn't he find a ram caught by his horns in a thicket?"

"Ah, yes. You're right." Saba smiled as he rested his hand on Zaki's shoulder. "You're a very clever boy. And you remember your Torah, that's good."

"At least there's no shortage of building stones in Jerusalem," Joel said. "But it's going to take a trememdous amount of work to clear this plateau."

"Our first task is to find the site where the bronze altar stood," Saba said. "It's where Abraham's sacrifice also took place. Once we rebuild the altar, we can offer the daily sacrifices again."

"I think we'll have to wait until the Samaritans simmer down before we rebuild anything," Joel said.

Saba turned on him. "No, Joel! We dare not wait a single day! If we want God's guidance and help, we must ask for our sins to be forgiven through the sacrifices." He strode off to work with the other priests, moving stones to make way for the altar. Zechariah had plenty of time to think as he helped pull weeds from between the cracks and clear away some of the smaller rocks. He wondered when the Almighty One would speak to him again and tell him what he was supposed to do next. The God of Abraham had won the tug-of-war between Zechariah's father and grandfather, proving that He was real by providing a second exodus from slavery. But the threat from their enemies that Zechariah had witnessed this morning and the enormous amount of rubble piled in front of him made him question his role in the Almighty One's plan.

Late that afternoon, they retraced their steps to their campsite in the valley, hot, weary, and thirsty from the day's work. Apart from a few mounds of gathered brush and some shifted stones, the temple mount looked little different from before. "Our job is going to be really hard, isn't it, Saba?"

"The Almighty One brought us back to our land, but we still have to do our part to conquer it, just like our ancestors did under Joshua. Our task is to build His temple, and the Holy One's enemies will do everything they can to try to stop us."

"Like they did this morning?"

Saba nodded. "Each obstacle we face is like an ancient Canaanite king who needs to be defeated, or a walled city like Jericho that we need to tear down. You and I and the others have already conquered the first strongholds by choosing to leave the comfort of Babylon and the pull of family ties and by turning our backs on its paganism."

Zechariah remembered Yael's entanglement with sorcery and looked away. The guilt of her secrets felt like his own. They soon reached the ruined Water Gate and headed down the ramp toward their camp.

"Will we let all these obstacles stop us?" Saba continued. "Or allow the hard work of rebuilding to discourage us?"

"No, Saba." He smiled as he imagined himself as part of Judah's army, going into battle, defeating their enemies. Or commanding teams of oxen as they hauled building stones into place for God's temple. "What's my job going to be from now on, Saba?"

"Your job is to study the Torah."

"What?" Zechariah halted. He must have misunderstood. "But . . . but that's what I did back in Babylon. I want to be a soldier and learn how to fight. And I want to help rebuild the temple."

"The way we conquer our enemies is by obeying God's Word. When Joshua obeyed, the walls of Jericho fell down. But how can we obey if we don't know what God's Word says? That's your job, Zechariah—to learn what it says."

Zechariah couldn't believe it. He would spend his days in this new land studying the Torah? Not learning how to use a sword or how to build, but studying? He couldn't disguise his disappointment as they started walking again. So far, his return to Jerusalem wasn't at all like he had imagined.

Chapter 12

The screams startled Yael awake. She sat up, clutching her blanket, her heart pounding. Should she run? Hide? Had the Samaritans attacked? The terrifying cries came from the tent right beside hers—from Zaki's grandfather. Abba leaped out of bed to go see what was wrong, and so did everyone around them, it seemed. Yael heard the mumble of voices as Iddo reassured everyone that he was fine and sent them back to their beds.

"He had a nightmare," Abba said when he returned a few minutes later. "Go back to sleep, Yael." He lay down again.

It seemed like a long time passed before Yael's heart stopped pounding. Her skin still had a funny, tingling feeling from being frightened half to death, as if ants were crawling all over her. As the camp settled down again, she could hear Iddo and Dinah talking softly. "All the way here, three long months of traveling and I never had a single nightmare," Iddo said. "I'm so ashamed . . . I-I don't understand it."

"There's no reason to feel ashamed. This is where your real nightmare happened. I'm sure the others realize that."

"I thought the dreams were gone for good."

"Maybe this will be the last one now that you've returned and faced what happened in the past."

"Or maybe God is punishing me with these nightmares because of all the mistakes I've made."

"Go to sleep, Iddo."

"I can't. I may as well get up."

Yael heard shuffling as he left his tent. She couldn't fall asleep, either, and she lay on her back, staring at the dark tent hovering above her head. One edge of the animal-skin covering was attached to their cart, the other to poles, with the excess hide hanging down to form sides that reached to the ground. Abba slept close to the cart, but Yael liked to sleep near the open side of the tent. She inched over to it, trying not to make too much noise, dragging her blanket with her for warmth. Maybe if she lifted the covering she would be able to see the stars.

The hide had the strong odor of animals and stank nearly as bad as the donkey that had pulled their cart. She managed to lift a flap of the heavy skin and look up at a small patch of star-flecked sky and the brilliant full moon that illuminated the roofs of the other huddled tents. Parthia had taught Yael about the phases of the moon and said that people could be "moonstruck" or even become "lunatics" during a full moon. Was that what had happened to Zaki's grandfather? He didn't believe in the moon goddess and refused to worship her, so maybe the nightmare was her punishment. Yael wondered when Iddo's birthday was. If the moon was rising in his star sign, that could cause even more trouble. Or maybe the dream was a warning to him. Parthia said the gods spoke through dreams.

Yael inched a little farther outside the tent. How beautiful the stars looked tonight! She knew how to read some of their mysteries and secrets, but she longed to know all of them. "*The heavenly bodies and celestial events all have powerful effects on what happens to us on earth,*" Parthia had said. And all of that information could be found on the star charts she had given her. Using pictures and symbols, the charts showed the lunar months and the sign of the zodiac that was dominant each month. Before Abba had decided to move to Jerusalem, Parthia had taught Yael how to locate the signs of the zodiac in the night sky. She closed her eyes for a moment, remembering the soft tinkling of Parthia's jewelry, the sweet smell of her incense.

"Once you learn to read the charts," Parthia said, *"you can warn people of trouble ahead or advise them of the best times to pursue love or financial success."*

Yael glanced over at Abba. He had rolled onto his side, facing away from her, and she could tell by his soft snoring that he had fallen asleep. She sat up, the tent roof skimming the top of her head, and reached for her bag, the one she had packed to take to Parthia's house when she'd run away to live with her. Good thing Abba hadn't looked inside it or taken it away from her when he'd dragged her here. Yael pulled the bag close and quietly rummaged inside until she found the charts. Then she felt around for something else—the little stone figurine of the moon goddess that Parthia had given her. It was small enough to fit in the palm of her hand, and it felt comforting, somehow, when she gripped the smooth, polished stone figure in her fist. *"Hold it tightly whenever you are afraid or in danger,"* Parthia had told her. *"And someday when you're giving birth to a child of your own, she will protect you."* Yael studied the little naked figurine in the dim light, then tucked it back inside the bag. It would have to stay hidden for now.

She inched toward the opening again, carrying the star charts. She lifted the tent flap to stick her head out, then pulled the moonstone amulet from beneath her dress. The smooth white stone looked as radiant and luminous as the real moon. She wished she could wear it on the outside of her clothing, but she was afraid that Iddo or Zechariah would see it and ask questions. Safta Dinah had noticed it once when Yael was bathing but Yael had lied and said that the necklace had been a gift from her mother.

The scroll made a crinkling sound as she unrolled it. Yael glanced at Abba again. He was still asleep. He probably wouldn't care what she did—after all, he had consulted Parthia and other Babylonian seers when Mama was sick. But now that he had moved back to Jerusalem, maybe he didn't believe in them anymore. Yael couldn't take that chance.

She looked down at the open chart, hoping that the moon would give enough light to read it. But the light was still too dim, the tiny figures on the scroll too small, even when she held the parchment close to her eyes or tilted it toward the moon's light. It was the month of Ab, which meant that the constellation of the lion was dominant in the sky. She heard movement in the next tent, but before she could hide the charts again, Zaki poked his head out from beneath the flap.

"Yael? . . . What are you doing?" he whispered.

"Nothing." The scrolls rustled like dry leaves as she quickly rolled them up again. Zaki moved toward her on his hands and knees.

"Are you doing sorcery or something?"

"No—I'm just looking at the stars, that's all."

"What are the scrolls for?"

She sighed, wondering if she could trust him. "They help me figure out what the stars are saying."

He moved closer and lowered his voice even more. "If they catch you doing those things here, you know what the punishment will be? Death! The Torah says to stone a sorceress to death!"

Her heart beat a little faster. Was he telling the truth? "You can't tell anyone, Zaki. You promised." She shoved the charts into her bag again and pushed it beneath the tent flap.

"You have to get rid of those scrolls before someone catches you."

"No, I don't. They're mine. I need them." She would never be able to explain how much she longed for guidance in this strange new place. Ever since Mama died, her life had felt so uncertain, like being tossed around in the back of a runaway cart with nothing solid to hang on to. The stars remained the same no matter where she traveled. "Good night, Zaki."

Yael ducked beneath her tent and lay down again, but she was still too restless to sleep. When she heard Zaki settle down in his tent, she lifted the flap and poked her head out one more time to look up. A falling star streaked across the sky and she made a wish on it, wishing for a new friend now that Zaki was so bossy.

The most important star, the one that all of the others circled around, shone brightly above her. Parthia had taught her how to find it by looking at the constellation that resembled a huge dipping gourd. The morning star was an important one, too, but it hadn't risen above the horizon yet—or else the mountains across the valley blocked it from sight. The longer Yael looked at the sky, the more stars began to appear, as if they'd been hiding behind their mother's skirts like shy children. Soon the heavens were white with them. How beautiful they were, holding secrets she longed to discover.

At last her eyes grew tired, and she rolled back inside the tent and tucked her moonstone amulet inside her tunic again. She would have to find a way to grab a few moments to herself during the day so she could study the charts without being seen. Then she could find the constellations more easily at night. Someday she would know all of the stars' secrets.

Wrapped in her blanket, Yael finally drifted off to sleep.

Chapter 13

Iddo didn't sleep for the rest of the night, his mind racing back and forth like a weaver's shuttle between the ghosts of his past that haunted the ruins of Jerusalem and excitement for a future he never dreamed he would see. The nightmare left him badly shaken. Why had the dreams started again after so many months without one?

At breakfast, his hands still shook, and he nearly spilled the bowl of roasted grain as he reached to take it from Dinah. "Are you sure you're all right?" she asked, steadying it for him. "Your face is as white as your beard. The circles under your eyes look like bruises."

"Thank you for that fine description. Now I have no need of a mirror."

"Iddo, no one will mind if you stay here and rest today. You've barely slept for two nights and—"

"You don't need to remind me or anyone else about my nightmares." Wasn't it bad enough that he had awakened half the campsite with his screaming last night? Why remind everyone of his weakness as they sat together, eating?

Dinah passed him the basket of figs next, watching him closely. "Will you promise not to work so hard in the hot sun today?"

He didn't reply. How could he promise such a thing when the Holy One had given him a job to do?

"May I go with you again today?" Zechariah asked.

"I'm sorry, Zaki, but I promised the other priests that I would help catalogue the temple treasures, and it will take us all day. Stay here and help Safta." He ate a few more bites of food, aware of everyone's scrutiny, then decided to leave.

Iddo hated the way his legs trembled as he climbed up the path to the city. Thankfully, he would sit all day as he recorded the treasures, making sure that everything on the long list of silver and gold items had arrived safely from Babylon.

"Prince Sheshbazzar has called for a meeting first," the others told him when he arrived at the treasury. "He wants to make an announcement."

The prince got right to the point as soon as everyone had assembled. "After time to reflect on recent events, I've decided that we need to build houses for ourselves and our families right away. Our work on the altar will have to wait a little longer."

"Wait," Iddo interrupted. "Build houses? Shouldn't rebuilding the temple be our top priority? Isn't that what the Holy One brought us back here to do?"

"Yes, and it still is a priority, Iddo. But the anger and hostility we saw in the Samaritan mob the other day is a serious concern. They see us as invaders, and there have already been some attacks. Some livestock has disappeared from our caravan during the night, and we fear these attacks will escalate. We're too vulnerable living in tents. We need to build houses, and I believe the safest place is up here on the ridge, in what used to be the old City of David." Sheshbazzar wasn't finished, but Iddo interrupted him again.

"The Almighty One didn't set us free so we could live comfortable lives in stone houses. We were comfortable and safe in Babylon."

"Yes, but I feel it's important to stake our claim to Jerusalem by building a permanent settlement here and—"

"We can stake our claim—and the Almighty One's claim—by rebuilding His temple."

"And we will do that, Iddo. This delay is only temporary. Once we're all out of the valley, we will return to our projects on the temple mount." Sheshbazzar was losing patience with him, but Iddo didn't care. He had to convince him and the others that this decision was a mistake.

"Listen," Iddo said, "if our enemies are a threat, then restoring the daily sacrifices becomes even more urgent. Without the sacrifices, what right do we have to petition the Almighty One for protection?"

Sheshbazzar stroked his white beard, his face stern. "I'm sorry, Iddo, but I didn't call this meeting to discuss the issue. I called it to announce that I'm suspending our work on the temple mount to give everyone time to move out of the Kidron Valley and into permanent homes. I ask for your patience."

"Let's hope the Almighty One will be patient." Iddo felt helpless. Sheshbazzar was a royal prince and the official governor of the new territory of Judah. His decision was final.

When the meeting ended, Iddo went to work tallying the temple treasures, taking all morning and part of the afternoon to account for every article. As he was rolling up the finished scrolls, the high priest drew him aside. "Can you stay and work a little longer? The leaders of some of our wealthier families have come forward to give freewill offerings to help rebuild God's house," he said. "We could use your help recording those donations."

The totals were staggering. Iddo counted sixty-one thousand drachmas of gold and five thousand minas of silver—all worth hundreds of years of wages. The patrons had also contributed one hundred linen garments for the priests to wear. Iddo laid aside his scrolls for a moment to examine the beautiful clothing, running his hand over the luxurious fabric. There were turbans of fine linen, headbands, and undergarments of finely twisted linen. Sashes of blue, purple, and scarlet yarn, exquisitely embroidered. As a slave in Babylon, he had never worn garments of such fine quality, but one day he would wear these. "The treasures we catalogued today need to be put to use to serve God," he told Jeshua, "not locked in a storehouse. These garments need to be worn."

"And they will, Iddo. In time. Can you come with me, please, so I can show you one more thing?" The high priest lit a small oil lamp and led Iddo into the windowless treasury. He set down the lamp inside and picked up a slender object about four feet long wrapped in a linen cloth. He carefully unwound the wrapping to reveal a straight, slender tube with a flared end, made from hammered silver. He handed it to Iddo. "According to our temple records, the men in your family once played these silver trumpets."

"Yes, I remember . . ." As Iddo ran his fingers over the cool, smooth metal, tracing the instrument's flared bell, he recalled standing in the temple courtyard as a boy, listening to the penetrating trumpet call that sounded from the pinnacle. His father had been the one blowing it.

"These trumpets will announce the appointed feasts and New Moon festivals and will be an important part of our worship. The Torah says that the sound of the trumpet shall be a memorial for us before our God. We need you and your sons to carry on the tradition of your forefathers."

Iddo handed back the instrument. "I-I'm sorry . . . but I don't know how to blow it. I was too young when . . . when the end came."

"I understand," Jeshua said, wrapping the linen cloth around the trumpet again. "I've asked around and unfortunately, none of the other priests remember how to play it, either. Even so, I would like you to take a shofar home to practice on. Someone needs to learn how to play it again." He picked up one of the long, curved ram's horns that were lying with the trumpets and handed it to Iddo. "Maybe by the time the Feast of Trumpets comes in a few months, you'll be ready."

Iddo carried the ram's horn down to his campsite in the valley when the workday ended. It didn't weigh much, but it felt heavy in his hands, weighted with responsibility. "Is that a shofar?" Zechariah asked as he ran out to meet him. "What's it for, Saba?"

"Yes, it's a shofar. The high priest asked me to learn how to play it, so I can blow the silver trumpets the way our forefathers once did. You'll play the trumpets one day, too."

"May I hold it?" Iddo handed it to Zechariah and watched him turn the horn over and over in his hands, studying it carefully before looking up at Iddo again. "You never told me that our ancestors played the shofar."

"I had forgotten all about it until today. Do you remember where the tradition of the ram's horn comes from?"

"Um . . . from when Abraham offered to sacrifice Isaac on Mount Moriah?"

"Very good. But don't make your answer sound like a question next time. Now tell me, what does the sound of the shofar remind us of?"

Zechariah thought for a moment. "God's salvation?" Iddo frowned, and Zaki quickly changed his reply from a question to a statement. "It reminds us of our salvation."

"Very good. In faith, Abraham told his son that God himself would provide the lamb for the sacrifice. And the ram that took Isaac's place and saved him was captured by its horn—like this one."

"Will you play it for me, Saba?" he asked.

"I don't remember how." He lifted the small end to his mouth and blew air into it but nothing came out except a sound like the wind. "I will have to learn how," Iddo said. But who would teach him?

That night another nightmare catapulted Iddo from his bed. He'd been so weary after two sleepless nights that he had fallen into an exhausted sleep only to be jolted out of it in terror. Once again, his screams awakened his neighbors, who came running. "I'm fine, I'm fine," he assured all of them. "I'm sorry for disturbing you again."

Iddo put on his outer robe and went outside his makeshift tent to sit on the broken block of stone that served as their table. He gazed across the valley at the Mount of Olives, afraid to close his eyes again. He would be barred from the priesthood if his nightmares were seen as a mental defect.

A moment later, Dinah came out to sit beside him. "I'm sorry for waking you," he told her. "Please go back to bed." Instead, she nudged him to move over so she could sit beside him.

"Maybe if you talked about your dreams you would get past them, back to the good memories of when you lived here."

"I can't talk about them."

"Iddo, we've been married nearly forty years, and I've never asked you to tell me about your nightmares or what those terrible memories were. But I'm asking you now, for your own good." When he didn't reply, Dinah placed her hand on his cheek and made him turn to face her. "If you tell me what your dreams are about, maybe they'll stop."

He hesitated. What if he told her the truth? Would she despise him? It was a risk he had to take. The dreams had to stop. He needed to sleep. He needed to wear that linen robe and embroidered sash to serve as a priest. He looked over his shoulder at the shofar, lying where he'd placed it just inside his tent last night. It was his family's job to play it.

"What's the earliest thing you can remember?" Dinah prompted.

"My earliest memories are in Anathoth, the village in the mountains where my family lived. I remember how green it was, and how the wind rustled as it blew through the trees. I used to listen to the birds singing at dawn every morning." He couldn't recall any birdsong in Babylon.

"Is the village far from here?"

"No, only a few miles. We would walk from there to Jerusalem in about an hour's time. My father used to carry me on his shoulders until I got too old to be carried. Then he carried my brother."

"You never told me you had a brother. What's his name?"

Iddo had never told anyone. He hadn't wanted to think about his brother or remember his last moments with him. "His name was Jacob," he said after a long pause. "He was two years younger than me. My father said it was my job to watch over him, to help take care of him. . . ." He bent forward, holding his stomach as the ache of regret gnawed at him.

Dinah rested her hand on his back, rubbing gently. "What else do you remember?"

He waited for the dull pain to ease before sitting up again. "We moved from Anathoth into the city when the Babylonian soldiers invaded our land for the final time. Everyone did. No one dared to stay outside the walls. And once we were safely inside Jerusalem, we remained there for two and a half years while the city was under siege. We had nothing left to eat in the end. I remember how thin my brother became, how his bones seemed to poke through his skin. I suppose I looked the same, but I didn't think about it at the time. . . . My mother had grown very thin, too, except for her stomach. She gave birth to another baby the final year of the siege but he was stillborn. How could he live when my mother gave all of her food to my brother and me? It was my fault—"

"No, Iddo. You know that you would do the very same thing for our children. Any parent would." He gave a small shrug, admitting the truth of her words. "Tell me about your father," she continued.

"I used to hear him crying at night after he thought we were asleep. His own father had been captured during the second exile along with a group of priests that included Rebbe Ezekiel. My father kept weeping and saying, 'We were wrong . . . we were wrong . . . and now my family will pay the price.' I didn't understand what he had done wrong. Even now I'm not sure."

When he paused, Dinah squeezed his hand. "And then . . . ?"

Iddo looked up at the sky. It was a lighter shade of black above the mountain across from them. The stars were gradually fading, and morning would soon dawn. "And then the end came," he said. "The Babylonian soldiers broke through the walls and flooded the streets. My father told us to stay hidden inside the house while he and the other chief priests went up to defend the temple. We tried to hide, my mother and Jacob and me, along with dozens of other people who crowded together in the house. It had once been a beautiful home with polished stone floors and plastered walls, much finer than our tiny home in Anathoth. But several families lived there with us—women and children and old people. I don't even know who they all were. But after the Babylonians broke through the walls, all we could do was cower there together, hoping they wouldn't find us."

Iddo realized that his shoulders had slumped forward again as if he was trying to hide, trying to make himself small so he wouldn't be seen. His voice dropped to a near whisper. "A long time passed," he finally said. "Jacob and I huddled close to my mother, her arms around us. I put my fingers in my ears to shut out the sounds from the streets outside, screams and cries and shouts. Then thick black smoke began leaking past the shuttered windows and doors and into the tiny room where we hid.

We tried so hard to be quiet, but the smoke grew thicker and thicker until we coughed and choked on it. Then part of the roof collapsed in flames, right in front of us. Our house was on fire and we had to get out! We had to run!"

Iddo stopped. He didn't want to remember any more, but Dinah gave his hand a firm squeeze, encouraging him to continue.

"We ran into the maze of streets, everyone scattering as we tried to escape the flames. Jacob and I each clung to one of Mama's hands, and I could see the terror in her eyes. She led us toward the stairs to the temple, up to where my father was, groping through the smoke. My eyes stung and watered from it. The air felt as hot as the *khamsin* winds that blow in from the desert. But we never made it to the temple. A group of soldiers appeared through the haze, marching straight toward us. Mama tried to turn around and run the other way, but there were soldiers behind us, too. Mama pushed Jacob and me to the ground, shoving us beneath something on the side of the road—a cart or a table, I don't remember what it was. But she didn't have time to hide with us. The soldiers attacked her. One of the men threw her to the ground, climbed on top of her . . ."

Iddo no longer tried to stop his tears. It was impossible. Dinah rested her head on his shoulder. "When the soldier was finished, he pulled out his knife and killed her. He slit my mother's throat in the same cold, practiced way that my father sacrificed sheep." He stopped and covered his face with his hands, unable to speak.

After a moment, he felt Dinah lean away from him. She pulled his hands down from his face and said, "Then what happened, Iddo?" He shook his head, unwilling to tell her the rest. "Please," she said softly. "Tell me."

He drew a breath. Exhaled. "Jacob and I had been clinging to each other, but my brother suddenly broke free and crawled out of our hiding place before I could stop him. He went to

Mama, calling for her. . . . And the soldier killed him, too. He lifted him up in the air by one leg and . . . and smashed his head against the stones." Iddo closed his eyes to shut out the image, but it was still there. It would always be there.

"And all that time," he said when he could speak again, "all that time as I watched them kill my family, I stayed hidden. I was a coward, Dinah, so I hid."

"No. You were a child."

He shook his head. "In all of my nightmares, I'm hiding beneath that cart again. I always tell myself to get up this time, to help my mother, to save her before the soldier kills her. I promise to hang tightly to Jacob this time and not let go. But even in my dreams I can't move. I don't help my mother, and I don't stop my brother from crawling out and going to her. Night after night I'm too cowardly to move."

"You were just a child," she said again. "How could you defend them against soldiers with swords? No one could possibly blame you for what you did."

"No one has to. I blame myself." Iddo ran his hand over his face, wiping his eyes. "Now you know why I never wanted to talk about what happened. I didn't want you to know the truth. I was too ashamed to tell you that I was a coward. And my cowardice is the reason why I lived while all the others died." He looked up at Dinah, her face clearly visible now in the dawning light. He expected to see revulsion in her eyes. She would despise him from now on, and he deserved it. Instead he saw pity. And love.

"Yes, you lived, Iddo," she said, stroking his face. "And now our nation and our people will live, too. We have three beautiful children who wouldn't be alive today if you had died. Seven grandchildren—maybe eight by now if Deborah had her baby. Think of all the generations who will live after you because you had the wisdom to stay hidden."

"It was cowardice."

She shook her head. "And where does the Almighty One fit into your story? If He thought you were a coward, why did He allow you to survive?"

"So He could punish me with exile. And He is still punishing me by sending these nightmares, forcing me to relive my shame."

"Your nightmares come from your own imagination, not from the Holy One. Thousands and thousands of our people were either killed or exiled by the Babylonians. And from what I can see, the same fate met those who believed in God and those who didn't, good people and bad people, heroes and cowards. Even Daniel the Righteous One was sent into exile, wasn't he? He certainly wasn't a coward, am I right?"

"Yes. You're right," he mumbled.

"But you said it yourself, Iddo—our punishment has ended and God is restoring us. If it was His will to destroy our people, He had plenty of chances to do it. But do you believe that He's showing mercy now?"

"He must be because we're back in Jerusalem." Where the sky was growing brighter and brighter, painting the dawning sky pink, turning all of the scattered building stones into gold.

"Then if He's showing you mercy, nothing else matters. Put the past behind you."

She was right. God's people weren't merely coming home, they were rebuilding the temple. Soon, when the altar was finished and the first sacrifices were slain, Iddo could ask God to forgive him for all his sins.

Dinah took his hand again. "Afterward, Iddo. What happened afterward?"

"What do you mean?"

"After you crawled out from your hiding place?"

"I don't know . . . I . . . I remember staying hidden for a very long time . . . until I got hungry. The soldiers finally left, and I couldn't bear to stay there any longer and see my mother and my brother, so I crawled out to search for food. I walked through streets that were black with smoke and blood and soot. Day or night? I didn't know. I had to step over countless bodies because there was no way around them. I was trying to find my way to the temple to look for my father, but none of the streets looked familiar.

"Eventually, I reached the open square at the base of the temple mount where the stairs and the empty ritual baths were. I found a group of survivors all huddled together, guarded by soldiers. But when I saw that these people had food, I didn't care about the soldiers. I was so hungry that I ran toward the survivors and grabbed a piece of bread from a woman's hand. She didn't stop me. She was half-crazed with terror and grief, and she let me have her bread. She kept calling me Gideon, thinking that I was her son. She wanted so much to believe that I was him, so I let her. I never learned her name. She took care of me all the way to Babylon, but she lost her mind from grief not long after we arrived. She had suffered so much abuse that she didn't know who she was anymore, let alone who I was. By then, the Jews who had been carried to Babylon during the first and second exiles all had homes in the city and they took care of all the women and orphans after we arrived, making sure we were fed and had places to live. You know the rest, Dinah."

"Yes, I know the rest."

Morning had come, and it was time to start the workday. Iddo heard the shuffling and murmuring of people moving around in some of the nearby tents, women grinding wheat between stones to make flour, the crackle of kindling when it caught fire. He wrapped his arm around Dinah's shoulder and pulled her close. As a lonely orphan, Iddo had never imagined that he would love another person again. Or be loved by anyone.

"All my life I've hated the Babylonian people," he said. "Hated being among them, looking at them face-to-face. I saw in each one of them the features of the man who slaughtered my family."

"I understand," she said. "And now that you've told me the very worst of it, Iddo, tell me what you remember from before the Babylonians invaded."

"When we still lived in Anathoth?"

"Yes. Tell me what you remember about the good days."

He lowered his head into his hands again. His head ached, hammering as hard as it had during those long months in Jerusalem when he was always thirsty, always hungry.

He heard Dinah's cousin Shoshanna singing as she prepared breakfast in a neighboring tent, and he remembered that his mother used to sing, too. "My mother loved Shabbat. She used to say it was her favorite day."

"Why?"

"Because she didn't have to cook or clean or wash anything for an entire day. She could rest and play with us, sing to us."

"And your father?"

Iddo reached through the open tent flap behind him and picked up the ram's horn that the priest had given him to use for practice. As he ran his fingers down the shofar's long, gentle curve, another buried memory suddenly came to him. His father had taught him to make a buzzing sound with his lips, making them vibrate against each other. Iddo imitated the sound, stiffly at first, but it became easier and easier as he continued doing it, letting his lips relax. Dinah watched him, saying nothing.

"That was how my father played the shofar. He said his lips did all the work. The horn simply made the buzzing sound louder so it would carry into the distance."

"Show me, Iddo."

"I'll wake the entire caravan."

"Do it softly, then."

He repeated the buzzing sound with his lips, then lifted the shofar and pressed the narrow end of it against his mouth. The shofar gave a short *toot*. "Abba said he used his tongue to make the calls. He would go 'tu, tu, tu' with his tongue against the mouthpiece. I remember now!" Iddo held it to his lips again and made another soft *toot*, wary of blowing too loudly and waking his neighbors—or sending the ones who were already awake into a panic. He lowered the horn to his lap. It was a start.

Dinah leaned against him, and he wrapped his arms around her, holding her tightly. Across the valley from them, the sun had risen in splendor behind the mountain, so blindingly bright he had to look away.

"What would I ever do without you, Dinah?" he murmured. "When God created the paradise of Eden, He said that everything was good except for one thing—it was not good for the man to be alone. So He created Eve to be Adam's helper. And He gave you to me when I was all alone. Do you know what that word *helper* really means?"

She pulled back to look into his eyes and shook her head.

"It means so much more than simply baking my bread and sharing my bed. Moses used the same word to describe what God does for us. 'He is your shield and helper and your glorious sword.' You're stronger than I am, Dinah. You always have been. I need you in the days ahead to help me face all of my battles. I'm so blessed to have you by my side."

Chapter 14

Sunlight leaked through the crack beneath the tent covering when Yael opened her eyes. She smelled smoke from the campfire, the aroma of flatbread baking, and heard the low mumble of voices outside. Her father's sleeping mat was empty. She sat up beneath the sagging roof, rubbing the sleep from her eyes, then lifted the tent flap to look outside. Safta Dinah had spread the rug on the ground for breakfast and Zaki, his grandfather, and her own father all sat around it, eating.

For a second night, Iddo's nightmares had awakened Yael, and once again she had poked her head outside the tent to study the night sky for a while. She had lain awake for so long that now she had overslept. She quickly put on her outer robe, tied the belt around her waist, then crawled outside to sit beside Abba on the rug. No sooner had she sat down when Iddo and Zaki both stood.

"Are you ready to go, Mattaniah?" Iddo asked.

"Go without me," Abba said, waving him away. "I have plans."

"What plans are more important than morning prayers?"

Abba looked away for a moment, then up at Iddo. "I'm going to walk over to the local village this morning."

Yael was suddenly wide awake. "May I go with you, Abba?" He didn't seem to hear her.

"What is your business in a Samaritan village, if you don't mind me asking?"

Abba looked uneasy as he ran his fingers through his beard. Yael could tell that he did mind Iddo's question. "Well . . . I went for a walk while you were gone yesterday and found a nice piece of land that I would like to farm. I've decided to talk to the village elders about leasing it or buying it from them."

"Wait. You're *buying* the land? We don't have to purchase land, Mattaniah. The Holy One gave all of it to us."

"I understand," he said, rising to his feet. "But I'm going to offer to pay for it as a gesture of goodwill. The villagers aren't happy about us 'invading' their country, as they see it, and so—"

"That's a very bad idea, Mattaniah. You're setting a bad precedent for the rest of us. The local people will expect everyone to pay for land from now on."

"Look, the patch of land I have in mind already has a small grove of olive trees and a few fig trees on it. The property is neglected and overrun with weeds, but it's close enough for me to farm and still live here in Jerusalem. It's also close to the local village, so I thought I would make friends there."

"Come to prayers with us, first. I think you should discuss this with our leaders."

"There's nothing to discuss," Abba said. "My mind is made up."

Yael tugged on his robe to get his attention. "Abba, may I please—?"

He held up his hand, warning her to wait and not interrupt. "I want this piece of land, Iddo, and I'm going to make the elders an offer."

Iddo exhaled. "Listen, aside from the issue of buying or

not buying, we need builders with your experience to help us with the temple. We have plenty of men who can farm the land already."

"I understand. But I became a builder by necessity, not by choice. Our fathers were brought to Babylon as slaves and put to work. None of us had a choice."

"I thought you liked your work as a builder. You had a good business in Babylon."

"It was work, nothing more. None of us could own land in Babylon, and I want to work the land. I've agreed to live near Jerusalem and to perform my duties as a Levite, and I'll keep that promise. But in between those duties I want to grow wheat and olives and grapes."

The two men studied each other for a long moment. Yael took advantage of the brief silence to tug on Abba's robe again. "May I come with you today? Please, Abba?"

He looked down at her in surprise, as if he had forgotten she was there. "Don't you have work to do here with Safta Dinah?"

Yael stifled a groan at the thought. How could she make him understand how she felt, confined like a sheep in a pen that was too small? She longed to explore the world the way she used to do in Babylon, to meet interesting people like Parthia and learn fascinating things instead of cooking all day. She stood and went to Safta Dinah, wrapping her arms around her for a rare hug, hoping to win her over. "You don't mind if I go with Abba, do you, Safta? Please?"

She brushed a strand of hair from Yael's eyes. "Are you sure that it's safe to go near the Samaritans, Mattaniah?"

"I'm not afraid," Yael said.

"The pagans often choose wives as young as Yael," Safta added. "And she's a lovely girl."

Abba appeared to be thinking. "Well . . ." Yael tensed, preparing to beg some more. "I guess you can come with me," he finally said. "I might seem less threatening to the Samaritans if I have my little daughter along."

Yael squirmed out of Safta's arms and quickly fetched the wooden comb. She stood submissively while Dinah untangled all the snarls and braided her thick hair into a long plait that hung down her back. It was a small price to pay for a chance at freedom. A few minutes later Yael skipped along the Kidron Brook beside her father, thrilled to leave their campsite, the braid thumping against her back. They took a different path than the one the women took when they went for water and headed toward a cluster of low stone houses across the valley. The sun grew hotter and hotter as it climbed in the sky, but Yael didn't care. She felt like dancing beneath it.

As they came to the outskirts of the village, Yael spotted a small shrine similar to the ones she'd seen in Babylonian neighborhoods like Parthia's. "Look, Abba. Someone made an offering to the gods. Do they worship Marduk and Ishtar here?"

"Don't ask questions, Yael. Just stay beside me and keep quiet." He reached for her hand.

A group of men sat on a rug outside the unwalled village as if guarding the entrance. Yael paid no attention to the conversation as Abba stopped to talk with them, gazing instead down the main road into town. The stone houses sprawled in a haphazard circle with an open area in the middle, where ragged children played and chickens pecked in the dirt. Another group of squealing children chased after a goat, waving their arms as they tried to herd it back to its pen. The village looked dirtier than the Jewish community where Yael had lived in Babylon. Rubbish littered the street and the stench of manure made her want to pinch her nose closed. She turned back to her father as the sound of the men's voices grew louder, and she heard one of them say, "You must talk to Zabad, our village leader. The land belongs to him. Come. I will take you to his house."

Yael gripped Abba's hand tightly as they entered the village, crossing the open area. The children stopped to watch as they passed, staring wide-eyed as if they'd never seen strangers before. Yael smiled and wiggled her fingers in a friendly wave but none of them returned the gesture. The man led them across the plaza and down a shadowy lane. The house at the end of it was the largest one in the village and stood apart from the others. They walked through an open gate and into a broad, sunny area paved with cobblestones and bustling with activity. It reminded Yael of Zaki's house back in Babylon, with women of all ages laboring busily over their chores. One woman ground grain, another kneaded dough, a third shaped the dough into flat rounds and laid them on a hot stone to bake. An elderly woman with a face as brown and wrinkled as a raisin ran a shuttle back and forth through the long, vertical threads of a loom. Beside her, a wispy girl with dark, curly hair tried to spin a clump of wool into a strand of yarn. It seemed as though none of the women dared to look up as she and Abba halted in front of the door to the house. A boy Zaki's age stood guard.

"This is Mattaniah, one of the new Jewish settlers," their guide told the boy. "He would like to speak with Zabad."

"This way," the young man said.

Abba let go of Yael's hand. "Wait out here with the women," he said as he followed the others into the house.

Yael looked around again. The women glanced shyly at her before quickly lowering their heads. She wandered over to the girl who struggled to spin the yarn. "Slow down, Leyla," the old woman chided. "It takes patience to spin. If you go too fast the yarn will turn out lumpy and will be useless."

The girl concentrated on her work but the strand of yarn frayed and snapped. "Oh, I can't do this! It's too hard!" She dropped everything into her lap and looked up at Yael. "Do you know how to spin?" she asked.

"No, and I don't want to learn either, but Safta Dinah says I have to."

The girl laughed. "My name is Leyla. What's yours?"

"Yael."

Leyla laid her work aside and stood. Her pale skin was nearly transparent, the color of the moon on a bright, sunlit day. Her dark eyes looked large in her thin face, the way Mama's had before she died. Yael could see fine, blue veins beneath Leyla's skin.

"I've never seen you in our village before, and I know everyone," Leyla said. "Are you one of the people from that big caravan that's camped in our valley?"

Yael nodded. "We used to live in Babylon, a long way from here."

"How old are you?" Leyla asked.

"Ten."

Leyla smiled. "We're the same age." But she looked very small and frail to be ten years old. They talked for a while, and Leyla explained that her father had three wives and several sons but she was his only daughter. She pointed to the boy who had led Abba inside—he had emerged from the house again to stand in the doorway—and said, "That's my brother Rafi. He's going to inherit everything Abba owns someday. Rafi is the only friend I have." Yael could see the resemblance between the two. Rafi had the same beautiful wide eyes, the same head of dark, loosely curled hair. He wore it longer than Jewish boys did, and it encircled his head like a thick halo. "Abba doesn't let me play with the village girls," Leyla continued, "because he's afraid I'll get sick if I run around outside. Will you be my friend?"

"I would love to!" Yael remembered the wish she had made on a falling star and was pleased that the moon goddess had answered it so soon. "I don't have any sisters or brothers at all," Yael said. "I used to have a friend named Zaki, but he never wants to have fun anymore."

"Then I'll be your friend from now on. I think the stars must have brought us together." Yael's heart beat a little faster. The stars? Was Leyla a believer, too? She followed Leyla around to the side of the house where a little pen held a small herd of goats. Yael leaned against the fence, petting the goats that wandered over to her. Their heads felt knobby beneath their stiff, rough fur. "You and your father are Jews, aren't you?" Leyla asked after a while. Yael hesitated before finally nodding. "My father is Jewish, too," Leyla said.

"He is? I thought all of the Jews went to Babylon."

"My father's family didn't. His grandfather hid in the mountains when the soldiers came so he wouldn't get taken away. Soldiers brought my mother's family here from a different country. Mama died when I was born and so my grandmother—the one who's trying to teach me to spin—takes care of me now."

"My mama died, too," Yael told her.

"We're so much alike, aren't we? Both the same age, and we both lost our mother. We're going to be best friends, I just know it." Leyla reached for Yael's hand. "Come on, let's go back and sit in the shade. I get dizzy if I stand in the sun for too long." They walked back to Leyla's grandmother and sat on a rug beneath the overhanging roof. Vines climbed up the wooden supports and hung over the top making a cool, shady place to sit.

"Your necklaces are very pretty," Yael said, admiring the pretty stones and feathers and other objects hanging from thin leather thongs around Leyla's neck.

"They're amulets." Leyla fingered the one that looked like a small embroidered pouch. "I get pains and fevers sometimes, and my grandmother says the amulets bring good luck from the gods and keep the fever away."

"My friend Parthia gave me this moonstone for good luck." Yael pulled it out from beneath her tunic to show her.

"It's beautiful. The moon goddess is very powerful."

Yael's heart beat a little faster. "Do you worship the moon goddess?"

"Yes, my grandmother and I do." Leyla eyed her curiously. "But I didn't think Jews like you did."

"Most of the people I know don't believe in her," Yael said, "so I have to keep it a secret. But my mother worshiped her and so do I."

Leyla smiled. "You don't have to keep it a secret here. Why don't you live in our village from now on? We could be best friends."

"I don't think I can live here, but Abba wants to plant a garden near here. If I get a chance, I'll study my star charts and see what the stars say about—"

"You know about astrology?"

Yael jumped when Leyla's grandmother interrupted them. She had forgotten that the old woman was sitting right behind her. Why had she blurted it out? Zaki said Jews would kill a sorceress and Leyla's father was Jewish.

The older woman came to crouch beside her. "It's all right, Yael. We look to the stars for guidance, too."

Yael gave a sigh of relief. This was all too wonderful—finding a new friend and people she could share her beliefs with, without fear. "I'll bring my star charts the next time I come," she said. "We can study them together."

"And I'll make an offering to bribe the goddess so she'll let you come back again," Leyla said. "We'll be best friends."

Abba's voice interrupted before Yael could reply. "Time to go, Yael." He stood in the courtyard with Leyla's brother, beckoning to her.

"Can't we stay a little longer, Abba?"

He shook his head. "Come on." She gave Leyla a quick hug then rose and took Abba's hand as they left the village and started across the valley to their campsite.

"I liked that village, Abba. Can we live there? I made a new friend."

"We need to live with our own people."

"Leyla's father is Jewish like us."

"Yes, I know. He told me. I made him an offer on that piece of land I want to buy, but he says he needs a few days to consider it. But even if I buy or lease the land from him, we're still going to live with Iddo and Dinah and the others in Jerusalem."

"Will I get to play with Leyla again?"

He gave her braid a playful tug. "I have a feeling that maybe you will."

That afternoon Yael sat with Safta Dinah beneath the shade of their tent as the hot summer sun blazed above them. The air around their campsite felt like the inside of an oven. "Iddo says that we'll start building our new house tomorrow," Safta said, fanning herself with the edge of her head scarf. "A real house, not a tent." She seemed like a different woman to Yael, as if the happy, contented woman she'd known in Babylon had stayed behind with the others while a pale, unhappy shadow of that woman traveled here.

"You hate it here, don't you, Safta? You wish you were back home with your family."

Safta glanced around as if worried that someone would overhear them. "Yael, I never said . . ."

"You pretend that you're happy, and you don't let anyone see your tears, but you wish you had never left Babylon."

For a moment, Dinah's fan stilled, her gaze never leaving Yael's. "Where did you get such an idea?" she finally asked.

Yael shrugged. "Sometimes when I look at people it's like I'm looking through their skin. I can see what's on the inside and not just the outside. Parthia said I had a special gift. I can tell what people are thinking and feeling even though they don't say a single word out loud."

Dinah looked away. "It probably doesn't take a special gift to see that I miss my children and grandchildren." She stared into the distance as she slowly fanned the stifling air. "The Persian soldiers will be returning to Babylon any day, and I keep dreaming of traveling home with them."

"You would really walk all the way back there?" Yael asked. "After it took months and months to get here?"

Safta didn't reply, but Yael knew the answer was yes. She would travel twice that distance to go home. Safta didn't seem to care at all about the Jewish God the way that Iddo and Zechariah did. Yael decided to take a chance.

"If you want me to," she said carefully, "I could look at your stars and see if you ever get to go home in the future."

"What?" Dinah stared at Yael, but her expression was one of surprise, not shock or disapproval.

"I learned to read the stars when we lived in Babylon. And Parthia was right when she told you about your future once before, remember? She said you'd be torn away from home, and you were." Dinah nodded and looked away, but not before Yael saw the sheen of tears in her eyes.

"I don't need to look at the stars to know that I won't be going home." She stood and went inside to begin preparing supper.

When Yael saw Zechariah returning with Iddo later that afternoon, she left her half-finished chores and hurried to meet him, longing for someone to talk to.

"What did you do today, Zaki?"

"Nothing . . . We spent the day figuring out where to build our house and where the new house of assembly is going to be." Yael sank down on the ground in the open space in front of her tent and pulled him down beside her.

"You explored the ruins? That sounds like fun." But Zaki's expression looked as gloomy as Safta Dinah's had. He picked up a stick of kindling wood from the pile and drew marks in the dirt with it. "What's wrong, Zaki?"

"Saba is worried because we're supposed to be building the Almighty One's house, not our own."

"Oh," she said with a shrug. "Well, I went to the Samaritan village today and made a new friend. Her name is Leyla, and I can't wait to go back to see her again. You should come with me next time, Zaki. She has a brother your age named Rafi. Maybe we could all play together like you and I used to do, remember?"

"I can't. They're building the house of assembly so they can start a *yeshiva*. I'll have to go there every day to study the Torah when it's ready."

"Every day? Why?"

"Because when our ancestors stopped studying the Torah, they fell into sin."

"They fell . . . where?"

"They started doing things that the Torah forbids. Their biggest sin was worshiping false gods."

Yael rolled her eyes. He would probably call her little carved moon goddess a false one. She was about to ask him why his grandfather had moon dreams if the goddess wasn't real, but Zaki wasn't finished. "Worshiping idols was one of the reasons why Jerusalem was destroyed and our ancestors were carried to Babylon. We have to be very careful to study the Torah from now on."

"But all day?"

Zaki poked in the dirt so hard that the stick cracked in two. "I'm going to be a priest, and it's the priests' job to teach the Torah to everyone. We're supposed to dedicate ourselves to living a holy life as an example to the people. That means I have to know all the rules and everything."

"It seems to me that your God of Abraham is a very gloomy god."

"Yael! Shh! You shouldn't say such things!"

"Why not? Is He going to strike me dead on the spot or something?" She looked up at the sky, shielding her head in mock fear.

Zaki looked uneasy. "Let's talk about something else."

She leaned closer to him and whispered, "Have you had any more dreams about the future?"

"I don't know . . . I had a crazy dream the other night about a Torah scroll flying through the air like a bird."

"That's what happens when you study too much. What do you think it means?"

"What difference does it make? It's just a dream."

"Parthia said that all our dreams have meanings if you know how to interpret them."

"Listen, Yael, you need to forget all those things that wicked woman tried to teach you." He stabbed at the ground again with his broken stick as if he was mad at her.

"Zechariah?" Iddo called. "It's time to pray." He and Abba were getting ready to leave.

"You're praying *again*?" Yael asked in disbelief.

Zaki stood and dropped the stick on the ground. "I have to go."

Yael remained seated. She probably should help Safta Dinah, but she didn't want to. Instead, she looked up at the pale, daytime moon and thought of her new friend, Leyla. Maybe she was looking up at the very same moon. The thought made Yael smile.

Chapter 15

No one could possibly expect Dinah to live here, could they? She looked at the jumble of toppled stones and weed-filled holes that Iddo pointed to, then up at her husband in disbelief. Was he joking?

"We chose this spot because the foundations of these houses aren't too badly damaged," he said. He was still short of breath after the uphill climb from their camp in the valley, and Dinah felt winded, too. "We can rebuild this house with a little work."

"This?" she asked, spreading her arms. "I don't see a house, Iddo. I see huge rocks that are too big for us to move and hundreds of small stones that will take a lifetime to move, and brambles growing where you say my kitchen courtyard will be, and—"

She was afraid she was going to cry, and she didn't want to lose control in front of the others. Zechariah and Mattaniah rummaged among the weeds within earshot, and Yael was making a game of balancing on the foundation walls, leaping over the gaps between them, scaling the higher walls using the ragged stones for steps. "Yael, be careful!" she scolded, venting her frustration.

"I won't fall," she called back. "Watch this!" She struck a pose on one leg, balanced on a teetering wall of rocks, then grinned and leaped across a void to another pile of stones, as graceful as a gazelle on a mountain slope. Dinah turned her back. Yael's father needed to discipline her, but he wasn't paying attention.

Dinah looked at the pile of rubble in front of her again. "I don't understand why we can't build a house down where our camp is in the Kidron Valley. Wouldn't it be easier to build near the spring or the brook?"

"Are we wiser than our ancestors?" Iddo asked. "King David built Jerusalem on this hill for protection."

"Are we in danger down there?"

"Don't put words in my mouth. I didn't say we weren't safe."

But Dinah could always tell when he was avoiding a subject by the way he played with the fringes on the corners of his garment. He was twirling them now. "Tell me the truth, Iddo. I have a right to know."

"Some of our Samaritan neighbors are a little . . . discontented," he said, lowering his voice. "They see us as invaders. Once they learn about King Cyrus' decree, things will settle down and . . ." He paused as Zechariah made his way back to them.

"Saba, are those caves over there on that hill?" he asked, pointing to a spot across the valley.

"I haven't seen them up close," Iddo said, "but I'm told they're tombs."

"Real tombs?" Yael asked. She jumped down from a nearby foundation wall with a graceful leap. "Do they have dead men's bones inside them and everything? Let's explore them sometime, Zaki. Want to?"

Iddo replied before Zechariah could. "Our families are priests and Levites, Yael. The Torah has rules about becoming ritually unclean from dead bodies."

"Oh. That's too bad," she said with a sigh. She climbed onto the low wall again, then jumped down to the other side and crouched to pick up pieces of broken pottery. "I'm finding some really big pieces, Zaki," she called. "Come see."

He went to kneel beside her, and a few minutes later Dinah heard him shouting, "Saba! Come look what I found! I think it's an arrowhead!"

Iddo climbed over the rocky foundation stones and took the metal object from Zechariah's hand. "Yes, I think it is. I imagine you'll find more of them, if you look. But listen, if you see any bones, don't touch them. They need to be handled with respect and dignity, and buried by men who aren't priests or Levites."

The talk of arrowheads and bones made Dinah shiver. "Tell me the truth about the Samaritans, Iddo," she said when he returned to her side.

"Mattaniah seems to think we can trust them. But our leaders decided that the sooner we move up here from the valley the better."

"I never felt threatened back home in Babylon," she said.

"Joel and your cousin Shoshanna are moving right next door to us. You'll have family close by again and—"

"Will this be our main room? Right here?" Dinah interrupted. She needed to stop him before he tried to tell her that it would be just like home. It wouldn't be.

"Yes. We'll build on these foundations." He traced the outline with a sweep of his hand. "One room will be enough at first, for you and me and Zechariah. As soon as we clear away these stones and repair these walls, we can put our tent covering over it for a roof and live here. I want to get settled as quickly as possible so we can start working on the temple again." He climbed over the low wall and into the space he had indicated, then held out his hand to Dinah as if inviting her into their home.

"It's very small . . ." she said, stepping over the rocks.

"I know. But it's just for now. I'll build you an outdoor hearth near that spot where Yael is digging. I found some blackened stones over there, so I think that's where a hearth used to be. This second, adjoining room will be for Mattaniah and Yael. And we'll repair this alcove back here for storage. There's even a cistern beneath the floor, chiseled out of the bedrock. Once we clean it out and re-plaster it, it'll be as good as new."

"Maybe we'll find buried treasure inside," Yael said. She wandered over to peer inside the cistern, and when she stood, Dinah smoothed her tangled hair away from her face and out of her eyes.

"You need to let me braid your hair again," she said. "You're such a pretty girl, but your hair needs to be tamed and untangled."

"It's fine," she said, shrugging away Dinah's hand. Dinah looked up at Iddo to see if he noticed Yael's unruliness, but he was much too engrossed with his building plans.

"Eventually, we can build a wooden roof over these rooms," Iddo continued, "and channel water into the cistern when it rains. That will spare you the long walk down to the spring every day. Once we plaster the walls and the roof . . ." *Don't say it!* But she couldn't stop him in time. "It will be just like our house in Babylon."

Dinah sighed and closed her eyes. This would never be like their house in Babylon, overflowing with children and grandchildren. Why did Iddo talk as if it would?

"Good morning, Joel," Iddo called out. She looked up to see her cousin Shoshanna and her husband walking toward them.

"This view is beautiful!" Shoshanna said. "Just think—we'll get to wake up to this incredible sight every morning." She halted beside Dinah, linking her arm through hers. "And there's a nice cool breeze up here, too. Won't it be wonderful to live in a real house again, side by side? It will be just like back home."

Dinah gritted her teeth. Not Shoshanna, too!

They cleared stones and weeds all morning, piling rocks on top of the foundations to make the walls higher. The hardest things to clear away were the thick thatches of brambles with roots that seemed to go all the way to the base of the mountain. Dinah heaped the pulled weeds into a pile to dry out and use for kindling. When she lifted a medium-sized building stone, the ground beneath it squirmed and writhed with snakes. Dinah cried out and dropped the stone, nearly falling as she quickly backed away. Some of the eggs in the nest were still intact, some half-open, and some had already hatched, sending innumerable small snakes slithering over and under the rocks. Everyone came running, even Shoshanna and her husband. "What is it, Safta?" Zaki asked.

"There's a nest of snakes under that stone. Be careful!" Dinah stood at a respectful distance, but Yael crouched close to see.

"Can I pick one up?" she asked.

"No, don't!"

Iddo hefted a sizeable rock and began crushing the living snakes and the eggs. So many of them slithered around that Zaki and Yael had to help him. Dinah looked away with a shiver.

They worked all afternoon until it was time to return to their camp. "We've made good progress on our house," Iddo told her as they ate together that evening. "Tonight will be the last night we'll sleep down here beside the cart. Tomorrow we'll carry our goods up the hill and live there from now on. We'll be settled in our house in time to celebrate Shabbat in two days."

Dinah closed her eyes. She couldn't imagine celebrating the Sabbath in a pile of rubble. The caravan had rested on the Sabbath all the way here, and it had been good to stop for a day and not have to pack everything up. But as badly as she needed the day of rest, Dinah knew it wouldn't be a proper Sabbath without her family gathered around her, laughing and eating and celebrating life.

The first night she spent in their half-finished house, Dinah felt so weary and discouraged that she couldn't stop her tears. Her blistered hands were scraped and sore, her muscles so tired from moving rocks all day, that she didn't know how she would carry a water jug to the brook and back. Her body ached from bending and lifting stone after stone, and there were still so many of them left to move. Did the earth grow new ones while she slept?

The men had stretched the tent covering over the foundations to form a roof, weighing it down with rocks. Dinah had to crawl inside on her hands and knees since the walls were barely three feet high—and she couldn't forget the snakes.

She had known the splendor of Babylon, and even though her neighborhood of mud-brick houses hadn't been much, it had been home, the place where her children had been born and where they'd grown. Iddo noticed her tears as he watched her unroll their sleeping mat for the night.

"What's wrong, Dinah?"

"We gave up our home, our family, for this?"

"We're doing this for our children's sakes. We sacrificed what we had so that they can have a better future. So they can worship the Almighty One in His temple."

"But our children aren't here. And to tell you the truth, I don't think they'll ever come." She brushed away a tear and shook out their blanket. "I keep thinking of Rachel and wondering if she's expecting a baby yet. Deborah's baby must have been born by now, and Shoshanna and I weren't there to help her. I'll probably have a dozen more grandchildren someday, babies that I'll never see, never hold, children whose first steps I'll never watch—"

"Don't, Dinah." He took the blanket from her and gripped her hands in his. "You told me to forget the past, remember? Now you must do the same."

"I can't forget our children and grandchildren, Iddo! You can't ask me to forget them."

"We won't forget them. But the Almighty One told us to come here, and we chose to obey Him. Blessings come from obedience. Sarah and Abraham left their families, and didn't God bless them?"

"Sarah didn't leave children and grandchildren behind." Dinah pulled her hands free and finished spreading the blanket. Her tears still fell as she lay down to sleep.

The next morning Shoshanna greeted Dinah with a smile, as cheerful as always. "Let's prepare Shabbat together today," she said. "We'll make all the food and then eat it together. Want to?" Dinah didn't know what to say. Shoshanna walked through the opening where the courtyard gate would be and bent to admire the hearth that Iddo had made. "We should cook everything on your hearth," she said. "Yours looks much nicer than mine."

"Yes. Iddo finished it for me last evening. It . . . it will be nice to work together. Thank you, Shoshanna. It will be very nice."

"It was Iddo's idea. He came over this morning and suggested that I ask you."

Of course. Dinah turned away so Shoshanna wouldn't see her tears. Iddo was trying so hard to make her happy, offering her everything except what she wanted most—to go home.

Shoshanna slipped her arm around Dinah's shoulder. "What's wrong, Dinah? You seem so sad."

"This place will never be home. I miss my family, and I miss delivering babies, don't you?"

"The babies will come, you'll see." She smiled and rested her head on Dinah's shoulder. "And so will our families. In the meantime, we get to prepare a new home for them."

"I hope you're right." She heard a rustling sound behind her and turned to see Yael emerging from her tent. "There you are," Dinah said. "Shoshanna and Joel are going to have Shabbat with us. We're going to cook the meal together."

"Then you don't need my help." Quick as a cat, Yael jumped

up on a half-finished wall to scamper away. But Dinah was just as quick and grabbed Yael's slender arm to stop her.

"Oh no, you don't! It's going to take all three of us if we want to be finished by sundown."

She gave Yael several jobs to do—sorting lentils, grinding grain into flour, peeling cloves of garlic. Each time Yael finished a task she would ask, "Now are we done? Can I go now?" Her shoulders would sag like a weary old man's every time Dinah replied, "No, Yael, there's still more work to do."

Late that afternoon, the three of them walked down to the spring to draw extra water for tomorrow's day of rest. It was a much longer walk than the one Dinah used to make to the well in Babylon, and the trip home would be uphill, carrying the heavy jars. Yael tried to balance a jug on her head like Dinah and Shoshanna but it kept slipping off. "Careful!" Dinah chided. "You'll have more potsherds to add to your collection, and I'll have one less water jug."

"I hate doing women's work like cooking and carrying water," Yael said with a sigh.

"I promised your mother I would turn you into a proper young woman and find you a good husband—"

"I don't want a husband!"

Shoshanna laughed. "You make it sound like Dinah was offering to find you a scorpion."

"The two are just as bad." Yael's jar slipped off her head again, and she caught it moments before it hit the ground. Dinah looked away.

"You may not be thinking of a husband now," Shoshanna said, "but someday a young man will catch your eye and your heart will be drawn to him, and he'll be the only thing you can think about."

Dinah remembered feeling that way about Iddo. She had been overjoyed when their betrothal was announced, and had floated on a cloud of happiness for days. She hadn't been able to stop smiling, and her sisters said she even smiled in her sleep. That happiness had never faded after all these years—until now. Now her joy seemed to die a little more each day, replaced by resentment as bitter as vinegar. Dinah was aware of what was happening, but she didn't know how to stop it.

"One day the young men will be fighting for your hand, Yael," Shoshanna continued. "Just like they fought for Dinah's. She was such a beautiful woman—and she still is. My husband Joel certainly thinks so. He wanted to marry her—did you know that? But Dinah was in love with Iddo. Only Iddo. I've always envied you, Dinah. I know I'm short and plump and that my hair is a frizzy mess—"

"But Joel loves you," Dinah said. "I can tell he does."

"Why do I have to get married at all?" Yael asked. She gave up trying to balance her jug and carried it in her arms.

"Because that's what we were created for," Shoshanna said. "When the Almighty One made the world, He saw that everything was good except for one thing. He said it was not good for the man to be alone. So he gave Adam a wife to be his helper."

"Adam just wanted someone to do all his work," Yael mumbled.

When they reached the bottom of the long, steep slope that led from the city, Dinah saw a crowd of women gathered around the spring. "Look at all the people!" Shoshanna said. "I hope it won't take too long to fill our jugs. Shabbat is coming."

"I'll run ahead and save us a place," Yael said.

"No, Yael! Wait—" She didn't listen. She took off ahead of them, running down the road like a deer.

"I apologize for Yael," Dinah told Shoshanna. "Her family let her run wild when Miriam was dying, and the girl picked up some terrible habits. I'm trying to tame her, but I hardly know where to begin."

"We all have a little too much Babylon in us. But you're doing a good job, Dinah. She'll soon settle down. Just keep loving her."

But Dinah wasn't sure if she wanted to risk being a mother to Yael if it meant losing her someday the way she'd lost her other daughters.

They reached the spring and saw that a group of local women had formed a circle around the reservoir, standing with their water jars, blocking the way. Dinah and Shoshanna joined the growing crowd of Jewish women huddled off to the side looking bewildered and frightened. "What's going on?" Dinah asked one of them.

"We've been waiting for our turn, but they won't let us through. We can't get past them to draw water."

Shoshanna stepped toward the women who were blocking the way, smiling as she said, "Excuse me, please. Our families need fresh water."

"This spring is ours, not yours," one of the local women shouted back.

"I'm sure there's enough for everyone if—" But the women drowned out her words with loud cries, waving their arms as if trying to chase away a flock of birds.

Dinah's pulse began to race. "Let's go home," she told Shoshanna. "We need to get out of here." She scanned the crowd of women, searching for Yael.

"Dinah's right, we may as well leave," one of the other Jewish women said. "They're going to block the spring until the sun goes down, and it'll be too late to draw water, let alone carry it all the way up the hill."

"Where's Yael?" Dinah asked, her panic swelling. "Do you see her?"

"Maybe we should walk back to the caravan camp and draw water from the Kidron Brook," Shoshanna said.

"There isn't enough time," Dinah said. "It's too far, and we need to be home before the sun sets. . . . Yael! Yael, where are you?" she called. The local women were still shouting their fearsome cries. Dinah wanted to run.

"I'm right here," Yael said, weaving through the crowd.

Dinah sagged with relief. "Come on. We're leaving." She turned to hurry back the way she'd come, with Yael and Shoshanna and the other Jewish women following her. "It was a mistake to move back here," she said as she walked. "This land and the spring belong to the local villagers. They've been living here all their lives, and we just arrived."

"Everything will work out," Shoshanna soothed. "We're all a little frightened right now. But they'll share the water with us, you'll see."

"I hope we'll have enough to last until Shabbat ends."

"Why can't we just come back tomorrow?" Yael asked.

"Because it's the Sabbath," Shoshanna replied, "and the Almighty One is giving us a day of rest."

"He sure has a lot of rules to remember," Yael said. "Doesn't He know it's impossible to obey them all? Besides, I don't see why we need to rest for a whole day. I'm not tired."

"We don't rest because we're tired," Shoshanna said. "It's a privilege to be able to stop working whether we're finished or not—and you know our work is never finished. The Holy One gives us an entire day of freedom. Believe me, you'll be thankful for it tomorrow when we can rest and not worry about cooking food because it's already prepared."

By the time the men returned home from their prayers, Dinah and Shoshanna had the rug spread out with the food arranged in the middle of it and the Sabbath lights kindled. The courtyard was open to the sky, and as everyone sat down to eat, the first stars began to appear above them. Iddo recited the blessings over the wine and the bread, the way he had every Friday evening in Babylon. Dinah closed her eyes, remembering her family, picturing them gathered for the meal with their little ones. Were they still keeping Shabbat without them?

She told Iddo what had happened at the spring as they lay in bed together later that night. "From now on we'll send guards with you to protect you. Our women can all go to the spring together later in the morning, after the local women are finished."

"By then the day will be too hot. That's why we go early in the morning or before dusk."

"Everything will be fine, Dinah. Don't worry. God will protect us."

That wasn't what Dinah wanted to hear. She shifted on the sleeping mat, unable to get comfortable beside Iddo.

The Day of Atonement was coming in a few months, the day when Dinah was supposed to confess all her sins and ask the Holy One for forgiveness. She was supposed to reconcile with those she was angry with and ask their forgiveness. But as she looked up at the goatskin ceiling hovering a few feet above her head, it seemed to her that Iddo was the one who needed to ask for forgiveness. He was the one who had dragged her here so far from home.

CHAPTER 16

Yael thought of her friend Leyla every time she saw the pale daytime moon. "When are we going back to Leyla's village?" she asked her father again and again.

"When our new house is finished," he told her. "I'm much too busy to return now." But at breakfast one morning, Iddo had declared their house fit to live in.

"I'm going back to work on the temple mount," he told everyone.

"Now can we go down to Leyla's village, Abba?" she begged. "Please?"

"Not today. I promised to help Iddo."

Yael fingered the round lump of her moonstone, hidden beneath her dress, and closed her eyes, asking the goddess to please make a way for her to see her friend Leyla. In the meantime, she would have to help Dinah with all the tasks that she hated like cooking and carrying water.

Their group of women left late in the morning to walk down the hill to the spring, knowing that the local women would be gone by then. Two Jewish men accompanied them to act as guards. When they arrived, one local woman sat on the stone lip of the reservoir, and Yael recognized her dark, wrinkled face right away—Leyla's grandmother! She broke into a run.

"Yael, stop! Come back!" she heard Dinah yelling behind her, but she kept on running.

"You're Leyla's grandmother, aren't you?" Yael said breathlessly. "I'm her friend, Yael."

The old woman rose to her feet. "Yes, I know who you are. I've been waiting to speak to you."

"To me? Why?"

"Leyla is sick, and she's asking to see you. Will you come to the village with me?"

"I would love to!" The moon goddess had heard her prayer. Yael set her water jug on the ground, ready to leave it behind and go. But a moment later, Dinah gripped her arm.

"What are you doing, running off?" She gave Yael's arm a little shake. "Didn't you hear me calling you?"

"My friend Leyla is sick, and she's asking for me. Can I please go with her grandmother to visit her? Please?"

Dinah backed up a step, pulling Yael with her. The pressure of her fingers made Yael's arm hurt. "We have to ask your father. I'm sorry," she said, addressing Leyla's grandmother. "It's up to him to give permission."

"Tell him that Zabad has personally made this request for his daughter's sake."

"I will. If Mattaniah agrees to let her come, he'll bring her to your village." Dinah continued to step backward as she spoke, tugging Yael with her.

"Ow! You're hurting me. And what about my water jug?"

"I'm not letting go of you again, Yael. Every time I do you run off instead of obeying me." She moved forward so Yael could retrieve her jug but Leyla's grandmother was already walking away, heading down the road to her village alone.

Since Dinah refused to release Yael's arm, Shoshanna had

to fill all three jugs and hand them out. Dinah still wouldn't let go as they retraced their steps up the hill. When they reached the top, she sent one of the guards to fetch Yael's father from the temple mount.

"What's going on?" he asked breathlessly when he arrived twenty minutes later. Iddo had come with him. "Is everything all right?"

Dinah finally released Yael, and she ran to her father, flinging her arms around his waist. Her words came out in a rush of tears. "Leyla is sick, and she's asking for me. Her grandmother was waiting for me at the spring to take me there but Safta wouldn't let me go. Can I please visit Leyla? Please, Abba?"

"Who's Leyla?" Iddo asked. "The guard said the old woman was one of the local Samaritans."

"She is," Abba replied. "Leyla's father is the man I spoke with about that piece of land I want to buy. He's the village leader. I think I'd better take Yael there."

"Will she be safe?" Dinah asked. "I thought the local people hated us."

"Some of them do. But I think we can trust Zabad."

"Thank you, Abba! Thank you!" Yael hugged her father tightly, then ducked into their makeshift house to fetch her bag. Maybe she could use her star charts and the little moon goddess to help Leyla get well. "I'm ready," she told her father a moment later.

On the long walk down to the village, Yael wavered between excitement at seeing her friend and fear for her health. Leyla's brother Rafi met them at the gate to the compound, and she started to ask him a thousand questions, but Abba put his fingers over her lips to stop her. The last time she'd visited, she'd noticed that men spoke only with men and women with women.

"Thank you for bringing your daughter," Rafi said to Abba.

"I will take her inside, and you are free to go. I know my sister will be very happy to see her."

Abba laid his hand on Yael's head. He seemed reluctant to leave. "I'll come back for you in a little while, Yael. Try . . . try to remember all the things that Safta Dinah taught you."

Rafi led Yael through his courtyard and into the large central room inside the house with doorways leading off from it. Rafi opened one of those doorways and gestured to where Leyla lay sleeping on a pile of cushions. Her skin looked even paler than the last time, and a fine sheen of sweat glistened on her forehead. A flood of memories washed over Yael of how her own mother had lain ill this way for such a long time. She felt a stab of fear—and then anger at the thought of losing Leyla, too. She knelt by Leyla's side and took her hand. It felt very warm. Leyla's eyes fluttered open, and she smiled.

"Yael . . . you came back. . . ."

"How are you feeling?"

"Better now that you're here."

They talked as if no time had passed at all, as if they had known each other all their lives. But after a while, a loud argument outside the bedroom door interrupted them. Yael opened the door and saw Leyla's grandmother holding a pottery cup in her hands while Leyla's father tried to wrest it away from her.

"Leyla needs this," her grandmother insisted. "It's a special potion made with goat's milk."

"And blood! You mixed it with blood!"

"It will give her strength."

"My religion forbids us to drink blood!"

"And mine prescribes it! Do you want your daughter to get well or don't you?"

Yael went back to Leyla's bedside. "I hate it when they fight because of me," Leyla whispered. "Grandmother knows lots of potions from her ancestors, but Abba doesn't like me to use them."

"When my mama was sick, my father was willing to try anything, even if our neighbors said it was forbidden." Yael didn't want to tell Leyla that nothing had worked. Or that she still blamed her Jewish neighbors and their unbelief.

The old woman eventually won the argument and brought Leyla the cup. Yael helped her sit up so she could drink it. "Don't sip it, Leyla," her grandmother said. "Drink it all at once." The potion was pale pink. Was she really drinking blood? Leyla took a sip and made a face.

"How does it taste?" Yael asked.

"It doesn't matter," the old woman said, frowning at her. "Just drink it down. It will make you well." Leyla obeyed, gulping the contents, then sank down on the cushions again as if the effort had tired her out.

"I have something to make you better, too," Yael said after the old woman left again. She lifted the moonstone necklace from around her own neck and slipped it around Leyla's. "You can borrow this. It'll help you get better."

"Thank you." Yael could tell by her voice that Leyla was growing tired.

"I brought my charts, too," she quickly continued. "The stars can tell us all kinds of things about your future. When's your birthday?"

"The tenth day of Ab. I turned eleven a month ago."

"That means you were born under the sign of the lion."

"Is that good?"

"Yes! It means you're strong and courageous like a lion."

"I think I'll sleep now."

Yael spread the charts on the floor beside the bed after Leyla drifted to sleep, trying to remember everything Parthia had taught her. She wouldn't let her friend die. Parthia had been wrong about Mama getting better, but she'd said it was because Zaki's family lived next door. Would it be the same in this village? Would Leyla's father hinder the stars' power?

"I see you brought your astrology charts." Yael whirled around when she heard the old woman's voice. Leyla's grandmother searched Yael's face as if trying to look inside her. Parthia had looked at her that way, too. "Don't worry, Yael," she finally said. "I believe in the power of the stars, too."

Yael sagged with relief. "I only know a few things. I was just learning to read these charts when we had to leave Babylon."

"May I see them?" She reached out with her wrinkled hand, and again Yael felt a moment of panic. What if the old woman was lying? What if she tossed them into the fire before Yael could stop her? But she didn't. She carried them over to the window where the light was better, to study them. "Where did you get these? They are beautifully done. I didn't think Jews like you consulted the stars."

"I knew a seer in Babylon. She gave them to me."

"I might be able to teach you a little more. But don't let Leyla's father see them."

They studied the charts as Leyla slept and discovered which heavenly bodies currently decided Leyla's fortune. "This is very good," her grandmother said. "Now that we know which gods we must influence, I'll go and prepare the proper offerings to make Leyla well." She rolled up the scrolls and handed them back to Yael, smiling.

Yael sat by Leyla's side all day, telling stories about life in Babylon when she was awake, describing how she and Zaki used to explore along the canal. Some of Yael's stories made Leyla laugh, and her grandmother said that was the best potion of all. Yael didn't want the day to end, but she could see the sun sinking lower in the sky, the shadows in the room growing longer. When she heard the door to the room open, she looked up to find Abba standing there beside Rafi.

"Time to go home, Yael."

"Oh, please let her stay. Please?" Leyla begged.

"Yes, please, Abba?"

Leyla's grandmother spoke to Yael's father without looking at him, her eyes never leaving the floor. "My lord, Leyla's father would be honored if you would allow your daughter to stay with us for a few more days until Leyla is stronger. Yael is very good medicine for her. Her stories cheer my granddaughter and help her forget her pain."

"Are you sure she's not a bother?"

"Not at all, my lord."

"Well . . . then I guess she may stay."

Leyla smiled and gave Yael's hand a squeeze. "Thank you."

"Please, wait a moment longer, my lord," her grandmother said, "while I fetch some gifts to send home to your family to show our appreciation."

"I thank you as well, my lord," Rafi said. "I sometimes stay with Leyla when she's ill, but I had to work for my father today. Thank you for letting your daughter take my place."

For the next few days, Yael spent all her time in her friend's room. At times, Leyla burned with fever and whimpered from the pain in her bones and joints. Yael told story after story to distract her friend and even sang songs to help soothe her to sleep. While Leyla slept, Yael studied the star charts with her grandmother. The old woman reminded Yael of all the things that Parthia had taught her, things she had forgotten in the months since leaving Babylon. At night, they walked outside into the open courtyard and studied the sky. "That's Leyla's sign, the lion," her grandmother said. She pointed to the sky overhead as Yael picked out the stars in the constellation. "But see the position of the moon within her constellation? And the moon's phase? What does that tell you?"

"The moon is waning! That's why Leyla is sick, isn't it!"

"Very good. You have a gift for this, Yael."

"If anyone finds my charts back home, they'll take them away from me."

"How foolish! Your own people once knew the power of the stars. David, your most famous king, wrote a psalm of praise to God about learning from the stars. He wrote, 'The heavens declare the glory of God; the skies proclaim the work of his hands. Day after day they pour forth speech; night after night they display knowledge. There is no speech or language where their voice is not heard. Their voice goes out into all the earth, their words to the ends of the world.' So, no matter where we go, no matter what age we live in, the heavens will speak to us and give us wisdom."

"I knew Parthia was right! I knew it! Wait until I tell Zaki!"

"Be careful who you share your insights with, Yael. The spirit of unbelief can be a powerful force."

"That's why my mother died. It's why Parthia's spells didn't work."

The old woman nodded sadly. "And it's why Leyla's mother died, as well. But we can use the knowledge from the heavens to protect Leyla. I'm so glad you're her friend and that you're a believer."

By the time Abba returned for Yael a few days later, Leyla was well enough to sit outside and look up at the stars with them. Her father, Zabad, was so pleased that he agreed to sell Mattaniah the parcel of land he had asked for.

"Come back and visit every chance you get," Leyla begged as they hugged each other good-bye.

"May I come back, Abba? Please?"

"Well . . . you're supposed to help Safta Dinah with the cooking. You have to do your share of the work."

"You must let her come," Zabad insisted. "She has brought happiness to my daughter and made her well again. She is good for Leyla."

"Then of course she may visit."

Grandmother loaded Abba down with gifts: almonds and figs from their trees, vegetables from their garden, a skin of aged wine, and fresh goat cheese wrapped in grape leaves. "Bring your charts when you come again," she whispered as she kissed Yael's cheek.

"I will."

Yael hoped her father hadn't heard her mention the charts, but on the way home he asked, "What does she want you to bring when you come?"

"Nothing."

"Yael, you know we don't have much, and Leyla's father isn't giving me the land for free. By the time I pay for it with a portion of our crops, we'll barely have enough to eat ourselves. What are you promising to bring her?"

"Abba, they have plenty of food. Didn't you see how much? And their home is three times bigger than ours was in Babylon. They don't need anything like that from us. Leyla just wants to be my friend. She only has brothers, and her mother died just like Mama did, and so she wants us to be friends." Yael held her breath, hoping he wouldn't ask again.

"Just be careful what you promise. Her people are very suspicious of us as it is, and we need them if we're going to survive here in the land."

"Why can't we all be friends like Leyla and me? Why don't her people and ours get along, Abba?"

"It's complicated. I would like it if we all got along, but I guess our biggest disagreement has to do with religion. We believe our God gave this land to us, and they believe their gods gave the same land to them. Religion can cause the biggest divisions of all."

Yael remembered the argument between Leyla's father and her grandmother over the potion that Leyla drank. And she knew she had to hide the little figurine and the charts that Parthia had given her from people who didn't share her beliefs. Yael had learned a lot from Leyla's grandmother, and soon she would be able to read the future in the stars and make decisions for herself. In the meantime, she couldn't wait to return to the village and visit her friend.

Chapter 17

Zechariah held the weighted cord next to the stone wall of his house and let it dangle freely. As he had feared, the last course of stones weren't quite straight. He would have to remove them and build all over again—and his arms already ached from lifting them into place. He groaned aloud in frustration.

"What's wrong, Zaki?" Yael peered around the corner of the house from where she'd been working with his grandmother.

"My studies ended early today, and I wanted to get this part of the wall done before Saba comes home. I wanted to surprise him. Now I have to take all these stones down again."

"Why isn't your grandfather working on the house with you?"

"Because he's rebuilding the temple, and that's much more important." Zechariah lifted a stone from the top row and dropped it to the ground.

Yael came to stand beside him, one hand on her hip. "I don't understand why you have to take them down."

"Because the wall isn't straight. See?" He held up the weighted cord to show her. "If it's just a little bit off in the beginning and you don't correct it, it will get further and further off as you build higher. The entire wall could collapse." He reached up to remove another stone and set it on the ground. Yael sat down on a large rock to watch him, idly jiggling her foot. "Aren't you supposed to be helping my grandmother?" he asked her.

"She went to borrow something from Shoshanna. You and Abba got a lot done while I was visiting Leyla," she told him. "The walls in my room are higher than my head now. I can stand up under the tent covering."

Zechariah removed another block, then held up the cord again. "Saba says the Torah is like this plumb line. We can measure our lives with His word to see if we're living straight. And if we stray from the Holy One's laws just a tiny bit, pretty soon our whole life will be off course."

Yael gave a long, loud sigh. "All you ever talk about is the Torah. Don't you get tired of studying sometimes? Don't you want to do something different for a change?"

Zechariah remembered going to the canal in Babylon with Yael, watching the ships sailing past, feeling free. He remembered walking to work with his father and watching the laborers unload cargo from all over the world. Now he spent all day studying with the handful of boys his age who had come to Jerusalem with their parents.

Yes, he wanted to tell Yael. Yes, he did wish he could do something different for a change, but he didn't dare say so out loud. "Studying the Torah is very important," he said instead.

Yael exhaled again. "My friend Leyla has a brother your age, and he doesn't study all the time."

Zechariah felt a stab of jealousy, envying Yael's freedom. He turned his back on her and continued working. "What do you do when you visit your friend?" he asked.

"Well, we couldn't play the last time I was there because Leyla was too weak to get out of bed. So I told her stories about how we used to go exploring in Babylon. Remember? She wants to go with us when she's better. She gets sick a lot, so I gave her my—" Yael stopped so abruptly that Zechariah glanced over his shoulder to see why. She had her hand over her mouth, a guilty expression on her face.

"You gave her your . . . what?"

"Never mind."

"No, I'm curious. What did you give her?" He stopped working and leaned against the wall, waiting.

"Just a necklace I had. She's much better now. You should come with me sometime and meet her brother Rafi."

Zechariah would never be allowed to go. He felt another stab of jealousy and wished he could do something to erase the contented smile from Yael's face. "You should stay away from that village," he said. "Those people are our enemies."

"That's not true. Abba and I made friends with them."

"They're idol worshipers, you know. They don't worship the same God we do."

"That's not true, either. Leyla's father is a son of Abraham."

Zechariah couldn't ruffle her contentment, and now he felt more irritated with her than before. He leaned close to her to whisper, "Did you get rid of your pagan stuff, yet?"

"I don't know what you're talking about," she said with a shrug.

He returned to his labor, reaching up to remove another stone from the top of the wall. "Well, instead of sitting there, why don't you gather up some of those smaller rocks to stuff between the cracks?"

She did what he asked, picking up a handful of smaller stones and carefully wedging them between the larger ones. "Don't you ever wish we could go exploring like we used to?" she asked as they worked.

"I'm not a child anymore. I'm a son of the covenant now—and I like studying. Every time I think I've learned all of the lessons from one passage in the Torah or studied all of the words in one verse, I discover that there's another layer of meaning beneath it and—"

"You're no fun anymore. Why did you come to Jerusalem, anyway? You could have studied the Torah back home." She struck her usual pose, her hand on her hip, a look of disapproval on her face.

Had he imagined that the Almighty One had spoken to him? Zechariah could barely remember the feeling of His presence on the day of his bar mitzvah. He did remember being in the tug-of-war between Saba and his father, remembered the dull pain he used to get in his stomach when they had argued about him. But God had proven that He was real, and Zechariah had obeyed His call to come. If only God would speak to him again and tell him why. What was he supposed to be doing here—besides studying? Every night he tried to remember the dreams that disturbed his sleep, hoping God would speak to him through them. The dreams seemed weighted with importance, but Zechariah could never remember them when he woke up, their content and meaning floating just beyond his grasp.

He lifted another stone from the top and dropped it to the ground. What would he be doing if he had stayed in Babylon? Would he be working with his father by now? But staying would have meant disobeying God's call. "Maybe after we finish building our house I'll have time to explore again," he told Yael. At least he hoped it was true.

"Promise? Promise that we'll do something fun when we have time?"

Zechariah hesitated, aware that he had fallen into Yael's trap before by making rash promises. But he missed her and longed to spend time with her again. Most of all, he longed to convince her to give up her sorcery. Before he could stop himself he replied, "I promise."

"Thank you!" She scampered off to finish preparing dinner

while he grabbed another rock from the last course of stones and tossed it onto the ground. Yael had reignited a longing for adventure that still nagged him as he sat through prayers at the house of assembly later that evening. The longing intensified when Mattaniah stood up after the prayers ended and addressed all of the assembled men.

"Listen, I received a message today from my new friend Zabad, the leader of one of the local villages. He asked me to extend his invitation to all of you to attend a celebration in his village tomorrow night."

"What kind of celebration?" the high priest asked.

"It's an annual festival to celebrate the olive harvest. But Zabad is also celebrating his daughter's recovery. She was very ill, and he seems to think that my daughter, Yael, contributed to her recovery somehow. That's why he's inviting all of us."

A chill went through Zechariah. What could Yael possibly have done to help her friend recover? Was it sorcery?

"Zabad has also agreed to let me farm that patch of land I wanted," Mattaniah continued. "Our neighbors are offering to make peace with us, so I think we all have a reason to celebrate."

Zechariah listened as the men discussed the invitation, and when they eventually agreed that a delegation should attend for the sake of goodwill and friendship, he longed to go with them. But the frown of disapproval on Saba's face told him that he would never be allowed to go. The restrictions Saba placed on him chafed like ill-fitting sandals, and he silently bemoaned the fact that Yael would certainly be going to the festival. Then he remembered that he did have the freedom to go. He was a man now. He could decide for himself what he would do, just as he'd made the decision to leave Babylon.

"I want to go with you tomorrow night," he told Mattaniah as they walked home.

Saba halted and pulled Zechariah to a stop beside him. "No,

son. I can't let you go. Priests of God have no business going to pagan celebrations."

"But I'm not a priest yet . . . and Zabad is a son of Abraham, and . . . and I want to go." His voice shook as he defied his grandfather for the first time. He saw Saba's surprise and disappointment, but he drew a steadying breath and said, "I'm old enough to make my own decisions now."

"You may be old enough, but you're not showing much wisdom. Did you pray and ask for guidance before deciding? I believe you should." Saba started walking again, but Zaki slowed his steps and turned to Mattaniah. His mind was made up. "I'm going with you," he told him.

The following evening as the sun was setting, Zechariah walked to the festival with Yael and Mattaniah and a dozen other Jewish men. This was the first time he had ventured away from their caravan camp and their settlement in Jerusalem, and his heart raced with excitement as they hiked across the narrow valley. The unwalled village, perched at the foot of the Mount of Olives, was little more than a cluster of plastered stone houses, but at least he was away from his studies and seeing something new, something different. A snaking path led uphill from the town, and Zechariah saw the glow of flames halfway to the top and a knot of men gathered around a stone altar. The aroma of roasting meat filled the air. A tingle of shock rippled through him. Were they worshiping at a high place?

"What are they cooking way up there?" he asked Mattaniah.

"I think they're making a sacrifice. It's an ancient tradition from the time before there was a temple—and since the temple is gone, where else can they offer sacrifices?"

A pagan image from the pages of the Torah had sprung to life right in front of Zechariah. "But the Torah says—"

"We're guests here, Zaki," he said, lowering his voice. "Let's not start preaching the Torah to our hosts."

A group of elders stood at the entrance to the village to greet them, ushering Zechariah and the other men into the open village square. Yael, the only girl in the delegation, was sent off to join the village women. A variety of rugs and woven mats had been spread out in the square, and when the sacrifice on the high place ended, the men sat down to feast. The women brought platters and trays and bowls of food and laid them before the gathered men, then disappeared again. Someone handed Zechariah a cup of wine as he sat down beside Mattaniah.

"Welcome, my esteemed guests," Zabad said, lifting his cup. "Please eat and drink your fill!"

Zechariah waited for his host to recite the traditional blessings on the bread and wine, but he never did. Zaki mumbled the blessings himself as the other men dug in, using their bread as a spoon as they ate from the common dishes. Every time one platter emptied, the women quickly set a full one in its place. Mattaniah gestured to a heaping plate of roasted meat and said, "Help yourself to some lamb, Zaki."

It smelled delicious, roasted to perfection and seasoned with fragrant rosemary. But as he reached to take a portion, he remembered the altar and the high place above the village. What if this meat had been sacrificed to idols? He had just studied the Fellowship Offering and knew that portions of that sacrifice would be offered to God while the rest would be eaten by family members and guests. He had no way of knowing if he was feasting with the Almighty One or with idols. No one had mentioned the God of Abraham or offered blessings to Him. Zaki shook his head at the mouth-watering lamb and nibbled on the eggplant and lentil dishes instead. Wine flowed as freely as the food. Mattaniah and the other Jewish men seemed to be having a good time, but Zechariah worried about the dozens of ways he was being tempted to disobey the Torah.

Toward the end of the meal, a troupe of musicians began

to play. Zaki didn't recognize any of the songs. When the men rose to allow the women to clear away the remnants of the feast, he decided to look around for Yael. "Most of the women are out there," a boy his age told him. He pointed to the village entrance. Zechariah watched from a distance and saw that Yael was surrounded by a group of women. They seemed to be coming and going, talking to Yael and an elderly woman for a few minutes, looking up at the stars together and pointing toward the heavens, then leaving again. Yael held a scroll in her hands, and when he remembered the ones she had consulted on the night of Saba's nightmare, he felt sick inside. These village women were coming to Yael to have their fortunes read in the stars.

He had to stop her. He and Mattaniah needed to leave with Yael before the other men from Jerusalem saw her practicing astrology. He hurried back to find Mattaniah, wishing with all his heart that he hadn't seen what Yael was doing.

The music and drinking had continued after the feast, and the celebration was growing very rowdy. As he searched the crowd for Yael's father, Zechariah saw several young couples lurking in the shadows away from the torchlight, their arms entwined. The thundering drumbeat and the dancing weren't like any Jewish celebration he'd ever attended. All the men sat back to watch the young women dance—and the girls were bare-armed and bare-legged. Their movements were so sensuous that Zechariah felt his face grow warm. He quickly looked away, not knowing what to do or where to turn. He remembered the story in the Torah about how the Midianites had tempted his ancestors to take part in an orgy and knew Saba had been right. Zechariah never should have come. He found Mattaniah watching the dancers and hurried over to whisper in his ear. "I don't want to stay here. I want to go home."

Mattaniah turned around to face him, his eyes bleary, his

face flushed from too much wine. "What? . . . Look, I'm sorry. I didn't realize this was how they celebrated."

Zechariah nodded. "I'm leaving. Should I take Yael with me?"

"Yael?" Mattaniah gazed into the distance toward Jerusalem for a long moment, then sighed. "No . . . No, I can't let the two of you walk home alone. . . . I'll go with you." He slowly rose to his feet as if hoping Zechariah would change his mind. He wouldn't. If anything, he was even more anxious to leave as the dancing and pounding drums continued. "Give me a minute to thank our host," Mattaniah said.

Zaki followed him as he wove through the crowd and crouched to speak in Zabad's ear. A moment later Zabad's voice boomed above the noise. "No, my friend! Must you leave so soon? The night is just beginning."

"I'm sorry, but I didn't realize the celebration would last this late. . . . Have you seen my daughter?"

Zabad gestured to the village entrance. "She and Leyla are out there with the women."

Mattaniah thanked Zabad again, clapping him on the shoulder. His steps were unsteady as he turned to go, and Zechariah took his arm as they made their way from the square. Outside, Yael and the other women were still stargazing. Maybe Mattaniah would see what she was doing and take away her scrolls. Maybe he would forbid her to ever return to this village. But Yael's father took no notice at all of the pagan charts she still held in her hands. "Time to go home, Yael," he said.

"Can't I stay? I could spend the night with Leyla."

He looked as though he might concede until Zaki pulled on his sleeve and whispered, "She needs to leave here. Now." He gestured to the revelry and Mattaniah finally seemed to understand.

"Not tonight, Yael. You need to come with us." She pouted

all the way home, but at least they had rescued her from that terrible place.

Zechariah knew he should warn Yael's father not to let her go back there, ever. But how could he do that without explaining the reason why and breaking his promises? Zechariah also knew he should tell his grandfather about the festival so they could warn the other men about being lured into temptation—but then he would have to tell Saba what he'd seen, and he was ashamed to do that.

The music faded in the distance as Zechariah walked up the hill, the path becoming harder and harder to see as he made his way into the dark night.

Chapter 18

Two days after the festival, the lingering images still hadn't faded from Zechariah's mind. Since none of the other Jewish men reported what they'd seen and done, he decided not to say anything to his grandfather about that night. Yet his guilt and his fear for Yael wouldn't go away.

He had just drifted to sleep for a Sabbath afternoon nap like everyone else when someone shook him awake. "Zaki! Wake up!" He opened his eyes to see Yael crouching beside his mat. "Come on, let's go," she whispered.

"Huh? . . . Go where?" She tiptoed from the room without answering, as quietly and gracefully as a cat. Zechariah rubbed the sleep from his eyes and followed her out to the courtyard. "Go where?" he asked again, still groggy with sleep.

"Exploring! You promised, remember?"

He glanced around, worried that someone had overheard, but his grandparents and Yael's father were all napping. Even so, Zaki kept his voice low. "We can't go anywhere. It's Shabbat."

"So? We used to go exploring on Shabbat when we lived in Babylon, remember?"

"That was different."

"How? How was it different?" She stood with one hand on

her hip the way she always did when she argued with him. She was so sassy for a girl, but he liked her that way, even if her daredevil spirit scared him. "You promised," she said. "Are you going to break your promise again?"

The worst image from the festival that he hadn't been able to erase was of Yael telling fortunes beneath the stars. The memory made his stomach knot up. If he went with her now maybe he could convince her to stop practicing sorcery. "Well . . . I guess we could go somewhere," he said. "As long as we don't go more than a Sabbath day's walk."

"Whatever you say," she replied with a shrug. "Come on, I want to show you something." She took off at a brisk pace, and Zechariah had to hurry to keep up. They went through the destroyed Water Gate and down the ramp, then turned up the path that led across the valley, heading in the direction of Leyla's village.

"Wait. Isn't this the way we went the other night? I don't think we should go back there—"

"We're not going to the village. Quit worrying."

They kept walking—much farther than a Sabbath day's walk—but he was afraid that if he turned back now she would continue on without him. The valley was unnaturally quiet; the metallic ring of chisel against stone that could be heard up in the city on most days had been silenced for the Sabbath. Even the birds weren't stirring on this warm fall afternoon. They passed a mere stone's throw from the village, and Zechariah was relieved when they didn't enter it. He should talk to her now, but he didn't know how to begin. "Um . . . what were you and the village women doing outside at the festival the other night?"

"Just admiring the stars."

"But you had your scrolls . . . your astrology charts . . . didn't you?"

"What if I did?"

"Yael, you have to get rid of them. You can't worship idols—"

She halted in front of him, blocking his path. "Do you still want to be my friend or don't you? I didn't invite you to come with me so you could argue with me."

"Of course I want to be friends, but—"

"Then just be quiet and have fun for once in your life."

They walked on, and a few minutes later he saw a stone cliff ahead of him with carved entrances that looked like doorways leading into the rock wall. He realized where Yael was taking him and stopped.

"Wait. These are the tombs that we can see from up in Jerusalem, aren't they?"

"Yes. I've been dying to see them up close, but Abba is always too busy to bring me here."

Zechariah could tell that this graveyard had once been very beautiful. But like everything else in Jerusalem, the cemetery was overgrown with weeds and brambles and scrub trees. The Torah said he shouldn't go near a cemetery. It would make him unclean.

"Well? What do you think?" Yael stood looking at him as if eager to see his reaction. Maybe she was waiting for him to take the lead in exploring the tombs the way he had led in all their other explorations in Babylon. Zaki wanted so badly to impress her. To show her that he was fearless and brave and adventurous.

But he hesitated just a moment too long, and before he could stop her, Yael turned and pushed her way through the weeds and graves, stopping in front of the entrance to a tomb that had been carved into the face of the cliff. "Hey, come look! This one has been pried open. If we squeeze through this crack we can look inside."

"I can't go in, Yael. Saba says priests can't touch unclean things."

"You aren't a priest yet, are you?"

"Well, no . . ."

"Then what difference does it make? Come on. I'm going in." She shoved several rocks aside to make the opening larger, grunting with the effort, then dropped to her hands and knees to squeeze through the narrow opening. One minute she was moving broken stones out of the way and the next minute she had vanished.

"Yael?" he called. No answer. Other girls would never dream of doing the crazy things she did. They would be too scared of spiders and snakes and ghosts to crawl inside a burial cave. "Yael?" he called again. He felt the foolish urge to impress her and followed her into the cemetery. He crouched down to peer into the hole, but it was too dark inside to see anything. Zechariah hesitated, then got on his hands and knees and followed Yael through the opening. He bumped into her a few feet inside. The cave was damp and stale-smelling—and darker than nighttime.

"I can't see anything," Yael said as they both stood up. "It's too dark." Judging by the flat sound of her voice and the lack of an echo, the space was small, the ceiling low.

"Me either. Let's get out of here." He started to turn around, but Yael grabbed his arm.

"No, wait. Our eyes will get used to it in a minute." She clung to his arm while they waited, not because she seemed scared, but probably because she didn't want him to change his mind and leave. As Zaki's eyes adjusted, he saw that the room was rough-hewn, like a cave. Massive stone tombs the size of wagons were arranged in a semicircle around the walls. Sealed inside those boxes were the bones of several generations of families.

"See? There's nothing in here but tombs," he said. "Let's go."

She released his arm and moved forward a few more feet. "I want to look for treasures, first."

"There won't be any treasures. Someone already broke into this place before we came. If there were any treasures, I'm sure they must be long gone. That's what grave robbers do, you know."

But Yael groped her way around the tiny space for a few more minutes—just to be contrary, he was sure—brushing cobwebs out of her hair as she went. She even tried to lift the stone lid from one of the burial boxes without success. At last she sighed and said, "All right, we can go." She led the way as they ducked outside into the sunlight again.

Zechariah shaded his eyes against the brightness and bumped into Yael a second time as he stood up. She had halted directly in front of him. "Why are you stopping—?"

And then he saw why. They faced a ring of boys his age, maybe a little older. Eight of them. And they weren't wearing kippahs on their heads. Their garments had no tassels.

Samaritans.

He and Yael were in trouble.

Yael recovered from her surprise first and marched forward. "Get out of our way," she demanded.

"Who's going to make us?" One of the boys stepped in front of her, planting his hand in the middle of her chest, shoving her backward. "What are you doing down here, anyway? You're Jews, aren't you?"

"Sure they're Jews," a second boy said. "Can't you tell? Just look at his stupid little hat and the fancy fringe on his robe." He walked up to Zechariah and shoved him backward until he was up against the rock wall. The boy was taller than he was, stronger. No one would hear him if he yelled for help. And he couldn't expect the Holy One to answer his prayers after he'd broken the Sabbath laws by walking here and entering a tomb.

"You don't belong here!" the biggest boy said. "This is our valley." The circle of boys moved closer, trapping them.

"My father has land near here," Yael said. "Let us through so we can go home." She sounded defiant, not frightened. Zechariah wondered if she was really that brave or if she was as terrified as he was.

"Home? You must mean back home to Babylon. That's where you belong."

Zechariah tried to step sideways and slip past the boy who blocked his way, but he wouldn't let him. "You're part of that locust swarm that invaded our land. And you know what we do to insects that invade our land? We crush them!" He pushed Zaki backwards again, slamming him against the rocks.

"I think we need to give them a message to take home to their friends," the leader said. "Then they'll know better than to come down here again."

Two boys suddenly moved in from both sides and grabbed Zechariah, pinning his arms. He struggled as hard as he could, kicking and flailing, but they were too strong for him. A third boy reached for his kippah and yanked it off his head. "Yael, run!" Zaki shouted. She was small and nimble and as fast as a deer. She could easily get away. "Run!" he shouted again. But the three boys had crowded in so close that he couldn't see around them to see if she had escaped.

Someone grabbed Zaki's fringes, tearing them off, ripping his robe. "What do we have here?" the boy mocked. "Aren't they pretty?"

"Stop it! Leave me alone—" His words were cut off by a punch to his mouth that split his lip and smacked his head against the stone. Before he could recover, someone punched him in the gut, knocking the breath from him. He tried to double over, but they jerked him upright. A second punch to his stomach left him reeling with pain.

"Rafi, tell them to stop!" Yael yelled. Zechariah couldn't see if the others were hurting her or not as the three boys pummeled him with blows. He was desperate to free himself, to help Yael, but he couldn't draw a breath.

"Rafi, it's me," Yael said. "Tell them I'm Leyla's friend!"

"What about you?" one of the boys holding Zechariah asked. "Are you Leyla's friend, too?" They struck him again and again, punching, kicking, and laughing at his futile attempts to free himself.

"Rafi, make them stop!" Yael yelled.

"Hey! She's the seer, isn't she," one of the boys said. "The girl who reads the stars."

"Yes, I am! And you'd better let us go before I put a curse on you!"

Zaki's attacker punched him again before saying, "Come on, let's go." The boys released him and he fell to the ground, too injured to stand, humiliated that Yael had rescued him instead of the other way around. He should have protected her. One of the boys kicked him in the back, another in his side, the third one kicked his head. The pain was excruciating, his punishment for disobedience.

"We delivered our message. Let's go."

"Don't come back here again, or you'll really be sorry!"

His tormenters shuffled away, and Yael ran to him, kneeling beside him. When he saw that she was uninjured, he closed his eyes in relief. "Zaki! . . . Zaki, say something! Are you all right?"

He nodded, but it wasn't true. He lay stunned and bruised, every inch of his body in agony. "I'll go get help," she said, but he reached for her arm, stopping her.

"No, don't. I'll be okay in a minute."

"You're bleeding!" She touched his bloodied lip, then wiped blood from his eye. It came from a gash on his forehead. "Does that hurt?"

He didn't reply. He didn't want to lie, but he didn't want to admit the truth, either. Yael stood and offered her hand to help him up, but he shook his head. "I can stand by myself. I just need a minute to catch my breath."

"You better hurry in case they come back."

He crawled to his feet, leaning against the rock wall to support himself. The ground swayed beneath him. He looked down at his robes, bloody and torn, and waited for the world to stop spinning. "How am I going to explain my clothes?" he asked. He looked around for his kippah but didn't see it anywhere. "They took my head covering."

Yael bent to pick up the fringes that the boys had ripped off his garment and handed them to him. They were supposed to remind Zechariah of God's laws—and he surely must have broken several of them to deserve this. "That's why David cut the fringes off King Saul's garment," he said. "To remind Saul that he was sinning."

"What are you talking about? Are you sure you're okay, Zaki?"

He was too old to cry so he let his emotions spill over in anger. "I shouldn't have listened to you! This is all your fault!"

She took her usual, brassy stance. "That's a fine way to thank me for saving you!" She turned around and strode away.

"Yael, wait!" He took a few feeble steps, limping in pain. The bruises to his stomach and ribs made him double over. He would never make it home without her help. "Yael, I'm sorry. . . . Thank you for saving me. I'm sorry!"

She stopped and waited for him, and he saw her pity. "You can barely walk. Come on, lean on me and I'll help you." They wrapped one arm around each other and headed toward home. It seemed a hundred miles away.

"I thought they were going to kill you," Yael said, and for the first time, her voice trembled with tears.

"Well, Saba is going to kill me when he finds out what happened."

"I can help you make up a story."

"No, don't. Lying will make everything worse." He remembered how one of the boys had called her the seer, and he felt sick inside. What if his fellow Jews found out? He was scared for her and for himself because he loved her—and he knew that he shouldn't love a sorceress. He should have nothing to do with her.

"Are you sure you're fine?" she asked. "They punched you so hard."

Zechariah suddenly felt nauseated. The pain was so excruciating that he had to bend over and vomit. It was one more humiliation in front of Yael. When he was finished, he wiped his mouth on his sleeve, leaving a streak of blood from his cut lip.

"Come on, we'd better walk faster," Yael said, "in case the boys decide to come back without Rafi." He draped his arm around her shoulder again and limped home as quickly as he could manage. "Maybe everyone will still be napping," she said as they neared the spring, "and I can help you clean the blood and dirt off your clothes before they wake up. I can sew your fringes back on, too." But Zechariah knew it was hopeless. Safta was certain to notice his cut lip and the gash above his eye. He couldn't even stand up straight.

His grandmother was awake and sitting outside in their courtyard when Zechariah hobbled home. She covered her mouth in shock when she saw him. "Zaki! What happened?"

"He fell," Yael said. "We were climbing on some rocks, and they shifted and—"

"Don't," he said, silencing her. Saba came out of the house as Safta was looking him over, examining the cuts on his lip and his head, the bruises on his arms.

"I'll get some water and bandages," Safta said.

"What happened?" Saba asked.

"I know you're going to be angry with me," Zechariah said, "and you have every right to be. I shouldn't have gone there, and I'll never, ever do it again."

Safta returned before he could finish explaining, and she

made him sit down on the low stone wall. She fussed over him, washing the blood off his face, holding a compress against the gash on his forehead. "Can you move your arms and legs?" she asked. "Are any bones broken?"

"I don't think so." His eye was swelling shut, but he could still see the tears in his grandmother's eyes as she worked. When she finished, she helped him lift his torn robe over his head. His grandfather stood watching with a sad expression, waiting for Zechariah to finish explaining.

"Yael and I went down to the valley for a walk," he said. "A gang of boys from the village attacked us. . . . They attacked me, I should say. Yael is fine."

"One of the boys was Leyla's brother," Yael added. "He wouldn't let them touch me. And he told the others to stop hitting Zaki."

Zechariah looked up at his grandfather, waiting for the scolding that was certain to come. Instead, Saba beckoned to him and said, "Come. It's time for prayers."

"He can't go like this!" Safta said. "He's hurt. He needs to lie down!"

"And my kippah and fringes are gone," he said, reaching up to feel his bare head. It required a great effort not to cry.

"I have a kippah you may borrow," Saba said.

"Iddo, no!" Safta said. "Can't you see that he's injured?"

"You can wear your old robe until Safta repairs that one. Go get changed, Zechariah. We don't want to be late for prayers."

"How can you be so cruel?" Safta said. She threw Zaki's tattered robe on the ground and strode across their courtyard, hurrying through the opening where the gate would be. She kept going, walking faster and faster, weaving between the half-finished houses in their neighborhood until Zaki lost sight of her.

Saba didn't call to her or chase after her. "Change your clothes," he said. "Quickly."

Every movement caused him pain as Zechariah ducked inside his room and put on one of his old robes. He couldn't stand upright as they walked uphill to the house of assembly. The pain in his belly and ribs made him feel nauseated again. "I'm so sorry, Saba," he mumbled. "I never should have gone down there." The Day of Atonement when he would have to confess his sins was still a few weeks away, but he knew that his guilt would easily last until then.

"I planned to start teaching you how to blow the shofar tomorrow, remember?" Saba asked. "Now we'll have to wait until your lip is no longer swollen."

Zechariah walked with his head lowered, wiping the tears that slipped down his cheeks. "I'm so sorry," he said again.

"Yes. I can see that you're sorry. And the Holy One sees it, too. But true repentance, true *teshuvah*, means that we turn around and walk in a different direction from now on."

"I know, Saba. And I will."

His grandfather halted for a moment and said, "Let me ask you something. Do you believe that the Almighty One called you to follow Him? To return to Jerusalem and become a man of God?"

"Yes . . . I believe it."

"You know that following God means all or nothing, don't you? A man of God does the right thing whether it's popular with the rest of the crowd or not. He speaks the truth and isn't afraid to challenge others when they're doing wrong. Men of God don't look for power or riches or man's approval but for God's approval. Each day in a hundred different ways you must choose all over again whether you still want to follow Him or not."

"Yes, Saba . . . I understand." And that meant he couldn't listen to Yael or anyone else who enticed him to do wrong. He should have nothing more to do with her.

But that was impossible. They'd been friends forever, and he loved her . . . and he needed to find a way to win her back to God before he lost her forever. Because if the other men in their community ever discovered what Yael was doing, they would stone her to death.

Chapter 19

The stench hit Iddo before he and Zechariah reached the house of assembly for morning prayers. They both covered their mouths and noses with the sleeves of their robes. "What's that terrible smell, Saba?" Zechariah's face was mottled with purplish bruises, and the cuts on his lip and eye were still healing from the attack three days ago.

"Something dead. But what is it doing so close to the sacred temple area?" Iddo hurried toward the ritual baths, where a group of his fellow priests stood talking, their faces shielded, as well.

"Vandals dumped rotting animal carcasses into the *mikveh* last night," one of the men told him. "We just finished repairing and refilling it, and now it will have to be drained and purified before we can use it for our ordination."

"Another delay," Iddo said, his jaw clenched. Anger, along with the stink, nearly suffocated him. He could barely breathe.

"We sent for volunteers who aren't priests to clean it out." But the nauseating smell contaminated the nearby house of assembly as well, invading the half-finished building like an invisible enemy and making everyone's eyes water. Their prayers and the yeshiva classes would have to be cancelled for the day.

"Can I go to work with you, instead?" Zechariah asked.

"You haven't been back to the temple mount since we first arrived, have you?" The boy shook his head. Iddo knew that Zechariah's decisions to attend the festival and to explore the tombs were symptoms of a restlessness that needed to be satisfied. "All right. Come on, son. Let's hope the air is fresher up there."

They climbed the stairs to the temple mount together and thankfully the stench wasn't as strong higher up where a fresh breeze blew. Iddo paused to let Zechariah see the progress they'd made in the past few months. The site resembled a beehive of activity with hired workers lifting and moving stones. "We've finally cleared away the place where the bronze altar once stood," Iddo said. "And we'll build the new altar on the same foundations. When it's finished, it will measure thirty feet square and be fifteen feet high with a ramp leading to the top."

"Will it be ready in time for the Feast of Trumpets?"

"I pray that it will be, but the feast is barely a week away. We should have begun much sooner, but we allowed enemy opposition to delay us. Now we're running out of time."

"Have they started rebuilding the temple, Saba?"

"Not yet. We haven't even cleared away the rubble or the trees and scrub bushes. It's a much bigger job than we ever imagined." Iddo closed his eyes for a moment, remembering the façade of Solomon's temple adorned with gold; the tall bronze pillars that supported the portico; the huge Bronze Sea, fifteen feet across, where the priests would wash in living water. Looking around now, a ferocious sense of urgency gripped him. They had to complete the task God had given them. The sabotaged mikveh was the latest reminder that the Holy One's enemies didn't want them to succeed.

"If that's going to be the new altar," Zechariah said, interrupting his thoughts, "what's that other platform for?" He pointed to a stone structure near the eastern edge of the temple mount, not far from the stairs.

"That's for the musicians. When the month of Tishri begins, we'll sound the silver trumpets for the first time to announce the Feast of Trumpets."

Zechariah looked at him and smiled. "Everyone in the City of David will be able to hear you, Saba. They'll probably hear you down in the valley, too, and in all the local villages."

"Yes, that's what we're hoping." He rested his hand on Zaki's shoulder for a moment, aware that not too long ago he would have rested his hand on his head. The boy was taller than his grandmother now, nearly as tall as Iddo.

They made their way across the recently cleared plaza where the worshipers would soon stand. Every morning Iddo and his fellow priests met where Solomon's porch once stood to discuss the day's tasks with Jeshua the high priest. The chief priests and Levites used to hold meetings there before the destruction, and Iddo remembered it as an open portico supported by pillars. Of course the roof was gone, and shattered sections of carved pillars and columns lay strewn across the weedy ground. He and Zechariah sat with the others on the remnants of broken pillars.

"We must concentrate on finishing the altar in time for the fall feasts," Jeshua began. He looked weary and worried, as if required to carry one of the huge pillars on his back.

"Won't the altar have to be sanctified?" someone asked. "Will there be enough time for that?"

"Yes, it must be made holy before it can be used to atone for sin. But I assure you that we'll be ready for the sacrifices on the Day of Atonement if we have to work day and night to do it. This is the beginning of our service to the Holy One. It's what we came here to do. After the feast, the daily morning and evening sacrifices will continue from now on. The altar fire will never be allowed to go out again."

"Is there any chance that the vandals who desecrated our mikveh will be caught and punished?" a voice called out.

"That's probably impossible," Jeshua said, shaking his head. "Nor can we be certain that there won't be more acts like it. I'm posting guards on the mount day and night to make sure no one desecrates the new altar."

"I thought when the local villagers invited us to their festival they were making peace with us. What happened?"

The high priest lifted his hands in a gesture of helplessness, then let them drop. "I don't know what happened."

"It was a ruse," Iddo said. "They let us think we were at peace so we'd lower our guard. And it worked. Now we have to start all over again with the mikveh."

"I'd like to think such an act couldn't happen again," Jeshua said, "but the walls around the city and the temple mount have too many breaches. And we have only 139 gatekeepers who must be divided into shifts. They can't possibly guard the hundreds of places where vandals could sneak in. And you know all too well that there are no city gates to close. We must post more guards from now on, so I'll need everyone to volunteer for a shift."

"I can't possibly spare any of the men under my supervision," Joel said. "They still need more training before they're ready to slay the sacrifices correctly. And we're all exhausted. Every priest has been assigned at least two jobs already."

"What about your musicians, Iddo?"

"I have 128 temple musicians," Iddo said. "Most of them are already doing more than one job, but I'll ask for volunteers."

"We could ask the yeshiva students to help us," one of the priests said, gesturing to Zechariah.

Iddo jumped in before anyone else could. "It's much more important for our young men to study. Weren't our ancestors punished because they didn't know the Torah or follow it?"

"But the students are eager to help," the other priest insisted.

"We should let our young men be part of this. We won't ask them to do anything as dangerous as standing watch in the night. Besides, they'll have all winter to resume their studies."

"I disagree," Iddo said firmly. "We would be sending the wrong message. There is nothing more important than knowing the Torah. Besides, if these vandals are anything like the gang that attacked my grandson . . ." He didn't finish.

"I heard about that incident," Jeshua said. "It was near one of the local villages, wasn't it? You have recovered, I hope?" he asked Zechariah.

"Yes, sir. I'm fine."

No broken bones, thankfully. That's what had frightened Iddo the most. Any lasting damage such as a limp or a broken arm that failed to heal straight would have made Zechariah a cripple and ineligible to be a priest.

"Have you received justice from those who were responsible?" Jeshua asked.

Iddo shook his head. "The only witness was Mattaniah's daughter, and the Samaritans would never accept the testimony of such a young girl."

"We need the yeshiva students' help," the other priest argued. "These acts of terrorism emphasize the importance of celebrating the feast on time and starting the schedule of daily sacrifices. God's enemies will do anything to try to stop us."

The high priest looked from Iddo to the other priest, as if trying to make up his mind. "I'm sorry, Iddo," he finally decided, "but we need the students' help. We'll only recruit young men like your grandson who have come of age."

The decision upset Iddo. He could tell that Zechariah and some of the others were losing interest in their studies, and taking them out of the classroom now would only fuel that disinterest. But the decision had been made, and Jeshua was moving on to the next topic.

"We won't give in to fear," he said. "There's work to be done, and we'll divide it among the four divisions of priests. This altar must be finished in time for our national day of repentance."

"What about building the storehouses?" someone asked. "The Jewish families who returned with us and settled in hometowns such as Tekoa and Bethlehem will be coming to Jerusalem with their offerings. We need a place to store the tithes that belong to us and to the Levites."

"Wait," another priest interrupted. "We have to build pens for the sacrificial animals first. We'll be sacrificing a goodly number of animals throughout the eight days of the festival—bulls and rams and lambs. We need pens for these animals and—"

"And the men who'll perform these sacrifices need to be fully trained," Joel added.

"And there's another reason why we must be finished on time," Iddo said. "The feast includes a ceremony to pray for rain. The early rains should begin next month, and we need the Holy One's blessing."

"We must explain all these needs to every able-bodied man in the community," Jeshua said. "Ask for additional volunteers and recruit the yeshiva students. One last thing before you start: I'm pleased to report that the workers have moved enough debris for us to see where the temple foundations once were. Unfortunately, we won't have a chance to begin laying the new foundation until next spring when—"

"What?" Iddo interrupted. "Why not?"

"We have to wait until after the winter rains end."

"Why? Why can't we work through the winter?"

"The ground will be too muddy for one thing, and the hired laborers will never agree to work in the rain and the cold."

"How can we expect the Holy One to protect us from our enemies if we aren't doing what He sent us here to do?"

"The delay can't be helped, Iddo. We'll start rebuilding the temple next spring. That's all for today. We have work to do."

Iddo's temper simmered all day. As much as he enjoyed his grandson's company, he knew it was a mistake to keep the young men from their studies. It was also a mistake to delay the rebuilding during the winter months, but he was helpless to change things.

His mood hadn't improved by the time he arrived home that evening, and he could tell right away that Dinah was still angry with him. She knelt alone in their courtyard, mashing chickpeas into a smooth paste, but didn't greet him or even lift her head as Iddo came through the gate. He watched her for a moment, remembering how she had stormed away from him the day that Zechariah had been injured, furious with him for not coddling him, refusing to understand that the boy needed to face the consequences of his actions. She had remained angry with him ever since. The crack in their once-strong marriage seemed to widen every day. They used to be so close, two people who were truly one. Iddo had no idea how to repair the widening rift.

"You used to sing while you worked," he said quietly. "I've noticed that you don't sing anymore." Iddo moved into the courtyard and sat down on the low wall, facing her. She continued working without looking up. "What are you thinking about, Dinah? You look so sad."

"I miss our family."

"I miss them, too."

She finally lifted her chin and he saw reproach in her eyes. "It doesn't seem that way. You never talk about our children and grandchildren. You don't seem to notice how different our Sabbath meals are without them. It's as if . . . as if they never existed for you."

"Of course I notice the difference. But don't you understand how important this work is? We're rebuilding this temple for their sakes and for future generations so that the Almighty One will dwell in our midst again."

She huffed and bent over her work again, the grinding stone crushing harder, moving faster. Iddo lost his patience. "Don't you see that anything we put in place of God or that keeps us from serving Him with all our heart and strength is an idol? Even if it's our own children and grandchildren?"

He saw by her reaction that he had said the wrong thing. She slammed down the bowl and pestle, spilling some of the food onto the ground, and rose to her feet. "Your heart has turned to stone, Iddo." He tried to catch her arm so he could hold her, but she twisted away. "Leave me alone!" She fled into their tiny house, and if they'd had a door, she would have slammed it in his face.

He would celebrate the Day of Atonement soon. Worshipers were supposed to examine themselves and search their hearts for all the ways that they had sinned—sins against God and against other people. It was a time for repairing relationships, but Iddo had no idea where to begin with his own wife.

He walked the short distance to where Shoshanna and Joel lived and found them sitting in their outdoor courtyard. "May I please speak with you, Shoshanna?" he asked. "It's about Dinah."

Iddo couldn't talk to another man's wife alone, so Joel would have to hear this, too. Since Dinah could have married Joel instead of him, it embarrassed Iddo to admit that she was unhappy. But he had to do something to make her happy again besides taking her back to Babylon. Iddo would never do that.

"Yes, of course," Shoshanna replied. "Won't you sit down?"

Iddo shook his head. He fingered the fringes on his robe as he spoke. "I know you spend a lot of time with Dinah, and I wondered if you've noticed a change in her."

"Yes . . . I've noticed."

"She seems . . . despondent . . . and I don't know how to cheer her up."

He saw compassion in Shoshanna's eyes as she looked at him. "Dinah was a leader among the women in Babylon, dearly loved and respected. I know I'm biased because I'm her cousin, but she was strong and wise and everyone admired her. She loved her work as a midwife, and all of the young mothers depended on her. But she has nothing to do here. She barely leaves her house, barely speaks. She doesn't even join our conversations at the spring."

"Does she ever say what's wrong?"

"She used to have her children and grandchildren with her all day, and now she only has Yael—who can be difficult at times."

"What can I do, Shoshanna?"

"I don't know. I wish I did. . . . It might help if she could work as a midwife again. Maybe once she has new babies to bring into the world . . . Maybe Dinah needs a child to hold and care for."

"Won't it make it worse for her, remembering her own children?"

"I don't know. We'll have to wait and see."

Iddo had been right in guessing that Dinah was despondent, right about the cause. But what should he do? "Thank you for your time, Shoshanna." He went home, his feet heavy, his heart heavier still. Dinah knelt in the courtyard again, mashing the chickpeas. "We must talk," he told her. She nodded but didn't look up from her work. "You barely look at me anymore. Are you truly that angry with me?"

"I'm tired, Iddo. You know I haven't been sleeping very well."

"I know. I used to be the one who couldn't sleep." Now Dinah was often awake in the night, and she would climb out of bed to wander outside and stare up at the cold night sky. "What can I do to make you happy again?" he asked her.

"Nothing."

"I don't know what to say or what to do. In all the years we've been married, we never struggled like this to talk to each other. We were always close."

"I'm sorry for disappointing you."

"Dinah, please. Yell at me, get angry, whatever it takes—but tell me what I can do to help."

She finally looked up at him and the deadness he saw in her expression frightened him. "I've done everything you've asked me to do, Iddo. Followed all the rules, made the sacrifice of this move, started my life all over again. But there's no meaning in what I do. No life from it, no joy. I used to be so satisfied, so full. Now I simply do what you expect of me. Don't ask for more, because I don't have anything left to give."

Iddo struggled to comprehend her words. How could she not see the higher purpose in coming here? What about all of God's promises, the gift of freedom their people had been given? "I thought you came here to serve the Almighty One," he said.

She shook her head. "I'm your wife. I had to come. It was never my choice to leave Babylon. That's where I truly want to be."

"And so now you're simply going through the motions without love in your heart?"

"There's nothing in my heart, Iddo. My heart is still in Babylon. But I could ask you the same question. Why are you enduring all this hardship? Why do you want to perform all those rituals at the temple? Is it from love or from duty? Is it merely to appease the Almighty One because you fear more punishment if you don't?"

Iddo didn't know what to say. Was it true that he served God only out of fear? Could he say that he loved God or that he believed God loved him? He wanted Dinah to walk beside him because she loved him—was it possible that God wanted the same thing?

"You asked why I'm unhappy," she continued. "Why don't you ask Zechariah the same question? Why don't you explain to him why you treated him so harshly after he was attacked?"

"I was only doing what any father would do."

"You believe that's how God treats us. We have to follow all the rules, do everything exactly right, or He'll punish our smallest misstep. And so you made the boy limp up the hill for prayers when he was in pain, and you humiliated him in front of all the others. You used to do the same thing with our sons. You were always criticizing them, making it impossible for them to keep all your picky little rules or to have a life of their own. The moment they were old enough to think for themselves, they walked away from your religion. They certainly saw no reason to uproot their lives to serve as priests for such a harsh, unloving God."

"That's . . . that's not true, Dinah." She was allowing bitterness to cloud her memories. He started to explain that he had raised their children according to the Torah, but she interrupted.

"All you think about is appeasing your God. What about the people in your life? You accuse me of making them into idols, but you don't care about them at all. People aren't important to you. Does your God see us as His slaves who are required to wait on Him at all costs? Even at the cost of the people we love?"

"Of course we aren't slaves. But we should be willing to sacrifice everything for Him."

"Why? And why is He so cruel that He demands everything?"

"He isn't cruel. . . ." Yet Iddo found he had no explanation for the horror he'd witnessed as a boy—horror that God had allowed.

"Well, I've sacrificed everything, Iddo, and it seems as if God still isn't pleased."

Iddo knelt down in front of her. "You haven't sacrificed everything, Dinah. We still have each other. And I love you." He took the bowl from her hands and set it on the ground, then gathered her in his arms. He clung to her tightly, but her embrace felt empty and rigid in return. She was angry with him and with God for losing her family. And in his heart, Iddo knew he was still angry with God for losing his family as a child. Was he doing the same thing Dinah was doing—going through the motions out of fear instead of love, holding anger inside?

He had wanted to rebuild the temple for the sake of his family and for the future of their people, the generations that would follow. But the coldness in Dinah's embrace made him wonder if he would lose his family all over again.

Chapter 20

Iddo left his house before dawn the next morning to take his turn as a guard near the Sheep Gate on the temple mount. "It's been a quiet night," the man from the last watch told him.

"That's the best kind," Iddo said. They exchanged a few words before the guard shuffled away to catch a few hours' sleep. Iddo didn't mind standing watch. The hours alone before dawn gave him a chance to pray about Dinah's unhappiness and the accusations she had made. He needed to pray for Zechariah, too. Iddo wished he knew for certain that it was merely youthful curiosity that had led him to go to the village festival with Mattaniah and to explore the tombs with Yael. The boy was wrestling with the call of God on his life, and like the enemy opposition his community faced, Zechariah faced testing, as well.

"Why can't I learn to shoot a bow and arrow," he had asked Iddo yesterday, "or fight with a sword? I want to help defend Jerusalem."

"Because it's a priest's job to intercede for the people in the temple. If we're obedient to Him, He'll fight all our battles. If we're not, then it won't matter if you're the most valiant swordsman in the world." But had that been the right answer? With all of the troubles they faced, maybe the young men Zaki's age should learn to fight.

A narrow rim of light had just appeared above the Mount of Olives when Iddo heard sheep bleating. He stood in the opening where the collapsed gate once hung and gazed down the darkened road. A man approached, walking like a drunkard with a swaying, limping step. A handful of bedraggled sheep followed him. What were they doing here? The shepherds weren't supposed to bring the sheep for the sacrifices until next week. The pens weren't even finished yet. Iddo watched warily as the odd little band drew closer, the sheep bleating piteously. Then he recognized the man. He was indeed one of the temple shepherds, and he wasn't drunk. He had been savagely beaten, his clothes torn and streaked with blood. Iddo rushed forward to help him.

"Are you all right? What happened?" He wrapped his arm around the man to support him as he helped him sit down on a large stone inside the toppled walls. "What happened?" he asked again.

"Hanan and I were guarding the temple flocks last night when we were attacked."

The man clearly needed help before being interrogated further. He looked ready to faint. Iddo remembered Dinah's accusation that he had a heart of stone, and he took pity on the man. "What's your name?"

"Besai."

"Stay here, Besai, and catch your breath. I'll go get help." The sheep seemed content to graze on the grass that still grew between the paving stones. Iddo left them and jogged as fast he could over the rough terrain until he reached the guard at the next breach in the wall. "Go wake the high priest," Iddo told him. "Our shepherds have been attacked. Gather some of the others and meet me back at the Sheep Gate. . . . And fetch some food and water and bandages for the poor man."

Besai was sitting on the ground when Iddo returned, his back propped against the stone, his eyes closed. Iddo let him rest until Jeshua and the others arrived.

"Tell us what happened, Besai," Jeshua said, after giving him something to drink and bandaging the worst of his cuts.

"We herded the sheep inside the stone pen for the night, as we always do, and we were taking turns keeping watch. Hanan stood guard first, so I lay down to sleep in front of the door to the enclosure. Our attackers came out of nowhere. Hanan barely had time to cry out before they jumped him and beat him. I woke up when he yelled, but before I could help him, two more men attacked me. They stole most of the sheep and left Hanan and me for dead. These are all that's left of the flock." He gestured to the handful he had brought with him. "They were too frightened to follow the strangers."

The sky was fully light now, and Iddo could see how badly Besai had been beaten, his face swollen and still oozing blood. He sat hunched over as if his stomach and ribs ached. One of his ankles had swollen to twice its size and was turning purple. "What about the other shepherd, Hanan?"

Besai shook his head. "They beat him worse than me. He was still unconscious when I left to get help. I hated to leave him, but I didn't know what else to do."

"And you walked all the way here in your condition?" Jeshua asked. "Don't the temple flocks graze on the other side of the mountain, at least three miles from here?"

Besai nodded. "There was no other place I could go for help. I didn't trust the people in the nearest village. They might have been the ones who attacked us."

"Don't worry. We'll send some men back to help Hanan," Jeshua said.

"You'll need a litter," Besai said. "He'll have to be carried."

"Where should we bring him? Do you know where he lives?"

"He and his family are still in the tent city in the valley. We both arrived with the very last caravan, and we've been too busy tending the flocks for the feasts to build proper houses."

"You can bring both men to my house," Iddo said. "My wife will know how to care for them. She and her cousin Shoshanna work as midwives."

Someone quickly fetched a tanned hide to use for a litter, and Iddo left with three other men to help the injured shepherd. The walk down through the valley seemed peaceful in spite of the violence Besai had just described. Birdsong filled the air as the sun dawned in the pale pink sky. Any other day, Iddo would have enjoyed the walk and the tranquility, aware that the pace at the temple would accelerate once the fall feasts began. But his concern for the injured shepherds and stolen sheep overshadowed the beautiful morning. What if there weren't enough sheep left for the sacrifices?

They reached the grazing lands on the other side of the mountain and found Hanan still lying unconscious, savagely beaten. The large flock of sheep he and Besai had tended had vanished. Iddo helped lift him onto the litter and carried him the three miles back to the city. By the time they arrived, Dinah and Shoshanna had cleaned and bandaged Besai's wounds, and he was resting inside Iddo's house. They laid Hanan's litter in the courtyard and both women knelt over him. "He has a very bad head injury," Dinah said. "It isn't good that he's still unconscious."

"Does he have a wife and family?" Shoshanna asked. "If so, we should send for them right away. And for Besai's family, as well."

"I'll go for them," Iddo said. "Besai told me that they're still living in tents down in the valley." It was time for morning prayers, and Zechariah was dressed and waiting to go. Dinah's criticism still worried Iddo—she'd said that the people in his life weren't important to him, that he'd been too strict as a father. Would it hurt the boy to miss prayers this one time? Didn't a priest need to learn compassion as well as laws and statutes? "Come with me, Zechariah," Iddo said at last. "I may need your help."

It took a great deal of searching, but they finally found the tents where the shepherds' families lived side by side among the hundreds of people still camped in the valley. Both of the men had young wives and small children—and they were astoundingly poor. None of the returning exiles had much, but at least Iddo had a roof over his head and something resembling a real house to sleep in at night. Dinah had a proper hearth where she could cook instead of a crude campfire.

The two shepherds' wives reacted with shock and tears when Iddo told them the bad news. They didn't seem to know what to do or which way to turn. "Do you have families here who can help you through this?" he asked.

"We left our families behind in Babylon."

Iddo's heart broke for these women and for the sacrifice they had made. "Gather your children and anything else you might need," he told them. "You can stay with us and be close to your husbands. We'll carry your household goods up to the city later."

Besai's wife wrapped a small baby in a sling and tied him to her chest so she could hold her little boy's hand. Zaki lifted Hanan's little girl and carried her for Hanan's wife, who was round with child. Iddo shouldered the few necessities they had gathered, and they all set off up the hill.

When they finally arrived, Dinah pulled Iddo aside to whisper, "Hanan is still unconscious. That's not a good sign."

"I was afraid of that. Listen, I'm sorry for making more work for you, Dinah—"

"No, it's the least I can do for these poor souls." She coaxed the frightened children to sit on the rug so Yael could give them something to eat. When they were settled, she concentrated on soothing the frightened wives.

By now Iddo and Zechariah had missed morning prayers. "The high priest will be waiting for news about the shepherds," he told Zechariah. "Come with me." They walked up to the temple mount together and found Jeshua conferring with several others about the stolen sheep.

"We don't have the manpower or the authority to find the thieves," he was saying. "Our stolen sheep are likely grazing in the Negev by now. We'll simply have to purchase more if we want to have enough for the Feast of Tabernacles. And this time we'll guard them well."

The injustice angered Iddo. So did his helplessness. "Listen, we owe it to those two shepherds to help them and their families. It's the least we can do. The rainy season is coming, and the very poorest of our people are still living in tents in the valley."

"I share your concern," Jeshua replied, "but what can we do? We barely have enough time or workers to finish everything at the temple."

"I know, and I've been thinking about that problem on the way up here. My grandson, here, helped me build our house. He knows the basics and how to use a plumb line."

"I thought you were against taking them from their studies," the high priest said.

"Learning compassion is also part of their studies. Yes, the altar and the sacrifices are our top priority. But it's also important to take care of the people in our community."

CHAPTER

21

Zechariah couldn't understand it. He stood on the temple mount on the tenth day of Tishri, jammed among thousands of pilgrims who had gathered for the Day of Atonement, his mind whirling with questions. Last night the young shepherd, Hanan, had died of his injuries. Why had the Almighty One allowed it? Why bring Hanan and his family hundreds of miles from their home in Babylon to have his life end in violence? Wasn't the Holy One supposed to save His people from their enemies? And why wouldn't their leaders, Sheshbazzar or Zerubbabel, go after the murderers and punish them? Hanan's killers would go free, just as the boys who attacked him had. It didn't make sense.

The courtyard was too crowded, Zechariah too far away from the altar to see the high priest conducting the ritual in his embroidered robes. He could only catch glimpses of movement and smell the occasional aroma of the sacrifices as they blew toward him on the breeze. But he knew from his studies that on this holy day, the Almighty One would forgive his sins and the sins of his nation if they repented. The sacrificial animals would die in his place. After nearly seventy years without an altar, without a way to cancel their sins, he and all of God's people would finally find forgiveness.

Had Hanan failed to repent? Had a terrible sin in his life led to his death? Or maybe they had all sinned by failing to build the temple right away. Or by compromising with pagans at the village festival. Maybe it was because Yael—and who knew how many others—still practiced sorcery.

If that was true, then Zechariah deserved to die, too. He was guilty of attending the village festival. He had broken the Sabbath by walking down to the tombs. The psalmist's words had echoed in his mind as he had fasted and prayed in preparation for this somber day: *"Blessed is the man who does not walk in the counsel of the wicked or stand in the way of sinners or sit in the seat of mockers."* Zechariah had made all of those mistakes. *"But his delight is in the law of the Lord, and on his law he meditates day and night."* He confessed that he hadn't delighted in his Torah studies in the past, craving adventure instead. And now his studies had halted. The elders had closed the yeshiva as Zechariah worked alongside the other Torah students in a dreary, gray rain, helping to build sturdier housing in the City of David for all of the people still camped in the valley. He and Saba added a room onto their own house for Hanan's widow and her two children, and another room for the surviving shepherd, Besai, and his family. But Zechariah now vowed to return to his studies with a different attitude when the week-long feast ended. Today's sacrifices would restore his standing with God.

He watched and waited throughout the lengthy ceremony, but nothing miraculous happened. No blinding light appeared to him, no sense of the Holy One's nearness overwhelmed him. Had he really heard God speaking to him back in Babylon? Why couldn't he feel His presence now that the altar had been consecrated and the sacrifices restored? The high priest was supposed to take the blood of the sacrifice into the holiest place on the Day of Atonement and sprinkle it on God's mercy seat, but there was no temple, no mercy seat.

The long ceremony dragged on and on, and Zechariah grew tired of standing. When it finally ended, his disappointment felt like a dull ache in his stomach, the same ache he'd felt after being punched and kicked. Their long journey from Babylon to Jerusalem, their hard work and anticipation, had ended with a crowded square, the sound of distant music, and the aroma of smoke and roasting meat. That's all. God's presence hadn't returned in a pillar of fire or a cloud of glory. If Zechariah's sins were truly forgiven, he felt no reassurance. He wondered if the other worshipers felt differently or if it was just him, if his sin still stood between him and the Almighty One like the huge stone blocks that littered the temple site. But who could he ask about it? Certainly not Saba.

The morning after the sacrifice, a nightmare jolted Zechariah from sleep. He sat up in bed, his heart racing. It had been the same dream he'd had in Babylon, the one that had come true. The Babylonian woman with her long, black robes and dangling jewelry had been pushing Yael into a large storage basket so she could hide. But in this dream, Zechariah had been helping them. The images had been so vivid that it took him a moment to realize that he was in his room in Jerusalem. There was no basket, no Babylonian woman.

He knew what the dream meant. By keeping Yael's secret he was helping her continue to sin. But what if he told on her and the elders stoned her to death? He didn't want Yael to die. Every time Mattaniah went down to the valley to work his land, Yael went to the Samaritan village to see her friend. And each evening when she returned she brought home gifts—a bag of pistachios, fresh goat cheese wrapped in grape leaves, a bouquet of rosemary—payment for predicting people's futures in the stars. He had to stop her, but how?

The sun had dawned. He heard voices outside in the courtyard and the sound of the women grinding grain. Zechariah tossed the covers aside and quickly dressed to join them. He glanced anxiously around the courtyard but didn't see Yael. Safta and the other women were baking bread and feeding the little children. Mattaniah sat on the rug finishing his breakfast. Zechariah hurried over to sit down beside him, keeping his voice low. "Are you taking Yael down to the village again today?"

"Yes, she asked to go. Why?"

How could he reply without telling a lie or betraying a secret? "Um . . . maybe Safta could use her help."

"She hasn't said anything to me about it."

"Well . . . but . . . Yael is gone so much of the time. She's hardly ever home."

"Her friend is the chieftan's daughter, Zaki. The villagers have asked her to come, and we need good relations with these people." He rose from his place, and a moment later Zechariah heard him calling to Yael, asking if she was ready.

He scrambled to his feet and went to the hearth where his grandmother baked flatbread on the hot stone. "Safta . . . I think Yael should stay home today and help you."

Safta made a huffing sound. "Yael does more complaining and sighing than she ever does helping. And she's not much help with the little ones, either."

"Well . . . I don't think you should let her go down to the village so often. They're not nice people. Remember how they beat me up?"

"If it was up to me, I wouldn't let her go," Safta said. "But it isn't up to me."

Zaki turned to his grandfather next. Iddo had just retrieved his prayer shawl from his room and was preparing to leave.

"Saba, don't you think it's dangerous for Yael to keep going down to that village all the time? What if that gang of boys—"

"Mattaniah assured me that she's safe. She's his daughter."

Dinah rose from her place by the hearth and said, "Mattaniah doesn't have sense enough to realize how beautiful his daughter is. Or the foresight to see what a village full of heathen boys might do to her."

"Dinah, please . . ." Saba murmured. "Don't talk of such things." He glanced at Zaki with a worried look. But Zechariah knew what his grandmother meant. He had read the story in the Torah of how a Gentile man had raped Jacob's daughter when she visited the local village. "Mattaniah wants to keep Zabad happy so he can plow and plant his land without worrying," Saba said.

"Is his land more important to him than his daughter?" Safta asked.

"Of course not. But it's none of our business, Dinah. Let the matter go. You have other women to help you now. You don't need Yael."

Zechariah could only watch helplessly as once again, Yael left with her father for the day.

On the fifteenth day of Tishri, Zechariah and his new extended family sat beneath the *sukkah* he had helped Saba build out of leafy branches for the Feast of Tabernacles. They would eat their meals and sleep outside in this booth throughout the week to remember their ancestors' long desert wanderings. "It's a blessing to eat and sleep outside," Saba said as he raised his cup of wine in a toast the first evening.

"How is it a blessing?" Safta asked. "Didn't we live in tents all the way here? Was that a blessing?" Everyone at the table seemed to freeze at her unexpected question. Every day, Safta's unhappiness became more apparent to Zechariah and tonight her demanding tone highlighted it. "Why eat in this flimsy sukkah when we just worked so hard to get out of our tents and build a proper house?"

"The booths remind us of how temporary our lives are," Saba replied. "How we are strangers and sojourners in this world. And they remind us how very much we depend on the Almighty One for all of our needs. It was too easy to forget Him when we were settled in Babylon living comfortable lives."

"Can't we be reminded some other way?" she argued, "without having to wave branches in the air and sleep outside?"

Zaki waited for his grandfather's reaction. Safta had never argued with him or questioned the Torah's commands when they'd lived in Babylon. His grandfather replied patiently. "Our rituals are what bind us together and sustain us as a people. They aren't meaningless, Dinah. They give hope to everyone in the community. And the sacrifices reconcile us with God. Each step we take brings us closer to the day that all the prophets saw, the day when we will have a restored kingdom with a son of David on the throne who will give us victory over all our enemies."

At the mention of enemies, Zechariah could no longer keep quiet. He glanced at Hanan's widow, still in mourning, and asked, "Do we have to wait until the Messiah comes before we fight back? Didn't the Almighty One tell our ancestors to fight against our enemies and drive them from our land?"

He thought it was a valid question, but Saba studied him for a long moment before asking, "Are you still thinking about the boys who attacked you? That happened weeks ago. You must let it go, Zechariah."

"But it isn't fair! They should be punished for what they did! And what about the men who attacked Hanan and Besai? Why can't we demand justice?"

Saba closed his eyes for a moment as if the memory pained

him. "We've been over this, Zechariah. That attack took place at night. If Besai can't identify the men who did it, how can we get justice?"

"Won't there be more attacks if these evil men keep getting away with it?"

"The prophet Isaiah wrote, 'The Lord has a day of vengeance, a year of retribution to uphold Zion's cause.' We need to leave revenge in the Almighty One's hands."

Zechariah had been told to let it go. He was causing pain to his grandfather and to Hanan's widow, seated beside Safta. But he couldn't drop it. "Why can't we ask the Persians to send their soldiers back to keep us safe? I'll bet they could find our stolen sheep."

"The Persian soldiers are not ours to command. Prince Sheshbazzar sent a report to Persia, but it will take many weeks to get a reply."

Saba's patience only fueled Zechariah's anger. "Then we need to form our own army in the meantime and defend ourselves."

"We're priests and farmers and shepherds, not warriors."

"King David was a shepherd, and he fought God's enemies."

"Let it go, Zechariah," Saba said again. "Didn't the Almighty One avenge the destruction of Jerusalem for us? He judged the Babylonians for what they did and sent the Persians to conquer them. And now He has brought us back to our land. We're going to rebuild His temple when spring comes. Let's just do the work He has given us, and in His good time our enemies will be avenged."

Zechariah was too angry to let it go. And he knew that the real source of his frustration was his failure to stop Yael from sinning and worshiping idols. The fresh figs on the platter in front of him were one of the many "gifts" she had brought home with her. If only he and the others could conquer that stupid village and raze it to the ground in revenge, then she couldn't go there anymore. He excused himself and went to sit alone outside the sukkah where he could see the night sky. The clouds had blown away and thousands of stars had taken their place. *"The heavens declare the glory of God,"* King David had written. *"The skies proclaim the work of his hands."* King David had talked to the Holy One beneath these same heavens and written his psalms of praise. He had worshipped the one true God, not the moon and the stars.

Zaki heard someone approaching and was afraid to look up, worried that it was Saba. It was Yael. She sat down on a stone beside him. "I heard what you and your grandfather were arguing about, and I don't blame you for wanting justice. See those stars up there?" She pointed to the sky. "The constellation Libra—the balance scales—is above us during the month of Tishri. If you want to see the scales of justice balanced, this is the time to do it, while Libra is high in the sky."

"Please, Yael, you've got to stop worshiping the stars," he said with a groan. "You're going to get into terrible trouble with all that nonsense."

"It isn't nonsense. The heavens can tell us the best times to do things, like when to plant our crops or choose a wife or get revenge on our enemies. And everyone wants to know the future, don't they? It gives us hope to see what's ahead."

"It's idolatry, Yael. And it's wrong. There's only one God—the God of our father Abraham. Only He knows the future."

She made a sound of contempt. "The moon goddess had a beautiful temple in Babylon. Why is your God's temple a pile of ruins?"

Her questions stirred his fear for her the way a stick stirs coals into flames. "It's in ruins because our ancestors stopped worshiping God and turned to idols, just like you're doing. The prophet Ezekiel watched the Holy One's presence leave the temple before it was destroyed. But all of God's promises about returning from exile and rebuilding the temple are coming true. That's why we're here."

"There. You said it. Your prophets are able to foretell the future, too. How do you know they didn't see it in the stars? Leyla's grandmother said that King David knew how to read the stars."

"No, he didn't."

"He wrote in one of his songs that the heavens give us knowledge at night."

Zechariah felt a chill run through him. Hadn't he just been thinking of that psalm? "'The heavens declare the glory of God . . . '" he quoted. "'Night after night they display knowledge.'"

"Yes! That's the one! King David wrote those words, didn't he?"

"Yes, but he must have meant something else because the Torah clearly says that sorcery and astrology are wrong."

"You can believe whatever you want," she said with a shrug, "but I can see things in the heavens, and what I see always comes true."

"Shh! Don't say things like that where people can hear you!" He sat very still, waiting to see if Saba or Joel or one of the other men had overheard. But the soft murmur of laughter and voices from inside the sukkah reassured him that they hadn't.

He struggled to think of a way to convince Yael that she was wrong, and he remembered that the prophet Ezekiel had also seen the Almighty One's glory and presence returning to the temple. The temple was still a pile of ruins of course, where no one was allowed to go. But what if Zechariah could sneak up there some night and find the place among the ruins where the Holy of Holies had been? Yael could go with him to help him avoid the guards and maybe they both would feel His presence. If only she could experience what he had on the day of his bar mitzvah, maybe she would finally give up her idolatry and sorcery. His heart raced as he made up his mind.

"Do you want to go exploring with me in secret?" He leaned close to ask.

"You're not going down to Leyla's village for revenge, are you?"

"No. Not there." His cheeks grew warm at the memory of how he had been beaten and humiliated in front of Yael. "I should warn you that it's dangerous to go where I want to go. We'll be in trouble if we get caught."

A wide grin spread across Yael's face. "I don't care. I'll go with you."

He shook his head at her daring. The threat of danger or trouble didn't faze her in the least. She had smiled! "You have to promise not to tell anyone," he warned.

"*I* can keep a secret," she said, emphasizing her words. "When do you want to go?"

His heart thumped faster. "How about tonight? After everyone is asleep." Before he lost his nerve.

"Sure. Where are we going?"

"Up to the temple mount."

She had been alert with excitement at the prospect of adventure but her shoulders sagged at his words. "That's not dangerous. You go there all the time for the sacrifices."

"The altar is on the eastern side of the mount. I want to explore the middle part, where the temple used to be. We're not supposed to go there, and they have guards who patrol all night. . . . You don't have to come if you're afraid," he challenged.

"I'm not afraid. If they ask me what I'm doing there, I'll say I'm looking for my father. He's been on night watch a couple of times."

"It's never a good idea to lie, Yael."

Her hands went to her hips. "Do you want me to come with you or not?"

Yes. He did. But how *would* he explain what they were doing if they got caught?

The hardest part was remaining awake until everyone else was asleep, and then being careful not to disturb one of the small children who seemed to awaken at every little sound. Yael had promised to keep the door to the room she shared with her father open a crack, and when Zechariah peered inside he saw her sitting up. He motioned to her to follow him.

"Let me lead the way. I'm better at this than you are," she whispered after they'd gone a short way. She was right. His nervousness made Zechariah clumsy, tripping over rocks and sending stones skittering downhill. Yael was as quiet and agile as a deer. She obviously enjoyed sneaking around in the dark and seemed to think that eluding the guards was a game. Meanwhile, Zaki's heart thudded as loudly as his feet. His stomach felt like he'd eaten snakes for dinner. But he hadn't changed his mind.

They crept between the clustered houses, moving up through the center of the settlement and staying away from the walls where guards watched over the breeches and fallen gates. They spotted one of the guards near the stairs to the mount where the ritual baths were, and waited until his back was turned. As soon as he walked in the opposite direction, Yael led the way to the bottom of the stairs, crouching low. Thankfully the clouds had returned, hiding the moon's light and making the shadows dark and deep. The darkness also made it hard to see where he was going. He and Yael climbed the newly-repaired stairs without being seen, feeling their way, but she held up her hand to stop him before they reached the top.

"Let me look around, first," she whispered. Zaki sat down on a step to wait until Yael returned a few minutes later. "The guard went toward the altar so the coast is clear."

"There's more than one guard—"

"I *know*!" He heard her impatience, even if it was too dark to see her roll her eyes.

Zechariah crawled to the top of the stairs and saw the altar looming ahead of them, illuminated by the soft, red glow of smoldering coals. A thin plume of smoke curled into the sky above it. He could smell the aroma of roasting meat, left to burn throughout the night. He pointed to the mound of rubble beyond the altar and they made a short, crouching sprint to Solomon's porch. Yael chose a good place to hide among the fallen pillars and Zechariah sank down to catch his breath. His breathlessness wasn't from running but from fear and anticipation. Then they crept along the western edge of the mount, staying in the shadows until they finally reached the point where piles of fallen building stones blocked their way. They sat down again to catch their breath, hidden among the enormous stones.

"The guards can't see us here," she said, her voice quickened with excitement. "Now, tell me why you wanted to sneak up here in the middle of the night. Is there buried treasure here?"

"No, nothing like that. This is a sacred place. The temple that stood here was like a map, showing us how to get back what we lost when Adam sinned."

"How can a building be a map? And what did we lose?"

"We lost the right to have the Almighty One living and walking with us. But if we rebuild the temple and follow all the steps that He showed us—offering the right sacrifices, and the incense, lighting the golden lamp, and laying out the bread of His presence, then the Holy One will dwell here with us."

Her sigh and shrug told him she was unimpressed. "So why did you want to come here?"

"I wanted you to see that the Almighty One is the only true God—and that your idols aren't."

"I don't see anything but broken stones."

"Not here. We need to go a little farther." He bent over and led the way as they scurried the last few yards into the rubble. The stones were difficult to climb over and nearly impossible to skirt around, especially in the dark. But eventually they reached an area where some of the stones had been cleared and the square outline of the former foundations had been exposed. Zechariah drew a deep breath for courage and climbed over the crumbled foundation to step into the sacred area. He was there! Inside the holy space. Standing where Solomon's temple once stood.

"This is as far as we dare to go," he whispered. "If we accidentally step on holy ground, the Holy One might strike us dead."

"You're making that up."

"No, I'm not. A Levite named Uzzah was struck dead just for steadying the Holy Ark when the oxen stumbled and the cart shifted. This is where I wanted to come. I want to pray here." He sat cross-legged on the ground and closed his eyes as Yael sat down beside him. He longed to bask in the warmth of the Holy One's presence again, and longed for Yael to feel it, too.

Where are you, Lord? he prayed silently in the darkness. *Why can't I feel your presence anymore? Why did you ask me to leave my family and come here? What do you want from me? . . . And why won't you tell me?*

Zechariah waited. Then waited some more, praying that the Holy One would draw close to them. The night was so still that he could hear the sacrificial animals stirring in their pens, the occasional bleating of sheep. Time passed.

If you won't come to me, he prayed, *then please come to Yael so she'll believe in you.* He waited a few more minutes but nothing happened. God's presence wouldn't return to a heap of broken stones. They would have to rebuild His temple first. Maybe then Yael would find Him—and so would he.

Zechariah opened his eyes. Yael had her head tilted back as

she gazed up at the stars peeking from between the filmy clouds. “That’s the central star,” she said, pointing to a bright one above their heads. “All the other stars circle around it.”

He felt tears welling up. He couldn’t let himself cry in front of her. “Let’s go home,” he said.

Chapter 22

The almond trees blossomed first, a sign of hope. Iddo breathed in the cool, scented air, excited to see winter end and spring arrive. At last, they would begin rebuilding the temple. Today was the eve of Passover, the anniversary of their deliverance from slavery in Egypt, and as Iddo watched Dinah and the two young mothers preparing breakfast, his wife seemed more content than she had for many months. Once again, she had children to care for, babies to hold in her arms.

Hanan's widow, Tikvah, had given birth to a baby boy, the first child that Dinah had delivered since coming to Jerusalem. "This travail is what our nation must go through," he'd told Dinah after the long hours of Tikvah's labor and delivery had ended. "It's always a struggle to give birth to new life. But our sorrows will be quickly forgotten when we can worship in the Holy One's presence again."

Now, as joy filled him at the prospect of their first Passover celebration in Jerusalem, he dared to catch Dinah's hand as she rose from tending the hearth and say, "Isn't the Promised Land beautiful in the springtime? The trees are in bloom, the poppies and wildflowers are flourishing among the ruins. Doesn't it make you feel . . . hopeful?"

"Yes, Iddo. It's lovely." She smiled her beautiful smile before shooing him out of the courtyard. "Now, go. We have a thousand things to do before tonight."

Iddo worked all day at the temple, helping the other priests slay the Passover lambs, one for every household. Each of the thousands of lambs had to be inspected to make sure it was free from blemishes, each one slain the proper way. The priests had been forced to purchase them from the local people at inflated prices to make certain they had enough for the feast. Pilgrims from all the scattered towns and villages in Judah were making the trip to Jerusalem as the Torah commanded. Shoshanna and Joel would join his family for the *seder* at sundown.

Dinah looked tired but content when they finally sat down together for the meal that evening. The people seated around her and Iddo weren't related to him by blood, but they had become family just the same. Mattaniah and Yael. The shepherd, Besai, and his wife, Rachel, and their children. Hanan's widow, Tikvah, and her children, who were learning the Passover traditions for the first time. Shoshanna and Joel. All the traditional elements of the meal were in place—wine and unleavened bread, roasted lamb, bitter herbs and salt water for tears, *haroset* to remember making bricks in Egypt. Iddo retold the exodus story, reminding everyone of the significance of this celebration and their deliverance from slavery in Egypt.

This time last year they had celebrated Passover in Babylon with their children and grandchildren, and it had been a somber meal. Everyone had been aware of the coming separation, and Iddo had worried about the long journey ahead. But Dinah showed no signs of sadness now as she played hostess for this meal and surrogate grandmother to all of the children.

Long before the lengthy meal ended, the children grew restless and were put to bed. But as the adults lingered at the table, Iddo learned that Dinah had been thinking about their children after all. She turned to Joel and asked, "Have any of the others heard news from home? Do you think our families will be coming from Babylon soon?"

"No one has heard any news since we left," he replied. "I wish we had a way to communicate with our families, but we don't."

"They would be leaving now, in the springtime like we did, wouldn't they?" she asked.

"We can only wait and pray," Shoshanna said. She and Joel were waiting for their grown children to arrive, too, but Iddo feared they would all be disappointed. If his sons had felt any longing at all to return to the Promised Land and rebuild the temple, they would have let nothing stop them from coming with the first group of returning exiles. Instead, they had recited a litany of excuses. Iddo doubted that they would ever come.

"Whether or not our families join us," he told the group, "we have many reasons to be excited about the months ahead. The construction of the temple will move forward at last. The high priest plans to begin next month, the same month that Solomon began building the first temple."

"I noticed a construction crane on the temple mount when I went to the sacrifice yesterday," Shoshanna said. "I wondered if it was the start of something."

"It is," Iddo said. "It took quite an effort to build a crane sturdy enough to lift and move those huge stones. Our workers went to great effort to cut timber from Israel's central forests and haul it up here to Jerusalem. They used the teams of oxen that were part of our caravan. Mattaniah can tell you how the crane works."

"It's a system of ropes and pulleys," Mattaniah said. "I learned to use a crane on construction projects back in Babylon." But Iddo could tell by the way Mattaniah looked down at his lap, avoiding everyone's gaze, that he would prefer to work his land rather than build. He had told Iddo once before that laboring with bricks and stones was a slave's job—a reminder that they had labored as slaves in Egypt and Babylon. Free men worked their own land and enjoyed the fruits of their labor.

"We've already hired masons and carpenters," Iddo continued, "and sent food and wine and oil to the people of Sidon and Tyre so they'll ship cedar logs to us by sea from Lebanon to Joppa. All the plans that King Cyrus of Persia authorized and funded are moving forward."

"The new foundations will be laid in the same location as the first temple's foundations," Joel said. "We're planning a celebration once the new foundation is finished."

Iddo reached for Dinah's hand, hoping she felt the contagious excitement in the room. "Rebuilding the temple is what we came here to do," he said. "And praise God, we're doing it at last!"

The work proceeded quickly in the days that followed the Passover feast. Iddo was overjoyed when the workers completed the new foundation in a few short months. Sheshbazzar, son of King Jehoiachin, who served as the official governor of the new territory, presided over the dedication ceremony dressed in his royal robes. It seemed to Iddo that all of the thousands of people who had been part of the original caravan from Babylon had returned to Jerusalem to celebrate the foundation's dedication. Perched on his platform where he played the silver trumpet, Iddo saw people jamming every inch of cleared space on the temple mount. Tears streamed down his face as the high priest in his embroidered robes and ephod gave the signal, and all of the people gave a great shout of praise to the Lord. Iddo didn't know if his tears were from joy or grief—maybe both. He had seen Solomon's temple as a child, and like many of the older priests and Levites, he knew that the new temple would have none of the splendor of the first one. The building stones would be much simpler and unadorned. No one had the skill or craftsmanship of those first artisans, and so the temple would be little more than a large boxlike structure. They also lacked the funds to adorn the structure with gold and bronze like the first one. King Solomon had been the richest man in the world, and the temple he'd built reflected his wealth. And so the older men like Iddo wept aloud when they saw the foundations of its humble replacement.

But at the same time, Iddo couldn't help shouting for joy, so loudly that his throat grew hoarse. The Almighty One had kept His promise. He had forgiven them and restored them. Iddo would worship and serve God at this temple for the rest of his life when it was finished. He had witnessed the horror of the first temple's destruction as a child, never dreaming that he would live to see this day. With the sound of deafening praise enveloping him, Iddo stood on the platform sounding his shofar, certain that the noise could be heard far, far away.

The lingering joy that Iddo experienced at the dedication was still with him the following day when a messenger summoned all the priests to an urgent meeting at Governor Sheshbazzar's residence. Along with living quarters for the two princes, workers had built a throne room where Sheshbazzar and his young nephew Zerubbabel held court and conducted business. The high priest and most of the chief priests and elders already had crowded into the simple, unadorned hall when Iddo arrived. He and Mattaniah found a place to stand alongside one of the cedar support pillars. Worry lines creased Governor Sheshbazzar's forehead as he opened the meeting from his modest throne at the head of the long, narrow room.

"I received a message from Shimshai, secretary to Rehum, the provincial governor of Trans-Euphrates. He requests a meeting with our leaders and priests, and with a delegation of Samaritan elders from the surrounding communities."

"Did they give a reason for the meeting?" the high priest asked.

"No. The last time we communicated was when I sent a formal complaint to Rehum after our shepherd was murdered. I provided details of our neighbors' terrorist actions, the thefts and beatings. If this meeting is in response to that report, it is very much overdue."

"If he's inviting the leaders of the local villages," Jeshua said, "maybe he's trying to smooth things over between us."

"Let's hope so," Sheshbazzar said. "Protocol would dictate that I respond to this request by inviting them to meet here in Jerusalem. Rehum once controlled all of Trans-Euphrates Province, and he wasn't pleased when I was made governor over this city and the territory of Judah. Prince Zerubbabel and I met with him in Samaria when we first arrived. We've lived here a year now, and this will be his first reciprocal visit. And so the question I ask you to consider is, where should we receive them? My governor's residence is still incomplete, this hall too small. And besides, we don't want them to see our treasury—or even suspect that we have one."

"We can't meet with them on the temple mount," Jeshua said. "It's out of the question. It's a holy place. The barriers that will separate the Court of the Gentiles from the sacred areas haven't been completed yet."

"How about down in the valley where the caravans first camped," someone suggested. "That area is vacant now that everyone has either moved to their ancestral villages or built houses in Jerusalem."

Mattaniah moved forward to speak. "I'm acquainted with one of the local village leaders, and he would view it as an insult if we met in the valley. He would think we were deliberately keeping him out of the city."

Iddo knew Mattaniah was right, but the idea of allowing the heathen governor or hostile local leaders inside Jerusalem worried him. "When we held the Feast of Tabernacles last fall,"

Iddo said, "we built a communal booth near the Water Gate. Why not erect another pavilion like that one, with a roof for shade, and offer to hold a feast for the leaders there? It would still be inside Jerusalem."

"Iddo has a point," Jeshua said. "An open-air pavilion would demonstrate the truth to them that we aren't wealthy and don't have much that's worth stealing."

"But won't they also see how vulnerable we are?" someone asked. "They'll see that our city has no walls or gates."

"Our neighbors already know it," Iddo said. "They were able to sneak in at night and sabotage our mikveh, weren't they?"

"Very well," Sheshbazzar decided. "We'll build a temporary pavilion as Iddo has suggested and prepare a small banquet to show our hospitality. As the leaders of our community, you priests and elders should all be there. One week should give us enough time to prepare, don't you think?"

Workers quickly erected the pavilion and outfitted the space with carpets and raised daises for Rehum and Shimshai at one end and Judah's most important dignitaries at the other. The Samaritans arrived in great splendor—and with a small escort of their own soldiers as if to emphasize their military superiority. Iddo sat with the other priests and listened impatiently to all the formalities as Prince Sheshbazzar and the governor of Trans-Euphrates exchanged lavish and insincere compliments. Mattaniah pointed out Zabad to Iddo, the leader of the local village.

"I apologize for the simplicity of our banquet hall," Sheshbazzar said. "Our foremost construction project is to rebuild the Holy One's temple, so we still aren't up to the standards that you're accustomed to in Samaria, even after living here nearly a year."

Governor Rehum lifted his chin as if a reply was beneath him. He was a short, swarthy man with the black, tightly curled hair and dusky complexion of Iddo's enemies, the Babylonians and Assyrians. His secretary, Shimshai, spoke for him. "Lord Rehum would be most interested in a tour of the city to see your progress. As you know, Jerusalem and the territory of Judah were under his jurisdiction for many years before you arrived."

"Yes, I am aware of that," Sheshbazzar replied. But Iddo was relieved when the prince made no offer of a tour. He remained cordial yet firm, and after more posturing and flattery and empty formalities, Governor Rehum finally got to the point of his visit.

"A year ago I received a copy of the proclamation from King Cyrus announcing the return of Jewish exiles from Babylon. Your intention, so it was stated, was to rebuild King Solomon's temple. I am aware of the recent flurry of commercial activity in my province as building materials have been ordered and shipped through my territory from Sidon and Tyre and Lebanon. And so I have come with my fellow officials from Samaria and with many of the local leaders to offer our assistance. Together we will all rebuild the temple that our sovereign, King Cyrus, has authorized."

Iddo's stomach made a sickening drop as if he had just stepped off the edge of a high wall. He gazed around at his fellow priests and knew that the look of shock on their faces probably mirrored his own. None of them had seen this coming.

"Like you," Rehum continued, "we also seek your God and have been sacrificing to Him ever since the time of Esarhaddon, king of Assyria. He brought our ancestors here and sent some of your priests to instruct us in God's ways. Now we're offering our manpower and our resources as we work alongside you."

Sheshbazzar stroked his beard for a long moment. He seemed to choose his words carefully as he replied. "Your offer is very generous, Governor Rehum, but unnecessary. King Cyrus has already made certain that we are well provided for. As his proclamation states, it's in his best interests to see that the Almighty

One is properly worshiped, and so he has provided everything we need."

Rehum's smile seemed stiff. "Nevertheless, since we'll be worshiping the same God as you, side by side with you once the temple is completed, we believe it's only fair that we help you build it."

His words were met with stunned silence. *No,* Iddo thought. *No.* The high priest couldn't possibly allow the half-pagan Samaritans and local people to worship alongside them, much less rebuild with them. It was unthinkable. Governor Rehum must have no place, no power, in God's holy temple. And that's what this really was, a blatant grab for power. When neither the high priest nor the prince replied, Rehum continued.

"We are willing and eager to work with you, sharing the costs and the labor. We have architects and expert craftsmen, experienced men, who will gladly work out all of the details with you."

Jeshua the high priest stood to reply, his voice so soft that Rehum had to lean forward to hear it. "We'll need time to consider your offer, Governor Rehum."

"To consider it!" Rehum looked as though he'd been slapped. "What do you need to consider? King Cyrus has decreed that we must all live together, and so we're simply following his majesty's wishes and offering to work together, as well. We've generously shared our land with you, as the king has requested. But I think you'll agree that the temple mount belongs to all of us."

Iddo began shaking his head. No. The temple mount belonged to the Almighty One, and He entrusted the Jews to rebuild His temple. But the high priest answered before Iddo could speak.

"I understand," Jeshua said. "But we don't make any decisions of importance without first consulting the Torah."

"We have the same Torah that you do," Shimshai responded. It was clear from the way that Rehum had slumped back in his seat with his arms crossed that he had been insulted and would no longer speak. His secretary would speak for him from now on.

"Even so," Prince Sheshbazzar said, "please allow our chief priests and scholars the time they need to consult God's Word. We would be honored if you would accept our hospitality at a second banquet tomorrow when we will give you their answer."

All work was suspended for the remainder of the day. Jeshua sent the Torah students home so he and the chief priests and Levites could meet in the house of assembly to formulate their reply. Iddo sent word home with Zechariah that the meeting would likely last the entire night. As the gathering convened, Iddo knew that the others recognized him as one of the leading Torah scholars. But he was astounded to learn that a handful of his fellow priests didn't see the Samaritans' offer the same way that he did—including his good friends Joel and Mattaniah.

"I know you must all share my great relief," Mattaniah began, "to learn that they're extending a hand of friendship to us. We won't have to worry and watch our backs as the construction continues. Or posts guards the way we did when the altar was being built."

"Yes. Let's come to a consensus quickly," Joel added, "before we insult them further with more delays."

"Wait," Iddo said. "I believe there's more to this 'friendly' offer than what we can see. Jeshua is right to proceed with caution. We need to pray and ask the Almighty One for guidance before we agree to compromise with them. Remember the trouble that Joshua and our ancestors got into when they made an alliance with the Gibeonites without consulting the Holy One? We don't know what these men's true motives are."

"Governor Rehum already told us his motives," Mattaniah said. "The Samaritans worship the same God we do and follow our Torah. Why not let them help us?"

"Anyone with eyes can see that we need their help," Joel

added. "Why build a second-rate temple for the Holy One when it can be as spectacular as King Solomon's temple with a little more help? I know that many of you share my disappointment with what we've built so far. If the Samaritans are willing to contribute money and manpower and skilled craftsmen, I say we should let them."

"It would be completed in much less time," Mattaniah said. "And wasn't that our goal in coming here? To complete the temple?"

Iddo hated to argue with his two friends, but he couldn't allow them to sway the others. All of the sacred scrolls were right here in front of him, and he quickly found the one that contained Israel's history, unrolling it as he spoke. "The Samaritans are a mixed race and their religion is also a mixture. According to these writings, when the Assyrians first exiled our people and settled outsiders here, wild animals attacked them because the people didn't know what the God of Israel required of them. So they asked the king of Assyria to send some of Israel's captive priests back to our land with the Torah to guide them."

"And like Governor Rehum said, the priests brought back our Torah," Joel said. "End of story."

"No, those priests from the northern kingdom had already fallen away from God, which is why the northern kingdom was punished first. I can show you here in Scripture how they worshipped golden calves in Bethel and Dan and built temples to Baal and Asherah. Their worship had turned corrupt long before the exile, and their priests were no longer descendants of Aaron. Yes, the Assyrians sent priests to them, but the Samaritans mixed the worship of our God with their pagan worship. You've all seen their shrines on the high places around here. The local people still have pagan ways."

"Why not teach them the right way?" Joel said. "Their young

men can study the Torah alongside ours so that the next generation will know what's right."

Iddo grabbed the fifth Torah scroll, appalled at the thought of Zechariah studying alongside the brutish boys who had beaten and mocked him. "It says right here, when Moses gave us instructions before reaching the Promised Land, 'Make no treaty with them, and show them no mercy.' We can't be deceived the way Joshua was."

"My friend Zabad traces his ancestry to the Jews who were left behind during the exile," Mattaniah said. "The Babylonians left some of the poorest people here to work the land, remember? Zabad is a son of Abraham just like we are, and he has a right to help us build and to worship God with us."

"Is he a pure son? Are his wives Jews or pagans? Are all of his ancestors pure?"

The exchange quickly became heated, and Iddo was grateful when the high priest entered the discussion, taking his side. "If Zabad can show us his genealogy and prove that his family hasn't intermarried with the Samaritans, then yes, he and men like him may worship with us. But not men of mixed race. They must remain in the Court of the Gentiles. And I'm sorry to say that includes Governor Rehum."

"Fine," Mattaniah said. "But I still don't see the harm in accepting their help and allowing them to work with us. Heaven knows we could use it. We don't have experienced architects and craftsmen, and they do."

"If we let them build with us, they can claim that the temple is rightfully theirs just as much as ours," Iddo said. "What if they want to introduce something foreign to our worship? Or change the way that the Almighty One has said to do things?"

"We can't allow it," Jeshua said.

"The Almighty One hates a mixture," Iddo said, waving one of the scrolls for proof. "We'll end up in the same mess that caused our exile in the first place. If their sons study with ours, they could become a bad influence on our sons instead of the other way around. We don't have very many young people among us as it is."

"Yes, and they still have a lot of Babylon's ways in them," Jeshua said. "We can't risk losing the younger generation to idols."

"Fine," Mattaniah said again. "Then their sons can study in their own schools. But we still should accept their help."

"And what if they want to install their own priests?" Iddo asked. "The Torah says only descendants of Aaron can be priests. The Samaritan priests aren't Aaron's descendants and haven't been for centuries."

"Then we'll make it clear from the start that we cannot allow them to serve," Joel said. "Only men who can trace their lineage to Aaron."

"But if the Samaritans have contributed money and experts to help us build, won't they claim they have just as much right as we do to make those kinds of decisions? Won't they expect their own priests to serve in worship?"

"Iddo makes good points," Jeshua said.

"And what about their women?" Iddo continued. "If we're worshiping side by side with Samaritans, won't our young men be attracted to their daughters and want them for their wives? How will we answer them? If we've compromised and worked together in other ways, our young men will see no reason not to compromise in marriage. Since these Samaritan women have been part of their life all along, why not marry them, they'll ask. I can show you right here," Iddo said, shuffling through the scrolls again, "where it says, 'Do not intermarry with them. Do not give your daughters to their sons or take their daughters for your sons, for they will turn your sons away from following me to serve other gods, and the Lord's anger will burn against you.'"

More and more priests joined the discussion, and Iddo was relieved to see that he had swayed nearly all of them with his arguments. Late that night, when they finally reached the decision to refuse all help from the Samaritan governor and the local people, only Joel and Mattaniah still disagreed.

"I will talk to Prince Sheshbazzar myself," Jeshua said, "and give him our reasons for refusing Governor Rehum's offer." Iddo thought the discussion was finished, but Joel and Mattaniah were still clearly upset.

"How will the prince dare to refuse the governor?" Joel asked. "Rehum controls the entire Trans-Euphrates district. He could cut off our supply routes, sabotage our caravans. You're going to be very sorry if you refuse." Iddo heard the anger in Joel's tone and wondered if he had lost a friend.

"Our authority comes from King Cyrus," Jeshua said. "Governor Rehum has no right to stop us. He will be welcome to worship with us in the Court of the Gentiles, but he will have no part in rebuilding."

"You're making a huge mistake," Mattaniah said. "We need the Samaritans and the local people in order to survive. What if they refuse to sell us their produce and livestock?"

"The Holy One will provide for our needs," Iddo said.

"He already has been providing for us through the Samaritans!" Mattaniah shouted. "Who do you think we've been buying oil and grain and livestock from? Do you want our families to starve?"

"Mattaniah is right," Joel said. "What if the local people turn against us in full force? There are more of them than us, especially now that we're spread out across Judah in dozens of struggling villages. None of our settlements have walls for protection."

"Should we allow fear to rule us? Is that how we make our decisions?" Iddo asked.

"No, but we need to be practical. We don't have weapons—and they do."

"Why did the Holy One send us into exile?" Iddo asked. "Wasn't it because of our idolatry? We now have a chance to start all over again, and the first thing you're asking us to do is compromise with idolaters? Any one of our Torah students can tell you the story of how our forefathers failed to drive all the Canaanites from the land, and how the next generation adopted Canaanite ways and Canaanite gods, just as Moses warned they would. We don't have the authority to drive the Samaritans out of our land, but we must remain separate from them."

"It isn't practical to remain separate. We are too few. We need them."

"We can't afford to need them, Mattaniah." The long discussion had made Iddo's head ache. He found the third book of Moses among the scrolls and handed it to Joel. "Read this yourself. You'll find that God says, 'You are to be holy to me because I, the Lord, am holy, and I have set you apart from the nations to be my own.' We must remain separate."

Iddo stayed behind in the house of assembly after Jeshua dismissed the meeting. It was after midnight, but he knew he wouldn't sleep. He lit an oil lamp and continued to study the Scriptures until dawn, praying that he was right, praying that when Sheshbazzar refused Governor Rehum's offer tomorrow that their tiny, vulnerable community of Jews was doing the right thing.

The following afternoon, Iddo sat in the banquet pavilion again, nervously awaiting the outcome. Prince Sheshbazzar was tactful in his refusal, assuring Governor Rehum that the priests had all the help and resources they needed to rebuild the temple. "We are very grateful for your offer, but we must refuse it." As everyone feared, the governor and his officials stormed away in anger. Amid the outrage and recriminations, the local leader, Zabad, stood up to shake his fist at Sheshbazzar.

"You want nothing to do with us?" he asked. "Very well! If we aren't good enough for you, then neither is our wheat or our wine or our olive oil!"

"I told you so," Mattaniah said glumly after the delegation left.

The high priest laid his hand on Mattaniah's shoulder. "I know. You did warn us, but we had no choice. Now I want to ask a favor of you, if I may. You've been friendly with these villagers. Would you go to them and tell them the truth about how you disagreed with us? Try to keep the lines of communication open. Be our eyes and ears in their villages."

"You're asking me to be a spy?"

"I'm asking you to keep us informed so we'll know if there's an imminent threat."

"You want me to pretend I'm still their friend to get information. That's being a spy."

"Moses sent spies into the Promised Land, and Joshua sent spies into Jericho. We would be wise to follow their example. You said you were concerned for our safety, didn't you?"

"You're backing me into a corner, Jeshua. I need time to think about this."

Iddo returned home after the disastrous banquet to tell his family what had happened. He wasn't surprised when Mattaniah didn't return home with him. Dinah met Iddo in the courtyard with a worried look on her face. "What's going on, Iddo? Shoshanna and I were standing here talking when Joel burst in and grabbed her by the arm and hauled her home with no explanation whatsoever."

Before Iddo could reply, Yael came out of the house and asked, "Where's my father? Why didn't he come home with you?"

Iddo closed his eyes at the enormity of the rift he had created.

What if Mattaniah moved out and took Yael with him? What if Joel wouldn't let their wives be friends anymore? Either move would break Dinah's heart—just when she was almost happy again, enjoying the female companionship she'd had in Babylon. "Sit down, Dinah," he said gently, gesturing to a small wooden stool.

"Why?" She remained standing as if bracing for a strong wind. Zechariah and the two shepherds' wives all gathered around to hear, as well. Feeling weary, Iddo sank down on the stool he had offered Dinah.

"You all know about the delegation of Samaritans and local elders who asked to meet with us. Well, they came to offer their help in rebuilding the temple, alongside us. The chief priests and Levites met last night, and we decided to advise Sheshbazzar to refuse their offer. I won't go into all of our reasons, but we used God's Law for guidance. Joel and Mattaniah both disagreed with our decision. Now they're upset."

"Where did my father go?" Yael asked.

"I think he went down to talk to the local leaders. The Samaritans were angry with our decision, too. He's worried there might be trouble."

"But we can't get mad at them!" Yael said. "Leyla is my friend!"

"Wait, I don't understand," Dinah said. "Why did Joel make Shoshanna leave our house?"

"Because I was the one who led the opposition. And I convinced all the others to reach this decision."

"Oh, Iddo," Dinah breathed. "What have you done? Just when things were going so well here."

"We must live according to God's Word and trust Him to protect us. Our leaders made the right decision. Mattaniah and Joel will eventually see the wisdom of it."

But Iddo couldn't deny that he was afraid. He had witnessed

the wrath of godless pagans as a child. Hanan's widow was a constant reminder of the local people's brutality.

The last thing Iddo had advised the high priest and the prince to do before leaving them was to be careful—and to double the number of guards.

Chapter 23

This wasn't what Zechariah had wished for. He may have longed to do something more besides study all day, but he never wished for his studies to stop altogether. But the day after Prince Sheshbazzar turned down the Samaritans' offer to help rebuild the temple, the elders decided to close the yeshiva. Not only was there no way to safeguard the Torah and the other sacred scrolls except to lock them away in the treasury, there weren't enough rabbis left to teach the students. The prince had conscripted every able-bodied man in Jerusalem to serve as a guard. The building supplies for the temple needed to be guarded day and night. The breeches in the walls and even the city streets needed to be guarded, and there simply weren't enough men to go around.

The elders put Zechariah and the older boys to work as watchmen during the day. His post, overlooking the Sheep Gate on the north side of the temple mount, had a view of the distant Judean hills. Zechariah sat atop a partially toppled watchtower with a small shofar in his hand. He was supposed to blow it at the first sign of danger.

He perched on his pile of rocks all day, swatting flies and wilting beneath the dizzying sun. He easily stayed alert and vigilant at first, energized with the excitement he used to feel when he went exploring. Along with the excitement, he also felt an undercurrent of fear. Mobs of angry Samaritans might converge on Jerusalem at any moment, and he was responsible for sounding the warning. But neither the excitement nor his heroic daydreams lasted long as boredom and the sun's heat wore him down. By the third day, he found himself wishing he was back in the house of assembly, exploring the Torah's many mysteries beneath a shady roof. When his replacement arrived at the end of the third day, he handed over the shofar and hurried to meet up with his grandfather for the evening sacrifice. Their prayers were needed now more than ever.

Afterward, he and Saba stayed to hear the troubling news that continued to pour in. "Reports of property damage, thefts, and threats are coming in from all over the district," the prince said. "It's no longer safe to go anywhere alone. In some places, food is becoming scarce after the local villages closed their markets to Jews."

"Our work of rebuilding the temple has been forced to halt before it barely got started," the high priest said.

"Halted! Why?" Saba asked.

"All of our supply lines have been cut off, our caravans are being attacked, our building materials stolen before they reach us. We can't continue to build without supplies."

"Or workers," one of the chief Levites added. "We relied on local workers for our manual labor, and they've all quit. And where is Mattaniah?"

Yael's father still hadn't returned home, and Saba's friend Joel refused to serve with the other priests or speak to Saba. The three men had been such good friends and co-workers, and now this.

One of the elders from Tekoa had come to complain about vandalism and sabotaged crops. "Our families are being forced to live in fear," the elder shouted. "What are we supposed to do?"

"Come back and live in the city for now," the prince urged.

"Then who will grow wheat for us or raise our flocks or tend our grapes? Why did you have to antagonize our neighbors?" And although Saba and the other priests explained their reasons once again, Zechariah saw that the unity of their tiny community had begun to fracture. The Almighty One had performed so many miracles during the first exodus. Why wasn't He helping them this time?

"I'm sorry for all this trouble," Prince Zerubbabel soothed. "We're all praying that tempers will cool and things will return to normal. The local people will soon realize that it's in their best interests to trade with us and work for us."

"Saba, there's something I don't understand," Zechariah said as they walked home afterward. "Didn't the Almighty One promise Abraham that all the people on earth would be blessed through him?"

"Yes, that was the promise."

"Then how can we be a blessing if we shut everyone out and refuse to let them worship with us?"

"They may worship with us, but they have to do it the way God prescribed, following His Law."

"I thought that's what the Samaritans were offering to do."

Saba shook his head. "We had no guarantee that they would give up their pagan ways and serve only God. If we allowed the Samaritans to help us rebuild, we would have to allow them to make decisions with us, and we couldn't take that risk."

"But . . . when I was reading through the scrolls of the prophets, they said that someday all nations would worship with us. How will that ever happen if we keep turning them away?"

They had reached home, and before Saba could reply, Safta came out to meet them. "There you are!" she said. "Dinner is waiting." Zaki saw his grandmother's relief each time he and Saba returned home safe and sound at the end of the day.

"There must be an answer to your question, Zechariah," Saba said as they washed their hands before the meal, "but I don't know what it is, yet. As soon as this trouble blows over, I promise we'll search the Scriptures together for the answer."

They sat down to eat, but the atmosphere around the table seemed tense. "Where's Rachel tonight?" Saba asked, looking all around. The shepherd's wife wasn't eating with them or working in the courtyard.

Safta leaned close to him and said, "You need to talk to her, Iddo. She's so worried about Besai that she can barely perform the simplest household chores."

"We sent as many men as we could spare out to the grazing lands to safeguard Besai and our temple flocks," Saba told her. "But he can't return to Jerusalem until all the ewes give birth and the new spring lambs gain strength."

"I hate being surrounded by so much fear and hostility," Safta said as she pushed away her plate. The worry crease on her forehead seemed to be permanent. "Armed guards came with us to the spring again today, but we're forced to wait until late in the day once again, until the local women are gone. We have to haul water up the hill at noon, in the heat of the day." Zechariah knew all about the sun's brutal heat—and he wasn't required to carry a heavy water jar like Safta. "Your decision has divided our community, Iddo, and we need each other now more than ever."

"I'm not happy about it, either. But when we do the right thing and obey God, we can expect opposition from the world. It's always easier to compromise. There's a difference between the easy way and the right way."

They were still eating when Mattaniah finally returned home for the first time in three days. Yael jumped up from her place and ran to him, clinging to him. "I didn't know where you were, Abba, or what happened to you!" Her words sounded muffled against his chest. She had been afraid for him all this time, Zaki realized, and hadn't let her fear or worry show.

"I'm fine, Yael. I'm fine."

"Have something to eat," Safta offered as she rose to wait on him. "There's plenty."

"No, thank you, Dinah. I can't stay. I only came back for some of my things. I need to leave again before dark." He disappeared into his room, and Zechariah could hear him shuffling around as he packed his belongings. No one seemed hungry anymore. Saba stood to talk with Mattaniah when he came out again.

"I hate this rift between us. Please stay. We've come to think of you as a son, your daughter as our granddaughter."

"I'm not leaving because I'm angry. My friend Zabad has agreed to keep renting the land to me. He even sold me a couple of goats so we'll have milk for the little ones from now on, and Dinah can make cheese. But I need to show good faith by living down there instead of here in Jerusalem. I'm building a house." He paused, looking down at his feet for a moment before continuing. "I've decided to do what Jeshua asked and be your eyes and ears. Not because I like the idea—I don't. But for our families' sakes."

Yael had disappeared into the room she shared with Mattaniah while he and Saba talked. She reappeared with her bag packed and her bedroll tied, and handed them to her father. "What's all this, Yael?"

"I gathered my things, like you said, so I can go with you."

"Not this time. Everything is too unsettled. You have to stay here with Dinah and Iddo for now."

"But I don't want to stay here. I want to be with you!"

"I'll be back and forth whenever I can. You'll see me."

"I haven't visited Leyla all week. When can I see her again?"

"Not anytime soon, I'm afraid. Wait until tempers cool." Mattaniah tried to hand back her things, but Yael let them drop to the floor, then stalked off to her room. Zaki thought he heard her crying. He felt enormous relief. The only good thing to come out of this mess was that Yael could no longer go to the village and read fortunes.

Zechariah was still in bed the next morning when his grandmother's shout awakened him. "Iddo! Iddo, come quick! Yael's gone! She's gone!" Zaki leaped out of bed and went to see. "I came in to wake her up," Safta said, "and look! Her room is empty. Her bag and bedroll are missing." This was much worse than when Yael had run away in Babylon. This time it was dangerous for anyone to go off by themselves, even grown men.

"Don't worry," Saba soothed. "She couldn't have gone far. We have guards all over the city to keep intruders out. She couldn't have gotten past them."

Zechariah knew better. Yael would make a game of sneaking past the guards. She was stubborn and fearless—and too young and naïve to know what a gang of village boys would do to her if Leyla's brother wasn't with them.

"We have to find her!" Safta insisted.

"We will, Dinah. As soon as I get back from the morning sacrifice."

"How can you go up to the temple when she's missing?"

"It's barely dawn. She couldn't have gone far. She would never leave in the dark. One of the guards has probably found her by now."

Zechariah needed to tell them that Yael wasn't afraid of the dark and that she knew how to evade the guards. But they would ask how he knew, and then he would incriminate himself. He remembered the beating he had suffered at the hands of the Samaritans and fear for his friend tied his stomach in a knot. For Safta's sake—and for Yael's—he had to say something.

"Saba? Yael is small and wiry. She loves to climb around on

rocks and things. I think she could easily sneak past the guards if she wanted to. I'll bet she went to be with her father."

"You have to go look for her!" Safta said. "Didn't Mattaniah tell us it was dangerous down there? Don't you remember the gang of boys who attacked Zechariah?"

"And haven't you been telling me how strong-willed Yael is? Perhaps suffering the consequences of her rebellion will teach her a lesson."

"Iddo! How can you say such a terrible thing?" The color seemed to drain from Safta's face. "How can you walk away when Yael might be in danger and say that she deserves it? She's a child! And we're responsible for her!"

Saba was maddeningly calm. "When I get back from prayers, I'll go look for her."

"No! You need to go look for her *now*, not mumble useless prayers!"

"Enough, Dinah. My mind is made up."

Zechariah accompanied Saba to the temple, but he couldn't concentrate on the sacrifice or his prayers. He wished the priests would hurry. Safta was right to be worried. Yael was too strong-willed, too fearless, for her own good. And Saba was wrong to waste time at the sacrifice when they should be searching for her. Again, Zechariah remembered his own brutal beating and felt sick inside. By the time the service ended, he had made up his mind to go down to the valley and search for his friend himself. "I want to help you find Yael," he told his grandfather.

"Absolutely not. If she did manage to leave the city to look for her father, I don't want you down there. Especially now, with all the trouble."

"I'm not afraid." He sounded braver than he felt.

"Zechariah—"

"I'm an adult now. I can make my own decisions."

"Yes, but this is a terrible one."

"Maybe so, but it's mine to make. If you don't let me come, I'll go search by myself after you leave—but I'd rather go with you."

Saba lifted the kippah off his head and ran his hand through his white hair before replacing his cap again with a sigh. "If you're determined to defy me, then I'd rather you come with me than go off alone." They returned home to tell Safta they were going to search for Yael, but they didn't mention that they were leaving the city.

Zechariah didn't realize how trapped and confined he had felt being cooped up in Jerusalem until he passed the guards at the checkpoint and walked down the road from the city. As the lush Kidron Valley spread out before him, he didn't blame Yael for wanting to escape. If danger lurked here, he didn't see it. He longed to run down the path in the bright sunshine, leaping like a calf set free from its stall. Much too soon they reached Mattaniah's patch of land, his sprouting crops laid out neatly in rock-bordered plots. Two goats grazed near the hut he had built, and he was already at work, bending over his grove of grape vines. If Yael was here with him, Zechariah didn't see her. Mattaniah stopped working when he saw them and stood up straight, wiping sweat from his brow.

"Is Yael with you?" Saba called out as they drew near.

Mattaniah froze for a moment before hurrying toward them. "What do you mean? No, she's not with me. I left her with you and Dinah."

Saba's shoulders sagged and for the first time, Zechariah glimpsed his worry. "Yael is missing," he said. "When Dinah went in to wake her up this morning she was gone. So were her bedding and her bag. We thought she might have followed you here."

Mattaniah appeared stricken. He glanced all around as if he needed to sit down somewhere. "I . . . I don't see how she could have left the city. I had to pass the guards myself when I came up to the city last night and when I left again."

"Zaki seems to think she could sneak past them."

Mattaniah lifted his arms, then dropped them again, helplessly. "The only other place I can think of where she might be is with her friend, Leyla. She hasn't been able to visit her and . . ."

"Do you want us to come with you, Mattaniah?"

"Not if you're going to be hostile toward them—especially if they have my daughter!"

"I can be calm," Saba said quietly. "They wouldn't hurt her, I don't think. The gang of boys left her alone the last time, didn't they?"

"Zabad's family has always treated her well. But what if she isn't there?" He looked as though he was about to panic.

"One step at a time," Saba soothed. "We'll find her. But I think we should send Zechariah back to the city first."

"No! I want to come with you!" He wanted to show the boys who had beaten him that he wasn't afraid, that he wouldn't cower in fear. And if they had laid a single hand on Yael, he wanted to be there to exact revenge.

"What do you think?" Saba asked Mattaniah. "Is it safe for him to come with us?"

"It doesn't matter. Let's just go!"

Mattaniah set a brisk pace as they walked across the narrow valley to the village.

The elders sitting at the entrance took them straight to Zabad's house. His son Rafi met them at the gate to the compound, and although Zechariah recognized him as one of the gang members, he wasn't one of the boys who had attacked him. Rafi led them into the house and into a dark, shadowy room where Zabad sat on a raised dais like a king on his throne.

"Mattaniah, my friend," he said, gesturing for him to approach. "I think I know why you're here. We were very surprised when your daughter came to visit Leyla without you." Zechariah felt his knees go weak with relief.

Mattaniah exhaled. "Then she's here. Thank you, my lord, for taking her in."

"Yes, she's here." Zabad smiled, a grin of superiority that held no warmth. "Unlike your people, we're careful to keep a close watch over our young girls, for their own safety."

"What Yael did was inexcusable, my lord. She was upset about the rift between our people and yours. We're all concerned about it—isn't that right, Iddo?"

Saba took a small step forward and gave a slight bow of his head. "Yes. There have been too many misunderstandings in the past, and what has happened most recently has all of my fellow Jews unhappy. Our leaders never meant to imply that you weren't welcome to worship with us. We would be happy to discuss it further—whenever you're ready to speak with us, of course."

Zabad took a sip from his cup without replying. He had offered none of the usual courtesies of hospitality.

"We won't take any more of your time," Saba said. "My wife is very concerned about Yael since she disappeared without telling anyone. I know it would be a great relief to her if we brought Yael home."

"Thank you, my lord, for taking care of her for me," Mattaniah added.

Rafi escorted them from the room again and back out to the courtyard. Yael was waiting for them there, bag and bedroll in hand. She looked defiant, but at a gesture from her father she remained quiet until they were well down the road away from the village.

"I don't want to go back to the city, Abba. I want to stay with you."

"That's out of the question."

"Why can't—?"

"Be quiet! You shamed me today! Zabad thinks that I don't

care enough about you to watch over you. He believes that our people don't value our women."

"But—"

"But nothing! You got away with too much in Babylon because your mother was ill, but that needs to change. You can't do whatever you want to here. And you can never, ever go off alone again. Do you understand?"

"When can I visit Leyla?"

"Not until I say so. That's your punishment. And if you run away again, I'll have you beaten for your own good."

Zechariah glanced at Yael, expecting to see tears. Instead, she was dry-eyed, her chin held high in defiance. What catastrophe would it take, he wondered, before her stubbornness was finally broken?

Chapter 24

Dinah was on her way to the spring late in the morning with Yael and the other women when she heard someone calling her. "Dinah, wait!" She turned to see her cousin Shoshanna hurrying to catch up. Dinah pulled her into her arms for a long embrace. "I've missed you so much," she murmured.

"I know. I've missed you, too. We may not be able to cook or eat meals together, but no one can stop us from walking to the spring together." They linked arms as they continued down the ramp toward the spring, balancing their jars on their heads. "We've been friends all our lives, Dinah, and that will never change."

"Of course it won't. But do you think this disagreement between our husbands will ever mend?"

"Joel is still furious with Iddo. He's convinced that the council made the wrong decision."

"Iddo told me about it, and I want you to know that I think Joel is right. Why refuse an honest offer to work together? Look at all the trouble Iddo's stubbornness has caused. Life here was hard enough without making it nearly impossible."

"I wish there was some way we could talk to the Samaritans'

wives," Shoshanna said. "Woman to woman. We have much more in common with them than our husbands have with their husbands. We're all mothers with families—we can better understand the Almighty One's love. We should be telling our neighbors about His grace, not turning them away in anger."

"The only thing Iddo ever talks about is God's wrath and punishment. And look where that's gotten us."

The women walking in front of them suddenly slowed. "Listen!" one of them said. "What's that sound?"

At first Dinah mistook the distant chattering for a flock of birds. But as she and the others rounded the bend she saw a mob of local women, faces shielded with veils, blocking the path to the spring. Dinah halted with the others, gripping Yael's arm to make her stop. One of the Jewish guards stepped forward to shout above the chattering, "Please! Move aside and let our women draw water!" The village women drowned out his plea with shouts and high-pitched cries.

"Why don't the guards just push them out of the way?" Yael asked.

"They don't dare," Dinah said. "If our men even got close to those women, there would be war." The mob had guards of their own—a gang of young boys Zaki's age who hovered in the background behind them.

The two Jewish men continued to walk forward, testing the local women's reactions, asking them kindly to move aside. When they were still several yards from the spring, the ring of women pelted them with rocks that showered down like hailstones. Dinah tightened her grip on Yael's arm as the men backed away.

"I can't imagine all this hostility over water," Shoshanna said.

"Let's go back to the city," Dinah said. "Come on. Iddo and the other men will just have to find another source of water for us. We shouldn't have to do battle this way."

"No," Shoshanna said. "I want these women to know that we aren't their enemies." She set her water jar on the ground and began walking forward. Dinah reached out to stop her.

"Shoshanna, wait! What are you doing?"

"Somebody has to be a peacemaker."

"No, don't! Stop!" But Shoshanna avoided Dinah's grasp and continued to stride forward, skirting around the two guards who now stood out of range of the stones. Shoshanna lifted her arms and spread her empty hands as if in surrender.

"We aren't your enemies," she shouted above the din. "We're wives and mothers just like you. Please, can't we—?" Her words were cut off by a hail of stones. Dinah saw a fist-sized rock smash into Shoshanna's head. A second well-aimed stone struck her face. Shoshanna toppled to the ground from the impact.

"No!" Dinah screamed. Her instinct was to run to Shoshanna's side, but Yael blocked her way, holding her back. All around them, the other women screamed and fled back toward the city as a barrage of stones rained down on them. Dinah heard the thudding rocks fall all around her but she was too grief-stricken to care. *"No!* Shoshanna, *no!"* she sobbed. "Somebody help her!" The two guards braved the barrage and ran to Shoshanna. Dinah would have run with them, but Yael was surprisingly strong.

"Stay here, Safta. Stay here," she begged. She was crying, too.

"Let me go, Yael!"

"The men will help her. You aren't strong enough to carry her, Safta." Dinah watched helplessly as the men reached Shoshanna and one of them lifted her in his arms. Stones pelted both men as they sprinted back toward Dinah and Yael, but thankfully neither man took a direct hit in the head as Shoshanna had.

"Safta! We have to run!" Yael suddenly cried. "The women are chasing us!" Through a haze of tears, Dinah saw that she was right. The rocks had stopped falling and now the local women surged forward, chasing them with angry shouts. Dinah was too stunned to move.

"Wh-where's my water jar?" She had no idea what had happened to it.

"Never mind, Safta. We need to run!" Somehow Yael got Dinah turned around and pulled her back to the city as fast as they could go. The two guards caught up with them, carrying Shoshanna, and Dinah saw her friend's lifeless face, streaked with blood. So much blood! It soaked Shoshanna's curly hair and ran into her eyes. The guard's tunic was stained with it.

"Bring her to my house," Dinah said when they reached the city. "It isn't far." The men carried Shoshanna into Dinah's courtyard and laid her down. She hadn't made a sound or opened her eyes in all that time. Dinah pressed her shaking fingers to Shoshanna's neck to feel for her heartbeat. It was weak, but she was alive. For her friend's sake, Dinah knew she had to pull herself together, to lay aside her shock and fear for a moment and tend to Shoshanna's wounds. *Please, God, let them be superficial. Please, when the bleeding stops and she wakes up again, let her be fine.*

"Her husband's name is Joel. He's a priest," Dinah told the two guards. Both men were bruised and bleeding from being struck by rocks, but they weren't hurt as seriously as Shoshanna. "Find him and tell him he needs to come right away."

"Do you know where he is?"

"No. He could be anywhere. The priests all work extra hours doing guard duty. Start at the house of assembly. Maybe someone there will know. But go! Hurry!"

Yael knelt down beside Dinah and wordlessly handed her a damp cloth. She cleaned the blood from Shoshanna's face and saw that her skin was badly scraped and her cheekbone probably broken. The larger wound above her eye, near her temple, was the one that worried Dinah. She gently dabbed away the blood, then probed the wound with her fingers. She felt the fist-sized dent in her friend's skull from the impact of the stone, felt sharp edges of fractured bone, and her stomach turned inside out. *No. Oh, God, no.* Shoshanna's skull was smashed in. There was nothing Dinah could do.

She bent forward, wrapping her arms around her friend, lowering her face to Shoshanna's chest. *Please don't take Shoshanna. She loved you, God. She wanted to come here so badly! How could you let this happen?*

Dinah was still weeping when the men returned with Joel. Shoshanna was alive, but she hadn't regained consciousness and probably never would. Dinah didn't know how to tell her husband. As the news spread and more people gathered in Dinah's home, Joel's grief turned to anger. He interrogated the two guards again and again, as well as the women who had witnessed the attack, including Dinah and Yael. Over and over they told him how Shoshanna had moved forward, trying to make peace. They were able to explain to him what had happened, but no one was able to tell him why it had.

"Don't just stand there," he told all the men who had come. "Go find the people who did this to her! Bring them to justice."

"It was a huge crowd of women and young boys," one of the guards said. "There's no way to know who threw that stone."

When Iddo arrived home, Joel lunged at him, his rage overflowing. "This is your fault! This never would have happened if it weren't for you!" It took three men to hold him back and keep him from striking Iddo. When Joel finally regained control, he lifted Shoshanna in his arms and carried her home. Dinah wept helplessly, understanding Joel's anger and grief, his need to blame someone. As far as she was concerned, Joel was right. Iddo was to blame.

"I heard that our women were attacked," Iddo said, moving toward her through the knot of people. "I was so worried about you, Dinah." He reached to take her in his arms, but she backed away from him.

"No. You started all this trouble by refusing to see anyone's point of view but your own. What kind of a hateful, unloving God do you serve?" She fled out of their courtyard and ran the short distance to Joel's house. She found him sitting on the ground with his wife in his arms, clinging to her as if his tears, his embrace, could make her well.

"Is she going to be all right, Dinah? Will she wake up soon?"

"I don't know . . . I don't know . . ." She sank down beside him and closed her eyes, weeping and pleading with the Almighty One to spare her friend. This couldn't be happening. They couldn't lose Shoshanna.

All day people quietly came and went, bringing food, offering their help, their prayers. "Just find the person who did this," Joel repeated. "That's the only help I need." Hours later, when night fell, he sent Dinah home. "I want to be alone with my wife."

Dinah did what he asked, but she dreaded facing Iddo. He was to blame for this as surely as if he had thrown that stone. When she arrived, she found Yael sitting outside their house with her back against the courtyard wall, looking up at the starry sky. Yael scrambled to her feet when she saw Dinah. "Is Shoshanna going to live, Safta?"

"I don't know . . . I wish I did." She wasn't ready to talk to Iddo, so she remained outside the gate with Yael as they both looked up at the stars.

"What month was Shoshanna born?" Yael asked softly.

"What difference does it make? Why is that important now?" But then she realized why Yael was asking. She knew how to see the future by studying the stars. The Babylonian woman had once seen Dinah's future, and maybe Yael could see Shoshanna's. "Can the stars tell us what will happen to her, Yael?"

"I'm not sure. I might be able to tell if . . ." She gave a little shrug.

"She was born in the month of Nisan, the same as me." Yael nodded and walked through the courtyard to her room. Dread filled Dinah as she waited. When she could no longer stand waiting, she followed Yael inside. She had lit a small oil lamp and knelt on the floor of her room to study a scroll unrolled before her, each corner weighted with a stone. When Yael looked up and saw Dinah, a look of guilt washed over her face—or maybe it was fear. "I won't tell anyone, Yael. What do you see?"

"All of the stars . . ." she said softly, " and even the moon . . ." She shook her head, and Dinah saw Yael wipe a tear. "They're all lined up against her, Safta."

Dinah closed her eyes as her tears began to fall again. Yael had only confirmed what Dinah had known all along. The rock had fractured Shoshanna's skull, shattering the bone, sending shards into her brain. She couldn't live.

When Dinah returned to Joel's house early the next morning, he was still holding his wife in his arms. But Shoshanna's body was cold and lifeless. "Joel . . . she's gone," Dinah whispered.

He couldn't be comforted. Dinah tried, but her own grief was inconsolable. She sobbed as she helped the other women prepare Shoshanna's body for burial. They held the funeral right away. Mourners gathered outside of Shoshanna's house afterward, bringing food and condolences, but Joel refused to let anyone inside. At last Dinah went home to confront Iddo, angry with him and his God. This was the second death among the returnees, and both Shoshanna and Hanan had died violently, attacked by their neighbors.

"Wasn't our people's punishment supposed to be over?" she asked. "We've been serving God, offering all the proper sacrifices. Why did He let this happen?"

"I don't know what to say," Iddo answered softly. His eyes were red with grief, but Dinah couldn't stop her angry words.

"Are you going to seek justice and punish the murderers this time? Shoshanna was trying to make peace with those people! We were all witnesses! They killed her for no reason!"

"Did you see who threw the stone, Dinah? Can you identify any of the veiled women? Did you see the boys' faces?" She didn't reply. Iddo already knew the answers. "Even the two guards couldn't identify her murderer."

"So you refuse to get justice?"

"No. I'm not refusing anything. I'm as outraged as you are. Our leaders will go to all of the local villages and confront their leaders. We'll do everything we can to get justice."

Dinah wasn't listening. "Why is God taking away everyone I love?"

"Dinah . . ." Iddo tried to hold her and console her, but she pushed him away.

"I blame you for this. You're the one who put that stone in the killer's hand!" Iddo turned and walked away.

As the days passed, Joel remained barricaded in his house, pushing everyone away. He refused to leave, refused to have anything to do with the other priests. "Please see if you can talk to him, Dinah," Iddo urged. "We're all worried about him."

She was worried, too. After breakfast one morning, she wrapped up a portion of food that she was too grief-stricken to eat and brought it to Joel. He sat alone in his inner room with all the shutters closed, his robes torn, his hair and beard disheveled. He looked up and saw her in the doorway, then looked down again. "Go away, Dinah."

Instead, she stepped into the room. "I know you hate Iddo, but please don't hate me. Shoshanna was much more than my cousin, she was my dearest friend. We brought hundreds of babies into the world together, and for as long as I can remember, she . . ." Dinah couldn't finish as she began to weep. "I miss her so much!"

"I know," he said hoarsely. "She loved you like a sister."

Dinah went all the way into the room and knelt down in front of Joel, laying the plate of food on the floor. "You were right, and Iddo was wrong. He never should have angered the Samaritans that way. I don't understand why he's so unbending, and I don't understand the God he worships."

"Shoshanna's death is so meaningless. She was so excited to come here, wanting me to be a priest and serve God. She's the one who convinced me to come. And look where it got her." When he covered his face and sobbed, Dinah wrapped her arms around him, weeping on his shoulder. She didn't care if the Law forbid her to hold him or to be here alone with him. They needed each other's comfort.

"Thank you, Dinah," he said when their tears finally ran out.

"I'll leave this food for you. Please try to eat something."

Every day that week Dinah put aside extra food for Joel and brought it to him after Iddo left for the day. Sometimes she talked with him for a few hours, reliving her memories of Shoshanna. Sometimes she simply held him and wept in silence. More than anything else, Dinah needed someone to hold on to and grieve with. Her sorrow required the warmth of another caring person no matter what the Law said. Joel didn't eat very much, and Dinah could see his handsome face growing gaunt. She was with him one morning when a group of priests came to his door.

"This never would have happened if you had listened to me instead of Iddo!" he shouted as he threw them out. "It should've been one of your wives who died, not mine! You're the ones who murdered her! You're all responsible!" Dinah tried to soothe him after they left, but he paced the small room, too angry to sit. "I'm leaving here, Dinah. I'm going home to Babylon."

She didn't believe he meant it at first, but she couldn't stop thinking about his words after she returned home and resumed her work with the other women. Joel was right; it could have been anyone's wife who had died. Surely no sensible man would want to stay here now, even Iddo. The local people would never make peace with them. Work on the temple had halted for lack of supplies and workers. No one would sell food to the Jews. Why not admit defeat and go back to Babylon? The Almighty One was clearly against them.

Thinking about Babylon quickly became an antidote to Dinah's grief. When she saw Yael standing outside their courtyard gate one evening, looking up at the stars, she went out to stand beside her. Yael seemed subdued since Shoshanna's murder, as if her death had killed Yael's usually lively spirit. Dinah looked up at the sky with her and said, "I know you can see things up there, and I need to know . . . I need hope . . . Am I ever going home?" Yael looked down at her feet, biting her lip. "You won't get into trouble, Yael, I swear. Your sorceress in Babylon was right about my heart tearing in two, and you were right about Shoshanna. If you know what the stars say about my future, please tell me. Are they against me like they were against Shoshanna?"

Yael reached to hold Dinah tightly. "Yes," she whispered. "Your stars are the same as Shoshanna's, since you were born in Nisan, and right now they're against you. But they'll change in time."

Dinah pushed free from Yael's embrace. "How much time?" Yael looked down at her feet again, but Dinah lifted her chin and made her look at her. "Will you tell me when the time is right? When I can go home?"

Yael nodded. "Yes. I'll tell you."

Two weeks after Shoshanna's funeral, Iddo tried reaching out to Dinah again as they lay side by side in bed one night, unable to sleep. She pushed him away. "Can you tell me why God took Shoshanna?"

"I don't know why. We can never fully understand the Almighty One—"

"Then why try? Why force Zechariah to study the Torah, and why go through all this effort to try to please Him, leaving our home and building a temple and sacrificing countless animals? Will He ever be satisfied? Why is He still punishing us, killing good people like Shoshanna?"

"Who are we to question the Almighty One?"

Dinah's temper flared. "Will you still defend Him after all this?"

"I'm sorry, Dinah. What I meant to say was . . . I-I can't answer your questions."

"You're supposed to be His priest. If you don't know the answers, then who does?"

Dinah spent more and more of her time with Joel, slowly coaxing him to eat and to come out of his room and sit in the sunshine. They talked for hours, sharing memories of Shoshanna and their life in Babylon, airing their dissatisfaction with life in Jerusalem. Joel's kindness and gentleness as they comforted each other made Dinah wonder what her life might have been like if she had married him instead of Iddo. Before long, she was spending all of her time with Joel, leaving home every morning, letting the other women do her daily work.

A month after his wife died, Joel finally seemed to find his way out of his grief. "Thank you for all your help," he said when Dinah brought him his breakfast one morning. He had changed out of his torn robes and trimmed his dark hair and beard. "I needed you and—"

"We needed each other. We helped each other."

"Yes, that's true. That's why I want you to be the first to know that I've made plans to go back to Babylon." Dinah's heart seemed to halt at his words, then speed up. "I have no reason to stay here anymore," he continued. "So I'm going back to warn my children not to come. God demands too great a sacrifice. If He would take a good woman like Shoshanna, then why serve Him?"

"Are you going alone? How will you get there?"

"I'm not the only one who's leaving. Several other families have decided to return, too. We're all fed up with the hardship here, the constant danger. It was a huge mistake to come. The temple will never be rebuilt now."

Dinah's heart beat so rapidly she could barely speak. "When are you leaving?"

"I've learned that the governor of Trans-Euphrates periodically sends caravans with tax revenue to the Persian capital. If I go to Samaria, I can travel with them for a fee."

Dinah flew into his arms, clinging to him, comfortable in his embrace after so many weeks, so many tears. "Take me with you, Joel! Please!"

"You aren't serious."

"Yes, I am! I never wanted to come to this godforsaken place to begin with. I never wanted to leave my family. I only came because I had to, because of Iddo. But after everything that's happened, I don't love him anymore. This is all his fault! I want to take my grandson back to Babylon before something terrible happens to him. I want to go home, Joel. Please take me with you. Please!"

He held her tightly and let her cry. "Of course, Dinah. Don't cry . . . Of course you can come with me. It will be justice, in a sense. I lost my wife because of Iddo, and now he can see how it feels to lose his wife."

Dinah wept with relief. She would start a new life with the man she should have married in the first place, back home with her children, her grandchildren. She and Joel were still holding each other when she heard footsteps. Dinah looked up.

Iddo stood in the doorway of Joel's house.

Chapter 25

Iddo stared at his wife, his friend. Surely this wasn't what it looked like. It couldn't be.

"What are you doing in my house?" Joel shouted. He released Dinah and strode toward Iddo, his fists clenched. "Get out!"

Iddo couldn't speak, couldn't breathe. *Dinah and Joel? Embracing?*

He had come to talk to his friend, to ask his forgiveness. To tell him that Prince Sheshbazzar was determined to meet with the local leaders and get justice for Shoshanna's death. Iddo came to urge Joel to go with them. He had never dreamed that he would find Dinah here alone with him, much less find her in Joel's arms.

"Joel is going back to Babylon," Dinah said. She walked forward to stand beside Joel, linking her arm through his. "I'm going with him."

Her words struck Iddo like a blow. *Dinah and Joel.* Iddo couldn't think, couldn't imagine . . . He turned and stumbled away, unable to say a word.

His heart felt like a dead thing inside him, a stone that grew heavier and heavier as he hurried away. He didn't know what to do, where to go, but he found himself trudging uphill toward the temple, then climbing the stairs to the top. One of his fellow priests spotted him and walked over. "You're not on duty today, are you Iddo?"

He shook his head. "I . . . I need to pray. Excuse me . . ." He couldn't find release with tears. Shock and rage had stranded him in an arid wilderness where his mouth, his tongue, his tears, had turned to dry sand. He hadn't wept as a child, either, even after all the horror he had witnessed. And he couldn't cry now. The deadness that he'd felt inside as a boy had crept through him again, overwhelming him, turning him to stone. *Don't think. Don't feel. Don't remember.* Once again, the people he loved were lost to him.

He skirted around the worship area and the altar, passing the abandoned crane and construction site until he reached the north side of the mount and the ruins of Solomon's temple. He sank down on a sun-warmed block of stone and hunched forward in grief, covering his face with his hands.

Dinah had told him months ago that she was merely going through the motions as his wife with no love in her heart, but he hadn't wanted to believe her. Now he'd seen the truth for himself. She didn't love him. She loved someone else. But what should he do about it? His heart and mind were so shattered by what he'd seen that he could barely think—he didn't want to think. But he would force himself to sit here and talk to the Almighty One until he came up with a solution.

If he refused to divorce Dinah, if he forced her to stay, she would hate him even more than she already did. Iddo would have to let her go. Back to Babylon. With Joel.

The realization doubled him over with grief. How could he live without Dinah? He loved her. Even now, even after what he'd just seen, even though jealous rage threatened to consume him, Iddo loved her.

But what should he do? Iddo's mind whirled in turmoil. The law clearly said that Dinah and Joel should both be stoned to death for committing adultery. And when he remembered seeing them in each other's arms, his rage screamed at him to do it. To condemn them both to a violent, painful death. As a priest, Iddo not only taught the Law, but was required to set an example in keeping it. Yet he couldn't kill Dinah. He couldn't inflict that horrible punishment on the woman he loved.

His fellow priests would tell him that God's justice must be served. She must be punished for breaking her marriage covenant, just as justice demanded that the person who had murdered Shoshanna must die. But Iddo had witnessed too many deaths, seen too much evidence of God's punishment in his lifetime. He couldn't bear any more.

Maybe Dinah was right. Maybe the Almighty One was cruel and unfeeling. Why else would He command such a law? Why else would His people suffer so much trouble? Where was the God of miracles who had parted the Red Sea and destroyed their enemies during the first exodus? Iddo had come to Jerusalem to be a priest, to serve God. He had wanted to undo the mistakes of his forefathers and rebuild the temple, teach the laws of the Torah. Instead, his sacrifice had cost him his children and now his wife. Why would God snatch his family away from him a second time?

The sun felt merciless as it beat down on Iddo's head. It would only grow hotter here among the shadeless ruins as the day progressed. *What do you want me to do, God?* He posed the question to the unfeeling skies, to a cold and distant God, never expecting an answer. But Iddo heard His reply, as clearly as if God had spoken the words to him face-to-face.

Forgive her.

Was his mind playing tricks on him? Forgive her? Even after she committed adultery? How could he forgive her? Wasn't he required to uphold the Law? And what about God's justice?

He thought back to the day when he first realized that Dinah's love for him was slowly dying. She had asked him whether he served the Almighty One from love or from fear. *"You believe we have to follow all the rules, do everything exactly right, or He'll punish our smallest misstep."* And her words had helped Iddo understand that God wanted his love, wanted a relationship with him, not mere obedience to the law.

Iddo stood, too agitated to remain seated, and paced the small area among the ruins. The huge blocks hemmed him in, frustrating him, and he felt like kicking them. But that would be wrong. These were the building stones of the Almighty One's temple.

He remembered where he was—in Jerusalem. He was here with thousands of other Jews because the Almighty One had forgiven him and offered him a second chance. No one could keep all 613 of the Torah's laws perfectly. No one. Especially Iddo. He had tried and tried, and yet measured against the plumb line of the Torah, he always fell short. That's why he bowed before God every year on Yom Kippur and confessed his sins. That's why the priests offered sacrifices twice a day. Iddo didn't deserve God's mercy and grace, but He offered it to Iddo just the same. What did God want him to do in return? Offer more sheep? More calves and lambs and grain offerings?

Forgive her.

Iddo sank down again. He remained seated on the broken limestone building block all afternoon, wiping the sweat from his face and neck, as the sun pressed down on him. He couldn't move, trapped between law and grace, afraid to take a step and make a mistake. How could the Almighty One give two conflicting commands?

As the sun finally began to sink in the west, Iddo heard the distant sound of music. The evening sacrifice. Was it that late already? He should leave. Zechariah must be waiting for him.

They had to attend the sacrifice and pray together. But Iddo couldn't move.

He recognized the words of the psalm that the Levite choir was singing: *"Give thanks to the Lord, for he is good . . ."* And the crowd of worshipers echoed the refrain, *"His love endures forever."* In verse after verse, God's wonders and miracles were retold and the refrain repeated, pounding into Iddo's heart like a hammer chiseling stone: *His love endures forever . . . His love endures forever . . . His love endures forever . . .* God hadn't left them in their sins in Babylon, separated from Him. They were here in Jerusalem because of His grace—with a job to do, a temple to rebuild.

At last the music stopped. And once more, in the silence that followed, Iddo heard God speak.

Forgive her.

Forgive Dinah.

When he was certain that the evening sacrifice had ended, he stood again, needing to walk, needing to escape the cramped confines of the temple's ruins. But he couldn't go home. He didn't want to go home. He made his way across the temple mount, down the stairs, down the hill to the house of assembly. He would search the Scriptures for answers.

Every evening the priests brought the sacred scrolls out of the treasury so any man who wanted to could study them for a few hours. Iddo wasn't the only one in the study hall. Jeshua the high priest already had several of the Torah scrolls unrolled in front of him, bending over them, reading them. Iddo randomly picked up one of the remaining scrolls and sat down to unroll it, not even sure he would be able to concentrate on it.

"The word of the Lord that came to Hosea son of Beeri . . ."

Iddo closed his eyes. He didn't want to read the book of Hosea's prophecies. He already knew the story of how God had told the prophet to marry a prostitute and then, after she was unfaithful to him, to take her back and love her again. God's message through Hosea was that God would take Israel back, even though His people had betrayed Him with idols. And here they were, back in Jerusalem.

Forgive her.

Iddo remained in the house of assembly all night, long after the other men left and the priests returned the scrolls to the treasury. He didn't need to read the other scrolls to know that they would all tell him the same thing. God's love was the theme of the psalms that he and his fellow musicians sang every day: *"He does not treat us as our sins deserve . . . For as high as the heavens are above the earth, so great is his love for those who fear him . . . You, O Lord, are a compassionate and gracious God, slow to anger, abounding in love and faithfulness . . . His love endures forever."*

Was God's law more important than His love? Did Iddo want justice for his shattered marriage or did he want Dinah's love?

He wanted her love. He still loved her and always would, in spite of everything. In understanding his own heart, Iddo began to understand God's heart. And he knew what he needed to do.

At dawn, Iddo finally went home. Dinah was awake, as he knew she would be, kindling a fire to prepare breakfast. She looked frightened when she looked up and saw him, as if she expected to be dragged before the chief priest and stoned to death. Her fear broke his heart. Iddo wished she could see how much he loved her, even in his anger. How much God loved her. But how could she believe in God's love when all Iddo had ever emphasized was His Law?

"Come with me, please," he said, gesturing to her. "You don't need to be afraid."

He saw Dinah's hands shaking as she set down the handful of kindling. Iddo led her the short distance to Joel's house. He was awake as well, and when he saw Iddo he shouted loudly enough to wake the entire neighborhood. "How dare you come back here? Get out of my house!"

For a moment, Iddo's resolve weakened when he remembered what he had seen yesterday. He was the one who should be shouting in anger, condemning Joel and Dinah for adultery. Iddo's face grew warm as rage boiled through him again. But God's command to him had been clear. *Forgive her.*

"Just give me a moment to speak, Joel. Then I'll go." Iddo turned to Dinah first, who cowered behind him. "When you return to our community in Babylon with Joel, you will be shunned and labeled a *sotah*. Our children will be put in a difficult place if they receive you back while you're still married to me. And so I want you to know that I'm offering you a divorce. You and Joel can marry—"

"Whoa!" Joel said, holding up both hands. "I never said I wanted to marry Dinah. My wife just died! You think I would replace Shoshanna?"

Dinah moved from behind Iddo and slowly walked toward Joel. "But . . . but you said you would take me back to Babylon with you."

"And I will. But not as my wife! Look, I needed comfort and you offered it. And deep inside, I also wanted to get even with Iddo. Until the day I die, I'll always blame him for Shoshanna's death."

"You used me?" Dinah asked, her voice hushed with disbelief.

"We used each other. Admit it, Dinah. You were as angry with Iddo as I was."

She stared up at Joel as if too stunned to speak, then turned and fled, brushing past Iddo as she ran out of the courtyard. He longed to run after her, but he didn't know if he should, if she would want him to.

"Get out of my house," Joel said again. "And don't ever come back!"

Iddo followed Dinah home and found her in their room, curled in grief, sobbing. He waved away the other women when they came to comfort her and closed the door. He knelt beside Dinah, asking God what he should do.

Forgive her.

He needed to forgive Dinah and take her back the same way God had forgiven His people after their unfaithfulness to Him. He needed to show his love to her. And that meant not only giving up his right to condemn her, but giving her what she longed for the most. Iddo would take her back to Babylon himself. He would prove his love by leaving Jerusalem a second time. That meant giving up his work as a priest, never worshiping in the temple, or having a part in rebuilding it. Did he love Dinah that much?

Yes.

A single tear slid down his face and into his beard. This was what God wanted him to do. Iddo waited until Dinah's sobbing tapered off, praying for the right words to say.

"I know you don't love me anymore, Dinah. But I've never stopped loving you. If you want to go back to Babylon, you don't need Joel to take you. I'll take you there myself."

She looked up at him after a moment, her beautiful face ravaged by sorrow. "Why, Iddo? Why would you do that for me?"

"Because I've made too many mistakes. You were right, I was too hard on our sons, and I want to make things right with them and with you. . . . And because it's what the Almighty One did, forgiving our people even after we went after other gods. I understand His love now, how deep and wide and everlasting it is. If He binds us tightly with laws and rules, it's for the same reason that we hold our children tightly in our grasp, to keep them from hurting themselves or being hurt. But God also gives us the freedom to leave His embrace and go our own way. He won't force His love on us, and I won't force mine on you. I'll take you back to Babylon, not so you'll forgive me, but so you'll forgive God. So you'll understand the truth about His grace."

"You would do that? After I turned away from you?"

"Yes." Another tear slipped down Iddo's cheek. He wiped it away.

Dinah stared at him as if waiting for him to say more. But he had spoken from his heart and said everything that he knew to say. He stood.

"I'll find out when the next caravan is leaving."

Chapter 26

The knowledge that she was finally going home to her family should have cheered Dinah, but it didn't. She sat by the hearth late in the afternoon, chopping garlic and leeks for their dinner and wondering how she had messed up so badly. How had she failed to see that what she felt for Joel was one-sided? He didn't love her. Their emotional attachment was bound by their grief for Shoshanna. He had used her to hurt Iddo, to get even with him. And she had done the same.

She pulled another garlic clove from the head to peel it. Iddo said he forgave her. He still loved her. He would take her home to Babylon. She was afraid to believe it, afraid it was a dream or that he would change his mind. For the past two days she had gone about her usual chores barely knowing what she was doing, her mind a confused mixture of thoughts and feelings. Even now she burned the vegetables and scorched the pot and had to begin all over again.

"What about Zaki?" she whispered to Iddo when he returned with Zechariah from the sacrifice that evening. "Does he know we're going home? Did you tell him?"

"Not yet. I thought we would tell him together. It was his decision to come here, so he must decide whether or not to return."

Of course Zechariah would return with them. Why would he stay here? "What about Yael?" Dinah asked.

"She'll do whatever her father says. I doubt if Mattaniah will want to return with us. Where is he, by the way?" Iddo asked, looking around. "He wasn't at the sacrifice."

"When Mattaniah came this morning to bring us some goats' milk, Yael talked him into letting her visit Leyla for the day. They should be home soon. Before dark, he said." Dinah had waited all day for a chance to ask Yael to consult the stars for her, to learn the best time to leave.

She and Iddo went through the motions of washing their hands, sitting down to eat together, and praying the blessing, but the others could surely see the strain between them. Their house was too small, the family too close not to notice the emotional upheaval. Halfway through the meal, Yael burst into the courtyard, upset and breathless, with Mattaniah trailing behind her. She went straight to Dinah and knelt in front of her.

"Safta, please! We need your help! Please, please come to Leyla's village with me. Please!"

"What's wrong?"

"Raisa is having trouble giving birth. I told Leyla's grandmother that you were a midwife and would know how to help her. Won't you please come, Safta?"

Dinah pulled her hands free from Yael's. "Why should we help them? These might be the same women who killed Shoshanna."

"Besides," Iddo added, "I'm not convinced that it's safe for either one of you to go down there after what happened."

"But maybe this is what we all need," Mattaniah said. "We could demonstrate our goodwill to them."

"But what if this woman or her baby dies?" Iddo asked. "Then what? They'll blame Dinah and say she did it for revenge."

"No, they won't," Yael insisted. "Leyla and her grandmother aren't like that. Please let Safta come. She knows what to do."

Dinah listened as the men continued to argue, her own thoughts turning one way and then the other. She pictured Shoshanna, bravely stepping forward to say, *"Somebody has to be a peacemaker,"* and knew that if she were alive, she wouldn't hesitate for a moment to go and help this mother. And Dinah also knew that if Iddo could forgive her, then she needed to forgive these village women, as well.

"Don't I have anything to say about this decision?" Dinah asked at last.

"Of course," Iddo said. "But for the good of our community we need to consider this carefully. I think I should consult Prince Sheshbazzar and see what he says."

"No. This mother needs me now. Delivering babies is what I do. I think I should help her."

Iddo stood and paced a few steps, crossing his arms then uncrossing them again, his turmoil apparent as he struggled to decide. "I'll come with you," he finally said.

"And do what, Iddo? Haven't I been a midwife for more than thirty years without your help? Mattaniah will take me there. He knows these people."

"May I come?" Yael asked. Dinah hesitated. There was an unspoken rule that girls Yael's age shouldn't witness childbirth or fear would overwhelm them when their own time came. But nothing seemed to frighten Yael.

"Yes, you may come if you'd like."

Dinah left the remains of her dinner and gathered up the things she would need. A few minutes later she was hurrying down to the village with Yael and Mattaniah. Dinah hadn't left Jerusalem in more than a month—since the disastrous day when Shoshanna had been killed. In all their years together as midwives, she and Shoshanna had rarely delivered a baby without each other, and Dinah mourned for her friend all over again as she walked. But remembering Shoshanna also brought a stab of guilt for the way she and Joel had behaved. Maybe going to this village and helping the people responsible for Shoshanna's death could help her earn forgiveness. Shoshanna would have forgiven everyone, even the person who threw the stone.

Night had fallen by the time they reached the village. For the last half mile, Dinah barely had been able to see where she was going in the dark. But oil lamps blazed in Leyla's courtyard and in several of the inner rooms when they arrived. Leyla and her grandmother led them to a room off the main courtyard where two women sat vigil beside a young girl, lying on a bed of cushions. Dinah stared at the white-faced girl, who was weak with exhaustion. She looked younger than Yael! "Is she Leyla's sister?" Dinah whispered to Yael.

"No, she's Leyla's stepmother."

"Stepmother . . . ?"

"Zabad has three wives. He married Raisa a year ago."

Dinah struggled to disguise her shock. How could any man marry a child who was young enough to be his daughter? But she couldn't think about that now. Raisa began writhing in pain, screaming as another strong contraction overwhelmed her. "How long has she been in labor?" Dinah asked.

"Since this time yesterday," Leyla's grandmother replied. She carried a cup of steaming liquid to the bedside.

Since yesterday. "You probably know that it's very bad for the baby as well as the mother when a birth takes this long," Dinah said. "I can't promise a good outcome, but I'll do everything I can."

"No one will blame you," the older woman said. "The stars foresee death for both mother and child."

Her words startled Dinah. The *stars*? Was everyone giving up because of the stars? Yet Dinah recalled consulting them when Shoshanna lay dying. They hadn't foretold anything that Dinah hadn't seen with her own eyes, but now her heart told her that as long as Raisa breathed, there was hope. Dinah would do everything in her power to save this mother and her baby, to prove that the indifferent stars were wrong.

"May I examine her?" Dinah didn't wait for a reply but knelt by Raisa's side and lifted the sheet that covered her. The contraction had subsided and she lay limp against the cushions again. Her pelvis was very narrow, and although Raisa was ready to give birth, the baby was positioned with its buttocks first instead of its head. There simply wasn't enough room for the child to be born.

"Am I going to die?" Raisa moaned. "I don't want to die. . . ."

The old woman knelt on the other side of her with the warm red liquid. "Help me lift her head so she can drink this," she told Dinah.

"What is it?" When the old woman didn't reply, Dinah rose to her feet and beckoned for Yael. "What is she giving her?" she whispered. "Raisa is in no condition to swallow anything. She could choke. And what's that burning smell?" Someone had lit a brass burner of incense and the acrid odor slowly filled the room. "They need to get that smoke out of here, Yael." Another woman draped two more amulets around Raisa's neck after helping Leyla's grandmother feed her the potion. Dinah recalled Yael's mother, and how all of the Babylonian rituals had been worthless. Her anger seethed. "Can't we chase everyone out of the room?"

"We'd better let them do these things," Yael whispered. "If Raisa dies, they'll say it was our fault."

She was right. And Dinah knew what she needed to do. "I'll need your help, Yael. I know a procedure that may or may not work, but it's our best chance of saving Raisa and her baby." She waited for the old woman to move away, then knelt beside the bed again. "Your baby is facing the wrong way, Raisa, and we're going to try to turn it around. I know you're tired and

I'm sorry for causing you more discomfort, but if it works, your baby will be born soon. Will you let me try?"

"I don't want to die. . . ."

"And I don't want you to die. Yael and I are going to help you change positions, rolling you over and turning you. We'll take it step by step, and maybe the baby will turn as well."

Raisa screamed through each of the maneuvers as her contractions continued. Each time Dinah moved the girl, she checked the baby, feeling hopeful each time there was a small change. Dinah had never done this without Shoshanna's help, and she missed having a second pair of eyes and hands. "We're almost there, Raisa . . . almost there . . ." Suddenly Raisa gave a blood-curdling scream that made Yael leap backward in fright. "She's all right, Yael. Just a hard contraction." It took more than an hour of maneuvering, but at last Dinah saw the baby's head starting to crown. "Everything's good, Raisa. Now, push . . . push!"

"I can't . . . I'm so tired. . . ."

"You can do it, honey. You're almost there." Dinah lost track of time as she worked to help Raisa, coaxing her, encouraging her, pleading with her. She wanted this mother to live, her baby to live.

At last she saw the baby's head emerging. But something was wrong—the umbilical cord was wrapped around the child's neck, choking it. "Wait, Raisa . . . Stop pushing, honey . . . wait . . . wait . . ." Dinah gently eased the cord out of the way and after one final push, Raisa's daughter was born into Dinah's waiting hands. The infant was a sickly, grayish-blue color—and she wasn't breathing. Dinah cleaned the mucus from her mouth. Slapped the baby's back. Slapped her again, harder. This child was not going to die now!

"Come on, little one. Breathe . . . breathe!" The baby finally gave a weak cry, and Dinah could breathe again, too. She laid the baby down for a moment and waited for the umbilical cord to stop pulsing, then tied it off and severed it. It was time to turn her attention back to the mother. Raisa couldn't afford to lose too much blood. The newborn gave another weak cry, and as Dinah picked her up to give her to the other women to care for, she saw that the baby's left leg was twisted at an odd angle, her foot pointing inward. Before Dinah could react, Leyla's grandmother grabbed the child from her.

"I'll take care of her now."

Dinah turned to concentrate on Raisa again. She was still moaning and writhing in pain, her last reserves of strength nearly gone. "Just a little more, Raisa. Can you push one last time for me?"

"It she having twins?" Yael whispered.

Dinah managed a smile. "No, she has to deliver the afterbirth. Then you can rest, Raisa. I promise. Did you hear your baby crying? It's a little girl." Dinah watched to make sure Raisa's blood clotted, then waited until her color slowly returned and she stopped trembling. Raisa would live, God willing, but she was about to faint with exhaustion. She needed to sleep.

"Where's my baby?" she asked. "Can I hold her?"

"Of course. I'll bring her to you." Every mother deserved the reward of holding her new child after hours of hard labor. But when Dinah turned around, the old woman and the baby were gone. "Where is she?" she asked Yael. "Where did they go?" Yael shrugged.

Dinah felt a chill, remembering the deformed foot. She hurried from the room and found Leyla's grandmother in the courtyard. She no longer carried the child. "Where's the baby? Raisa is asking to see her."

"The child died."

"No. I don't believe you. She was breathing fine. Where is she? Let me see her."

"It's too late to do anything for her. Besides, the father has rejected her."

"What do you mean?"

"Zabad saw his child, saw that she was a girl and that she was crippled, and he refused her. Even if he hadn't refused her, the baby was too weak to survive."

A cold fury rushed through Dinah. She grabbed the old woman's shoulders, shaking her. "What did you do with that baby? Give her to me!"

"The child will never be worthy of a dowry because she will never walk. It's better to let her die now. Better that Raisa grieves now than for her entire life."

"Raisa's baby is alive! She wants to see her child!"

"No. If she does, she will face an impossible choice. Her husband will divorce her if she keeps her child. Then neither one of them will survive."

"You cannot let that child die! Where is she?"

"We're grateful that Raisa will live, but now you need to leave us alone. This is our way. Our village. You have no right to tell us what to do." The old woman struggled to free herself, but Dinah wouldn't let go.

"Never! Give her to me!" Dinah was still wrestling with the old woman when she heard a faint cry. She released her and ran toward the sound. Dinah found the baby outside in the cold, stuffed in a basket and covered with a wet, suffocating blanket. She lifted the tiny, naked girl out of the basket and pulled off her own head covering to wrap her in. She held the child close, warming her, soothing her. "Don't cry, little one . . . don't cry."

There were many things that Dinah didn't understand about God, but she knew from her years of experience as a midwife that each life was precious to Him. Shoshanna had told her so repeatedly. If a child was born with a defect, Shoshanna would insist that the Almighty One had a reason for it—that a wonderful blessing would come from loving that child. She had often said that we became better people when we defended the weakest ones among us, the ones God entrusted to our care. Dinah remembered seeing tears in Shoshanna's eyes each time they saved a child's or a mother's life, as Dinah had done tonight. *"When we save one life, it's as if we've saved the entire world."*

Dinah looked up through her tears and saw the old woman standing in the doorway. "I'm leaving now," she said. "And I'm taking this baby with me."

"She will only die."

"Not if I can help it."

Yael and Mattaniah met Dinah outside in the street. She refused to go back inside the house. No one spoke as they followed the road up through the valley, up to Jerusalem, the baby whimpering softly in Dinah's arms. The sun was just dawning and the light reflected off the buildings, gilding the stones and making the destroyed city shine like gold.

"Were they really going to let the baby die?" Yael asked when they finally reached the top of the hill. Dinah could only nod. "How are we going to feed her without Raisa?"

"Hanan's wife is still nursing her son. I'm sure she'll be happy to be the baby's wet nurse."

"I can't believe they would have let her die," Yael murmured.

"I know." And Dinah realized in that moment that Shoshanna's death wasn't Iddo's fault, nor had God taken her life. The Samaritans had killed her, just as they would have killed this child. There was a difference between her people and the Samaritans and Babylonians, between their gods and her God—the God of Abraham. Iddo had been trying to tell her this all along, even when they'd lived in Babylon. She looked down at the tiny baby and understood for the first time why they had to leave Babylon and return to the Promised Land.

"We'll name her *Hodaya*," Dinah said. *God be praised.*

Iddo looked relieved when they all returned home safely—and shocked when he saw Dinah carrying a baby. "They were going to let her die," she told him. "I couldn't let her die." Tikvah offered to feed Hodaya, as Dinah hoped she would. She laid the baby in Tikvah's arms, then looked around for Yael. She found her standing all alone on the eastern side of their courtyard, gazing out at the sunrise above the Mount of Olives. Dinah had rarely seen Yael so quiet and subdued, as if she had been the mother who'd labored all those long hours instead of Raisa. Was she tired from being awake all night? Shocked after witnessing a birth for the first time? Dinah moved up beside her and slid her arm around Yael's waist.

"Thank you for helping me tonight. I'm not sure I could have saved either one of them without your help." Yael nodded but didn't reply. "What's wrong, Yael? Why so quiet?"

"I don't understand it," she said. "According to the stars, Raisa and her baby were both supposed to die. I read them myself."

Dinah saw the damage she had done by asking Yael to consult the stars for her. She never should have encouraged her belief in astrology. "God is more powerful than the stars, Yael. He's the one who gets to decide such things."

"What about Shoshanna? Did God want her to die?"

"No. God didn't decide to kill her, the Samaritans did. Just like they decided to kill this baby. They don't see the preciousness of life the way we do, or the way our God does. Maybe it's because they believe that their fate is in the hands of capricious gods and indifferent stars, and so they've become indifferent, too." She paused, wondering how to say what she was thinking. "Yael . . . I'm not going to ask you to consult the stars for me ever again. I don't believe in their power. I hope . . . I hope you'll see the truth one day, too." Dinah waited, wondering if she would respond. When she finally did, her words surprised Dinah.

"May I help you deliver babies again the next time? It was so . . . amazing."

"I hope it didn't frighten you. Most deliveries aren't as difficult as Raisa's was."

"I was afraid she was going to die—and I like Raisa. But I liked helping you, too. I think I'd like to be a midwife someday."

Dinah gave Yael a squeeze before letting go. "I would be happy to train you. You were a great help to me tonight. And now, maybe you should sleep for a few hours. We've both been up all night."

"May I hold Hodaya for a few minutes, first?"

Dinah watched Yael take the baby from Tikvah, surprised by how gentle she was. Iddo came to stand beside Dinah, watching Yael, too. "Did they reject the child because of her foot?" he asked.

"Yes. Her father rejected her, and so the women left her to die."

"But she'll thrive in your hands, Dinah, and she'll grow to live up to her name."

Iddo would accept this child as his own, love her. Dinah had never doubted for a moment that he would. She took his arm and pulled him outside the courtyard where they could talk alone. "Iddo . . ." she began. She was afraid to look up at him, afraid to face him, but she knew she had to. Her throat swelled with emotion as she spoke. "Iddo, I know you saw Joel embracing me, but I want you to know that we never committed adultery . . . not in a physical way." He closed his eyes for a moment and she saw his relief, his pain. "But I was still wrong to be with him, to turn to him for comfort instead of to you. And Joel and I were both wrong to blame you for what happened to Shoshanna. Can you ever forgive me?"

"I already have."

"And . . . and can God ever forgive me?"

"That's why we have an altar and daily sacrifices, so we'll have a way to come to the Holy One and ask for forgiveness. That's why our word for sacrifice also means to come near—to have a close relationship with someone. It's a lesson I'm just beginning to learn." Again, she saw lines of pain creasing his eyes and knew how very much she had hurt him.

"Iddo, I'm so sorry. Will you show me what I need to do to make things right? And . . . and will you make the offering for me?"

"I'll be the priest on duty in two days."

When that morning came, Dinah stood in the women's courtyard and watched Iddo take his place in front of the altar, his hair and beard as white as the turban and robe he wore. A scarlet sash was tied around his waist, and like the other priests, he worked barefooted. The daily morning sacrifice was a lamb, and Dinah watched Iddo expertly slit the animal's throat, watched the life, the blood, drain out of it. So much blood. She realized how close the two were—life and death. And knew she had come close to throwing something priceless away, just as the Samaritans had with Raisa's child.

Two priests assisted Iddo as he quickly removed the lamb's skin and inner parts.

Afterward, he walked up the ramp to the top of the altar and laid the offering on the fire. A cry of joy went up from the assembled men as smoke and fire ascended toward heaven. Dinah closed her eyes and wept as she prayed for forgiveness.

Iddo returned home much later than she did, after he'd completed his duties and changed out of his priestly robes. He came to where Dinah was kneeling, tending the fire, and crouched beside her, staring at the ground. She saw tiny crimson flecks of blood on his forehead that he had missed when he'd washed after the sacrifice.

"Has God forgiven me?" she asked.

"Yes. We're both free to start all over again."

This was the Holy One's way, substituting a life for a life, with priests like Iddo acting as His servants. There had been no sacrifices for forgiveness in Babylon.

"And you, Iddo? Can you forgive me?" She needed to hear him say it again to believe it was really true. She saw tears spring to his eyes.

"Of course, Dinah. I love you."

"And I love you," she whispered. She wanted to say she was sorry over and over again, to hold him, kiss him, but she feared that she had forfeited the right.

Iddo cleared his throat. "I was talking to some of the other men today, and I found out that we can take the main road north to Samaria and Damascus, then make our way to Babylon by joining up with local caravans each leg of the way. It might mean staying in one town for a few days while we wait for a trader who has room for us. But the road from Damascus to Babylon is a major trade route, so we'll get there eventually." He looked up as if to see if she was listening before continuing. "I have the names of reliable merchants and traders who can be trusted. Our return journey may take longer than three months, but we'll get there. Before winter, certainly."

Dinah thought of little Hodaya's birth and of the many births she had witnessed over the years. When mothers like Raisa struggled in pain, especially during the last hours of labor when the exhaustion and agony were unbearable, many of them wanted to give up. She always urged them to persevere because the most difficult and painful times were in the last moments just before birth. What if their struggles here in Jerusalem were the same? What if their tiny nation was just moments from being reborn? She and her people couldn't turn back now. They couldn't go back to the gods of Babylon. Not when the sacrifices were finally being offered again. Not when men like Iddo had just begun to serve the Almighty One in worship. Not before the temple was rebuilt and God could dwell among them again. If she returned to Babylon, she would soon make her family into idols all over again. She would find her joy and purpose in them instead of in God.

"Iddo," she said softly. "Iddo, we're not going back to Babylon."

He looked at her in disbelief. "What?"

She touched his cheek, stroked his white beard. "I don't want to go back. I want to stay here and serve our God."

Chapter 27

Yael sat in the courtyard in a patch of morning sunlight, rocking Hodaya in her arms. This tiny baby who had entered the world so dramatically two weeks ago had shaken Yael's world. She felt a fierce protectiveness and love for Hodaya that she'd never experienced before. Safta Dinah and Iddo had taken Hodaya to the mikveh and adopted her as their own daughter, but Yael loved her as much as they did.

"There, now . . . go to sleep, little one," she soothed, shifting Hodaya from her arms to her shoulder, patting her warm, narrow back.

"You're very good with that baby," Zaki said. "You always get her to sleep when nobody else can." He was about to leave for guard duty but she gestured for him to sit down on the low wall beside her for a moment.

"I watched her come into the world. It was so amazing. . . ." The memory still brought tears to Yael's eyes.

"Safta said that the Samaritans were going to kill her?"

"It's true. I was there." She hugged Hodaya a little tighter. "They told Raisa that her baby was dead, and they put Hodaya outside in a basket to suffocate."

"Because she was born with a crooked foot?"

Yael nodded and kissed her dark hair. "I don't know how anyone could kill a defenseless baby."

"Pagan people do it all the time, Yael. They sacrifice their children in the fire to idols. When our people began doing it, too—and even our kings did it—the Holy One punished us and sent us into exile."

"I wouldn't have believed it if I hadn't been there," Yael said. "I would have thought Safta was making it up."

"I never wanted to believe those stories in the Torah, either. How could people do such terrible things? But the stories aren't made up. And these Samaritans are our neighbors."

Hodaya's eyes were closed. She was asleep. Yael should lay her down and help Safta with the work, but she loved holding her, loved feeling the baby's warmth and life. "Hodaya has the same father as my friend Leyla," she said. "Yet Leyla didn't fight for her sister's life. I keep hoping it was because she didn't know about it. She was asleep when Hodaya was born. But Leyla's grandmother knew. She was the one who tried to suffocate her. I don't think I can ever face her again."

"Is that why you don't go to visit Leyla anymore?"

"No . . . I don't know . . . I mean, Leyla isn't cruel and she could never kill anyone, but she just accepts the way her people do things—like her father marrying a girl as young as Raisa. Leyla doesn't know any better."

"But we do. We know better. I'm starting to see why our people could never partner with the Samaritans to build the temple."

Yael didn't care about the temple. She simply was trying to understand her friend's family, people she cared for. "Leyla has been sickly ever since she was a child, but they didn't throw her away. Why was this baby different?"

"Maybe because Hodaya's defect is visible?" Zaki replied with a shrug. "I don't know, but Saba is always saying that we're different from the Gentiles. That we have the Torah to teach us right from wrong. And the Torah says that life is precious, every life, because we're made in God's image. Does your moon goddess say that you're made in her image?"

"Don't start preaching to me, Zaki."

"I'm worried about you, Yael. You need to worship the Almighty One, not the stars."

Yael no longer had her star charts. She had left them at Leyla's house the night Hodaya was born. She had felt lost without them at first, and longed to use them to look into Hodaya's future. She knew the day and hour of her birth and wished she knew which heavenly bodies had influence over her. And yet she didn't want to know. Part of her wasn't sure she still believed in the stars.

Yael heard footsteps and looked up, surprised to see Abba hurrying through the gate. He had just left for his farm a short while ago and now he was back. "Did you forget something, Abba?" she asked.

He shook his head, wiping sweat from his brow. "Leyla's brother just came to see me. His sister is sick and he asked you to come."

Yael shot to her feet, waking the baby. "Don't go," Zaki said, grabbing her arm. "Please."

"I have to. Leyla is still my friend. I'd never forgive myself if something happened to her and I didn't go to see her." She carried the baby inside and gave her to Safta, explaining where she was going.

"You can't go back there, Yael!" Dinah said.

"I need to face them. And I need to see Leyla." She turned away before anyone else tried to stop her and told her father she was ready. He took another long swig of water, and they left.

A mixture of emotions swirled inside Yael as she hurried down to the valley. Anger at Zabad and his village, at their heartlessness. Dread at the thought of facing Leyla's grandmother. But mostly fear for her friend who was ill enough to ask her to come. The moon hovered above the mountain, reminding her of Zaki's haunting question: *"Does your moon goddess say that you're made in her image?"*

Abba walked with Yael as far as the village entrance, and Rafi brought her the rest of the way to the house. All of her misgivings vanished as she knelt beside Leyla's bed and her friend looked up at her and smiled. "I was afraid you weren't my friend anymore."

"Of course I am. We're best friends."

"Why did you stop coming?"

So. Leyla didn't know about the baby. She wasn't to blame for her family's cruelty. "It was hard to get away. . . ." Yael said vaguely. "There's trouble between our people and yours."

"The last time I saw you was the night that Raisa nearly died. It was so sad that her baby died, wasn't it?"

Yael couldn't reply. The memory of the child's warmth and softness, her sweet smell, was still fresh. She longed to tell Leyla that her baby sister was alive, but she didn't dare. Instead, she changed the subject, and they talked as they always had until Leyla grew tired and drifted to sleep. Yael touched Leyla's burning forehead, gazed at her pale, blue-white skin, and wished she could pour some of her own life and vitality into her friend.

She heard someone come into the room. Leyla's grandmother. Yael's anger sprang to life. She looked away, refusing to face her, hoping she would leave. "I can see that Leyla already is better now that you're here," the old woman said. She fussed around the bed for a few minutes, plumping pillows and tucking covers before asking, "Are you hungry, Yael? Would you like something to eat?"

She shook her head, determined not to speak to her. But her rage finally got the best of her and she said, "Aren't you even going to ask about Raisa's baby?"

"I already know about her," she replied, unruffled. "She died at birth. It was very unfortunate."

"She didn't die! She's alive and thriving. Her name is Hodaya."

"Raisa mourned for her daughter, of course," she continued in a soft, sad voice. "We all did. Now Raisa is asking the moon goddess for another child. Raisa is strong and well again, thanks to your friend. We will always be grateful to her—and to you for bringing her here."

"Hodaya is a beautiful, healthy baby," Yael said stubbornly, "with dark hair and the most amazing brown eyes—" Tears choked her words. She couldn't finish. Leyla's grandmother turned away, and Yael hoped she would leave. Instead, she opened a little chest at the foot of Leyla's bed and took something out. Yael's star charts.

"These are yours, Yael. You left them here the last time you came."

Yael crossed her arms, refusing to reach for them. "They're worthless," she said. "They predicted that Raisa and her baby would both die. You and I read their stars together that night."

The old woman smiled. "My dear child, sometimes the stars show only what might happen if we fail to intervene. I offered sacrifices that night on Raisa's behalf once you showed us which heavenly bodies needed to be influenced. That's why she lived. Why are you upset over an answer to prayer?"

Yael stared at her. Could that be true? She knew the gods could be influenced, but Yael had never seen it happen so dramatically. Mother and child had both lived. If the people back in Babylon had this much faith, maybe Mama would have lived, too.

"I would be very grateful if you would look at Leyla's stars with me now," the old woman continued. "As you can see, she is very ill. I believe I know which powers are holding her in bed, but I would like your opinion." She held the scrolls out to Yael.

"And there are others in the village who are waiting for you, too. We have missed our seer these past few weeks."

Yael couldn't let Leyla die any more than she could have let Hodaya die. Zaki was right; every life was precious. She took the scrolls from the old woman and carried them to the window where the light was better, then slowly unrolled them.

Chapter 28

From his post on the watchtower, Zechariah saw the soldiers marching up the road to Jerusalem. The dark forms of men on horseback had emerged from a cloud of dust, their swords glinting in the sunlight. They carried the colorful banners of the governor of Trans-Euphrates Province. He counted at least a dozen men.

Zechariah had stood watch on this crumbling tower for so long, seeing nothing unusual on the roads day after day, that now he could scarcely believe his eyes. But as a chorus of shofars began to blow, he knew that the other sentries saw them, too.

His first impulse was to climb down and join the men in challenging these invaders. If only he had a sword. If only he knew how to fight. But his community had been warned of their arrival, and now his job was to stay here and continue watching for more trouble, or for a threat from another direction. He worried about the soldiers all day as he sat at his lonely post, and when someone came to relieve him from watch duty, he begged for news about the armed strangers.

"I was told that the delegation came from the provincial capital, from the governor of Trans-Euphrates," his replacement said. "The foreigners were escorted to the governor's residence to meet with Prince Sheshbazzar. That's all I know."

Zechariah ran all the way across the temple mount and found his grandfather waiting for him to watch the evening sacrifice. "What are those Samaritans doing here, Saba? Do you know why they've come?" he asked, still panting.

"I have no idea. They met with the prince in a closed meeting. Let's hope they're coming to help us get justice for Shoshanna and to restore peace."

When the sacrifice ended, the younger prince, Zerubbabel, came forward to speak to the congregation. "Governor Sheshbazzar and I are calling for a convocation here on the temple mount in two days' time, immediately after the morning sacrifice. We're sending messengers to our brethren in all the surrounding villages, asking them to come, as well. I know you've all seen the emissaries and are wondering what's going on, but the Samaritan governor has requested that we wait until everyone has assembled before making the announcement, so that rumors won't spread and cause even more trouble." He paused, and Zechariah saw him glance at the soldiers standing outside the courtyard. "The request comes at Governor Rehum's insistence."

"What do you suppose it's about?" Zechariah asked again as they walked home.

"Believe me, I wish I knew," Saba said. "It must be serious if they're asking men to leave their land and their crops and come to Jerusalem at this time of year, so close to the grape harvest. Two days will be a long time to wait."

A huge crowd filled the temple courtyards two days later, as large as on one of the feast days. Men from all over Judah stood beneath the burning sun, waiting to hear the provincial governor's announcement. The Samaritan emissaries and soldiers watched from the Court of the Gentiles as if standing guard. Zechariah stood with his grandmother and the other women while Saba stood with the chief priests to listen. "Depending on what the announcement is," Saba had told Zechariah, "I may need to meet with the priests afterwards. I need you to make sure the women get home safely."

The crowd quieted as Judah's two princes climbed onto the platform where Saba usually stood to blow the trumpet. Prince Zerubbabel stepped forward to act as spokesman. The elderly Sheshbazzar looked too weary and defeated for the task, which could only mean that the news must be bad. Zechariah remembered the night in Babylon when Saba had talked about the power of words and wondered what power these words would unleash.

"Thank you for coming," Zerubbabel began. "Governor Rehum of Samaria has asked me to read a copy of the letter he sent to King Artaxerxes in Persia. I've been told that Artaxerxes is the son of King Cyrus and as of a few months ago he now reigns as co-regent with his father." He paused to look across the plaza at the leader of the Samaritan delegation, and Zechariah saw the controlled fury on Zerubbabel's face, heard it in his voice. "Rehum shrewdly chose not to address his letter to King Cyrus himself but to his young son—for reasons that will soon become obvious. This is what Rehum's letter said:

"'To King Artaxerxes, from your servants, the men of Trans-Euphrates:

The king should know that the Jews who have moved here from Babylon are rebuilding the rebellious and wicked city of Jerusalem. They are restoring the walls and repairing the foundations. Furthermore, the king should know that if this city is built and its walls are restored, no more taxes, tribute or duty will be paid and the royal revenue will suffer. Now, since we are under obligation to the palace and it is not proper for us to see the king dishonored, we are sending this message to inform the king, so that a search may be made in the archives of your predecessors. In these records you will find that Jerusalem is a rebellious city, troublesome to kings and a place of rebellion from ancient times. That is why this city was destroyed. We inform the king that if Jerusalem is rebuilt and its walls are restored, you will be left with nothing in Trans-Euphrates.'"

Zerubbabel lowered the letter and faced the assembled people, his anger poorly concealed. "You'll notice that Rehum said nothing in his letter about the Holy Temple, which was the true reason that King Cyrus commissioned us to return. If Rehum had mentioned the temple, then the original proclamation could have easily been found. Instead, the governor deliberately misled the new king. Now I'll read King Artaxerxes' reply, which Rehum has just received." He unrolled a second scroll and began to read, his tone edged with bitterness.

"'Greetings. The letter you sent us has been read and translated in my presence. I issued an order and a search was made, and it was found that Jerusalem has a long history of revolt against kings and has been a place of rebellion and sedition. The city has had powerful kings ruling over the whole of Trans-Euphrates in the past, and they demanded that taxes, tribute and duty be paid to them. Now issue an order to these men to stop work—'"

"No!" The outcry raced through the crowd at his words. Stop working? They had just begun! The prince waited for the cries to die away.

"' . . . Issue an order to these men to stop work so that Jerusalem will not be rebuilt until I so order. Be careful not to neglect this matter. Why let this threat grow, to the detriment of the royal interests?'"

The crowd's outrage overflowed as the prince rolled up the letter. He finally held up his hand so he could continue. "Governor

Rehum and Shimshai his secretary and their associates are now compelling us to stop working through threat of force—you've all seen their *enforcers* among us." Once again, he glared at the Samaritan leader and the soldiers standing guard beside him. "It grieves me to tell you that their order includes all work on the temple." The loud cry came from the priests this time. Zechariah craned his neck to catch a glimpse of his grandfather and saw that he had covered his face with his hands.

"And since we can no longer build our city," the prince continued, shouting to be heard above the murmuring, "it also means that new immigrants will not be allowed to come."

At this, the crowd stilled. Zechariah caught his breath. His parents wouldn't be allowed to come? He might never see them again? He looked at his grandmother and saw her standing with her eyes closed, her hands covering her mouth as if to hold back her grief.

"Rehum has assured us that once we stop building the temple and stop repairing the city walls and gates, our neighbors will make peace with us," the prince continued. "The threats and the violence will end. The local people will trade with us again."

It wasn't a fair exchange. Zechariah knew they could survive without Samaritan food, but not without God's presence. Their lives would have no meaning at all without Him. Once again Zerubbabel had to hold up his hands to quiet the people, who seemed to grow angrier every minute, like a hive of bees that had been disturbed. This time Prince Sheshbazzar stepped forward to speak.

"We all know that King Cyrus has commissioned us to build the temple. Rehum knows it, as well. Once the king's original proclamation is found among the Persian documents, it will confirm our right to be here and to build here. I'm sending emissaries of my own to Persia immediately. This matter will be settled in our favor. Unfortunately, it will take time to get the justice that we deserve, and in the meantime, I'm sorry to say that all construction on the temple must cease."

"No . . ." Zechariah murmured. He repeated it, louder, joining the chorus of protests. "No! No! We can't stop building!" He felt his grandmother's hand on his shoulder and looked at her tear-streaked face. "Why won't the Holy One help us?" he asked. "He could do miracles!" Safta could only shake her head in reply.

Once again, Zerubbabel gestured for silence. The high priest had joined the other two men on the platform, waiting to speak. "The daily sacrifices and annual feasts will continue," Jeshua said. "No one can prevent us from worshiping God as we wait for the original proclamation to be found. In the meantime, we have much to pray about."

There was nothing that anyone could do. The courtyards slowly emptied. Zechariah walked home with his grandmother and the other women, staying with them all day as Saba had asked him to instead of going to the watchtower. Why keep watch when the enemy was already in Jerusalem, defeating them?

The sun went down and the stars came out, but Saba still didn't return home. Zechariah pushed food around on his plate at dinnertime, unable to eat as bitter questions churned inside him. He waited for his grandfather outside the gate to their courtyard, watching for him, and when he finally trudged down the street toward home, alone, Saba resembled a plant that had withered in the summer's heat. Zechariah ran out to meet him.

"I don't understand why the Holy One allowed this to happen, Saba!"

"Our enemies are very shrewd, Zaki. But they won't be able to stand in God's way for long."

He blocked Saba's path, needing answers before his grandfather talked to the others. "Why doesn't He help us? The Holy

One drowned all the Egyptians and their chariots. He struck their firstborn dead and—"

"The Holy One has a purpose in this. Maybe this time of waiting will be good for us."

"How can it be good for us? We should fight back instead of giving in to our enemies."

"I've been arguing about this all day, Zaki," he said, and his voice did sound hoarse. "I told them that we should obey God, who commanded us to rebuild the temple, and not the men who told us to stop. But Prince Sheshbazzar has the final authority, and he fears that because the Persians have labeled Jerusalem a rebellious city, they will retaliate with force if we disobey. He has decided to send emissaries to Persia and go through the proper diplomatic channels and wait for a reply. He wants to protect our people."

"But . . . but the Almighty One could protect us!"

Saba laid his hand on Zechariah's shoulder. "You and I are among the very few who believe that, I'm afraid. No one listened to me today. The last time the priests took my advice, our enemies attacked us and killed Shoshanna. Now our leaders are afraid."

Zechariah turned to slouch away, but Saba stopped him before he could open the gate. "Listen, every man among us—including you and me—has to settle this matter in his heart: Did God command us to rebuild the temple or did King Cyrus? If it was King Cyrus, then construction may stop for good. But if it was God, then this setback by our enemies is only temporary."

Zechariah rubbed his eyes, fighting tears. "I heard the prince say that new immigrants won't be allowed to come."

Saba put his arm around his shoulder and pulled him close. "You're worried about your parents, aren't you?"

"Abba said that he and Mama would come later, and now they can't."

"Your father made the mistake of waiting when he should have acted. And he wasn't the only one. When we hear God's call, we need to respond to it immediately. Now all of those people who stayed behind in Babylon will have to obey the Persian authorities because they chose not to obey God."

This wasn't what Zechariah wanted to hear. He tried to escape his grandfather's grasp, but Saba wouldn't let go. "Are you doubting that the Almighty One spoke to you, Zechariah?" He didn't reply. "Listen, son. Do you remember how God tested Israel in the wilderness? How He wanted to see what was in the people's hearts—fear or faith? God already knows what's in our hearts, of course, but He tests us so we'll see it for ourselves. Our forefathers should have used their time in the wilderness to learn about God, to learn that He would lead them and provide for them and fight for them. But they didn't. As soon as the bad spies gave their report, the people were ready to turn back to Egypt. Only Joshua and Caleb had faith. Do you remember what they told the others?"

"Don't be afraid of the people of the land," he said woodenly. "God is with Israel."

"That's what you and I need to be saying to all of the others now, while we wait for justice."

"How long will we have to wait?" Zechariah asked. He had been calculating in his head all afternoon and not liking the results. It would take at least three months for Prince Sheshbazzar's emissaries to travel to Persia. Weeks or maybe months longer to go through the proper diplomatic channels and get an audience with the king. More time would be spent waiting while the king's officials searched the archives for King Cyrus' original proclamation. And even if the king issued a favorable ruling, it would take another three months for the emissaries to travel back to Jerusalem with the news.

"How long?" Saba repeated. "I suppose it depends on how long it takes us to learn the lessons of faith."

"It's not fair! We just started building the temple!"

"Life is seldom fair, Zechariah. But we can use this time to nurture our faith or to nurture doubt. That's what these times of testing are all about. How long did David have to wait before becoming our king while his enemy, Saul, chased him around the wilderness? Was that fair? During those long years of waiting, David nurtured his faith, and now the words of his psalms can strengthen ours. 'Wait for the Lord; be strong and take heart and wait for the Lord.'"

"Why can't I learn to fight while we're waiting? We could make weapons and—"

"This is the Almighty One's battle, not ours. Your job is to study the Torah."

"What? . . . No!" This wasn't what Zechariah wanted to hear.

"We've decided to reopen the yeshiva tomorrow since Governor Rehum assures us that there's no need for guards as long as we obey the king's edict." Again Zechariah tried to leave, but his grandfather stopped him. "If you really want to fight for God, then find out what He is saying to us. Study His Word and learn about God's faithfulness in the past so you'll have the faith to trust Him now. Help me speak His truth to those who have no faith. Help me convince them that the temple must be rebuilt no matter who tries to stop us. Can you do that, son?"

Zechariah nodded. He may have to wait, but he wouldn't have to like it.

Part III

Jerusalem

You showed favor to your land, O Lord;

you restored the fortunes of Jacob.

You forgave the iniquity of your people . . .

Restore us again, O God our Savior,

and put away your displeasure toward us.

Will you be angry with us forever?

Psalm 85:1, 4–5

Chapter 29

Ten years later

There was so much to learn. Zechariah stood on the temple mount with his class of future priests, watching an older priest named Jakin demonstrate how to prepare a ram for the burnt offering. Jakin gripped the animal in a firm hold, subduing it, and tilted the animal's head, exposing its neck. "It's very important to place the knife in the proper position. The animal must not suffer unnecessarily."

Zechariah now spent part of each day in the yeshiva studying the Torah and the history of his people and the writings of Israel's prophets, and the remainder of his time on the temple mount receiving hands-on instruction from the older priests.

"Put the tip of the knife here and draw it back . . . like this."

His mind wandered as Jakin showed how to collect the sacrificial blood in a bowl. Beyond the altar, the temple ruins and the abandoned construction site looked the same as on the night Zechariah had snuck up here with Yael ten years ago, searching for God's presence. She had gazed up at the stars that night, pointing to them, because there was no temple to look to for meaning in life.

"When the blood has been drained and set aside, we . . ."

Everything was still in place. The crane stood ready to lift the building blocks onto the temple's new foundation, although the ropes had begun to rot. So had the piles of rain-soaked timber. Weeds and scrub brush had slowly crept back over the site, knee-high around the new foundation they had laid.

"Zechariah? Are you paying attention?"

"Yes, sir . . . I'm sorry."

Zechariah had to learn how to slaughter the sacrifices, how to skin the animals and remove their entrails, how to prepare the meat and the fat for the offerings. He had to know the differences between daily offerings, burnt offerings, fellowship offerings, and guilt offerings. Then there were the intricacies of the annual feasts to learn and the special rituals required for each one. And because Zechariah descended from a family of priestly musicians, he also had to learn the proper trumpet calls for the New Moon festivals, the yearly feasts, and most important of all, for the annual Feast of Trumpets. After his ordination in a few years, the rhythm of his ministry at God's altar would determine the shape of his days and years for the remainder of his life.

He glanced over at the ruins again, wondering if he could find the place where he had sat with Yael and prayed. He had told her that the temple was like a map, a way to find God's presence. But there was no temple, no map, and he feared that his lifelong friend was walking deeper into darkness with each passing year. And she was just one of the many people in Judah who needed to find their way back to God.

"Zechariah . . ." Jakin was staring at him, and so were all the others. "Would you stay behind for a moment, please? The rest of you are dismissed."

Zechariah could feel the heat from the great altar several yards away as he waited for Jakin to speak. "What's wrong, son? You're one of our best students. You have a brilliant mind for Torah study. But lately you've been distracted. Are we losing you like the others?"

"No, sir. You're not losing me." Three of Zechariah's fellow Torah students had recently quit, and in the past few months he'd heard of two more Jewish families who had decided to return to Babylon.

"Can you tell me what's wrong, then?"

He was about to say that he didn't know. But when he pictured Yael sitting among the huge, abandoned building stones, he suddenly realized what was wrong. "I'm fed up with all of this!" He swung his arms in a wide circle to take in the entire temple mount. "The more I learn what the Torah says the more frustrated I get because no one seems to believe any of it. They're just words on a page."

Jakin's shoulders stiffened. "Of course we believe it."

"No, you don't. The prophets Jeremiah, Ezekiel, and even Daniel the Righteous One all told us that God wanted us to come back and rebuild the temple—but we stopped building. If we truly believed these men spoke God's word—if we believed in a God of power and miracles—there would be a temple standing over there instead of rubble."

"That's not fair. Our leaders have been trying to get the king's edict reversed, but there have been setbacks. The Persian courts—"

"I know all about how our enemies in the Persian courts have sabotaged our requests. I've heard all the announcements about political intrigues and palace insiders in the Persian government working against us—the schemes and plots and important messages that were intercepted and stolen. Meanwhile, our work on the temple has been abandoned for ten years. Ten years!"

"Stop shouting, Zechariah. This is a sacred place."

He drew a breath to calm himself, inhaling the aroma of roasting meat. When work on the temple had first halted, Zechariah had worried that he'd be forced to wait for a year—an outrageously long time. No one, including his grandfather, had ever imagined that ten years would pass.

"We've waited long enough," Zechariah said. "Do we believe the Torah or don't we? Moses said not to look at our enemies and tremble in fear but to remember what the Almighty One did to Pharoah and his armies. We're supposed to remember His miraculous signs and wonders and God's mighty hand."

"The exodus from Egypt was a special time when—"

"See? Even you don't believe it."

"That's not true! I resent that!"

"I've heard Jeshua and some of the other priests saying that a restored altar is enough for now—"

"And it is, Zechariah. It has been."

"You can't tell me that God asked us to leave Babylon and travel all this way just to build an altar. If so, He played a cruel joke on us. The Almighty One promised to dwell among us and be our God, but how can He dwell here without a temple? If we really heard from Him all those years ago, then we need to finish what we came here to do."

"We had no choice. The Persian authorities ordered us to stop building."

"What about the words that we pray every morning: 'Some trust in chariots and some in horses, but we trust in the name of the Lord our God.' We have it memorized, but we don't believe it."

Jakin took a step back. "This is so unlike you, Zechariah. You need to talk to the high priest. Your anger and your . . . your accusations are unbecoming to a candidate for the priesthood."

"You're right. I'll do that. Right now."

Zechariah strode across the courtyard and down the stairs, knowing he would find Jeshua in the house of assembly this time of day. He felt a growing sense of urgency with each step he took, as if they were all inside a burning building, yet no one would listen to him and stop the flames. He wanted to shout at everyone, even the high priest. At the same time, he was angry enough to simply walk away and let them all perish in the fire.

The house of assembly was empty, the students dismissed for the day, but he heard Jeshua's voice coming from the room that he used to meet privately with people. Zechariah stood aside, waiting for him to finish. He didn't mean to eavesdrop but their voices were raised, and he realized that the high priest was talking to his son, Eliezer.

"I want your blessing, Abba. Why won't you give it to me?"

"I can't give it to you if you marry a foreign woman. You and your brothers are the next generation of priests. You'll be the Holy One's intermediaries after my generation is gone. But only if you remain pure."

"What difference does it make whom I marry? All we're doing is performing empty rituals. It's not real worship. If God isn't interested in what we're doing or answering our endless prayers, why not marry whomever I want?"

"A child from a foreign wife can never worship with us. Your sons can never be priests."

"It doesn't matter, Abba! We're just pretending to be priests for a God who doesn't even care about us. I want to find a little happiness for once in my life. I'm tired of all your laws and rules—there's no use at all in following them."

Zechariah hurried away, embarrassed for hearing as much as he had. If Eliezer had drifted away from the Almighty One just like Yael and so many others had, it was too late to sound the alarm. Flames already engulfed the building.

Zechariah's anger had a chance to cool as he walked home, replaced by sadness. When he entered his courtyard, his grandmother and the other women bustled around, finishing the preparations for the evening meal. He hardly knew where to stand so he wouldn't be in their way. The simple rooms that he had helped build when they'd first arrived had doubled and then tripled in size. More rooms had been added for Besai and his wife, Rachel, and their growing family, for Tikvah and her children, and for Yael and Hodaya. As the years passed, they had plastered over the building stones, inside and out; added a sturdy roof with steps up to the top, like they'd had in Babylon. They had expanded the outdoor courtyard where they lived and worked to include a larger hearth, an oven, and two more cisterns to capture rainwater.

"Where's Yael?" he asked Hodaya. The girl was a constant shadow at Yael's side and looked lost without her.

"She's visiting her friend in the village. They're having a festival."

He stifled a groan, remembering the pagan festival he'd attended ten years ago. Yael would eat forbidden things, watch the men worship on the high places, and be drawn even further away from the Holy One. She was already lost to him.

"Zaki! There you are," Safta said, pulling him aside. "Your grandfather is upset. Please, go see if you can talk to him."

"Where is he?"

She gestured to the roof. "Up there. I'll join you in a minute."

Zechariah would have known something was wrong with Saba even if his grandmother hadn't told him. Saba stood near the parapet on the eastern side of the roof, looking out at the darkening sky above the Mount of Olives, the worry lines etched deeply into his face. "What's wrong, Saba?"

"The Almighty One is testing us—and we're failing the test."

Zechariah had heard this refrain for ten years now. "Is there some new test I'm not aware of?" he asked.

"I may as well tell you. You'll hear about it soon enough. The high priest's son, Eliezer, has decided to marry a local woman. He was one of my Torah students back in Babylon. I've tried to change his mind, but he won't listen to me."

"I know. I overheard Eliezer talking to his father. He wouldn't listen to Jeshua, either."

"I've begged him to consider what he's doing to the priesthood—and to our people. We're such a tiny remnant as it is, and we'll disappear entirely if we intermarry with Gentiles. We only have four priestly family lines left, and we'll need every eligible man to serve once the temple is finished."

If it ever is finished. Zechariah didn't have the heart to say the words out loud and discourage Saba even further. The sky clouded over again, adding to the darkness and gloom. "Did Eliezer say when he wants to get married?" Zechariah asked.

Before Saba could reply, Safta joined them, breathless from climbing the stairs. "I came to tell you that dinner is ready. . . . And who did you say is getting married?"

"The high priest's son, Eliezer. He—"

"That's wonderful! Do I know the bride, Iddo?"

"No. She isn't one of our women. She's a Samaritan."

"Oh. No wonder you're upset." She turned to Zechariah as if desperate for him to do something about it. When he didn't, she resorted to one of her own familiar refrains. "Speaking of marriage, don't you think it's time for Zaki to find a good wife? He's already older than we were when we married."

Zaki wrapped his arm around her shoulder. "I'm waiting to meet a wife who is as perfect as you, Safta. I haven't found one yet."

"Why do you resist all my efforts?" she asked. "There are so many lovely young women in our community."

"And yet the high priest's son went looking outside our community," Saba said gloomily.

Safta gave him a worried glance before turning back to Zechariah. "Don't you want to get married and have children, Zaki? A good priest should be married, you know. You'll be ordained in just a few more years."

Several of the women Safta had found for him had been attractive, but none as beautiful as Yael. They shared a lifelong friendship and countless memories—but he could never marry her. A priest of God could never marry a sorceress. He couldn't explain this to his grandmother, especially with Saba feeling so discouraged, so he decided to make light of the subject. "When you find me someone as beautiful as you are, Safta, then I'll marry her."

She frowned at him. "There are other qualities to consider besides beauty. 'Charm is deceptive, and beauty is fleeting—'"

"'—but a woman who fears the Lord is to be praised.' I know what the proverb says, Safta. But can you find me a woman who can cook as well as the women in our house? I'm used to good food, you know."

"Why can't you take me seriously, Zaki?"

"Why pick on me? What about Yael? She's well past the age that most girls marry."

"I know. Can't you help me with her, Zaki? Invite some of the young men you know to come home and meet her. Or invite this Eliezer, the high priest's son, to meet her. If he saw how beautiful she is, he wouldn't be looking at foreign women."

"It's too late," Saba said, shaking his head. "Eliezer is determined to marry the Samaritan."

Zechariah had raised the topic of Yael to deflect attention from himself, and now he was sorry. He searched for a way out. "We all love Yael, Safta, but we also know that she's too independent to settle down and be a good wife. You see how she flits from our house to Mattaniah's house in the valley and then to her friend Leyla's house. Can you picture her staying home and cooking for a husband and children all day? Hodaya is only ten years old, and she's already a better cook than Yael."

"I know," Safta said with a sigh. "I suppose it's my fault for not controlling her when she was young."

"How can you control the wind?" Zechariah asked. "When she finally decides to settle down, believe me, Safta, the men will line up to marry her." But he recognized the jealous longing in his heart whenever he thought about Yael with another man. And as he went downstairs to dinner, he worried that Yael sat inside that burning building at this very moment. And it was probably too late to save her.

CHAPTER 30

Yael knelt in her room combing her hair and plaiting it into a long braid. The spring rain clouds had blown away during the night and the sun shone brightly this morning, making Yael eager to get out of the stuffy house. Abba said to meet him below the steps to the temple mount right after the morning sacrifice.

She heard the familiar thump and scrape of a crutch on the cobblestones as Hodaya came to stand in the doorway. "Are you going to see your friend Leyla today?" she asked.

"Yes, I am. It's been much too long since I've visited her."

"May I go with you?"

Yael searched for a kind way to refuse as she stood and went to Hodaya. "It's too far to walk, little one," she said, smoothing Hodaya's dark curls away from her face. "You would be exhausted before we were even halfway there."

"We could borrow your father's donkey . . . I could ride."

"That old donkey is too stubborn and grumpy to ride. He might get it into his head to throw you off, and I don't ever want anything bad to happen to you." She gave Hodaya a hug and felt her slender arms wrap around her in return.

Hodaya had grown into a strong, happy ten-year-old who

walked with her crutch nearly as well as Yael walked on two good feet. Her laughter and bright smile made everyone in the community love her. But Yael could never take her adopted sister back to the village where she was born. Leyla's family would know who she was the moment they saw her, not only because of her crippled foot, but because of her strong resemblance to her half sister Leyla and half brother Rafi. They all had the same thick curly hair and large dark eyes. Hodaya might see the resemblance herself, and Yael didn't want her to learn the truth about her birth. She belonged to this family now.

"Hodaya?" Safta called. "Where are you? I need your help."

"Why doesn't Yael ever help?" she asked as she turned to limp away. "How come she gets to run all over?"

Yael didn't wait to hear Safta's explanation. She tousled Hodaya's hair as she hurried past her saying, "See you later, little one."

Abba talked on and on about his barley crop as they walked to the Samaritan village together, describing how the plentiful spring rains had made it flourish. Yael listened patiently, smiling to herself, knowing how much her father loved his land. It had prospered under his hands these past ten years, and the land easily fed their extended family with enough food left over to sell.

Yael's father sat down with Zabad and the elders at the entrance to the village when they arrived, but Yael couldn't look at Zabad, hating him for ordering his infant daughter to be put to death. She hurried into the village as he and Abba talked, but her progress was soon slowed by the abundance of greetings from all the women and children who gathered around her. Yael's stature as a respected seer was well established, and people from other local villages now sought her advice, as well.

When she finally reached Leyla's house a few minutes later, she found her friend propped up in bed, looking pale and weak. But her face lit up with happiness the moment she saw her.

"Yael! I have wonderful news! And now I have my best friend to share it with."

Yael smiled as she walked to Leyla's bedside. They'd been best friends for more than ten years. "Tell me your wonderful news."

"I'm betrothed! I'm going to be married!" Yael could only stare in disbelief as her friend chattered on. "Abba made all the arrangements and settled on my dowry, and now I'm officially betrothed to my new husband."

"Who is he? Have I ever met him?" Foolish questions. The women in Leyla's village never socialized with the men. The fact that her brother Rafi sometimes came into Leyla's room to visit with her was highly unusual. Yael searched for something to say to disguise her shock and surprise. "Is he young and handsome?"

Leyla laughed. "If you mean as young and handsome as Rafi—no. But that doesn't matter. My husband is nearly as rich as Abba, and our marriage will seal their business partnership. I was lucky that Basam accepted me since I'm past the age when most women in my village marry."

"I see." Yael tried to smile and be happy for her friend, but she wasn't. How could her father use beloved Leyla to seal a business deal, in spite of her poor health? Yet Leyla seemed to think this was fine. At least her father hadn't married her off years earlier when she was barely grown.

"Promise me you'll come to my wedding, Yael. I want you to be my attendant."

"Of course I'll come. I would be honored." She was about to sit down beside the bed when the door opened and Rafi strode into the room.

"Leyla, I—" He stopped short in surprise. "Well, hello, Yael. I didn't realize you were here. Did my sister tell you her good news?" His smile made Yael's heart beat a little faster. She still thought of him as Leyla's brother and as a friend, the same way she thought of Zechariah as her friend. But Leyla was right; he had grown into a very handsome man. He wore his dark, loosely curled hair longer than Jewish men did and his dark beard was a little longer, too, framing his magnificent smile.

"Yes, we were just talking about it," Yael said. "I'm so happy for her."

"What I don't understand," he said, stroking his beard, "is why a beautiful woman like you isn't betrothed yet? Doesn't your father know he could ask a king's ransom for your dowry? Or is that the problem? Are the Jews in your community too stingy to pay what you're worth?" There was something about the way he looked at her today that seemed different—or was she imagining it?

"Believe me, Safta Dinah has tried to marry me off several times. She promised my mother she would find me a good husband but I told Abba that I don't want to get married yet."

Rafi's brows lifted. "Really? The fathers in our village would never allow our daughters to boss us around and tell us what to do."

The insult stung. She lifted her chin. "Besides, I'm too busy to think about a husband."

"Is it your work as a seer that keeps you so busy?"

"That's part of the reason. I'm also learning to be a midwife."

He grinned. "Ah, now I see what has you frightened of marriage—watching babies being born."

"Not at all!" His teasing made her heart race. She couldn't tell if it was annoyance or something else. She planted her hands on her hips and decided to tease him back. "And by the way, why aren't you married, Rafi?"

"I haven't met anyone I want, yet."

"Oh, so you get to choose who you'll marry and Leyla doesn't?"

"Of course. She's a woman, and I'm a man. That's the way God created it to be. The Torah clearly says that the husband shall rule over his wife."

"The Torah?" She would have to ask Zaki about that when she got home. He studied the Torah all the time. But somehow it didn't seem fair to be ruled over. "Are the men in your village ever allowed to marry for love?" she asked.

"We marry for a variety of reasons. Love is sometimes one of them." The way he looked at her was disconcerting, his dark eyes fixed on her as if memorizing her face. She needed to change the subject.

"Have you met Leyla's husband? Is he a good man? Worthy of my dear friend?" She had seen Rafi's love for his sister over the years, and knew how tender and protective he was. She had often wondered if he would have protected his other sister, Hodaya, if he had known about her. She couldn't imagine either Rafi or Leyla letting their baby sister die.

"I don't know Leyla's husband very well," Rafi said, turning away. "He's from another village. I should go. I'm keeping you ladies from your wedding plans."

"No, you're not," Leyla said. "Can't you stay?"

"Not today."

Leyla looked up at Yael and gave a sigh after he was gone. "I've always wished that you and Rafi would get married. Then we really would be sisters."

Yael couldn't speak. Why did the idea make her feel so funny inside?

"I've been waiting for you to come so you could read my stars," Leyla rattled on. "I need to find the best day for my wedding."

"Yes, of course." Yael fetched her charts from the little trunk at the foot of Leyla's bed and spread them out to get a look at Leyla's future. Zaki had warned her of the consequences if she got caught with her scrolls in Jerusalem, and so she kept them at Leyla's house most of the time. What she read in Leyla's stars today surprised her.

"I see so much happiness! It's . . . it's almost overwhelming! The moon, the stars, all of the heavenly bodies—they all line up to give favor and blessing. You will have a prosperous new life, Leyla, and many, many sons." Leyla's grandmother joined them and they bent over the charts together, choosing a favorable date for the wedding two months from now.

"There! It's settled," Leyla said happily when they were alone again.

"I still can't believe that you, my dear friend, will soon be married. Tell me more about your husband."

"I barely know him," Leyla said with a laugh. "His name is Basam. He already has one wife but she has only given him daughters. When I give him a son, he will be Basam's heir, and I'll become his primary wife. In time, we may even grow to love each other."

Yael couldn't imagine being married to a man she didn't know or love. The Jewish couples she knew all loved each other—her father and mother had. Iddo loved Dinah, Besai loved Rachel. She didn't know what to say to her friend without revealing her doubt—or her fear. "So, you don't mind that your father chose Basam for you?"

"Not at all. Rafi is right, you know. Women should never choose for themselves. Our fathers and husbands know what's best for us. They're wiser about these matters, so it's good that they should decide. We're wise to obey them." Sweet Leyla was so compliant and easy to lead—and so different from Yael. "You know what's the best part of all?" Leyla asked. "I'll have babies! I've always wanted to have lots of babies."

"Oh, Leyla . . ."

"What's wrong?"

Yael couldn't reply. She knew from helping Safta Dinah deliver babies that labor and delivery exhausted healthy women, much less one as fragile as Leyla. She also knew how much blood women sometimes lost. Leyla should never get pregnant, never have babies. Yael searched for something to say. "I'm going to give you my moon goddess for a wedding present. She'll bring you good luck and keep you strong and safe in childbirth."

"Don't you want her? Aren't you ever going to get married and have children?"

"Of course I am . . . someday. Then you can give her back to me."

As soon as she got home that evening, Yael pulled Safta Dinah aside to talk about her friend. "Leyla is betrothed to a man she barely knows. She wants to have a baby, but I'm so scared for her, Safta. You know how sickly Leyla has always been. Do you think she'll be strong enough to deliver a baby?"

"I don't know. She may never be able to get pregnant at all if she's that ill."

"It still bothers me that she didn't have a choice in the matter. Her brother Rafi and the other men in her village get to choose who they'll marry."

Rafi. He had been on Yael's mind all day like a melody that kept repeating. She thought of his smile, his halo of dark curls, his beautiful eyes. And most of all, the intensity of his gaze as he'd looked at her.

"You should be thinking about it, too," Safta said, interrupting her thoughts.

"Hmm? Thinking about what?"

"Marriage! Isn't that what we're talking about? As the daughter of a Levite, you could have the honor of marrying a Levite or a priest. I promised your mother—"

"I know, I know," Yael laughed, drawing Safta close for a hug. That was the easiest way to change the subject with Safta Dinah. "I promise I'll start thinking about marriage soon."

Rafi was still on Yael's mind as she helped the other women prepare for the evening meal. She couldn't stop thinking about what he'd said, that the husband was supposed to rule over his wife. She decided to ask Zaki about it when he arrived home from the yeshiva. She approached him as he prepared to wash his hands.

"Do you have a minute?" she asked. "I have a question for you."

"Yes, of course. What is it?" Sweet, responsible Zechariah, always so serious compared to Rafi, who didn't seem to have a care in the world. Zaki was a little taller than Rafi, but not as muscular, with the trim build of a scholar. He wore his dark hair cut shorter, his beard neatly trimmed, and his kippah slightly askew on his head no matter how many times he straightened it. He would be a priest in a few more years, but to Yael he would always be the solemn boy she had grown up with, the friend she had known all her life.

"Does the Torah really say that a husband should rule over his wife?" she asked.

"Yes, it does. The Almighty One told Eve, 'Your desire will be for your husband, and he will rule over you.'"

"But why? That doesn't seem fair."

"Well, because Eve tempted her husband to sin."

"I thought the serpent tempted them."

"The serpent tempted Eve and then *she* tempted Adam. But the Almighty One also said that Eve was created from her husband's side to be his partner. They're supposed to work together in love, two people becoming one."

"How can they do that if they don't know each other or love each other?"

"Why all these questions?" Zaki gave a slow, easy grin, and Yael saw the boy she'd long known behind the serious scholar. But concern for Leyla kept her from returning his smile.

"My friend Leyla is betrothed to an older man, chosen by her father. She doesn't even know him, but she says she has to obey him from now on. That doesn't seem right, does it?"

Zechariah grew serious again. "No. It isn't right. That's another difference between us and the Samaritans—one of thousands of differences. You already know they don't value human life, and they don't value their women, either. They see their wives as property, not as helpmates. I wish you wouldn't spend so much time there, Yael. Can't you make friends with some of our own women?"

"I asked a simple question," she said, growing angry. "I don't need a lecture on who to make friends with."

"We were friends once, weren't we?" he asked softly. "What happened?"

"We still are." She said it lightly, but it wasn't entirely true. Yael knew Zaki didn't approve of her astrology. The more renowned she became as a seer—and the closer Zaki came to becoming a priest—the more she distanced herself from him. He had once told her that the penalty for sorcery if she was caught was death by stoning.

Yael studied the married couples that evening as they gathered around to eat together, and their affection for each other was obvious in their looks and gestures. She wanted that sweet closeness for her friend—and for herself someday. She wanted Leyla to be happy. And healthy. She kept glancing at Hodaya with her dark curls and beautiful eyes and thought of Leyla.

And Rafi.

Yael stood at Leyla's bedside, her worry and frustration leaving her too tense to sit. "Can't the wedding be postponed?" she asked Leyla's grandmother. Her friend had fainted a few minutes after Yael arrived to help with the final wedding preparations.

"I'm fine," Leyla insisted. "Just a little dizzy." But Yael made her lie down, just to be sure, and now her fever was rising. She moaned from the pain in every joint in her body.

"It's too late to postpone the wedding," her grandmother said. "Her father would be shamed. The food is being prepared, the guests are coming in three days. It can't be changed now."

"Never mind his shame—what about Leyla's health?"

"I want to get married," Leyla said. "The stars are all favorable, remember?" It was true. Yael had consulted her charts again, and the stars showed no indication of illness.

Leyla spent the next three days in bed, drinking her grandmother's potions of blood and goat's milk, but she still wasn't completely well on the day of her wedding. A veil hid her pale face and bruised-looking eyes, but nothing could disguise the fact that she was too weak to walk unaided. Yael sat beside her as they waited for the groom's procession to arrive, trying to calm Leyla's nerves with empty chatter.

"Will I still be able to visit you?" Yael asked. "I don't even know where your new husband lives."

"In another village, only a short walk over the mountain from here. I promise that as soon as my marriage week ends, I'll send servants to bring you there for a visit."

"Have you seen your new home?"

"Not yet. Not until after the wedding. My father said that Basam added a beautiful new room just for me."

At last Leyla's groom arrived with an escort of musicians and singers and dozens of relatives and guests. Leyla was too weak for the traditional procession through the village and had to be carried on a chair decked with flowers. They proceeded to the village square for the formalities, followed by the marriage feast.

Basam was a portly, unsmiling man, older than his bride by at least fifteen years. Sitting side by side, they seemed opposite in every respect: Basam dark, and sturdy as an oak tree; Leyla pale, and frail as a willow branch. Yael remembered how fragile Mama had looked during her last months of life, and she felt a terrible foreboding for her friend. She turned to Leyla's grandmother, seated beside her and whispered, "How could her father agree to this? She's too ill to be married."

"The stars and omens have all been favorable, Yael. Remember?" Yes. It was true.

The huge feast lasted late into the night with roasted lamb and wine, followed by singing and dancing by torchlight. Yael's father had also been invited, and he sat with the men while Yael sat with the women from Leyla's household, including her young stepmother, Raisa. All three of Raisa's little children resembled Hodaya. As time passed, Yael watched her dear friend shrivel and droop like a tender shoot beneath a desert sun, but she could do nothing to help her. When Leyla's new husband escorted her to their bridal chamber, Yael packed up her star charts and left her friend's house for the last time, walking home with her father.

❖ ❖

Yael waited a full month after the wedding, worrying about her friend, wondering how she was doing, but the promised servants never arrived with an invitation to visit. She waited a second month, then a third. By now the early fall rains had begun. Yael told herself that the bad weather was making travel difficult. But when the weather cleared and the almond trees blossomed and she still hadn't heard from Leyla, Yael decided to walk to her village one morning and ask about her friend. She saw Rafi sitting among the elders at the entrance to the village and greeted him as she would any longtime friend.

"Rafi! How—?"

"Hush!" one of the elders shouted. "Do not speak!"

Rafi quickly rose from his place, shaking his head at her as if she had committed a terrible sin. The other men glared at her in disapproval. Rafi looked very uncomfortable as he motioned for her to walk a short distance away from the others to talk.

"What's wrong?" she asked.

"Women don't address the elders at the gate. And why did you come here all alone? Where's your father? Don't you know it isn't safe or proper for a woman to travel unescorted?"

"That's silly. You can see my father's land right over there across the valley. He was too busy to come, and besides, it only takes a few minutes to walk here." She didn't understand why he was making such a fuss. "Listen, I've come to ask about Leyla. How is she? I miss her."

"My family hasn't heard from her since the wedding."

"What? That was months ago!"

"Leyla's husband hasn't invited any of us to his home or allowed her to visit us."

Yael swallowed a lump of fear. "Is she . . . do you know if she's well? Does your grandmother visit her?"

He paused before replying. "Our grandmother died two months ago. We sent word for Leyla to come, but Basam wouldn't allow it."

"That's horrible! Poor Leyla!" This was worse than Yael had feared. Leyla had not only been cut off from her and Rafi but from her beloved grandmother. "I thought Basam and your father were business partners. Surely he's heard something."

"The partnership has ended. It's a husband's right to make decisions that concern his wife," Rafi said. "There's nothing we can do." But Yael could see Rafi battling to control his emotions, his concern even greater than her own. Basam held Leyla prisoner. But why had all the stars predicted that they would have a wonderful marriage?

"When you do see Leyla, please tell her that I was asking about her. I would love to visit her. I miss her." She felt powerless—and furious—as she turned to start walking home.

"Yael, wait. Don't walk back alone. I'll come with you." Rafi hurried to catch up with her.

"Won't they think that's even more scandalous?" she asked bitterly, gesturing to the elders with a tilt of her head. She was angry with them for being men and for their stupid, controlling rules that separated her from her friend.

"It isn't a question of scandal. I mean it, Yael. Don't ever walk alone again. Ever! Your safety is the issue." He tried to take her arm as they continued down the road away from the village, but she shrugged him off.

"My safety? I thought our people were at peace. There hasn't been any trouble in ten years."

"Yes, we're at peace. But that's not the point. Not all of the young men in the local villages have the same moral traditions that you do. And the truth is, many of your young men don't, either."

"What do you mean? All the men I know in Jerusalem follow the Torah."

"You may think so, but they don't. No one talks about it, so it's a dirty little secret, but our villages have certain . . . celebrations. Especially now, in the springtime. And many of your saintly Jewish men like to join us for the festivities. In fact, that's how one of your priests fell in love with a village woman. There will be more of these affairs in the months to come, I'm certain."

"I know all about the high priest's son. Everyone gossiped about him and the Samaritan woman he married."

"The marriage was a mere formality. He had already taken her as his concubine."

Yael felt her face grow warm. "What does that have to do with me walking home alone?"

"I guess I'll have to be blunt. There's a widespread belief among my people that an unaccompanied woman must be looking for . . . a partner. The local men believe they have the right to claim her. And a beautiful woman like you . . . ?" He shook his head without finishing.

"I never heard of such a thing." Nor could she imagine Zechariah and his fellow Torah students doing something so outrageous.

"Well, it's true. The Torah says that once a man 'takes' a woman, he's obliged to marry her or pay the bride price for her stolen virtue. But if the men don't follow the Torah . . . well, she may spend the rest of her life as a prostitute." Yael's cheeks burned from such candid talk. She didn't know how to reply.

Rafi halted suddenly and drew her to a stop beside him, resting his warm hands on her shoulders. "Now that you know, Yael, promise me you won't take chances again." He smiled at her for the first time since she'd greeted him back in his village, and the warmth from his hands seemed to spread all through her. He was such a handsome man. She had to resist the urge to brush his dark curls off his forehead the way she brushed Hodaya's.

"All right. I promise." Abba's land was just ahead. Yael could see the door to his stone house standing open and hear his goats bleating in their pen. "Thanks for walking me home," she said, then turned and ran toward the house without looking back. She needed to get away from him. The way her heart raced when she looked at him frightened her. Yael remembered a morning long ago, when Safta's cousin Shoshanna had told her, *"Someday a young man will catch your eye and your heart will be drawn to him, and he'll be the only thing you can think about. . . ."*

And a week after Yael went to Rafi's village, she still thought about him. She thought of him while she worked and when she walked to the spring for water and when she lay in bed at night. She was thinking of him as she sat with Safta Dinah and Hodaya and the others after the evening meal one night—and when she looked up, there he was, magically appearing at their courtyard gate as if she had conjured him with a spell. He asked to speak with her father, not to her, but she overheard their conversation.

"I need your help, my lord. My sister Leyla is very ill. She's asking to see your daughter, Yael. May she please come? I wouldn't dream of bothering you if it wasn't urgent, my lord."

Rafi hadn't addressed Yael or even looked at her, but she leaped up from where she'd been sitting. "Let me go with him, Abba. Please! You know I've been worried about Leyla."

"Of course," Abba said. "I'll go, too."

It seemed to take forever for Abba to get ready. Yael tucked her star charts in her bag and begged him to hurry, wanting to run all the way to her friend's house. The situation must be serious if Rafi came all the way to Jerusalem looking for her. How had he even found her house? She waited until they were outside the city walls and walking down the ramp before blurting out, "What's wrong with her, Rafi? Is she sick? Please tell me! I'm so afraid for her!"

"She's gravely ill," he said quietly. "You've taken care of her during her illnesses before, and she's asking for you. She wants you to read her stars and tell her which god to petition."

"Read . . . what?" Abba said. "What are you talking about?"

"It's nothing, Abba. Leyla has always been a little superstitious."

The night had grown dark by the time they reached Basam's house. It had been a tiring climb up a winding road that took them over the top of the Mount of Olives. No one offered any introductions when they entered the house, nor did Yael see Leyla's husband. Her heart hammered with fear as she left Abba and Rafi and followed one of the women into Leyla's bedchamber. Tears sprang to her eyes the moment she saw her friend lying on a bed of blood-soaked cushions. Her skin was as white as linen. Yael ran to her side and knelt down. "I'm here, Leyla. It's me, Yael." She was alive but only half-conscious. She didn't respond. Yael looked at the bloody mattress, the piles of bloody cloths, and asked, "What's wrong with her? What happened? This isn't one of her usual weak spells."

"I'm a midwife," an elderly woman said. "She is expecting a child, but yesterday she began to bleed."

Yael's anger exploded. "Leyla is much too frail to have a baby! Something has been wrong with her blood all her life. She never should have gotten married! Never should have gotten pregnant!"

"Can you help her?" one of the other women asked. "She wants this baby." Yael saw the amount of blood and knew the truth.

"The baby is gone. Your midwife can see that as clearly as I can. Leyla already lost the baby, and now she's losing too much blood. We have to stop the bleeding."

"We tried. Her blood won't thicken and clot."

"Did you give her yarrow to drink? Pack her womb with clean cloths?"

"We did everything we could. She was asking for you to come and consult the stars."

Yael ordered more lamps and spread out her charts. She even went outside to study the night sky. She couldn't believe what she saw. The stars and the other heavenly bodies all lined up favorably. Leyla's illness didn't even appear among the omens.

"Can you tell us which gods we must appease?" one of the women asked when Yael came inside again.

"I-I don't know. Appeal to all of them!"

She sank down by Leyla's side and took her pale hand in both of hers. Leyla held the little moon goddess that Yael had given her in her limp hand. "I'm here, Leyla . . . I'm here," she said over and over. Her helplessness felt like a deep ache inside her. Leyla was dying, just like Mama had, even though there were no unbelieving neighbors this time. Yael could do nothing but watch her friend bleed to death. Hours later, Yael was still holding her hand when Leyla took her last breath.

Yael covered her face and wept for a long time. Leyla's death was so senseless. How could the stars be so wrong? Dazed with grief, she slowly became aware of the other women gathering around Leyla's body, making preparations to wash her and anoint her with spices for burial. One of them held a long, white shroud in her hands. "Wait," Yael said. "Let her brother Rafi come in to see her. He'll want to say good-bye. And where is her husband? And her father?"

"That's not the way we do things," the midwife said. She helped Yael to her feet. "She is unclean from the blood. The men won't want to become defiled. You should leave now. There's nothing more for you to do."

The little statue of the moon goddess had fallen from Leyla's hand. Yael left it lying on the floor. She took one last look at her friend and fled from the room, carrying her useless charts, longing to run and run and never look back. She found her father waiting outside in the courtyard, watching the sky turn light. Rafi was gone. She linked her arm through Abba's, pulling him toward the gate. "We can go now. It's over."

The farther they walked, the more Yael's grief and anger soared. Anger at Leyla's father for forcing her to marry. Anger at Basam for not caring enough to stay by her side during her final hours. Anger at the stars for not speaking the truth to her. "I don't want to go home to Jerusalem yet," she said as they neared the city. "Can I stay at your farmhouse for a few days? I need some time alone to grieve."

"Why grieve alone? Why not let Dinah and Hodaya and the others comfort you?"

"I can't, Abba. . . . Hodaya looks too much like Leyla, and I just can't . . ."

He squeezed her arm. "I understand. We'll go to the farm. I'm on duty at the altar during the day, but I'll come back to stay with you at night."

Yael slept and cried for most of the morning after Abba left, then ate a little bread and wept some more. She couldn't understand why the moon goddess hadn't revealed the truth to her in the stars. Why had all the signs led her to believe that Leyla would be happy, that she would live? All these years Yael had been angry with Zaki's God for Mama's death, and now her own deity had let her down.

She was lying on her mat, staring up at the rough, wooden ceiling, when she heard a man's voice from outside calling, "Anyone home?"

She sat up, her heart racing. She decided to peek out to see who it was, then remain hidden if it was a stranger. She crept to the window, staying in the shadows.

Rafi.

"Is anyone here?" he called again. Yael wiped her face and smoothed her hair, then walked to the doorway, shading her eyes in the bright sunlight, fighting the urge to run into his arms for comfort. He looked relieved to see her. "Yael. I was hoping you were here."

She nodded, wiping fresh tears as they rolled down her face. She walked outside to stand near him and saw that his eyes were red-rimmed with grief. He suddenly pulled her into his arms, and she clung to him in return. Embracing him felt as natural as embracing Leyla.

"I needed to hold someone," Rafi said, his voice breaking. "I knew you would understand." Yael felt his body shake with silent sobs as she held him tightly, felt his tears in her hair as she wept against his chest. She didn't know how long they remained that way, but finally he released her. "Thank you," he whispered.

Yael took his hand and sat down with him on the low stone wall surrounding the courtyard. She stared down at her feet, too angry to look up and see Leyla's village across the valley, too frightened of her own emotions to look at Rafi. "I miss my sister," he said hoarsely. "She was my friend ever since we were small—and she was yours, too. Thank you for being so good to her. Leyla loved you. She wanted you to be with her in the end because she knew that I couldn't be."

"I wish I knew if she'd been happy these past few months."

"Basam will pay."

"Rafi, all the money in the world won't bring her back."

"A life for a life. He let my sister die. It's my duty to avenge her death."

Yael froze, chilled by his words and by the ice in his voice. He wouldn't really kill Basam, would he? This was anger and grief talking. "I miss her so much," Yael murmured.

"I know. Me too." He squeezed her hand a little tighter before letting go. Then he stood. "I'm glad I found you here. If it's okay, I'd like to come back tomorrow. The men in my village . . . we aren't supposed to show our grief."

"I'll be here for a few more days," she said.

"Thank you."

Yael remained sitting as she watched him walk away, following his progress across the valley.

He returned the next day and the next. When she shared her confusion about what the stars had said, she learned that Rafi didn't believe in anything. "We make our own destiny," he told her, "through our own power and strength. I don't believe in gods or stars or religion."

Yael didn't care what he believed. They talked and laughed and wept for Leyla, and by the end of the week, when he kissed her for the first time, she already knew that she was in love with him. She had thought her first kiss would be on her wedding night, but after Rafi kissed her that first, tender time, she knew she wanted his lips on hers, his strong arms around her, for the rest of her life. Rafi loved her. And she loved him. In spite of her overwhelming grief, Yael was happier than she'd ever been in her life. All around her the world turned green, the wildflowers sprouted, the sun warmed the land, and she felt like she was awakening, as well. Dizzy and breathless with excitement, she could barely wait for Abba to leave every morning and for Rafi to come. She knew that Leyla smiled down on them, laughing along with them at their unabashed joy.

"Do you want to know when I first fell in love with you?" Rafi asked. They sat beneath her father's fig tree on a rug she'd spread on the ground against the chill of the damp earth.

"When?"

"That day when you were at the tombs and I was with that gang of boys. You ordered them to get out of your way, and you didn't look one bit afraid. You stood with one hand on your hip and your jaw jutting out like this, and you said, 'Let us through!' You were formidable—and beautiful."

Yael laughed at his pantomime. "I didn't look like that!"

"Yes, you did."

"I may have acted brave, but I was terrified. They were hurting my friend. I never thanked you for helping us."

"I had never seen a girl stand up to a gang of boys like that. I remember thinking that no man could ever capture such a spirited woman's love, much less possess her for his own. It would be like trying to capture a flame."

"I'm yours now," she said, moving closer to him. "I love you, Rafi."

"And I'm the richest man in the world. I want you for my wife."

"Then let's tell our families. My father will be home before sunset. Let's tell him together. "

"That's not the way it's done in my village. I will tell my father that I've found a wife, and if he agrees, he'll go to your father and ask for a marriage contract. Do you think your father will accept?"

"Of course! I'll tell him he has to accept. I want to marry you."

Rafi left before Abba returned, but he promised to speak with his own father as soon as he could. Yael couldn't bear to wait through such a long, tedious process. She prepared a nice meal for Abba, and as soon as he sat down to eat it, she told him about Rafi. "I have wonderful news, Abba . . . I'm in love!" Her words bubbled out in a rush of excitement. "When Rafi's father asks you for my hand, please, please say yes!"

"Wait—you're in love? . . . With *Rafi*?"

"Yes, Leyla's brother Rafi. He wants to marry me! You know his father, Zabad."

"Yes. I know him." Abba had stopped eating. He set down his bowl and bread with a worried look. "When did all this happen?"

"I've known Rafi for years, Abba, and he's a good man. We've been friends, just like Zaki and I are friends."

"I don't think it's a very good idea to marry a Samaritan."

"Why not? I love him!"

"I need to talk this over with Dinah and Iddo."

His words outraged her. "You don't need their permission. You're my father!"

"I'm sorry, but I won't give you an answer until I've talked this over with them. You're their daughter as much as you are mine."

Yael knew what their reaction would be. Iddo and Dinah hated Samaritans. She waited until Abba fell asleep and got out her charts to study the stars, desperate to read what the future held for her and Rafi. She could make offerings to influence the heavens in her favor, if she had to. When the stars all told her that she and Rafi would be together, that they would be happy, she read them a second time and then a third, just to be sure. The stars had been wrong about Leyla's future. . . . Yael lay awake for a long time, doubting what she'd just read, questioning her ability as a seer—a seer who could no longer see.

She and Abba walked up to the city the next morning, and Yael was forced to wait with the other women all day until Abba and Iddo returned home. "Why are you so fidgety?" Safta Dinah asked. "What's the matter with you?" Yael didn't want to tell her until that evening when the four of them sat down together after the meal. Yael would find a way to be with Rafi no matter what anyone said. She had seen it in the stars.

"Yael thinks she's in love," Abba began.

"I *am* in love!" she interrupted. "With Leyla's brother Rafi. And he loves me. His father is going to ask Abba if he can marry me."

"And I told Yael that we needed to talk it over with both of you first," Abba said.

"You can't let her do this," Safta said, the first to object. "I promised Miriam I would find her a suitable husband, a Jewish husband—"

"Rafi is Jewish!" Yael tried to stay calm, but she wanted to stamp her foot in frustration.

"Our heritage comes through our mother's line," Iddo said, "not our father's. If Rafi's mother is a Gentile, then so is he. God gave our people a second chance after they strayed into idolatry, and now His enemies are trying to tempt us away from Him again."

"How could you possibly live with people who kill their own children?" Safta asked.

"Rafi isn't like that." But Yael couldn't forget his cold, stony face when he'd talked of making Basam pay for his sister's death.

"How do you know he isn't like them?" Safta asked. "Once you're married to him, he might turn out to be just like his father and all of the other men in his village. It's all he knows, Yael."

"Rafi is the oldest son, isn't he?" Iddo asked. "The heir? Someday, as village elder, Rafi will marry other wives for political alliances and prestige and as a display of his wealth. Why would you endure such humiliation?"

"He wouldn't do that. He loves me." But again Yael felt uneasy when she remembered how the women remained separate from the men in Rafi's household.

"What if he forbids you to come home and see your family," Safta continued, "like Leyla's husband did? Hodaya would be heartbroken. We all would be. Remember how you felt when Leyla's husband cut you off from her? And you know Hodaya would never be allowed to visit you."

"Rafi will let me come home. Our families are at peace." Yet Yael knew that Safta was right about one thing: Hodaya could never visit his village. And she would wonder why.

"What about your work as a midwife? You would need his permission to continue, you know."

"I'm sure he won't mind. The women in his village need midwives, too."

"But they don't share our values, Yael. You know that. You only have to look at Hodaya to remember what they're like. Do you really want to live with such people?"

Yael didn't want to think about all these things. She and Rafi loved each other. That was all that mattered. "We'll figure out a way to make it work."

"Yael, I'm saying this because I love you," Safta said. "You've always been stubborn and independent, but for once in your life, please listen to our advice. After the first rush of love fades, you'll be trapped in a village that's completely different from ours, living among people who aren't your family, people who think and believe differently than we do. And you'll have to obey your husband without fail for the rest of your life."

"But—"

"Dinah is right," Abba said. "I know how the men in that village think. You've always gone your own way, but not this time. I can't let you marry Rafi. It would be a mistake. I've known Zabad for more than ten years. I know how he lives and . . . and I can't let you live that way."

"Abba, no! Don't listen to Safta!" Yael's tears began to fall as she scrambled to her feet. "You can't refuse us, you can't! What will you tell Zabad when he asks for my hand? That his son isn't good enough for me? That our marriage would be a mistake? You'll start another war! Remember what happened when you said the Samaritans weren't good enough to worship with us?"

"My mind is made up, Yael. I won't listen to any more arguments."

She ran to her room where she could cry in private, hoping that Safta or Abba wouldn't follow her. But a few minutes later, Hodaya came in to comfort her.

"Why were they talking about me, Yael?"

"They weren't, little one, they were talking about me. They're trying to stop me from marrying the man I love, but I won't let them. Nothing can stop Rafi and me from being together."

"But they *were* talking about me. I heard them say, 'Look at Hodaya and remember.' Remember what?"

"Don't worry about it," Yael said as she pulled her close. But Hodaya wiggled out of her embrace.

"It has to do with my real parents, doesn't it? Why won't anyone ever talk to me about them?"

"This isn't the time. Everyone is upset about Rafi and me. Wait until all this blows over."

"When you move away with Rafi, can I go with you?"

Yael closed her eyes. It was impossible. Yet how could she walk away from Hodaya, whom she loved like a sister? She would miss her every time she looked at her husband and saw the resemblance. But it would destroy Hodaya if she ever learned the truth. Her father had rejected her. He had ordered her to be smothered to death beneath a soaked blanket. *Rafi's father.*

"There has to be an answer to all this," she said with a sigh. "I'll figure something out, I promise."

Late that night when everyone was asleep, Yael took her star charts and a lamp outside to the courtyard to see, once again, what the heavens had to say. But before she had a chance to study them, she heard the familiar thump and scrape of Hodaya's crutch on the cobblestones and quickly rolled them up. "Why are you up so late, Hodaya? Go back to bed."

"I can't sleep. I'm worried that you're going to leave me."

"I won't leave you." But Yael knew that she wouldn't be making that decision, Rafi would. Hodaya limped closer.

"What are you doing? What are those scrolls?"

"Nothing," she said. "Let's go back to bed."

For now, her future with Rafi would have to remain unknown.

Chapter 32

In living quarters as close as theirs, Zechariah could easily hear everything that was going on. Yael was in love with a Samaritan and determined to marry him. He heard all of his family's well-intentioned pleas and arguments, and he knew that his free-spirited friend would do whatever she wanted to in the end. Zechariah had tried for years to lure her away from the Samaritans and their astrology, but he had failed. Once she married Rafi and moved to his village, no one would ever see her again. He would never win her back to God. She would die with the pagans.

The morning after Yael arrived home with the news, a familiar dream jolted Zechariah awake just before dawn. But it had a different ending this time. The storage basket with Yael hidden inside was tightly bound with ropes so she couldn't escape. In the dream Zechariah cut through the ropes with one of the sacrificial knives he was learning to use and set her free.

He lay awake in the dark, staring at the ceiling, wondering what it meant. As the sky grew lighter, he heard his grandparents talking outside in the courtyard. "Iddo, we have to do something! You know what those Samaritans are like. It makes me sick to think of Yael living with them. They'll destroy her. She's like my own daughter, and I can't bear to lose her. We can't let her marry him."

"Don't worry, Dinah. Mattaniah assured me that he's going to refuse Zabad's offer."

"She'll run away with him—I know she will. We haven't convinced her that she's making a mistake."

"Mattaniah asked us to watch her and make sure she stays here. We can't let her go to the farm."

"She ran away from here once before, remember? She went all the way to the village to see Leyla. She's fearless."

"I know. But Mattaniah needs time to figure out an honorable way to decline Zabad's proposal. Yael was right when she said that a flat refusal will start another war. We can't risk insulting him and causing more trouble."

Zechariah climbed out of bed and hurried outside as the solution to the dilemma suddenly came to him. The dream had shown him the answer, and it seemed so obvious, so inevitable, that he wondered why he hadn't thought of it sooner. "Saba, I know of an honorable way for Mattaniah to decline Zabad's proposal. He can say that Rafi's proposal has come too late. That he already chose a husband for Yael and settled on a dowry. He can show him a signed marriage contract. Then if Rafi runs away with Yael, he would bring shame to his family. He would be stealing another man's wife."

"I cannot advise Mattaniah to lie,"

"He won't have to lie. Mattaniah can sign a contract with me. I'll marry Yael."

"No, Zaki," Saba said. "You should marry a wife who loves you—and who loves God."

"Yael is a Levite's daughter and—"

"Do you have proof that she's a suitable wife for a priest? Is she devoted to the Almighty One?"

Zechariah turned away, hoping Saba wouldn't read the truth

in his expression. Should he tell them about the dream he'd just had? Would they believe him?

"Yael's family dabbled in astrology and sorcery in Babylon," Saba continued, "and she's been mingling with the Samaritans all these years."

"I know. But the same is true of our entire nation, Saba. Our ancestors all drifted from the Holy One, didn't they? Yet He forgave us and offered us a second chance. Isn't Yael still a daughter of Israel? Doesn't she deserve a second chance?"

"But what kind of a marriage will you have," Safta asked, "if she loves someone else and not you?"

Zaki couldn't think about that right now. This was the answer, he was certain of it. "You both have to admit that this is the best solution to the problem. Everyone knows that Yael and I have been friends since childhood. We might have been promised to each other years ago."

"Let's not rush into this," Saba said, holding up his hands. "There must be a better solution. Once our emotions have calmed down, maybe we'll see it."

Zechariah drew a deep breath, his mind made up. "I'm my own man, Saba. The decision is mine to make. I'm going to offer Mattaniah my proposal so he can turn down Zabad's. If Yael and Rafi run off together, there's nothing we can do about it, but at least we tried."

"If they decide to run off, Yael would become his concubine, not his wife," Saba said. "I tried to explain that to her last night, but I don't think she was listening."

"I promised her mother—"

"I know, Safta." Zechariah rested his hand on his grandmother's shoulder. He was taller than her now by more than a head. "And I'm going to help you keep that promise."

"Wait," Saba said. "You need to pray about this some more and ask the Almighty One what to do."

"I already know what His answer will be," he said, remembering his dream. "The Torah forbids mixed marriages with Gentiles because we'll end up adopting their ways, worshiping their gods. Wasn't that why we were exiled? But He allowed us to return to the land to rebuild our nation. To marry and to have children—"

"Zechariah, listen to me—"

"I'm sorry, Saba, but it makes sense that I marry her. I love Yael, and I want to save her from making a huge mistake. I'm going to do this."

Zechariah returned to his room before his grandparents could argue further. He could see how upset Saba was, but Zechariah was surprised to discover that his confession was true. He did love Yael. He always had. He would do what he'd tried to do all his life and save her, even though it would cost him the priesthood. That's what the sacrificial knife had meant in his dream. He could never be a priest, never stand before the Almighty One and serve Him knowing that his own wife worshiped idols.

Chapter 33

Yael grabbed the front of her father's robe as she pleaded with him. "Abba, no! Please don't make me marry Zaki! I don't love him, I love Rafi!"

"It's done, Yael. I told Zabad I was sorry, but you were already spoken for, that you've known Zechariah your entire life. I showed him the betrothal agreement. He understands that it's a father's right to decide for his daughter."

"Was Rafi there? He would have fought for me, I know he would have."

"No, Rafi wasn't there. He had nothing to do with this proposal. In his village, the fathers arrange these matters."

The walls of the tiny room seemed to close in on Yael. Abba stood in front of the door, leaving no escape. How could this be happening? "Please don't do this to me, Abba! Please!"

"I'm sorry, Yael, but I honestly believe that this is what's best for you. Zechariah is a good man, and he'll treat you well. I can't say the same for Zabad's son. The Samaritans aren't like us, especially the way they treat women. How can I allow my only daughter to marry a man who sees nothing wrong with polygamy or with marrying a twelve-year-old child?"

"Rafi would never do that. He loves me."

"I know the men in his village, Yael. It's a sign of prestige to have more than one wife—and several concubines, too."

She clutched the front of Abba's robe tighter, trying to shake sense into him, but he was unmovable. "Abba, please don't do this!"

"It's done."

She remained in her room the rest of the day, refusing to speak to anyone, even Hodaya. She would figure out a way to be with Rafi. She would! Everyone watched her closely, making sure she didn't run away. Abba slept right outside her door that night, blocking her path. But just before dawn, when everyone slept, she managed to pry off the wooden shutters and squeeze through the tiny window in her room. She knew the way to her father's farm, even in the dark, and she waited there until it was light enough to walk to Rafi's village. Yael had promised him that she wouldn't walk across the valley all alone, but she had to. From now on they would be together.

Rafi wasn't sitting outside with the village elders as she had hoped. Yael lifted her chin, intending to walk past them without speaking but one of the young men who attended the elders stopped her. "What is your business in our village?" he asked. The way he and the others looked at her made her shiver, as if undressing her with their eyes. Jewish men would never gaze at a woman so directly, so disrespectfully.

"You know me," she told them. "I've been coming here with my father for years to visit with Leyla."

"Leyla no longer lives here."

"I know. But her family does." She turned and strode past them into the village, hoping they wouldn't stop her. Rafi said that her fearlessness had surprised him, and it must have surprised the elders, too, because they let her go. She hurried toward Rafi's house, her progress slowed by all the village women who rushed forward to greet her, touching her and begging her to stop and give them advice from the stars. "I-I'm sorry but I didn't bring my charts with me . . . maybe another time . . ." They followed her all the way to Rafi's house as if worshiping her.

Zabad's wives were working outside in the courtyard, their children playing in the dirt when Yael entered the family compound. They all looked up at her, then quickly looked away again as if afraid. She strode over to Raisa, who stood at the loom, working the shuttle through the threads, and said, "Good morning, Raisa. Is Rafi here?" When she didn't reply, Yael took the shuttle from her, halting her weaving. "Raisa, I helped save your life when your first baby was born, remember? Please. Send a message to Rafi that I'm here. That I need to speak with him." The women had all stopped working and even the children were still. Everyone seemed to hold their breath as they waited, watching her. Finally, Raisa summoned one of her sons.

"Go ask your brother Rafi to come here."

His brother. Yael felt the shock all over again at the reminder that this woman, ten years younger than Rafi, was his stepmother.

At last Rafi strode out into the courtyard. Yael had to resist the urge to run into his arms. She saw love in his eyes when he first saw her, then a look of pain. Then anger replaced all of his other emotions. "What are you doing here, Yael? You shouldn't have come!" Before she could reply, he glanced around at all the women and children who watched and listened, and made a sweeping gesture with his arm. "Leave us!" The courtyard emptied.

"Rafi, I love you. I came so we could run away together. Remember what you told me about claiming a wife? That if I was all alone it meant that—"

"No!" The anger in his eyes intensified. "No, Yael. That would bring shame on my family. My father is the village leader. Men of our standing pay a dowry for a suitable bride. They don't marry a sotah who throws herself at a man. And they don't steal a woman who is already betrothed."

"My betrothal is a sham."

"It doesn't matter. If I took you, you would become my concubine, not my wife. I need to marry a wife first. My heir can never come from a concubine."

"Do you love me, Rafi?"

For a moment his eyes glistened with unshed tears. "With all my soul," he said quietly. Then his face turned hard again. "Go home, Yael. Marry your Jewish friend."

"But you and I are free people. If you love me and I love you, we can defy our fathers. No one can stop us from being together."

"I would never defy my father. It would cost me my inheritance."

"Not even to marry me?"

He hesitated for a very long moment. "No. Not even for you."

Yael turned and fled—out of the compound, through the village streets toward home. Rafi didn't follow her. She felt real terror as she ran past the elders and the knot of young men surrounding them, remembering how they had looked at her, remembering Rafi's warning. Yael could barely breathe, barely see through her tears as she raced across the narrow valley, her legs pumping as fast as she could go. When she finally dared to look over her shoulder, she was horrified to see that three of the young men from the village were following her.

"Oh, God, no . . . please!"

Their steps were unhurried. They would easily catch her once she tired. She couldn't possibly make it all the way up the hill to Jerusalem, to safety. Even if she made it to her father's farm, Abba wasn't there to protect her. No one was. She heard the men's laughter behind her as they came closer.

"Oh, God, please help me!" She had no idea who she was pleading with.

She was nearly to her father's house when she saw a man burst out of Abba's front door, running toward her. "No!" she screamed. One of them must have left the village ahead of her, and now she was trapped. She veered away from the man, no longer knowing which way to run.

"Yael!" She heard the man calling to her. "Yael, wait!" She looked over her shoulder and saw through her tears that it was Zechariah. "Yael, run this way! Run to me!"

She did what he said, whirling around and staggering toward him as he closed the gap between them, falling into his arms. "You're safe now," he soothed. "I won't let them hurt you." But there were three Samaritans, and Zaki was outnumbered. She clung tightly to him, trembling with fear, as the men came within a dozen yards of them and halted.

"Yael is my wife," Zaki told them. "We're betrothed. Even you aren't low enough to rape a man's wife right in front of him, are you?" He turned Yael around, turned his own back on the men, and slowly walked with her the rest of the way to her father's house, still holding her tightly. He never looked over his shoulder.

When they reached the house, Yael stumbled inside and sank down on the floor, weeping. Zaki stood in the open doorway, gazing out, saying nothing. A long time later, she finally dried her eyes.

"You followed me," she said softly. "Why?"

"To save your life. It's what I've been trying to do all these years. That's why I've kept your secret for so long, so no one would know about your sorcery."

She couldn't comprehend it. "Thank you," she whispered.

He looked at her for a long moment, then came to crouch beside her. "Are you all right?"

"I begged Rafi to run away with me, but . . ." A long, slow tear traveled down her cheek. She brushed it away. "He refused.

He cares more about his inheritance than he does about me. He could have defied his father if he really loved me."

Zaki exhaled. "I'm so sorry, Yael. I don't know what else to say."

"We'd better go home. Everyone will be worried." She stood and they left her father's house to walk up the road to Jerusalem. She would do what Abba wanted and marry Zechariah.

Rafi didn't love her.

Chapter 34

Dozens of people filled the courtyard of Zechariah's house for his wedding—priests and Levites, his fellow Torah students, people who had made the long journey with him and Yael from Babylon. There was lively music and joyful dancing and a feast of food and wine, yet Yael's father looked worried and Zechariah's grandparents looked unhappy. Zechariah had misgivings himself, wondering if Rafi and his gang of ruffians would burst into their home to disrupt the celebration and steal Yael away. But the day passed peacefully. Rafi didn't come. Zechariah sat close enough to Yael to see the sorrow and pain on her face beneath her veil.

Late in the evening, he escorted her to their bridal suite—a new room added onto their house just for them. His chest ached as he closed the door behind them and set the oil lamp in its niche on the wall. Yael yanked off her veil and unpinned her hair. She was such a beautiful woman. No wonder the Samaritan had wanted her. But instead of moving toward her, Zechariah crossed to the other side of the room and sat down on the floor, leaning against the wall. "What are you waiting for?" she asked. "Just go ahead and get it over with."

He shook his head. "I know you don't love me. In fact, you

probably resent me for taking Rafi's place. It's supposed to be an act of love," he said, gesturing to their marriage bed. "Not a conquest."

"An act of love?" she repeated, and he heard the scorn in her voice. "Do you love me, Zaki?"

"I've always loved you. Ever since we were children. I love your spirit, your sense of adventure, your zeal for life, and I didn't want the Samaritans to destroy all those things. And they would have, you know. That's why I asked your father for your hand."

Yael stared at him for a moment, her defiant expression still in place. Then she closed her eyes, and he saw her defiance transform into grief as she sank down on their bed. "I loved Rafi . . . I really did." Her tears began to fall. Zaki longed to go to her and comfort her, but he stayed where he was.

"I believe you. But a few years from now, after the passion faded, your life with the Samaritans would have become a living hell. And you could never undo it or change your mind and come home. I know you don't see it right now, but I rescued you from a terrible life." She didn't look at him, didn't reply. "If you don't want to be married to me, if you still want to run away, I won't stop you."

Yael finally stopped crying. She wiped her tears and lifted her chin to look at him. "They're waiting for us to show them the sheets, the proof. No one believes that I'm a virgin. They think Rafi and I have already been together, but it isn't true."

"I believe you. But I won't seal our marriage until you're ready."

"Until I'm ready? You're my husband. Doesn't the Torah give you the right to rule over me? Why aren't you claiming your rights?"

"Because I'm guessing that the only way you can endure our marriage bed is by pretending that I'm Rafi. And I want you to be glad that I'm your husband. I hope you'll love me someday.

In the meantime, I saved a little bit of blood from one of the goats we slaughtered for the wedding feast. We'll put it on the sheets to fool them."

Yael lowered her face into her hands, weeping again. Her grief broke Zechariah's heart. He stood and went to sit beside her on the bed, wrapping his arms around her, comforting her the way he had after her mother died when they were children.

"Without love, we won't have a true marriage," he told her. "I see my grandparents, the love they share, and I want the same thing. Safta is devoted to Saba. And he couldn't survive without her. I know their marriage hasn't always been perfect, yet they stay together, work together, through the good years and the bad." He waited until Yael stopped crying, then stood again, pulling one of the coverings from the bed. He carried it back to his place in the corner and removed his outer robe. "I'll give you time to decide what you want to do, Yael. We're not married until you decide that we are." Then he lay down on the floor to try to sleep, exhausted from the strain of this long, emotional day.

With the lamp still lit, he watched Yael's shadow on the wall as she rose from the bed and crouched beside the bags that held all her belongings. Safta had moved Yael's things into their room earlier in the day, but now Zechariah was certain that Yael would gather them up and leave. Instead, he heard a rustling sound, and when he sat up on one elbow, he saw her sitting on the floor, bending over an open scroll. "What is that? What are you doing?" he asked.

"I need to see what the stars say about my future . . . I don't know how else to decide what to do."

He lay down again, disgusted. There was no point in telling her that the Torah forbade it—much less in a priest's house. Yael knew. He had told her many times before. Saba had warned him that he shouldn't marry her, that she still had idolatry in her heart, and here was the proof. He would resign from the priesthood as soon as his marriage week ended. He sighed and closed his eyes. "Good night, Yael."

❧ ❧

Yael bent over her star charts, searching for answers. She'd seen things so clearly when she'd studied the charts in the past, but tonight she couldn't make sense of all the signs. They seemed to contradict each other. Maybe she was too close to the situation to read them clearly. After all, these were her stars, her future. Maybe what she wanted them to say was getting confused with what they really did say. But Leyla's grandmother was dead, and Yael didn't know anyone else who could help her interpret them.

Frustrated, she left the lamp burning in the room and went outside to the courtyard. Maybe if she looked up at the real heavens, the answer would become clear to her. The cool night was beautiful, the sky sparkling and cloudless as if scrubbed clean, the moon so bright she could read her star charts without an oil lamp. More and more stars appeared as Yael gazed up, as if coming out of hiding to talk to her. And sweeping across the center of the sky was a sparkling white river of stars.

The heavenly bodies all said that the love she shared with Rafi was real. They had predicted a happy life together, forever. But the stars had been wrong, just as they'd been wrong about Leyla's marriage. How could she have been so mistaken? What was she doing wrong? Why wouldn't they give her guidance? Her future seemed unknowable.

She was still looking up at the stunning heavens when she heard a rustling sound near the gate. She turned, startled to see a man standing there. For a moment she froze, her heart quickening. Then she recognized him—his height, his stance, his beautiful curly hair. *Rafi!* Yael ran to him, throwing her arms around him, weeping tears of joy. "Rafi! You're here! You came for me!"

"Yes. I'm here," he said. But his voice sounded strange. And he didn't return her embrace. His arms hung stiffly at his sides. Yael released him and looked up at him.

"Rafi, what's wrong?"

"Where's your new husband?" The cold expression on his face made her shiver. He seemed different tonight, not the Rafi she knew.

"Zechariah isn't my husband yet," she told him. "We haven't consummated the marriage."

"I don't believe you." Again, that strange, icy voice. She embraced him again as if her love and the warmth of her arms could thaw his coldness.

"I love you, Rafi. Zechariah knows that. He said I could run away with you if I wanted to, and he wouldn't stop us. I came out here to consult the stars for answers, but now that you're here, I don't have to. Come on, let's leave." She tried pulling him toward the gate, but he was as immoveable as a pillar.

"He and your father signed a marriage contract, didn't they?"

"Yes, but—"

"Does your husband love you?"

"That's not important, Rafi. Please—"

"You didn't answer my question. That must mean that he does love you."

"I would have run away with you before the wedding. I told you that. Why didn't you come for me sooner?"

"I didn't come for you now, Yael."

"What? . . . What do you mean?" In reply, he grabbed her upper arm, holding it so tightly he would leave fingerprint bruises on her arm. This man was a stranger, not the gentle, loving man she knew. "Rafi, let go. You're hurting me."

He yanked her toward the door to her room, the door she had left open with a lamp burning inside. "You belong to me, Yael. You're mine."

"Yes, I already told you that. Why are you acting this way? You're hurting me."

"I don't like losing someone I love. Basam had to pay for Leyla, and now it's your husband's turn to pay." They reached the door, and he kicked it wide open. Zechariah sat up, startled. "Is that your husband?" Rafi asked her.

"I told you, it isn't a real marriage. Tell him, Zaki—"

But in one swift, strong move, Rafi pulled Yael against his chest, pinning her arms to her sides. Something cold and sharp pressed against her throat. A knife. "Neither of you make a sound," Rafi said, "or I'll slit her throat right now."

Fear washed through Yael, draining her strength. If Rafi hadn't been holding her, she would have collapsed. Her body trembled so violently she might have been standing naked in a snowstorm. As tears blurred her vision, she couldn't see Zechariah's expression in the dim lamplight as he slowly rose to his feet.

"Wait! Put the knife away, Rafi. Don't hurt her." He raised his arms in surrender.

"I should have let my friends beat you to death years ago. Of all people, I had to lose Yael to you. To *you*!" He spat out the words like bitter gall. "The suffering you caused me—it was like watching Yael die, knowing I could never have her. Now you'll have the agony of watching her die. It will be the last thing you'll ever see before I kill you, too."

"She loves *you*," Zechariah said calmly, "not me. She wanted to marry you. Why would you kill someone who loves you? Kill me if you want to, but why kill Yael?"

"Because you stole her from me. And because you love her. I want you to suffer the way I have."

Yael felt his grip tighten. The knife blade pressed against her flesh. She was going to die. "No, Rafi, don't!" she begged.

Iddo awoke from the dream, gasping.

"Shh . . . It was just a dream, Iddo," Dinah soothed. "Go back to sleep." He sat up, his clothing drenched with sweat. The nightmare had been so real that it took Iddo a moment to figure out where he was. In his bed. Beside Dinah. In Jerusalem. But why have a nightmare now, after all these years without one?

"Did I cry out and awaken everyone?" he asked.

"No one heard you but me. . . . Was it the same dream, Iddo?"

"Yes." He had crouched beneath the wagon as Jerusalem burned. The soldier was attacking Mama, and his brother had crawled out to help her. Iddo had tried to leave his hiding place and save the people he loved. He had tried to move, to crawl out and rescue them—but the dream had jolted him awake before he could move. He tossed the covers aside and climbed out of bed.

"Where are you going?" Dinah asked.

"Outside for some air. I'm sorry for waking you." Iddo left the room but even the canopy of glimmering stars couldn't erase the nightmare from his mind. Fear and dread lingered like a sour taste that couldn't be washed away. What could have triggered the dream? Yesterday had been a joyous occasion—Zechariah's marriage to Yael. True, Iddo hadn't wanted him to marry her, but even so, he marveled that he had lived to see such a day. Soon there would be children, reversing the curse of death and bringing renewed life. *"Look up at the heavens and count the stars—if indeed you can count them. . . . So shall your offspring be."*

But Iddo couldn't concentrate on the night sky. The lingering horror from the dream had left behind an aura of evil. He tiptoed around the courtyard, searching for—he didn't even know what he searched for. But he recalled the nest of vipers they'd found when building the foundation of this house, and like rooting out those snakes, he felt an urgent need to find the source of evil and destroy it.

He heard a sound. Voices. They came from the new room added on for Zechariah and Yael. He inched toward the sound and saw the open door and a light burning inside. A man stood silhouetted in the doorway. Not Zaki . . . he was shorter than Zaki. Not anyone from Iddo's household.

"Now you can watch her die," the man said.

Rafi. The Samaritan.

He was holding Yael against his chest. Iddo saw the glint of a knife.

"Don't hurt her, Rafi." Zechariah's voice. "Take your revenge on me, but don't hurt Yael. She loves you."

For a moment Iddo couldn't move, frozen in horror just as he'd always been in his dream. He had to save his family! Then he forced himself to move, glancing around the courtyard for a weapon. Dinah's heavy clay water jar stood near his feet. He picked it up and crept to the opened door, then smashed it into the back of Rafi's head with all his strength. Rafi tottered but didn't fall, momentarily stunned. And in that instant, Zechariah lunged toward Yael and snatched her from Rafi's grasp. Zaki stood in front of her, shielding her as she screamed and screamed.

Rafi whirled to attack Iddo, a short, double-edged knife in his hand. He was young and strong, but Iddo was strong, too. He had killed and skinned hundreds of bulls and rams for the sacrifices. Now he wrestled for his life and for Zechariah and Yael's lives—gripping Rafi's arms to keep away the knife.

"Stay back, Zaki," Iddo shouted. "He'll kill you." But Zaki attacked Rafi from behind, punching and beating him, then wrapping one arm around Rafi's throat as he tried to pull him away.

Yael continued to scream for help as the three men struggled, loudly enough to awaken the others. Besai and Mattaniah came to help, but they moved too slowly, still groggy with sleep and with wine from the wedding. In one swift, deadly strike, Rafi managed to free one hand and stab Iddo in the stomach. Iddo felt the force of the thrust, the warm, wet rush of blood. Iddo staggered backward as Rafi pulled out the knife and whirled to attack Zechariah, the knife raised.

"No!" Iddo roared. He fought for balance and hurled himself at Rafi, pushing him sideways with all his strength, away from his grandson. The other men piled on Rafi then, knocking him to the ground, kicking the knife from his hand. Iddo snatched up the dagger and plunged it into Rafi's chest. A moment later, Rafi went still.

Iddo had used up all his strength. A fire burned in his gut where he'd been stabbed. He leaned against the wall, then slowly slid to the ground.

"Iddo's hurt! He's bleeding!" someone shouted.

They helped him lie down, and Dinah bent over him, tearing open his robe to tend to his wound. The room whirled, dream-like. It was hard to breathe. "Lie still, Iddo," she begged. "Please don't move . . . Please be all right. . . ."

"I'm fine, Dinah. Don't worry. It was just a dream . . . But I saved them this time. . . . I killed the Babylonian soldier . . . and I saved them. . . ."

Iddo closed his eyes and let the darkness take him.

Chapter 35

Zechariah ran home from the evening sacrifice, desperate to be with his grandfather, unwilling to miss a single moment with him, knowing each one might be his last. Three long, agonizing days had passed since Rafi had stabbed Saba, and no one was able to say if he would survive or not. Zechariah raced into the courtyard, then into his grandfather's room and saw Safta sitting beside his bed. "He's asleep," she whispered. "There's been no change." She was trying so hard to be brave, staying by Saba's side, encouraging him to get well, never letting anyone see her cry. Zechariah had also remained beside his bed all night and had heard her murmuring to Saba in the darkness, "I love you, Iddo. . . . You must get well. . . . You must."

"I'll stay with him for a while," he said as he sat down beside the bed.

"Do you want something to eat, Zaki?"

"Maybe later." Worry had stolen his appetite.

Safta nodded and released Saba's hand as she stood. "I'll warm some broth in case he's hungry when he wakes up."

Zechariah closed his eyes after she left, silently pleading with the Almighty One to spare his grandfather's life. Why should Saba pay the price for Zechariah's decision to marry Yael?

As time passed, his mind began to wander, circling back to the events of that terrible night. No one in his household could comprehend the violence and hatred that had entered their gate. Rafi had tried to kill Yael. And him. And Saba. Who knew how many others he would have killed if Saba hadn't stopped him?

But Rafi was dead. At dawn, Mattaniah had sent for the elders from Rafi's village, asking them to come and see for themselves what Rafi had tried to do. The elders had carried his body home. And now all of Jerusalem held its breath, waiting to see if more blood vengeance and killing would follow.

In all the grief and confusion, Zechariah had barely spoken with Yael—his wife. Hodaya had been much better at comforting her than he was. What a terrible way to begin their marriage. If it ever truly would be a marriage.

Zechariah opened his eyes again when he heard his grandfather stirring. "Is the sacrifice finished, Zaki?" he asked in his whispery-soft voice.

"Yes. And everyone prayed for you. All of the priests and the people . . . How are you feeling?"

"Like I'm still dreaming. Like I'm half in this world and half in the next."

Lines of pain creased Saba's face. The wound had been deep, and so much blood had drained from his body that he was as weak as an infant, as pale and cold as snow. But Zechariah refused to allow his grandfather to give in to the pain and die. "Please stay in this world a little longer, Saba. We need you."

"That's up to the Holy One, not me. . . . In the meantime, tell me about today's Torah portion."

Zechariah swallowed his grief. "It's one of your favorites, the passage where the Holy One says to Abraham, 'Look up at the heavens and count the stars—if indeed you can count them. So shall your offspring be.'"

"Tell me—" He began to cough and Zechariah tensed, fearing the exertion would reopen his wound.

"Just rest, Saba. Don't try to talk until you're stronger. It takes too much of your strength."

"You know how we become stronger?" he asked, smiling faintly. "By studying the Torah."

Zechariah bit his lip. He longed to hear just one more of his grandfather's Torah lessons. Why hadn't he appreciated the wealth of wisdom and knowledge that Saba possessed? Who could ever take the place of this man of God when he was gone? Zechariah couldn't bear to think about it. "Then we'll study this passage together so you'll grow strong." He sat up straight, waiting for his grandfather to begin with a question. The room grew dimmer now that the sun had set, but Zechariah didn't want to light a lamp.

Saba drew a shallow breath. "What is the plain meaning of the passage?"

"The Holy One is telling Abraham that one day his descendants will be so numerous that we'll be like the stars in the heavens. Too many to count."

"And He always keeps His promises. . . . Don't let our tiny population fool you. Or our disobedience in failing to finish His temple. God keeps His promises even when we don't keep ours." He paused for a moment, then asked, "Do you see a deeper meaning?"

Zechariah smiled. Of course. There was always a deeper meaning. Saba had taught him this passage years before and was checking to see if he remembered. "The Holy One was not only telling Abraham that his offspring would be numerous, but also that we would shine like the stars. We would be a source of light in the darkness. The Holy One entrusted us with His

Word, and the world is enlightened by the Torah's wisdom and moral teachings when we live in obedience to it."

"Good. . . . Is there still another meaning?"

Zechariah thought for a moment but none came to mind. "If so, I'm certain that you know what it is, Saba." He bent closer as his grandfather cleared his throat.

"The Holy One asked Abraham to count the stars. An impossible task. But He knew that if Abraham attempted the impossible, his offspring would follow his example. We would also attempt the impossible if God asked us to. Because with His help, nothing is impossible. Do you believe that, Zaki?"

"Yes. Of course." This wasn't the time to share his doubts with his grandfather.

"We all believed it when we first came here," Saba continued. "We were going to rebuild Jerusalem and the temple and our nation even if the rubble and the weeds and the hatred of our enemies made it seem impossible. We started off so well and now . . . now for the past decade we've decided it was impossible. There were too many obstacles in our way, too many stars to count."

"The obstacles aren't imagined, Saba. We had to stop building, remember? The Persian king reversed his decree."

"Did the Almighty One reverse His decree?"

"No, but our enemies came with soldiers and threats and ordered us to stop. We had no choice." Zechariah tried to be gentle and not argue, even though he had once agreed with Saba when he'd argued with the priest, Jakin. "We're still under Persian control. We have to obey the king."

"Is he mightier than God?"

Before Zechariah could reply, Safta came into the room with a bowl of warm broth. "Are you tiring him, Zaki? He needs to eat something and then rest."

Zechariah stood to give her his place beside the bed. "I'll come back in a little while."

"No, Zechariah . . . wait . . . I'm not finished." Iddo motioned for him to kneel beside the bed again. "Nothing is impossible with God," he said. "Do you believe that or don't you?"

"I believe it." But he had wrestled with doubt and fear for so long that they had exhausted his certainty, just like they had exhausted the high priest and their nation's leaders and so many other people.

"Try to eat some broth," Safta said.

Saba shook his head. "God has His hand on you, Zechariah, for a very special task. I've always known that was true. . . . Tell me why you decided to come here."

"Because I felt God's presence. I heard Him telling me to come. I thought . . . I thought if we rebuilt the temple, then God's presence would dwell with us all the time, but then . . ."

"You haven't found Him?"

"No. Not yet." It shamed Zechariah to admit it.

"Are you certain about that? I think you've been searching for God in the wrong place when all this time He has been as close to you as I am."

"How? . . . Where?"

"We all want to meet God in a dramatic way like you did on the day of your bar mitzvah. But instead, the Almighty One quietly reveals himself to us in His Word. As you study it every day, you hear His voice and you see Him. You learn to know Him."

"Saba, I—"

"Don't wait for a new temple to be built or for another mystical experience like the first one. Listen to God now, son. Pay attention to His voice in the Scriptures." Saba closed his eyes. "And then when He tells you to do the impossible, go do it."

Zechariah left the room and went outside to the courtyard as his emotions overwhelmed him. Do the impossible? The others had sat down to eat the evening meal and they invited him to join them, but he wasn't hungry. Could Saba be right? Was God's presence truly as close as the pages of the Torah, the writings of the prophets? Zechariah's pain was so raw, his dread so great, that he could scarcely think, barely function. He fled to his new room—his marriage chamber—as he tried to pull his fraying emotions back together. He was still sitting there on the floor in the dark with his back against the wall when he heard the door open. He looked up. Yael came inside with a lamp and closed the door behind her. He waited while she set the lamp in its niche, not trusting himself to speak.

"We haven't had a chance to talk since that night," she said. "Since your grandfather . . ." He saw her swallow. "But I need to tell you how sorry I am for everything that happened. Can you ever forgive me?"

"For what? For loving the wrong person?" he asked with a shrug. "You couldn't have known what Rafi would do."

"I should have known. I ignored the signs because I didn't want to see them. Rafi would have killed both of us. And anyone else who tried to interfere." She walked forward a few more steps as if afraid to approach him. "Zaki, I know that what happened to your grandfather was my fault."

"It wasn't. I don't blame you. I shouldn't have interfered with your life by offering to marry you."

She moved closer and knelt in front of him. Tears streamed down her beautiful face. "If you hadn't interfered, I would have foolishly married Rafi. I would have married a man capable of murdering me. I should have listened to you and to everyone else. Please, please forgive me."

"Of course, Yael. Of course I forgive you." She was so distraught that he reached for her and pulled her into his arms, letting her sit beside him and weep against his shoulder. But in spite of his assurances, part of him did blame her for what had happened. And if his grandfather died . . . Zechariah wasn't sure he could ever look at Yael without thinking that she was partly to blame.

"I burned up my star charts . . . I threw them all on the hearth and watched them burn." Her voice sounded muffled against his robe. "I'll never look at the stars for guidance again. I'll worship your God from now on."

He didn't reply. She had spoken the words he'd waited to hear all these years. But at what price? His grandfather's life?

"Will you give me a second chance, Zaki?" she whispered.

"Of course."

Yael released him and leaned away to look at him. She took his face in her hands, touching his beard, stroking his hair. "When Rafi said he was going to kill you, he was a man I didn't know. A stranger. I could never have loved a man who would kill you. But in that terrible moment, I saw you, I knew you. You were Zaki, my friend. The man I've shared a lifetime with, the man I know so well. I love you, and I can't imagine a future without you. I'm so sorry for what I've put your family through. For what happened to your grandfather—"

"Shh . . . shh . . . Don't cry, Yael." He pulled her close again, desperate to stop her flow of words. He had promised to forgive her, the same way he had assured Saba that he believed in a God who could do the impossible—and Zechariah wasn't sure if any of it was true. He didn't know what he believed or if he could ever forgive. He needed to get away somewhere alone so he could think.

"I want to truly be your wife," she said, "if you haven't changed your mind."

"You are my wife, Yael. We're already married. I won't change my mind." But his heart, not his mind, needed to change. Especially if his grandfather died.

Her arms tightened around him. "I'm yours, Zaki. From now on. I'm yours."

"Yael, right now I . . . I need to go pray for Saba." He unwrapped her arms from around him and struggled to his feet. "I'll be back in a little while."

He left the house and walked through the dark streets, dodging the rubble still piled everywhere after so many years. Dim lamplight lit a few of the scattered houses, but not many. The inhabitants of Jerusalem were too poor to waste precious oil. Wanting to avoid the temple mount, he walked downhill to the reservoir that held the runoff from the Gihon Spring. The pool used to be inside the city walls, but they had all been destroyed by the Babylonians. Zechariah climbed onto a half-broken section of wall and sat down.

Across the valley, thin plumes of gray smoke curled into the night sky from Rafi's village. Zaki turned away from that view and gazed up the hill at the cluster of houses where he and the other settlers lived. Farther up the slope was the house of assembly and Governor Sheshbazzar's residence, and on the highest point above this mound of land where King David's city had once stood, Zechariah could see smoke rising from the Holy One's altar. It was the mountain where the temple should be.

He closed his eyes, lowering his face in his hands so he could think. Yael had given up her idolatry. She was ready to be his wife. But he knew she acted out of guilt and obligation and fear, knowing Saba might die. Zaki wanted her love. It had taken the crisis of nearly losing her, seeing that knife pressed to her throat, for him to realize how much he did love her. He had offered to trade his life for hers. As he opened his eyes again and gazed up at the place where the temple should be, he wondered if living with a wife without her love was like serving as God's priest without loving Him. Was this how God felt about Zechariah's halfhearted faith? Did He also want all or nothing, a relationship of mutual love, not mere guilt or obligation?

All or nothing. That's what his grandfather was trying to teach him. Did Zechariah believe all of the stories in the Torah, all of the impossible deeds that the Almighty One had done in the past, or didn't he?

He realized that he did. Because Saba was right—he had learned to know God through studying the Scriptures. What he saw was a God of love and miracles and laws, and he knew that a life without Him wasn't worth living. He would be no better than the dumb beasts of the earth. No better than the Samaritans.

Zechariah truly had experienced God's presence back in Babylon. The Almighty One had commanded him to return to Jerusalem and to Him. Zechariah had been longing for His presence ever since, searching for Him, waiting for God to tell him why he was here and what He wanted him to do. And as Zechariah gazed up the sloping hill, at the ruins, at the half-built city, at the empty place on the top of the hill where Abraham had offered up Isaac, the place where the temple should be, he suddenly knew exactly what God wanted him to do.

The impossible.

He jumped down off the wall and ran up the hill, hurrying through the narrow lanes as fast as he could in the dark. He raced through the gate into his house, passing the others still sitting in the courtyard, and went straight into Saba's room. His grandfather opened his eyes and looked up at him as Zechariah knelt beside the bed.

"We need to rebuild the temple," he said, still breathless from the climb. "Not because King Cyrus told us to, but because we long to meet with God. Because we love Him and are incomplete without Him. It's just like you said, Saba—God has been testing us with all these difficulties to see how important the temple is to us. Will we allow ourselves to be discouraged, or will we trust Him and do the impossible?"

A slow, gentle smile lit Saba's pale face.

"The Almighty One wants our love, Saba, not guilty obedience. That's what's been missing in my life—love. Instead of waiting for God's presence to come to me again, He wanted me to pursue Him the way the Torah says to do, with all my heart and soul and strength. Following rules and offering sacrifices is meaningless without love. Am I making any sense?"

Saba nodded, still smiling.

"We need to rebuild the temple. We need to trust the God of the impossible. It's so clear to me, so obvious—but how do I get the others to believe it?"

"You'll have to convince them."

"And you'll have to help me!" Zechariah gripped his grandfather's icy hand in both of his. "You have to fight to get well and to live so that we can do this together. It was your dream, and now it's mine for us to minister together in the Holy One's temple."

He felt the gentle pressure of Saba's hand in return. "I'll do my best."

And Zechariah would do his best, too, from now on. He would build his marriage with Yael and his faith in God—day by day, one loving, impossible step at a time. And then he would rebuild God's temple.

Part IV

The Temple

"Not by might nor by power, but

by my Spirit," says the Lord Almighty.

Zechariah 4:6

Chapter 36

Six Years Later

The relentless sun left Zechariah parched and thirsty as he made the six-mile trek home from the grazing pastures outside Bethlehem. The report that he and the others had just heard from the chief shepherd, Besai, had discouraged all of them. "Let's stop for a minute," Rebbe Jakin said. "I need to rest." Sweat rolled down his face, which was red with exertion from the uphill climb. Zechariah and the two other young priests-in-training halted in the stingy shade of a cedar tree, grateful for the rest.

"If it's this hot in the springtime, what will summer be like?" Zechariah asked the others. He took a drink from his dwindling waterskin, not expecting a reply.

Jakin gestured to the straw-colored landscape all around them. "The Judean hills look nearly as desolate as the wilderness by the Dead Sea. Have any of you ever seen the Judean wilderness?"

"No," Zechariah replied. "But I've walked this route before in the springtime and these *wadis* usually gush with water. It was a challenge to wade across some of them. Now they're all dry. Even the Kidron Brook has dried up."

The spring rains that usually filled the dry riverbeds to overflowing hadn't come. Neither had the winter rains or the early rains last fall. Drought baked the Promised Land's fertile soil, leaving it dry as ashes.

"Jeshua won't be pleased with our report," Jakin said. "The daily offerings will need to be scaled back yet again."

"And what about the Passover sacrifices? And the ones for my ordination?" Zechariah asked. No one knew the answer. He mopped the sweat from his brow, and they set off again for the last leg of their climb over the Mount of Olives. "I'm finally going to be ordained in a few weeks," he said to the others, "and now there may not be any lambs for me to offer."

When they arrived in Jerusalem, they went straight to the house of assembly to give their report. From inside the high priest's stifling room, Zechariah heard the young yeshiva boys' voices droning like a beehive as they studied, their heads bent over their scrolls. Rebbe Jakin told Jeshua about the effects of the drought and how so many of the ewes from the temple flocks had miscarried. "If large crowds come for the Passover Feast, Besai fears that we may not have enough lambs to go around," Jakin finished. "Let alone enough for the daily sacrifices."

The high priest closed his eyes for a long moment, the strain evident on his face. "I checked our storehouses this morning and our supplies of grain and oil are critically low. Those daily offerings may have to be halted as well, for the first time since we rebuilt the altar."

"The Almighty One won't get His portion and neither will we," Jakin said. "How will our families survive? We depend on the peoples' tithes, and ten percent of nothing is nothing."

"I don't understand why this is happening," Jeshua murmured, fanning himself with a dried palm frond.

Both Jeshua and Rebbe Jakin had seniority over Zechariah, and he knew better than to lecture his elders, but he could no longer keep still. "Ask the Lord for rain in the springtime; it is the Lord who makes the storm clouds. He gives showers of rain to men, and plants of the field to everyone." The men stared at him as if trying to place the Scripture he had just quoted. Where *had* it come from? The words had sprung to Zechariah's mind, but he couldn't place the verse, either. He scrambled to think of another one that he could quote. "I was reading and praying about the drought the other day, and I found a passage about it in the Torah. May I read it to you?"

"Yes, of course."

Zechariah hurried into the yeshiva, interrupting the lessons as he borrowed the scroll of the fifth book of Moses. He searched for the verse as he returned to the high priest's room, and although it wasn't the one he had just quoted, he read it aloud to the others. "'If you faithfully obey the commands I am giving you today—to love the Lord your God and to serve him with all your heart and with all your soul—then I will send the rain on your land in its season, both autumn and spring rains, so that you may gather your grain, new wine and oil. I will provide grass in the fields for your cattle, and you will eat and be satisfied.'"

"We're all familiar with that promise," Jakin said, his irritation apparent.

"Yes, that's why I've asked all our priests and students to examine their lives for sin," Jeshua added. "Can you say that any of us don't love Him or serve Him, Zechariah? How are we failing to obey God?"

Zechariah drew a slow breath as he gathered his courage. He had been trying to get someone's attention and say these words for the past six years as he'd served his apprenticeship for the priesthood. Maybe it was finally time. "With all due respect . . . I believe that we're failing because we haven't obeyed the Almighty One's command to rebuild the temple. I think He sent this drought to get our attention."

The high priest's fan stilled. He leaned back in his seat, studying Zechariah for a moment. Zechariah's heart began to race. Maybe the others would finally listen to him. But when Jeshua spoke, his words were disappointing. "Prince Zerubbabel and I met recently to discuss the temple, and we both agreed that the time hasn't come for the Lord's house to be built."

"I disagree! The time to build was nearly twenty years ago when we first arrived. We're disobeying God and—"

"Zechariah!" Jakin interrupted, his voice sharp. "You're an outstanding Torah scholar, and you're going to make a fine priest. But I think you're forgetting that it was an edict from the Persian king that forced us to stop in the first place. Neither Jeshua nor Zerubbabel dares to come against the might and power of the king."

And Zechariah shouldn't come against his elders, but he couldn't stop the flow of words as another Scripture verse came to him: "It's not by might nor by power, but by my Spirit, says the Lord Almighty."

The men stared at him as if he had spoken another language. Where had *that* verse come from? One of the prophets? Zechariah couldn't recall. He had studied the Scriptures diligently, had memorized large portions of it, and it upset him that he couldn't recall where he had read this verse, imprinted so strongly on his mind. He was still trying to figure it out when Jeshua said, "The prince is concerned about the safety of our people. He's responsible for us. He doesn't want to risk retaliation from the king or from our enemies. We stopped rebuilding for the sake of peace."

"But we haven't made peace, we've simply compromised with our enemies," Zechariah said. "We're not fulfilling our purpose for being here in the land. We're supposed to glorify the Holy One among the nations. He wants to fulfill His promise to Abraham that through his offspring all nations would be blessed!"

"What does that have to do with rebuilding the temple?" Jakin asked.

"It has everything to do with it! Our worship at the temple demonstrates the way to find fellowship with God. He promised to dwell here among us. The rebuilt temple isn't just for us, it's so that the whole world can know the Almighty One. We're meant to bring life and hope to the world the same way we brought life from the rubble. The Babylonians and Samaritans have no hope because they don't know God. That's why they cling to superstition and try to see the future in the stars."

"If they wanted to find God," Jakin said, "they wouldn't have opposed us when we began to rebuild."

"No, I know some of those stargazers, and they're searching for Him whether they realize it or not. Listen, during the first exodus from Egypt, the Almighty One commanded our ancestors to utterly destroy all the inhabitants of the land. This time He didn't say that. I believe God wants us to live in such a way that we'll draw all men to Him. So they'll give up their idolatry and find the living God." The way Yael had, after all these years.

Zechariah got the impression that only Jeshua, out of all the men in the room, was truly listening and trying to understand what he was desperate to say. "We're supposed to remain separate from the other nations," Jeshua said.

"I know. But we haven't remained separate. In the name of peace we've gone to their pagan festivals, and we've eaten food sacrificed to their idols and followed their customs instead of showing them the right way to live and how to worship properly. My grandmother gave one of the bravest examples of how we're to conduct ourselves among unbelievers when she saved a newborn baby that the Samaritans tried to kill. She could have reasoned that killing the child was just their custom and she shouldn't interfere, but she didn't. She told them that human life is precious to our God, and she adopted the child as her own."

"We all admire her for her brave example," Jeshua said.

"We *all* need to become examples," Zechariah continued. "This is what the Lord Almighty says: 'Men from all languages and nations will take firm hold of one Jew by the hem of his robe and say, "Let us go with you, because we have heard that God is with you."'"

"Where is that written?" Jakin asked. "I'm not familiar with that verse."

Once again, Zechariah couldn't remember. Where had it come from? "I-I'm not certain . . . but God showed the prophet Isaiah a time when foreigners would seek Him. He said, 'My house will be called a house of prayer for all nations.' We need to rebuild His house! This drought is His way of getting our attention. The fact that we barely have enough offerings for the sacrifices should tell us that He isn't pleased with our worship."

"You've certainly given me much to think about," Jeshua said. But then he sighed and laid down his fan, and Zechariah could see that he was dismissing the topic. They were all hot and tired. Jeshua had other work to do. "Right now I need to figure out how to hold the Passover feast with this shortage of lambs," he said. "If the drought continues after the holiday, Prince Zerubbabel and I will call for a day of prayer to seek the Almighty One's will. Thank you all for your report."

Zechariah had been dismissed. But instead of going up to the temple mount with the others, he remained behind in the yeshiva to study the scrolls of the prophets, determined not to leave until he found the prophecies that had imprinted so strongly on his heart. He would prove the truth of God's Word to Jeshua and Zerubbabel. *"It's not by might nor by power, but by my Spirit, says the Lord Almighty."*

Chapter 37

Dinah rooted through the storage room, opening baskets and clay storage jars to see how much food was left. What she found—or rather, what she failed to find—dismayed her. "Look at this," she said to Yael, who had followed her inside. "Every jar is nearly empty. I wanted to prepare an enormous meal for this joyous occasion but how can it be a feast with so little food?"

"Zechariah understands, Safta. He doesn't expect a huge feast in the middle of a drought." Yael stood with one hand on her pregnant belly, the other pressed against her aching back. Dinah could see that the baby had dropped into position. It would be born any day.

"But we have guests coming," Dinah said. "We have to feed them."

"Besai and Rachel said they would bring what they could," Yael said. The couple would travel from Bethlehem where Besai cared for the sacrificial flocks, bringing Hanan's widow, who had remarried, with them. "And Abba will bring what he has from his farm. They're coming to watch Zechariah become a priest, not to dine like kings."

Dinah lifted a nearly empty jar of grain in one arm, a

dwindling basket of figs in the other. "Let me help you with those," Yael said.

"No, dear. I can manage. You need to rest and stay off your feet."

"Rest? With two little ones to chase after?" Yael asked, laughing. "That isn't likely to happen." Dinah smiled, knowing she was right. The two daughters who had been born to Yael and Zechariah—five-year-old Abigail and three-year-old Sarah—were every bit as lively and mischievous as Yael had been as a young girl, exhausting their mother, their Aunt Hodaya, and everyone else in the household.

Dinah carried the supplies out to her courtyard kitchen and set them beside the hearth. She would begin cooking for tonight's feast as soon as she returned from the morning sacrifice. Today Zechariah would minister as a priest for the first time, serving at both sacrifices. "Iddo says the Almighty One is trying to get our attention with this drought but that we're not listening."

"Well, so far we've had enough food to feed our family," Yael said, grabbing little Sarah who had escaped from Hodaya's grasp, and lifting her into her arms. "I'm sure there will be enough for this celebration, too. We didn't have very much for Passover this year but it was still a joyous occasion, wasn't it?"

"Abba said that sharing a meal with the people you love is what makes it a feast," Hodaya said. She had pulled Abigail onto her lap so she could comb the tangles from her hair.

"Yes, Iddo did say that," Dinah replied. "He said it wasn't the amount of food *on* the table that mattered but the amount of love *around* the table."

"In that case," Yael said, "tonight we will dine like kings."

"When did Besai and Rachel say they would arrive?" Hodaya asked.

Yael laughed and gave Hodaya's braid an affectionate tug.

"Why are you asking, little sister? Are you wondering about the lamb they're bringing or their handsome son, Aaron?"

Dinah watched Hodaya's cheeks turn bright red and wondered if she had missed something. Was there a budding romance between sixteen-year-old Hodaya and the shepherd's eighteen-year-old son? But Dinah couldn't worry about that right now. If she didn't hurry, they would be late for the morning sacrifice. Zechariah and Iddo had already left before dawn.

She quickly checked to see how much water was in the jars and sighed when she saw they were nearly empty. There hadn't been rain for such a long time that the cisterns beneath everyone's homes had dried up, forcing the women in Jerusalem to walk all the way to the spring for water. Hodaya couldn't hobble that far and Yael could no longer go in her condition, which meant that Dinah had to do it alone every day. Everyone told her it was too much for a woman her age to fetch water, but Dinah didn't feel old. "It might take me longer to get there and back," she had told her family, "and I may have to carry a smaller jug, but I'm still mistress of this household, thank you very much." Typically, Yael hadn't listened to Dinah and had recuited several neighbors to each carry an extra supply for them. Dinah knew that by the time she returned from the morning sacrifice, the jars would be mysteriously full.

"Is everyone ready?" she asked. "We should leave very soon if we want to get a place up front where we can see Zechariah." She turned to Yael and saw her gripping her stomach, a look of surprise on her face. "Yael? Are you in labor?"

"No, it's nothing. Just one of those false pains. And not a very strong one. This baby wouldn't dare to arrive on his father's big day."

Dinah coralled her two great-granddaughters and they all set out for the uphill walk to the temple mount. They would have to walk slowly for Hodaya's sake, and for Yael's, who stopped often to rest. "I can't believe Zechariah turns thirty years old today," Dinah said the first time they paused. "A grown man, already."

"Remember the day of his bar mitzvah in Babylon?" Yael asked—and then caught herself. "I'm so sorry. I know you don't like to talk about Babylon."

"Never mind, dear. It's okay. And yes, I do remember that day. We had a big celebration for him. Naomi and Sarah and I cooked for a week. I only wish we could do the same for this birthday."

Abigail tugged on Dinah's arm. "Come on, Safta. I want to see Abba." They started walking again.

"I still wonder about my family in Babylon," Dinah said, "but I've learned that children are only loaned to us for a short time. A husband, especially the right one, is given by God for a lifetime. Yes, it was hard to leave my family, and I grieved for a long time. But even if Iddo and I had stayed in Babylon, there were no guarantees that we wouldn't suffer sorrow and loss. I'm glad we came to Jerusalem."

"You are?" Yael asked.

"Yes. Don't look so surprised. If Iddo and I hadn't come, Zechariah wouldn't be serving as a priest today." She took Hodaya's hand for a moment and added, "And Hodaya wouldn't have come into our lives."

Dinah's adopted daughter was growing into a lovely woman with beautiful dark eyes and thick, curly hair that was the envy of the other girls her age. She could maneuver so well around their house with her crutch that no one dared to call her crippled. Hodaya knew she was adopted, but she didn't know the terrible details of her birth. So far, Dinah had been able to evade her daughter's questions with vague replies.

The women rested again at the bottom of the stairs leading to the temple mount, then began the ascent. Dinah's anticipation grew with each step. She never thought she would live to see this day. Iddo was well past the age of retirement, but the other priests had invited him to put on priestly robes today and assist his grandson with the sacrifice.

At last they reached the Court of Women and walked all the way to the front so they could see over the barrier to where the sacrifice would take place. They arrived just in time to see Zechariah emerge from the robing room and stride across the courtyard to stand beside the altar. His linen robe and turban looked dazzling white against his black hair and beard. A red sash encircled his waist. Iddo walked forward behind him, his hair and beard as white as his robe, his shoulders a little stooped. He had never regained all the weight he'd lost after being stabbed six years ago, but by the grace of God he had survived. Dinah watched them perform the sacrifice together with tears in her eyes, her heart so full she feared it might burst. Zechariah climbed the ramp and laid the offering on the altar and the crowd gave a shout of joy as the smoke and fire ascended. But Yael gave a sharp gasp and doubled over. "You're in labor," Dinah said. "We need to get you home."

"I'll be fine. Let's watch for just a few more minutes."

They did, but as soon as the sacrifice came to an end, Dinah made everyone start for home. She kept a close eye on Yael as they walked, the journey easier downhill.

"I can't go into labor today," Yael said. "I don't want to miss the evening sacrifice or ruin the celebration tonight. Besides, you need my help with the preparations and—"

"I'll have plenty of help. Hodaya is a better cook than all of us put together."

Yael's face was flushed and beaded with perspiration by the time they reached home. Dinah sent her into her room to check for spotting, but she knew the truth even before Yael returned. Her labor had begun. She insisted on helping Dinah with a few simple cooking chores, but by noontime, Yael had to give in and lie down in her room.

"Hodaya, I'm putting you in charge of the children while I go fetch the midwife." Dinah had trained another woman as well as Yael, and rarely delivered babies anymore. But she was thrilled to help deliver this one.

Yael's third child arrived faster than her first two babies had, but her labor still took all day. At the hour that Zechariah slew the evening sacrifice, his first son entered the world. Dinah delivered him with her own hands, her third great-grandchild. How could she be so blessed? "He's a beautiful, healthy boy," she told Yael as she laid him down beside her.

"I hope he's not going to be a troublemaker," Yael said with a smile. "He already made us miss his father's big day."

"I don't think Zechariah will mind in the least once he sees why."

Dinah's neighbors helped her finish preparing the meal, and by the time everyone arrived home from the evening sacrifice, the feast was ready. Dinah ran to embrace her grandson. "I'm so proud of you, Zechariah! So proud!"

"Thanks, Safta." He looked all around the crowded courtyard and asked, "Where's Yael?"

"In your room. She has a surprise for you." Dinah followed Zaki into the room, wishing she could see his face when he saw Yael lying in bed with their baby beside her.

"You have a son, Zaki," Yael told him. "And he has the same birthday as you do."

Dinah turned away to give them privacy as Zaki fell to his knees beside the bed to hold his wife in his arms.

Yael was dozing later that night when Zechariah finally said good-night to his family and guests and came to bed. When she opened her eyes he was sitting beside their bed, gazing at her. "Why are you staring at me?" she asked.

"Do you have any idea how beautiful you look, lying here?" He bent to kiss her.

"You're just saying that because I gave you a son."

"No, I'm saying it because it's true. I love you so much, Yael. How are you feeling?"

"Tired. At least my labor was quick this time. Just as grueling, but faster than the other two. I'm sorry I missed the evening sacrifice."

"You had a good excuse. And you'll have a lifetime to watch me offer sacrifices."

"How was your first day on your new job?"

"I can't even begin to describe my joy! All the long years of apprenticeship are over, and it's like I'm beginning a brand-new life. How many times do we get to begin new lives?"

"I can think of a few. When we arrived in Jerusalem . . . when you and I got married . . . when we became parents—"

"You're right, you're right," he said, laughing. "And now I'm beginning my ministry for God. Saba says priests stand as peacemakers between the Almighty One and His people. I didn't think my joy could be any more complete while I was working today, but then I came home to you . . . and our son."

"You should have seen Safta trying to prepare a meal and deliver a baby at the same time," she said, smiling.

"I told her what a wonderful feast it was—and in the middle of a famine, no less." He bent to kiss her again, then asked softly, "Are you happy, Yael?"

"Can't you tell? I can't stop smiling!"

"I don't mean right now but every day. Do you ever feel . . . trapped?"

"Zaki! Why would you ask such a question?" When he didn't reply, she nudged him. "We've been married for six years. Why are you asking me if I'm happy?"

"I used to feel trapped when we first arrived in Jerusalem and

I had to study all day. I envied your freedom. You didn't seem to want a life like my grandmother's or the other women's. Safta despaired of ever getting you to settle down. And now that you have, I sometimes wonder if . . . if you ever regret it. Do you long for more than this life we have? Tell me the truth, Yael."

"I didn't feel 'free' at the time, I felt like I was always running and never getting anywhere. Like I was missing out on something, so I had to keep looking for it. My life felt so uncertain after my mother died that it was like being tossed around in the back of a runaway cart. I couldn't find anything solid to hang on to. I tried to control my future because I didn't know God or trust that He had me in His care." She reached to take his hand. "And now I've finally found something solid."

"Are you sure you don't long for an adventure or two?" He was typical Zaki—so serious as he asked the question.

Yael smiled. "Marriage has been an adventure, don't you think? And raising children certainly has been!"

"But you never seemed to want this life, and now . . . here you are."

Yael studied him for a moment in the dim moonlight, wishing she knew why he was asking her these things. Was he thinking about Rafi after all this time? "I love you, Zaki. I know you must wonder if I still think about Rafi." She saw his surprise and added, "I can read your mind, you know."

"I thought you gave up your Babylonian sorcery." At last he smiled.

"I don't need to be a sorceress. I know you very well. You always think too much, worry too much. When good things happen you always question them, waiting for something bad to happen to balance them out. Your grandfather is the same way. You have such a brilliant mind that you over-analyze everything. Just enjoy the moment, Zaki, enjoy this day. Isn't that what the Almighty One tells us to do?"

"Yes, but you're my wife. I need to be certain that you're happy."

She gazed down at their son, running her fingers over his soft, downy head, then back at her husband. "You want to know why I was so restless and wild, exploring the tombs and getting mixed up with all that Babylonian stuff? I think I was testing the limits, wanting to be stopped. Because we're not free when there are no boundaries—we're in great danger. I see that so clearly with our children. If I allowed Sarah and Abigail to run wild without limits, they would end up getting hurt. But once I learned what the Almighty One was really like and why He sets boundaries, I saw that His way is the best way to live. Without Him, we'd be just like the murderous Samaritans." She waited for Zaki to speak, and when he didn't she said, "Now tell me what's really prompting all these questions."

He looked up at her, tears shining in his eyes. "I'm just so incredibly happy today, and I want you to be as happy as I am."

"But today was an exceptional day, Zaki. Do *you* ever feel trapped?"

"Just the opposite. I feel like my life is on the brink of breaking through into something huge . . . something enormous. I've been holding my breath, expecting a miracle or a sign, and I think our son is that sign. Especially because he was born today, at the beginning of my new ministry."

Yael wasn't sure she followed him, but his words flowed out faster than he could stop them. He needed both hands to speak. "I understand why Saba wanted my father and uncle to come with us to Jerusalem. Why he was so happy when I decided to come. The God of the universe condescends to have His dwelling place here, in the temple we're supposed to be building. And it's my calling—our son's calling—to serve as His priests. Every time I see that empty foundation where the temple should be

I want to stand up and shout at everyone to wake up! It's time to do what God told us to do!"

"Shh! Zaki! You really will wake everyone up."

"But do you understand what I'm trying to say? I don't think I'm saying it very well."

"Yes, I understand. You've found joy because you're doing God's work. And I'm trying to tell you that I've found joy, too. Because if we obey God, then our lives do have meaning, even if all He asks us to do is cook lentils and raise children."

He looked down at their son. "Today we brought another priest into the world," he said, holding the baby's tiny hand. "He's another star in the sky that our father Abraham saw."

Yael reached up to stroke his cheek. "I love you, Zaki. I never dreamed I could be this happy. And every day I thank God that you're my husband and not Rafi."

CHAPTER 38

Zechariah held his grandfather's arm, steadying him as they made their way to the priests' room to change into their white linen robes. Drenched with sweat from the relentless heat, Zechariah didn't know how they would manage to peel off their damp street clothing. But Prince Zerubbabel and the high priest had asked every able-bodied priest to minister at the evening sacrifice and to pray. Saba would sing with the Levite musicians.

Since Zechariah's ordination four months ago, the drought had continued its devastation. Khamsin winds had blown in from the desert, creating dust storms of gritty sand and scorching hot air. No hope remained for their withered crops, but the leaders had asked the nation to pray for God's mercy, for an end to the wind and the drought and the famine.

Zechariah bent to untie his sandals. The priests ministered with bare feet according to God's instructions, but today he worried that the overheated cobblestones would burn their feet. "This heat, these winds—they're the Almighty One's judgment, aren't they?" he asked his grandfather.

"The Torah says that drought and famine are curses for our disobedience."

"And we're disobeying by not completing the temple. Why can't our leaders see that?" Iddo didn't reply as he struggled to pull the white robe over his head. Zechariah helped him with it, then tied his red sash for him. "I wish I could do something to wake everyone up," he continued, "but I don't know what to do. You told me to wait until I finished my training as a priest. Will I have to keep waiting until I work my way up through the ranks and earn the respect of the other priests and leaders? Why can't they see that we're disobeying Him by not completing His temple?"

Saba picked up a linen towel and wiped his face and brow before fastening on his turban. "You need to pray the way you did as a boy and ask God to give you the answer. Ask Him to tell you what you should do."

Zechariah finished dressing and helped his grandfather walk to the platform where the musicians would stand. Thankfully, someone had laid down a layer of straw to protect their feet from the burning pavement. "I'll meet you here after the service ends, Saba." He crossed to where the other priests stood, his chest tight with anger as he glimpsed the gaping, weed-filled hole beyond the altar where the temple should be. The elderly Prince Sheshbazzar had died without completing his task. His nephew Zerubbabel had taken his place as governor. A new emperor sat on the Persian throne, a new provincial governor ruled the Trans-Euphrates Province in Samaria. Why couldn't Zechariah's fellow Jews see that the time had come to do the impossible, to trust God and start building?

While he waited, a verse of Scripture sprang to mind, as clearly as if he'd read it from a scroll or watched it happen:

> *The seed will grow well, the vine will yield its fruit, the ground will produce its crops, and the heavens will drop their dew. I will give these things as an inheritance to the remnant of this people.*

As you have been an object of cursing among the nations, O Judah and Israel, so will I save you, and you will be a blessing. Do not be afraid, but let your hands be strong.

What a beautiful promise. But which prophet had spoken those words? He would search for it after the sacrifice and share it with the others—if he could find it. There had been so many other promises and warnings that he'd longed to share but he hadn't been able to locate the verses.

The high priest performed the sacrifice himself, leading the congregation in prayer, asking God to renew His favor and blessing on His people. The Levite choir sang, "*Restore us again, O God our Savior, and put away your displeasure toward us. . . . Show us your unfailing love, O Lord, and grant us your salvation.*"

Zechariah bowed his head and did what his grandfather advised, asking the Almighty One to speak to him the way He had in Babylon. *Show me what to do, Lord.* Were he and Saba the only ones who believed that they must rebuild?

By the time the service ended, the sky blazed with a crimson sunset. The motionless air radiated with heat, as fiery hot as the altar coals. The congregation would return home to their sweltering houses and bare storerooms and meager dinners. But before Zechariah or any of the other priests had a chance to move from their places, a man stepped forward from the crowd. Nothing in his appearance made him stand out. Middle-aged, no taller than the other men in the crowd, wearing simple robes, he could be anyone's brother or father or uncle.

"Listen!" the man shouted. "Listen, Zerubbabel and Jeshua. The Lord Almighty has something to say." The courtyard went so still that Zechariah could hear the doves cooing in the treetops. The man took another step forward. "Why do you keep saying that the time hasn't come for the Lord's house to be built? Is it time for you to be living in your paneled houses, while His house remains a ruin?"

Zechariah wondered if the heat had made him hallucinate. This stranger spoke the words of his own heart. He might look like an ordinary man, but his words carried power and authority. "Now this is what the Lord Almighty says," the man continued. "'Give careful thought to your ways. You've planted much, but have harvested little. You eat, but you never have your fill. You put on clothes in the winter, but you're never warm. You earn wages but you may as well put them in a purse full of holes.'"

The awareness of God's holy presence slowly filled Zechariah, just as it had when he was a boy. But instead of warmth this time, it seemed as though a rain cloud had burst open, pouring life-giving water over him, water that could turn the dry riverbeds into rushing streams. Zechariah glanced around and saw that the others seemed just as spellbound by the force of the man's words. He was more than a man—he was a prophet! Was this what it was like to hear Isaiah or Jeremiah preach? Zechariah scarcely dared to breathe as the prophet continued to speak for the Holy One.

"'Give careful thought to your ways. Go up into the mountains and bring down timber and build my house, so that I may take pleasure in it and be honored,' says the Lord. 'You expected much, but see? It turned out to be little. What you brought home, I blew away. Why?' declares the Lord Almighty. 'Because of my house which remains a ruin, while each of you is busy with his own house. Therefore, because of you the heavens have withheld their dew and the earth its crops. I called for drought on the fields and the mountains, on the grain, the new wine, the oil and whatever the ground produces, on men and cattle, and on the labor of your hands,' says the Lord."

As abruptly as he had appeared, the man turned to leave. The awareness of God's presence vanished with his final words. Zechariah raced across the searing courtyard, the first of the priests to move, calling to the man to wait. He caught up with him before he disappeared into the crowd. "Please, we want to hear more. Come back and speak with us and with our leaders." He took the man's arm and led him to Prince Zerubbabel's platform. The prophet's entire body trembled as he crossed the pavement, but Zechariah didn't think it was from fear. The man's prophecy clearly had exhausted him, as if he'd expended a day's worth of effort in the past few moments.

The other priests gathered around the prophet, as well. Zechariah wondered if they were as deeply moved by his words as he was, or if they were angry at his rebuke, upset that their ceremony had been disrupted. "What's your name?" Prince Zerubbabel asked the man.

"Haggai."

"You spoke God's word to us today, Haggai."

"Yes, my lord. He told me to say, 'I am with you,' declares the Lord."

Zechariah felt a shiver go through him. *I am*—the name God used when He spoke with Moses.

"You are a prophet," Jeshua said. But it didn't seem to be a question. Haggai clearly was, the first prophet anointed by God since the exile. God was with them once again, speaking to them. Zechariah could no longer keep quiet.

"We need to do what the Holy One said! Our fathers didn't listen to the prophets, but we need to listen to Haggai! The Holy One has been waiting for us to get desperate enough to seek Him—and today we finally did. He answered through Haggai, His messenger." Zechariah was the newest priest to be ordained, yet he was shouting at the others, shouting at the prince! No one silenced him.

"You say that God wants us to resume building the temple?" Zerubbabel asked.

"Yes," Haggai replied. "You don't need the Persian king's

sanction. You have the Almighty One's sanction. *'I am with you.'* That's what He's telling us."

"But what if it brings renewed attacks by our enemies?" one of the priests asked.

"We can't give in to fear!" Zechariah replied. He wanted to say more, but everyone began talking and arguing at once. Zerubbabel held up his hands for silence.

"Listen," he said. "I'm allowed to govern Judah and Jerusalem, but I'm under Persian authority. All building projects require their approval. If we resume building without it, they could interpret our actions as a rebellion. I don't want to risk another invasion and exile."

"If we don't obey, the drought will continue," Haggai said. "We'll slowly starve to death. Shall we submit to Persian authority or to God's?"

Once again, Zechariah couldn't resist speaking. "The governor of Samaria who made us halt the construction is dead. So is the emperor who issued the order. God is telling us to rebuild, and He's promising to be with us. What more do we need? Let our enemies try to stop us! 'It's not by might nor by power, but by my Spirit,' says the Lord Almighty."

"I need time to think about this," Zerubbabel said. He turned to leave, obviously wishing to postpone the decision, but Zechariah couldn't let that happen.

"Wait! Do you believe the Holy One has spoken through Haggai today, my lord?" He didn't know where his sudden boldness came from, but he couldn't keep quiet. "We came together here to pray about the drought—so do you believe this was God's answer to us or not, my lord?"

It took the prince a long time to reply but he finally said, "Yes. The Holy One spoke through Haggai today. . . . And I admit that I'm afraid to disobey Him—but I'm also afraid of the consequences if I do obey Him."

"Why not trust God—who brought us out of captivity in Babylon by His mighty hand—and begin building?" Haggai asked. "Yes, our enemies will send a report to the emperor, telling him what we're doing. But let them wait for the slow movements of justice this time. Meanwhile, we'll keep building—and we won't let our enemies stop us again."

"Put me in charge of it," Iddo said. "I've been waiting for this day for nearly twenty years."

Zechariah wasn't surprised when several of the other priests began to argue against the idea, joined by many of the laymen who had come to Jerusalem to pray for the drought. But most of the people seemed to be siding with him and with Haggai, urging the prince to trust the Almighty One. The arguments grew louder and angrier until at last the prince held up his hands for silence once again.

"The decision is mine alone to make, and I'll bear the responsibility for it. Your arguments for and against won't sway me. I need to discern the word of the Lord for myself." He paused, and Zechariah sent up a silent prayer as he waited in suspense. "Today I believe that I have heard from Him," the prince finally said. "It's time to rebuild the temple."

The gathered men were silent for a long moment as if trying to comprehend the importance of what the prince had just said. Zechariah didn't wait for anyone else's response. He sank down on his knees on the scorching pavement and praised God.

Iddo presided over the first meeting to discuss rebuilding the temple. He assigned workers to assess construction needs, delegated specific tasks to engineers and laborers. And the next day, the terrible khamsin winds died away.

Restless to begin, he made it his goal to have constuction under way before the Feast of Tabernacles in less than a month.

But he knew that the real labor couldn't begin until new materials arrived and new timbers were brought up from the forests. They had to repair the crane after letting it sit idle for so many years, and hundreds of building stones had to be cut and shaped. Iddo kept a record of costs and expenditures and noted in his log that work on the house of the Lord began on the twenty-fourth day of the sixth month. On that day he went to the yeshiva and recruited all of the Torah students to pull weeds and chop away the growth that had accumulated around the temple's foundation. Iddo led the work himself.

"We're not going to hire laborers to do this," he told the young men and boys, "because we need to do it ourselves as penance for allowing the work to stop and these weeds to grow so huge. Sin is like these weeds, with roots that go down very deep and require great effort to uproot. And it will require renewed diligence on our part to keep the weeds of unbelief and apathy from taking over our lives again the way these have. And vigilance! We may think we've eliminated sin, but if even a very small seed of it remains, it quickly takes over our lives."

As Iddo and his students paused for lunch a few hours later, the first rain clouds appeared on the western horizon, rising from the Mediterrean Sea. The students pointed to them, whispering with excitement. The clouds continued to thicken and soon concealed the sun, darkening the sky above Jerusalem. But the weeding and Iddo's Torah lessons continued. "The rain never came last year, remember?" he asked. "Just a few spitting drops from clouds that had no substance, no life-giving water. That's what we must seem like to the Holy One. We've been all talk and hot air when it comes to our faith and to rebuilding His temple, but with no life-producing results."

They managed to clear away a good portion of the undergrowth by the time the first raindrops began to fall. Neither Iddo nor his students stopped working. The rain felt refreshing after the long, hot summer. "Why does the Holy One need this temple?" Iddo asked the group. "What does Scripture tell us?"

He listened with satisfaction to the lively buzz of voices as his students discussed the question for a while, offering Scripture verses that supported their arguments. One of the brightest boys replied that the Almighty One didn't need it, quoting from King Solomon's prayer during the dedication for the first temple: "'The heavens, even the highest heavens, cannot contain you. How much less this temple I have built!'"

Another student shouted out, "It says in the psalms to 'Exalt the Lord our God and worship at his footstool; he is holy.'"

"So, if the Almighty One's temple is in the heavens and if earth is His footstool," Iddo challenged, "why does He need us to rebuild the temple?"

The discussion continued, the students' voices loud at times as they argued and quoted Scripture. At last, one of the young men summarized their collective conclusion: "Because we're the ones who need it, not Him. It's a place where our sins can be forgiven so we can approach the Holy One. A place where we can meet with Him and recover the fellowship we lost in Eden."

"It's a privilege and a blessing to have the Holy One dwelling among us," another added. "He promised Abraham that He would be with him and his descendants always."

"Very good. But do we really want the Holy One to be with us?" Iddo asked. "Do we want Him badly enough to work with all our strength in spite of persecution or threats from our enemies? Is our longing for Him so great that we're willing to defy an emperor's decree?"

Every young man and boy agreed that obeying God at all costs was more important than giving in to fear. The rain was falling harder now, but no one wanted to stop the discussion or the work. If the winter rains truly had begun, Iddo was determined to build throughout the entire rainy season.

"Now comes the hardest question," he told his students. "This temple was destroyed because our ancestors stopped obeying God's Law. They became just like the Gentiles—promiscuous, filled with hatred and greed, worshiping false gods. Are we willing to live in such a way that the Holy One will remain with us this time? Will we make sure He won't turn His back on us in wrath again? Each one of you needs to answer that question in his heart and then decide if you want to come back and work here again tomorrow—and the next day, and the next. Will you come back when our enemies attack us and try to discourage us?" The rain poured down now. Everyone was getting soaked. But so was the land. They continued working until time for the evening sacrifice, singing psalms of praise as they did.

Dinah reprimanded Iddo when he returned home that evening. "You'll make yourself ill! You're too old to be standing outside in the rain and getting soaked."

"It isn't rain, Dinah, it's God's blessings. We obeyed Him, and He heard our prayers."

"But look at you! You're drenched to the skin."

"And it feels glorious!" Iddo went to bed that night knowing that if he was the only man who showed up tomorrow, he would pull weeds and prepare to build all by himself.

He awoke the next morning to the sound of rain pattering on the roof. In spite of the weather, an enormous crowd assembled for the morning sacrifice, not caring that they were getting wet. The clouds still poured when the sacrifice ended and Iddo walked back to the temple's foundation to resume clearing weeds. He stared in astonishment. Not only his yeshiva students, but young men of all ages filled the site. And they already had begun to work, filling baskets with weeds that pulled easily from the rain-softened earth.

Chapter 39

On the first day of the seventh month, Zechariah stood in the rain on a special platform and blew the silver trumpet to announce the Feast of Trumpets for the first time in his life. As the sound echoed off the distant mountains, the Holy One's presence filled him, just as it had back in Babylon. He closed his eyes and thanked God for the rain and for speaking through His prophet, Haggai. Work on the temple had resumed. The first course of cut stones would soon be ready to place on the foundation.

Zechariah had waited all these silent years, wondering why God wouldn't speak to him again, and now he understood. The Holy One hadn't been silent—He simply hadn't changed His mind. He had told Zechariah to leave Babylon and rebuild His temple, and those instructions hadn't changed. Today Zechariah sounded the trumpet with all his might, praying that it would awaken God's people from their spiritual slumber, praying that they would believe He was the God of the impossible.

On the twenty-second day of Tishri, the last day of the Feast of Ingathering, Zechariah stood on the temple mount again for the sacred assembly. The festival celebrated a harvest that had never come, and instead of slaying multiple sacrifices, the high priest offered a single male goat for a sin offering. Yet Zechariah and the others praised the Almighty One, joining with the Levite choir and musical instruments in singing, "*Give thanks to the Lord, for he is good. His love endures forever.*"

Zechariah hated for the service to end, but when it finally did and the last strains of music died away, Haggai stepped forward from the crowd once again. Zechariah's heart sped up. The milling worshipers who had been preparing to leave fell silent.

"Who of you is left who saw God's house in its former glory?" Haggai asked, gesturing to the newly cleared foundation beyond the altar. "How does it look to you now? Doesn't it seem like nothing to you? 'But now be strong, O Zerubbabel,' declares the Lord. 'Be strong, Jeshua son of Jehozadak, the high priest. Be strong, all you people of the land,' declares the Lord, 'and work. For I am with you,' declares the Lord Almighty. 'This is what I covenanted with you when you came out of Egypt. And my Spirit remains among you. Do not fear.'"

Zechariah saw determination and renewed hope in the faces of the priests and the people in the courtyards. Haggai gazed solemnly at the temple's foundation as if seeing into the future as he continued to speak. "This is what the Lord Almighty says: 'In a little while I will once more shake the heavens and the earth, the sea and the dry land. I will shake all nations, and the desired of all nations will come. I will fill this house with glory,' says the Lord Almighty. 'The silver is mine and the gold is mine,' declares the Lord Almighty. 'The glory of this present house will be greater than the glory of the former house. And in this place I will grant peace.'"

It was what Zechariah hoped for, longed for. Not only would God's presence return, but the Messiah would come to this temple. And unlike the kingdoms of the world that God was about to shake from their places, His kingdom would never end.

Haggai turned to walk back into the crowd, and once again

Zechariah chased after him. "Haggai, wait! May I speak with you, my lord?" The prophet looked exhausted as he shivered in the cold, autumn rain. "Let's go someplace dry," Zechariah said. "The yeshiva is vacant today because of the holiday. We can go there and talk. Will you give me a few minutes to change out of my robes and meet you there?" Haggai agreed and a short time later they sat together at one of the yeshiva's study tables.

"I know you're a prophet because your words carry the anointing of God," Zechariah said. "It isn't you we hear speaking, but the Almighty One. Did you notice that we've obeyed God's word and resumed the construction?"

"Yes, I did notice. Clearly, God has stirred men's hearts."

"But even before you spoke that first time, I felt something . . . unusual . . . going on in my life. When I was a boy back in Babylon, I once felt the Holy One's presence in a very dramatic and powerful way. The experience made me decide to come here and help rebuild the temple so I could worship in His presence again and again. I've been searching for Him all my life, and ever since I discovered that I could know Him through the Scriptures, I've been reading and studying them with renewed diligence. Whenever I open the pages to read, He is there. Not quite in the way I experienced Him as a boy, but I hear Him speaking to me, teaching me, just the same."

Zechariah paused, afraid to ask if he was making sense. But Haggai nodded and said, "I understand. Go on."

"And now, even when I'm not reading but ministering as a priest—especially then—I hear His voice clearly and forcefully. It's like I'm hearing Scripture verses that I've memorized . . . 'Thus saith the Lord' . . . But the words I hear aren't found anywhere. I've searched all the prophets and the writings." Zechariah gestured to the Aron Ha Kodesh, where the Torah and the other sacred scrolls were kept. "I keep looking for the words I've heard to no avail. I'm beginning to think that maybe

I've studied too much and I'm losing my mind. But along with the words in my head I felt an urgency to start rebuilding the temple, even before you spoke to us. An urgency to tell the others that we need to return to God. To seek Him with all our heart and soul and mind."

"You're hearing the same message from God that I'm hearing."

"I know! When you spoke that first time I wanted to shout along with you. We should be dissatisfied with the stale, routine way we've been worshiping and seek His presence. We should build the temple and build a relationship with Him that's genuine and real."

"Yes. Exactly." Haggai listened intently, leaning toward him. His dark eyes seemed to read Zechariah's heart. "Go on."

"I thought this . . . this craziness I've been experiencing would end once we started building, once the others decided to listen to you and obey God. But if anything, it's becoming more intense. The words surge through my mind like . . . like a pot boiling over on the hearth. I can hardly stop them from coming, let alone ignore them. And God's presence and warmth always come with them, the same way I experienced Him as a child. And so I wanted to ask if . . . if you can help me figure out what's going on. Am I losing my mind?"

"No, Zechariah. Far from it! From what you've described, I believe the Holy One wants to speak through you the same way He speaks through me. He's calling you to be His prophet."

"His . . . His *prophet*?" Zechariah shook his head, unable to grasp it. "That's impossible. I'm not old enough or mature enough . . . Certainly not righteous enough!"

"None of that matters. You said yourself that you've learned to know God and to understand what He wants from us. Now you need to open your mouth and allow His words to flow through you."

"Is . . . is what I described . . . is that what happens to you?"

"Not exactly, but it's similar enough."

Zechariah hesitated, wanting to pepper Haggai with questions, yet he was afraid of exposing his own shallow faith. "May I ask . . . how did you know it was the right time to come forward? Where did you get the courage to speak?"

"You're afraid that people will ridicule you," Haggai said.

"No, I'm not afraid of ridicule, exactly. . . . My concern is that everyone knows me. They've watched me grow from a boy of twelve into a man, watched me become a priest, watched me make mistakes. Many of these men are the rabbis who taught me the Torah. Prince Zerubbabel and the high priest are both older than I am, and have far more wisdom and maturity and experience. How dare I come along, saying outrageous things, daring to speak for God? You came as a stranger to nearly all of these men. Your anonymity gave you a measure of credibility. They listened to you."

"It's the Spirit of the Almighty One speaking through me that gives me credibility. Speak His words, Zechariah. People may laugh, they may refuse to listen, but every prophet of God has faced those reactions."

Zechariah had read the stories of Jeremiah and Isaiah and Ezekiel. He knew Haggai was right.

"But if God wants to speak through you," Haggai continued, "how can you keep silent? Trust His Spirit. Be faithful to the message He puts in your heart and on your lips. After that, every man who hears you is accountable to God for heeding His word or for ignoring it. If they judge the message by the messenger, that's to their shame, not yours."

"May I share with you what I hear God saying? To confirm that I've truly heard?"

"Certainly."

Zechariah inhaled. "I believe the Almighty One is saying,

'Return to me!' We've slowly drifted away from Him and become distracted by things in our lives that just aren't important. We've allowed fear of our enemies and our own lack of faith to distance us from Him. We've been enticed away from Him by the temptations of the surrounding nations, first in Babylon and now here. God says 'Return to me.' He's waiting to bless us when we do."

A slow smile spread across Haggai's face. "Yes. You've heard from God. I see His Spirit in you. We'll accomplish His work together, my friend. The Almighty One now has two witnesses to speak for Him." He stood and embraced Zechariah as he prepared to leave.

"Wait . . . I have one more question. How will I know when it's time to speak?"

"You'll know. The Holy One will tell you."

Haggai's words both encouraged Zechariah and terrified him at the same time. Was it truly possible that he, Zechariah son of Berekiah, son of Iddo, was called to be God's prophet? It seemed impossible, like counting the stars. He told no one about his conversation with Haggai—not his grandfather, not even his wife. But he continued to pray, asking for God's will, offering himself as His servant.

Work on the temple site resumed after the feast, and Zechariah met his grandfather there at the end of each day so they could walk home together. The noisy site bustled with activity, and he could see the rapid progress they'd made, the piles of stones that had been cut and shaped, the newly repaired crane ready to lift them into place, the support timbers sized and waiting. Today, like many days, Zechariah had difficulty getting Saba to quit and come home. As they descended the stairs from the temple mount, Saba asked him, "Will you come with me to the house of assembly tomorrow morning? Jeshua and Zerubbabel called for a meeting after the morning sacrifice, and

I'm dreading it. I'm too old to waste my remaining years and dwindling strength arguing with dolts."

Zechariah couldn't suppress a smile. "Which dolts is the high priest meeting with?"

"Jeshua described them as 'concerned citizens' from several Jewish villages. He suspects that their concern is that we've angered the Samaritans by rebuilding."

"I'll be happy to come," Zechariah replied, and he felt a strange stirring rustle through him, the same restless anticipation he'd felt on the night before his ordination and on the morning that he'd sounded the silver trumpet for the first time. The odd feeling continued to distract him after he reached home and washed his hands and gathered with the others to eat. Yael called his name three times before he heard her.

"What's the matter with you, Zaki?" she asked. "You're a million miles away."

The people he loved sat gathered around him—his grandparents, his wife and children, young Hodaya—and he didn't know what to say to them. They had readily accepted Haggai as God's prophet, believing that he spoke the Almighty One's words. But what would they think if he told them he might be called to be a prophet, too? He could scarcely believe it himself—why should they?

"Nothing's wrong," he finally said. "I just have too many things on my mind." He smiled and joined the conversation. But he awoke before dawn the next morning and went out to sit alone in the courtyard to pray. He felt the same unease as when the weather was about to change and a thunderstorm was about to rumble through. He ate breakfast without tasting a bite of it, kissed his wife and children, and left with his grandfather.

The visiting men who gathered to meet in the house of assembly with the prince and the high priest later that morning revealed their concern in their restlessness and angry voices.

Their spokesman, a portly man named Adin from the village of Lod, began without preamble. "Why weren't all the family heads and local leaders consulted before the rebuilding began? You've put all of us in danger—our wives, our children. The construction must stop immediately until we receive proper authorization from the Persian emperor."

"Were any of you here when we sought the Holy One in prayer for the drought?" Prince Zerubbabel asked. "Or for the Feast of Ingathering? Did you hear God's prophet, Haggai, speak?"

"No, but we heard reports about him. Even if this man is a prophet, your decision to immediately resume building was foolhardy and premature. Samaritan settlements surround all of our villages," he said, gesturing to the other men. "We've lived in peace with them these past few years because you obeyed the emperor's edict and stopped building. But now that word of your violation has spread, we're back to living on a knife's edge!"

Iddo slowly stood to address the men, and Zechariah could see his barely controlled fury. "Why did you gentlemen return to this land with your families?" he asked.

"Because the land belongs to us," Adin said. "The Almighty One gave it to our forefathers."

"Were you afraid of the Samaritans when we first arrived and began to build?"

"Not at first. We had permission from King Cyrus to be here. Then you foolishly refused the Samaritans' offer to help and unleashed a firestorm of trouble."

"Did the Samaritans also cause the drought and the famine we've been experiencing?" Iddo asked.

"Of course not!"

"Then why do you suppose we've been suffering? Why have our crops and our harvests failed?"

"I don't know! Why are you asking these foolish questions? Are you going to listen to our concerns or aren't you?"

"I'm asking," Iddo said, "because I'm trying to determine what the Holy One's promises mean to you and what part you believe He plays in all of this. Did you return to the land because you wanted to walk with God the way our father Abraham did or because you were tired of living in Babylon? Because you thought you'd have a comfortable life here?"

His words were met by a storm of angry shouts and protests from the other men. When Jeshua finally calmed them down, Iddo continued. "I was an eyewitness to God's wrath and the destruction of Jerusalem. And also an eyewitness to His miracle that allowed us to return. If the Almighty One brought us here, and if we walk in obedience to Him, then He promises to give us victory over our enemies and send rain in due season. But for the past few years we've wanted peace with our enemies more than we've wanted God."

"How dare you!"

Iddo ignored Adin's outrage. "God spoke through His prophet Haggai and told us it was time to rebuild. We obeyed, and the rain we desperately needed began to fall. Was that a coincidence?"

"I have no idea, but—"

"Those of us who heard Haggai believe he spoke a message from the Almighty One, and so we obeyed Him. Were we wrong to do that? What would you have done?"

"Of course we would obey if we heard God speaking to us, but we haven't heard Him and—"

Without thinking, Zechariah shot from his seat, knocking the chair backward with a crash. "Then hear the word of the Lord Almighty!" It was his voice, and yet it wasn't. He couldn't have stopped the words from coming any more than he could have stopped a thunderstorm. "The Lord was very angry with our forefathers. He told me to tell you and all the people, 'Return to me,' declares the Lord Almighty, 'and I will return to you,' says the Lord Almighty. 'Don't be like your forefathers who heard the prophets proclaim: "Turn from your evil ways and your evil practices," but they wouldn't listen or pay attention to me,' declares the Lord. 'Where are your forefathers now? And the prophets, do they live forever? But didn't everything my prophets warned about overtake your forefathers? Then they repented and said, "The Lord Almighty has done to us what our ways and practices deserve, just as he determined to do."'"

Zechariah paused to catch his breath and saw a stunned look on everyone's face. Everyone except his grandfather. Saba's eyes were closed, his head bowed, his face wet with tears. Zechariah drew another breath. "'Don't be like your forefathers,' declares the Lord Almighty. 'Return to me, and I will return to you!' says the Lord Almighty."

He groped behind him for his chair, turned it upright again, and sank onto it, exhausted. Minutes passed, but no one stirred or spoke. Then the prince slowly rose to his feet. "We've heard the word of the Lord from *two* of His prophets. I believe that's all that needs to be said, gentlemen."

CHAPTER 40

Zechariah shivered on a cold winter morning as he stood beside his grandfather to inspect the progress on the temple. "You left for work awfully early this morning, Saba. The sun wasn't up and neither was anyone else."

"I wanted to get a head start on the work before the morning sacrifice. Today we'll finish laying the first course of stones. The work will go faster as we become surer of ourselves, and as more people join us. Mattaniah finished planting his winter crops last week and has been an enormous help to us."

"It looks amazing, Saba. It's hard to believe you started building only three months ago." He took his grandfather's arm and gestured toward the altar, where the morning sacrifice was about to begin. "I'm not on duty as a priest today. I thought we could watch it together." They walked across the mount and found a place to stand in the men's court. Zechariah was aware of the shy whispers and turned heads as he passed.

He had spoken his first prophecy more than a month ago, and had worried at first that the older men he knew and respected wouldn't take him seriously. But as the news spread throughout the community that the Holy One had anointed Zechariah son of Berekiah, son of Iddo to be His prophet, the opposite had been true. The other men looked at him with respect and even deference. Unaccustomed to such treatment, he found their reaction unsettling.

"I feel a growing distance between the other priests and me," he told Saba as they waited. "As if they're afraid of me or something."

"They're in awe of you."

"They should be in awe of the Almighty One, not me."

"But He has made you His spokesman. They recognize that. Our forefathers refused to listen to the prophets that He sent us, remember? And they were punished for it. These men don't want to make the same mistake."

"Even Yael seems . . . well, shy with me. So does Safta. And you've acted a little differently around me, too."

"We're all amazed by you, Zechariah. You became a man of God when we weren't looking. And a man of His Word. That's why He chose you. We were all too close to you to notice the gradual change in you, but we recognize it now, and we're amazed."

As the priests performed the morning sacrifice, Zechariah looked around the courtyard and noticed Haggai standing with the other men. He watched the prophet closely, and his heart surged with anticipation when the service ended and Haggai stepped forward to speak. Everyone quieted to listen.

"This is what the Lord Almighty says: 'Now give careful thought to this and consider how things were before you began rebuilding the Lord's temple. When you looked for a heap of twenty measures there were only ten. When you went to your wine vat to draw fifty measures, there were only twenty. I struck all the work of your hands with blight, mildew and hail,' declares the Lord, 'yet you did not turn to me. But, from this day on, from this twenty-fourth day of the ninth month, give careful thought to the day when the foundation of the Lord's temple was laid.

Give careful thought: Is there yet any seed left in the barn? Until now, the vine and the fig tree, the pomegranate and the olive tree have not borne fruit. But from this day on I will bless you.'"

"That was a warning to us not to quit again," Saba whispered. "He must have heard about our meeting with Adin and the other village leaders."

"Oh, I'm certain he has."

Once again, the worshipers turned to leave the temple mount and begin the day's work. But a procession of men ascending the stairs to the mount hindered their progress, forcing everyone to move aside to allow them to pass. The delegation of government officials carried the standards of the Persian emperor and were escorted by a small cadre of Persian soldiers. They approached the governor's platform where Zerubbabel had been preparing to leave. Zechariah and his grandfather followed them, arriving in time to hear the regal-looking man in a richly embroidered robe being introduced as Governor Tattenai of the Trans-Euphrates Province, along with Shethar-Bozenai and their associates.

"We knew opposition was coming the moment we ordered supplies and timber," Saba said. "The new governor was certain to hear about it—and here he is."

"Nothing is done in secret," Zechariah said. "The question is, will Prince Zerubbabel stand strong, considering all that he and his family could lose? Will he believe the Almighty One's promise that his ancestor, King David, will always have an heir on the throne?"

"The eye of our God is watching over us," Saba whispered.

Tattenai stepped forward, addressing Zerubbabel. "Are you the official in charge?"

"Yes, I'm Zerubbabel, Governor of Judea and Jerusalem."

"I was recently made aware that a large-scale construction project was taking place here. Since I hadn't been informed of any building permits being issued, I decided to come and see for myself." Tattenai gestured to the sprawling site, the piles of materials. "This is no ordinary structure you're building."

"That's right. We're rebuilding the temple that King Solomon built here many years ago. A temple to the one true God, whom we serve."

"I see. Well, on behalf of Emperor Darius, I demand to know who authorized you to rebuild this temple and restore this structure?"

"The God of heaven and earth did. We're His servants."

"*God* did?" Tattenai asked, his tone scornful. The two men stood face-to-face, as if neither was willing to give an inch or acknowledge the other's superiority. They reminded Zechariah of two dogs circling each other, hackles raised, waiting for the other to either pounce or yield in submission.

"Our fathers angered the God of heaven," Prince Zerubbabel continued, "and so He handed them over to King Nebuchadnezzar of Babylon, who destroyed this temple and deported our people. However, King Cyrus issued a decree in the first year of his reign permitting us to rebuild this house of God. He even gave us the gold and silver treasures that Nebuchadnezzar had taken from God's temple and entrusted them to my predecessor, Sheshbazzar. Cyrus appointed him governor, and told him to return the articles to Jerusalem and rebuild the temple on its site. So Sheshbazzar obeyed and laid the foundations of the house of God. From that day to the present it has been under construction but isn't yet finished."

"King Cyrus is dead. Darius is king now."

"So we've heard."

"You need authorization from King Darius." When the prince didn't reply, Tattenai said, "I'll need the names of all the men who are constructing this building."

"My name is Zerubbabel. Shall I spell it for your secretary?"

"And my name is Iddo." Zechariah's grandfather stepped

forward. "I'm overseeing construction and recording the costs and expenditures."

"I'm Jeshua, son of Jehozadak, high priest of the Almighty One." More and more men stepped forward, priests and laborers alike, telling the Samaritan secretary their names. Others too far back in the crowd to approach began shouting out their names, as well.

Tattenai held up his hands, clearly frustrated. "Wait. Don't all talk at once. My secretary can't record all these names."

"He's going to need many hours and dozens of scrolls to record all of our names," Zerubbabel said. "More than forty-two thousand of us returned to our land from Babylon, and we're building this temple together, as one man."

Tanttenai gestured to his secretary to stop. He locked gazes with Zerubbabel, his forehead creased with a frown. "My men will inspect the project now, as part of my report."

"They will have to do it from a distance," Jeshua said. "This is a holy site."

Zechariah saw Tattenai's chest heave with anger. He seemed reluctant to object, reluctant to tread on holy ground. "I'll be sending a report to King Darius immediately," he finally said. "You'll receive a copy of it, as well, Governor Zerubbabel. In the meantime, all construction must halt until you receive official authorization."

Zerubbabel shook his head. "With all due respect, Governor Tattenai, we intend to continue working. We already have authorization from King Cyrus and from our God. We must obey Him."

"Well done," Iddo whispered as Tattenai stalked away with his retinue.

"I had no idea our prince was so courageous," Zechariah said. "He just took an enormous risk."

"I know. If his actions are interpreted as a rebellion against the Persian emperor, he and his family will be hauled back to Persia in chains and executed as traitors."

"And so will you, Saba . . . And yet you don't seem at all afraid," he added with a grin.

"The eye of our God is watching over us."

The show was over, and the people prepared to leave for a second time. But the prophet Haggai surprised everyone when he stepped forward once again. "The Lord Almighty spoke to me again and said, 'Tell Zerubbabel governor of Judah that I will shake the heavens and the earth. I will overturn royal thrones and shatter the power of the foreign kingdoms. I will overthrow chariots and their drivers; horses and their riders will fall, each by the sword of his brother.' And because of your courage and your willingness to obey God, the Lord Almighty declares, 'I will take you, my servant Zerubbabel, son of Shealtiel, and I will make you like my signet ring, for I have chosen you,' declares the Lord Almighty."

"Praise God," Zechariah whispered. "The Almighty One has reversed His curse!"

"Is that what Haggai's prophecy means?" Iddo asked.

"Yes. I've been reading the prophecies of Jeremiah, and the Holy One told our last king, Jehoiachin, that even if he was a signet ring on God's right hand He would still pull him off and hand him over to his enemies. God said Jehoiachin would be recorded as childless and none of his descendants would sit on the throne of David."

"Ah, yes. I remember."

"But now the Holy One has made Zerubbabel His signet ring. It's His pledge that someday the Messiah will come, a descendant of King David. An heir will once again sit on his throne."

"What a day this has been," Saba said with a sigh. "But now I have work to do. Do you have time to help me, Zaki?"

"Give me a job to do, Saba. I'm ready."

Chapter 41

It was one of those rare, peaceful moments for Yael when dinner simmered on the hearth and both of her daughters napped. She sat down to rest in her room as well, nursing her son and thinking about her husband. Ever since prophesying, Zechariah had become a man of standing in their community, a man everyone looked up to. Yael was proud to be his wife but also a little awed by him. Imagine, the God of heaven and earth speaking through her husband!

She was still marveling over it when she heard a knock on her door. A moment later, Hodaya peeked inside. "Can I ask you something, Yael? I'm not disturbing you, am I?"

"Not at all. Come sit beside me. I have plenty of time to talk while this little glutton fills his belly." Hodaya limped into the room and sat down on a cushion beside Yael, propping her crutch against the wall. She paused for such a long time that Yael finally asked, "What is it, Hodaya? What's wrong?"

"I want to know who I am," she said, her pretty face creased with determination. "I want to know who my parents are and how I came to live here with all of you."

Yael closed her eyes for a moment, searching for an escape. She and Safta Dinah had become experts over the years at changing the subject and avoiding Hodaya's questions by assuring her that she was dearly loved and part of this family now. But judging by Hodaya's determined look, she wasn't going to be content with vague assurances this time. "Why are you asking, Hodaya? Haven't we told you countless times how much we love you? That you belong to us?"

"Yes, but this time I need to know the truth. It's important."

"Can you tell me why?" Yael asked, still stalling.

Hodaya met Yael's gaze, her beautiful dark eyes shining. "Because I'm in love with Aaron son of Besai. And he loves me."

Yael's mouth fell open as she stared at Hodaya. How had the tiny baby she and Safta carried home from the Samaritan village grown up so quickly? Sixteen years old already, and in love with Besai and Rachel's son, Aaron, who was eighteen. He lived near Bethlehem now and worked with his father as a shepherd, but Hodaya had known him all her life. They had grown up together and now saw each other during holidays and celebrations. Yael had noticed their tender glances and shy conversations, but she wasn't prepared to have Hodaya fall in love and marry and move to a home of her own.

"Aaron thinks I'm pretty," Hodaya said when Yael didn't reply. "He doesn't even care about . . . you know . . . my crooked foot."

"You are pretty. And none of us cares about your foot. Every one of us has things about us that aren't perfect—it's just that yours is a little more noticeable than ours."

"I don't look like any of you," Hodaya said.

"What difference does that make?" Yael said with a shrug. "My daughters don't look like me either, and—"

"That's not what I mean! I know who I *do* look like, and I want to know the truth!"

"Who do you think you look like?" Yael waited, dread making her skin prickle.

"Remember that night when Iddo was stabbed? I saw the man

who did it. The man who died. I saw his face when he was lying on the ground, before they covered him up. I peeked out of my room—and he looked like me! His hair looked just like mine!"

Yael floundered for words.

"Am I related to him? Am I a Samaritan, too?"

"None of that matters," she managed to say. "Why are you so concerned about who you look like?"

"Because the man who died was Rafi, the man you wanted to marry, wasn't he? But they wouldn't let you marry him because he wasn't Jewish. If I'm related to him . . . if I'm not Jewish . . . then they won't let Aaron marry me, either."

"Oh, Hodaya . . . of course you're Jewish. Iddo and Dinah adopted you. They took you to the mikveh and made you ours. Of course Aaron can marry you."

"The Almighty One won't accept me if I'm not Jewish."

"Hodaya, you worship in the Jewish Court of Women with us all the time. You know God accepts you."

"Aaron told me that the Samaritans aren't allowed to worship with us. He said that was why they made us stop building the temple. And why they're trying to stop us again. I heard all about it, Yael."

"Listen, we'll ask Zaki about it when he comes home, but I guarantee that he'll say you're allowed to worship with us and that the Almighty One accepts you." She hoped that would end the matter and put a stop to these questions, but Hodaya gave a huff of frustration.

"I want to know the truth about my parents and why I was adopted. I have a right to know, and so does Aaron. Why won't you tell me?"

Hodaya had raised her voice, and the baby stirred. Yael propped him against her shoulder and rubbed his back to soothe him to sleep. "We never wanted to tell you because we were afraid you would be hurt. And none of us ever wants to hurt you."

Hodaya struggled to her feet. "Then I'll find out the truth some other way if you won't tell me. Aaron and I will walk down to that Samaritan village and ask them why I look like Rafi."

"No, Hodaya! Don't ever do that! You and Aaron need to stay far away from that village. Sit down again, please. . . . I'll tell you the truth." Hodaya sank down on the cushion again.

Yael wondered if she should send for Safta Dinah, if maybe they should tell Hodaya the truth together. Safta had long worried that this day would come. "Let me get Safta, first—" she began, but Hodaya interrupted her.

"No. I want you to tell me."

Where to start? Yael took a moment to decide, praying for the right words. "Remember my good friend Leyla? The Samaritan girl I used to visit all the time? You're her half sister. You both have the same father. That means that Rafi, the man I wanted to marry, was your half brother. That's why you noticed a resemblance. I loved both of them, Hodaya. They were good friends of mine for many years until Leyla died and everything went wrong with Rafi."

"Who is my mother? Did she die, too?"

It would be less hurtful to say yes, that she had died giving birth, but it would be a lie. And Yael knew that lies always ended in grief. "Your mother's name is Raisa, and she nearly died giving birth to you. Both of you would have certainly died if Safta Dinah hadn't gone to the village that night to help. Your mother was very young when she married your father—younger than you are right now. Too young to be giving birth. You were her first child."

"Did she give me away because of my foot?"

Yael realized the truth for the first time. "No. Your mother didn't give you away at all. In fact, she loved you and asked to hold you. But Leyla's grandmother—who is no relation to you—believed that you were too weak to live. She told your mother that you had died to spare her the pain of loving you and then losing you. No one expected either you or Raisa to live."

"What about my father?"

Yael sighed. "His name is Zabad, and he's the village leader. He's mostly Jewish, a descendant of the people who stayed here in the land when everyone else was carried off to Babylon."

"But my mother is a Samaritan?"

"I presume so, but I don't really know. I never asked her." Again, Yael hoped this would be the end of Hodaya's questions. It wasn't.

"Why did my father let you take me?"

Yael sighed again. "He wanted a son."

"And I was a girl—with a crooked foot?"

Yael nodded and laid the baby down on the bed. She took Hodaya's hands in hers. "Everyone thought you would die that night. But Safta Dinah said she would make sure you lived if it was the last thing she ever did. And so we brought you home. . . . I was there when you were born, Hodaya. Watching you come into the world was the most amazing experience I'd ever had. I fell in love with you that instant. We all fell in love with you." Tears sprang to Yael's eyes. "And now, if we have to give you away again, I can't imagine a more wonderful, worthy man to give you to than Aaron son of Besai."

Chapter 42

From his foreman's shelter on the temple mount, Iddo watched a team of workers raise a huge building block with the crane, the ropes creaking and groaning beneath the strain. It twisted in the air for a moment before the men steadied it and lowered it into place on the wall of the sanctuary. The satisfaction Iddo felt was as enormous as the block. Across the valley on the Mount of Olives, clouds of white almond blossoms sprouted on the trees, announcing that winter would soon yield to spring. The days would grow warmer and longer, providing more hours of daylight in which Iddo and his teams could work. Fields of barley and flax ripened in the distant fields thanks to the plentiful winter rains, signaling God's grace and goodness, His pleasure in their obedience.

Iddo was about to turn back to his lists of supplies and expenditures when he saw Zechariah striding across the courtyard toward him. "If you're coming to inspect our progress," Iddo said, smiling, "we just laid another stone in place." He pointed to where the workers maneuvered the limestone block.

Zaki shook his head, his expression serious. "That's not why I'm here. Prince Zerubbabel received a dispatch from Samaria this morning. It's a copy of the letter Governor Tattenai sent to the Persian emperor about us. I thought you might want to come with me and hear what it says."

Iddo slowly rose to his feet. "Tattenai certainly didn't waste any time sending his report, did he?"

"No. As the proverb says of evildoers, 'their feet rush into sin.'" Zaki took Iddo's arm as they walked across the plaza, then descended the stairs from the mount. It frustrated Iddo to have grown so frail and in need of an arm to cling to for balance. He could accomplish so much more if he were as young and fit as his grandson.

"I'm sure it will take a few months for Tattenai's message to get to the emperor," Zaki said as they paused at the bottom of the steps to rest. "Then a few more months to receive his reply. How much progress do you think we can make during that time?"

Iddo wasn't optimistic. "Even if it takes a year to hear back from the Persians, that still won't give us enough time to finish. My best guess is that it will take three or four years to complete the entire temple."

They walked the short distance to the throne room in the governor's residence where Zerubbabel conducted business. The high priest and most of the chief priests and elders had crowded into the long, narrow hall already. Zechariah found a place for them to stand alongside one of the support pillars. "In the end, it won't matter what Tattenai's letter contains," Iddo said. "I'm going to continue building no matter what."

Zerubbabel stood to quiet the men. "As you've heard, this morning I received a copy of the letter that Governor Tattanai sent to King Darius. When I finish reading it to you, we can consider what our response, if any, should be." The prince unrolled the letter and began to read.

"To King Darius:
Cordial Greetings.

> The king should know that we went to the district of Judah, to the temple of the great God. The people are building it with large stones and placing timbers in the walls. The work is being carried on with diligence and is making rapid progress under their direction."

Iddo leaned close to whisper to Zechariah. "I consider that a high compliment."

> "We questioned the elders and asked them, 'Who authorized you to rebuild this temple and restore this structure?' We also asked them their names, so that we could compile a list of their leaders for your information. This is the answer they gave us . . ."

Zerubbabel looked up from the letter and said, "Tattenai gives a fairly accurate account of our reply, saying that we're building this temple for our God and that we have authorization from King Cyrus. The letter continues:

> "Now if it pleases the king, let a search be made of the royal archives of Babylon to see if King Cyrus did in fact issue a decree to rebuild this house of God in Jerusalem. Then let the king send us his decision in this matter."

"Good," Iddo said, loudly enough for those around him to hear. "If they search, they'll find the proclamation. And he'll also see that exiles from other nations were allowed to return and rebuild, not just us."

"Are there any questions?" the prince asked as he rolled up the scroll again.

The captain of the temple guards asked to speak first. "What if the Samaritan governor sends soldiers to force us to stop? We don't have the manpower or the strength to fight them."

"True," Zerubbabel replied. "And you can be sure they noted

our lack of defenses when they came to inspect the building project. But for now, the province of Judah is still my territory, and the Samaritan governor has no right to send troops unless the Persian emperor orders him to."

Iddo lifted his hand to be recognized. "We should not—we *will* not—stop building while we wait for the emperor's reply."

"My concern is also for your safety, Prince Zerubbabel," the captain continued. "As the legitimate heir to the throne, you could be executed or carried back into exile if your actions are seen as rebellious."

"Thank you for your concern, but I'm trusting the Almighty One's promise that David's throne will endure forever."

"Have there been any reports of trouble with our Samaritan neighbors?" someone else asked.

"Dozens of them, just like before. They're waging a war of terrorism, using fear as a weapon. I've asked for volunteers to guard the temple mount again. But I believe that the Almighty One has commanded us to build, and we need to fear Him more than our neighbors."

Iddo returned to the temple mount after the meeting, but work ended an hour early that afternoon so the workers would have time to prepare for the Sabbath. He arrived home to find Dinah, Yael, and Hodaya scurrying around as they put the finishing touches on the Sabbath meal. But Dinah pulled Iddo aside for a moment, still holding a loaf of fresh bread in her hands. "We heard about the letter from the Samaritan governor," she said. "Some of the women are afraid there will be trouble again."

"Our cisterns are full from all the rain, aren't they?" he asked.

"Yes. Thankfully we won't need to go to the spring for water, but—"

"Let's eat in peace, Dinah. I've prepared something to say to everyone at the end of our meal." Iddo had thought about Tattenai's letter all afternoon. His family's safety was his responsibility, yet he knew he was helpless to protect them. Over and over, he had prayed to let go of his worry and fear and to trust their safety to God's hands—a prayer he would likely pray for the rest of his life.

They broke bread, sipped wine, and feasted by lamplight. Singing the traditional songs of his ancestors filled Iddo with hope and courage. Afterward, the children quieted to hear him talk about the weekly Torah portion, his custom on Shabbat. "Our portion this week is very fitting for this time in our nation's life," he told them. "In this passage, the Holy One has brought Moses and our ancestors out of Egypt, just as He brought us out of Babylon. Then the Holy One says, 'Then have them make a sanctuary for me, and I will dwell among them.' He revealed to them exactly how to build this sanctuary and the people obeyed, freely offering their treasures of gold and silver and precious stones, fine linen and wood and spices. Today we're again obeying the Lord's command to build His sanctuary, even as our enemies try to stop us. Tonight I want to ask each of you: Do you trust God? Are you willing to obey Him, no matter the cost? Because this time the Holy One's dwelling place may cost not only our gold and silver but our lives, as it did with Shoshanna. Will you offer up your fear and let Him replace it with faith?"

Dinah replied first. She sat beside Iddo, holding a very sleepy Sarah in her lap. "When the Holy One asked me to sacrifice my family and leave them behind in Babylon, I admit I wasn't willing. But that's because I didn't understand why we had to come here. Now I do, Iddo. We would have become just like all the other nations if we had stayed in Babylon. I'm willing to obey now. And I won't let fear stop me."

"I agree with Safta," Yael said. She held the baby against her shoulder, gently rubbing his back. "I used to study the stars because I wanted to know the future, while all that time, the Holy One was leading us into our future. The prophets said

He would restore our people, and here we are in our land. He said we would be as numerous as the stars, and He has blessed Zaki and me with three children. I know that God is with us, not with our enemies, and so I'm not afraid, either. That's why we named our son Joshua, because the Lord saves."

"What about you, Hodaya?" Iddo asked. She looked away, and he saw her eyes fill with tears. "Are you afraid? There's no shame in admitting it if you are."

"It's not that," she said, shaking her head. Iddo waited until she finally looked up at him again. "Yael told me about my real parents. I know I'm not Jewish. I know I'm a Samaritan, which means I'm one of your enemies. I'm not allowed to help you build the temple."

Yael handed the baby to Zechariah and tried to pull Hodaya into her arms. "You aren't our enemy! You're one of us! Tell her, Zaki. I can't explain it to her the right way."

"I know the story from the Torah," Hodaya said, pushing Yael away. "When Israel came into this land after leaving Egypt, the Holy One told them to kill every man, woman, and child. He said not to marry anyone who wasn't Jewish."

"This is my fault," Yael said. "I didn't explain it to her very well. I'm so sorry."

"Hodaya, look at me," Iddo said. He waited until she did. "The Holy One told us to totally destroy those nations for the same reason that Jerusalem was destroyed and the Jewish people taken into exile—because we had all become corrupt, worshiping false gods, doing immoral things, sacrificing our children to idols. But it has always been the Holy One's plan to bless all the people on earth through our nation. He made that promise to Abraham and repeated it to Isaac and Jacob. In the past, I didn't want to see that prophecy fulfilled because I hated the Babylonians for what they did to my family and to this city. But then you came into our lives, and the Holy One began to show me how much He loves all people, not just the sons of Abraham. You became one of us, worshiping our God and obeying His Torah. And in the future, that's what will happen with all the people on earth—they will all worship our God and obey Him."

He paused, looking at Hodaya's beautiful face in the flickering lamplight, realizing how much he had grown to love her as his daughter. "Are you listening, Hodaya? Do you understand what I'm saying? The reason we couldn't let the Samaritans help us rebuild was because they still practiced a mixture of religions. But any Samaritan who turns wholeheartedly to God is always welcome to worship with us. You're Jewish because you belong to us. But even if you weren't ours, you would be welcome to worship with us and marry our sons because you serve our God."

"Yes, Saba is right," Zechariah said. He leaned close to Hodaya and took her hand. "The prophet Isaiah wrote that in the last days the mountain of the Lord's temple will be established as chief among the mountains, and all nations will stream to it. He said that foreigners who serve and worship the Lord and keep His covenant will be accepted by Him, and His temple will be called a house of prayer for *all* nations."

"That's why we're working so hard to finish it," Iddo said. "And why our enemies want to stop us. They're rebelling against God. But you, Hodaya—you are the firstfruits of God's promise. His prophecies are being fulfilled in you."

Hodaya looked around at all of them and smiled faintly as she wiped her tears. "So . . . does that mean . . . you'll let me marry Aaron when his father asks you for my hand?"

"Yes!" Iddo said, laughing. "Yes, my dear girl. I'll dance with joy at your wedding."

"But not for another year or two," Dinah added with a worried look. "You're still much too young."

Everyone at the table laughed, and Hodaya's face was flushed with happiness.

Chapter 43

That night Zechariah's son awakened him from a restless sleep, crying to be fed. "Stay in bed," he told Yael, who snuggled beneath the covers on this cold, late-winter night. "I'll fetch him for you." The stone floor felt icy beneath his feet, the room chilly as he lifted Joshua from his basket and laid him beside Yael. But instead of returning to bed, Zechariah put on his outer robe and slipped his sandals onto his feet. He felt wide awake for some reason, even though dawn was still a long way off, judging by the lightless sky outside his window.

A multitude of thoughts had tumbled through his mind all day, everything from the letter that Governor Tattenai had sent to the Persians, to Hodaya's concerns about God's love for the Gentiles. He would pray about all of these things, he decided. And rather than pace the floor of his room and keep Yael from sleeping, he closed the door behind him and tiptoed outside to the courtyard.

And there stood a man.

Zechariah backed up a step, startled, remembering the night that Rafi had come. But without moving or saying a word, the man conveyed peace to Zechariah as if he had poured it from a pitcher, saturating him with it. Zaki walked slowly toward him, his legs a little shaky. And as he stepped into the open courtyard and glanced around, it was as if a curtain had been drawn back and instead of seeing the houses and streets of his neighborhood, Zechariah stood in a ravine among myrtle trees. He saw a man riding a red horse, and behind him were red, brown, and white horses. He knew he wasn't dreaming because he could feel the stone floor beneath his sandals, the night breeze ruffling his hair. But the vision in front of him was as real and vivid as the cobblestones. He heard the pounding hooves of the horses, smelled their scent. The wind rustling his hair rustled the leaves of the myrtle trees, as well.

He turned to the man in the courtyard and knew he was an angel without knowing how or why. Zechariah gestured to the horses and asked in a hushed voice, "What are these, my lord?"

"The Lord has sent these to go throughout the earth." The power of God filled the angel's voice, and Zechariah's entire body resonated in tune with it the same way his body vibrated when he blew the silver trumpet. "I asked the Almighty One how long He would withhold mercy from Jerusalem and the towns of Judah," the angel continued, "and He said, 'I will return to Jerusalem with mercy, and there my house will be rebuilt. My towns will again overflow with prosperity, and the Lord will again comfort Zion and choose Jerusalem.'"

Zechariah's heart raced with excitement. He wanted to run into his grandfather's room and awaken him with this good news, but he heard a sudden noise above him and when he looked up, he saw four horns, emblems of political power and might. "What are these?" he asked the angel.

"These are the horns that scattered Judah, Israel, and Jerusalem so that no one could raise his head. But now the nations that destroyed you are about to be destroyed."

Another sound got Zechariah's attention, and when he looked in that direction the scene had changed. He saw a man with a measuring line in his hand as if preparing to build. Zechariah felt a prickle of excitement, remembering all the building they had done when they'd first arrived, and how Jerusalem had risen from the ashes. He had learned to use a measuring line like the one this man held, and a plumb line to make sure the walls were straight. But then their enemies had brought the construction to a halt. "Where is that man going?" he asked the angel.

"To measure Jerusalem, to find out how wide and how long it is. Jerusalem will be a city without walls because of the great number of men and livestock in it. 'And I myself will be a wall of fire around it,' declares the Lord, 'and I will be its glory within.'"

Did this mean that more exiles would be allowed to return? Zechariah was about to ask, but it was as if the angel had read his thoughts. "'Come! Come! Flee from the land of the north,'" he shouted. "'Escape, you who live in Babylon. I will surely raise my hand against the nations that have plundered you,' declares the Lord, 'for whoever touches you touches the apple of my eye.'"

Zechariah wanted to shout along with the angel at God's comforting words, but the vision hadn't ended. "'Shout and be glad, O Daughter of Zion. For I am coming, and I will live among you,' declares the Lord. 'Many nations will be joined with the Lord in that day and will become my people. I will live among you and you will know that the Lord Almighty has sent me to you. Be still before the Lord, all mankind, because he has roused himself from his holy dwelling.'"

Zechariah sank down on the courtyard wall, overcome with emotion. He had left his home and his parents to seek the Lord's presence, and now He was promising to live among them. Even more, as if in answer to Hodaya's concerns, God promised that the people of many nations would become His, as well. Zechariah sat on the wall for a long moment, his eyes closed as he silently praised God.

When he opened them again, the angel beckoned to him.

"Come with me." They walked only a few steps—and there was Jeshua, the high priest. Zechariah wanted to touch him to see if he was real, but the scene had changed to that of a courtroom. The Accuser stood at Jeshua's right side as they stood before the angel of the Lord. Zechariah felt the cold chill of evil in the Accuser's presence. "The Lord rebuke you, Satan!" the Lord's angel said. "The Lord, who has chosen Jerusalem, rebuke you! Is not this man a burning stick snatched from the fire?"

The high priest wore filthy clothes as he stood before the angel and his fellow priests, robes that only the lowest beggar would wear. But the angel of the Lord ordered those standing near him to take off his filthy clothes. He said to Jeshua, "See, I have taken away your sin." And as Zechariah watched, Jeshua was clothed in a clean white robe. A spotless turban was placed on his head. "This is what the Lord Almighty says," the angel told Jeshua. "'If you will walk in my ways and keep my requirements, then you will govern my house and have charge of my courts, and I will give you a place among these standing here. Listen, Jeshua and your associates—you are symbolic of things to come: I am going to bring my servant, the Branch. And I will remove the sin of this land in a single day.'"

Zechariah's heart beat so rapidly he feared it might burst. The angel spoke of the promised Messiah, the seed of the woman who would crush the serpent's head. Before Zechariah could react, the images faded into the night as if dissolving into a pool of dark water. When they had all disappeared, Zechariah stood in his familiar courtyard again, surrounded by the homes and streets of his neighborhood. It seemed as though days had passed, but the night sky was still black, the mountains to the east still cloaked in darkness. Exhausted, he sank down in the courtyard with his back against the wall and closed his eyes. The next thing he knew someone was shaking him. He looked up and saw the angel.

"What do you see?" the angel asked.

Zechariah scrambled to his feet. "I see a solid gold lampstand with a bowl and seven lights. And two olive trees, one on the right and one on the left of the lampstand."

"This is the word of the Lord to Zerubbabel," the angel said. "'Not by might nor by power, but by my Spirit,' says the Lord Almighty. 'What are you, O mighty mountain? Before Zerubbabel you will become level ground. Then he will bring out the temple's capstone to shouts of "God bless it!" The hands of Zerubbabel have laid the foundation of this temple and his hands will also complete it.'"

Zechariah could scarcely wait to see Saba's joy when he told him this news. But the lampstand and olive trees still puzzled him. "What are these two olive branches?" he asked the angel.

"These are the two who are anointed to serve the Lord of all the earth." The king and the high priest. God's anointed servants.

Suddenly Zechariah heard a noise like flapping wings or rattling parchment, and when he looked up he saw a huge scroll, fifteen feet wide and thirty feet long, flying through the air above him. He recalled dreaming of this as a boy. "What is that?" he asked the angel.

"This is the curse that's going out over the entire land. It will enter the house of every thief and everyone who swears falsely, and whatever they attempt to build will be destroyed, left with nothing but timbers and stones. Now look there, Zechariah."

He looked where the angel pointed and nearly laughed out loud at what he saw. It was a measuring basket, and when the cover of lead was lifted, there sat the sorceress from Babylon who used to visit Yael's house next door. She was dressed in black, and Zechariah heard the soft jingling of her bracelets and amulets. "This is wickedness," the angel said as he pushed the lead cover back into place over the woman. Zechariah watched in amazement as two women with wings like storks lifted the basket and flew away with it.

"Where are they taking her?" he asked.

"Back to Babylon where she belongs. God will remove wickedness from this land."

Zechariah watched until the winged women were out of sight, and when he turned back to the angel, the scene had changed again. Four chariots rode out from between two mountains of bronze, each chariot pulled by a team of differently colored horses—red, black, white, and dappled. He could hear the horses snorting, their hooves thundering, the chariot wheels creaking and rumbling as they raced forward. "What are these, my lord?" he asked.

"These are the four spirits of heaven, going out from standing in the presence of the Lord, going throughout the earth. Look, those going toward the north country have given God's Spirit rest in the land of the north."

Once again, Zechariah felt the Holy One's peace wash through him. This was a sign to him and to His people that whatever happened—today, tomorrow, or the next day—the Almighty One was in control, working for the good of His people and not for harm.

The sound of the chariots faded in the distance and once again the vision dissolved into blackness. Zechariah found a place to sit down, leaning against the courtyard wall so he could watch the sunrise above the Mount of Olives when it finally came. The next thing he knew, someone was calling his name, shaking him awake.

"Zechariah . . . Zechariah . . ." His grandfather, not an angel. A flesh-and-blood man, not a vision. "Are you all right?" Saba asked. "Why are you sleeping out here in the cold?"

Zechariah slowly pulled himself to his feet. "I wanted to pray, so I got up and came out here. But then . . ." He had no words to describe what he'd seen last night but he knew he had to try. "The Holy One sent an angel who spoke with me, Saba. He showed me things in visions that were so real that I could smell them and touch them. I need to get parchment and some ink so I can write them down and tell everyone." But Zechariah knew that God had etched the visions on his heart as if on stone. He would never forget what he'd seen and heard. He ran his hands through his hair as Saba stared at him in amazement.

"What you and I are doing here in Jerusalem is so much bigger than we can ever dream, Saba. I saw time pulled back like a curtain last night, and I glimpsed eternity. The things the angel showed me . . . it was like . . . like I could finally make sense of everything that's happened to you and to me and to our people. And God reassured me that we *will* finish building His temple. Zerubbabel will lay the capstone himself. Our enemies can't stop us. The Lord Almighty said, 'Not by might nor by power, but by my Spirit.' I need to tell Jeshua and the others that the defilement of the past is gone—washed away! The Accuser of men has nothing to say to us now that the Holy One has cleansed us and forgiven us."

"Praise God," Saba murmured.

The women joined them in the courtyard as Zechariah spoke. He looked at his beautiful wife and smiled to himself when he recalled the vision of the Babylonian woman who had nearly enticed Yael away. Now the woman of wickedness was gone. Their land was being purified. He gestured to Hodaya to come to him and rested his hand on her shoulder. "The Lord promises that many nations will be joined with Him," he told her. "They will become His people. You are His, Hodaya. You belong to Him." She wrapped her arms around him and hugged him tightly.

"Zechariah?" Yael asked. "What . . . how . . . ?"

"The Holy One opened eternity and showed me visions to encourage us, Yael. We shouldn't be disappointed if the work we do seems small in our eyes. The future will be so much more than this temple we're building. The Holy One is coming! He is coming and will live among us!"

It was all Zechariah could say. The enormity of it—*God with us*—took his breath away.

Chapter 44

Iddo watched his team of carpenters shape a cedar tree into a massive beam for the temple, their planes and adzes producing mounds of fragrant shavings. If only they could work faster. If only he had more expert craftsmen like these. Iddo sighed, resisting the urge to rush his workers, telling himself to be patient. The work was going well, considering their limitations and the summer's heat. The temple was slowly rising from the ashes of Jerusalem, the workers encouraged by the prophecies of Haggai and Zechariah. Iddo's grandson had just returned from traveling to other Judean towns and villages, calming people's fears with the messages he'd received from the Holy One, telling them of the glorious future that awaited them. Their salvation from exile had been a mere taste of God's worldwide salvation to come. The restoration of the temple and the nation was a picture of the restoration that the Messiah would bring one day.

Imagine! Zechariah, his own grandson, a prophet of God. Iddo wondered if his son Berekiah would hear the news someday. Would he be proud of his son and glad that Zechariah had obeyed the Almighty One and returned to Jerusalem? Did Berekiah and Hoshea ever regret their decision to remain in Babylon? Iddo sighed again, knowing he shouldn't dwell on the past when the future continued to unfurl before him like a magnificent carpet rolled out before a king. Iddo turned his attention back to the cedar beam that was taking shape and saw in it a symbol of the Holy One's work as He slowly cut and shaped Iddo's life to fit His purposes. The cutting had been painful at times, but how else could he be made to fit into the place God had for him?

When Iddo looked up again, he saw Zechariah weaving his way across the work site, coming to fetch him.

"I know, I know," Iddo said as Zaki approached. "I'm late. And I'm in trouble, aren't I?"

Zechariah grinned, holding his hands up as if in surrender. "Don't ask me, I'm just the messenger. Safta sent me to tell you—and these are her exact words—that you will still be building the temple tomorrow and the next day, but this is the only day that Hodaya will ever get married."

"But not until this evening. There's still plenty of time."

"Do you really want to risk Safta's wrath?" Zaki asked. "I certainly don't, and I'm under orders not to come home without you."

Iddo gripped Zaki's arm for support as they began the long walk across the plaza. Hodaya was getting married. Unbelievable. She had turned seventeen this spring, and Dinah had run out of excuses to make her and Aaron wait any longer.

As he and Zaki descended the stairs from the mountaintop, Iddo caught sight of a small caravan approaching the city from the northwest with horses and chariots and banners waving. "Look at that," he said, stopping to catch his breath. "That's not something you see every day."

Zechariah shaded his eyes. "Those are the banners of the Samaritan governor. Maybe he finally received a response from the Persian emperor. It's been nearly eight months since Tattenai sent his letter."

Iddo's stomach suddenly felt hollow. "I've been dreading this day. And it's not a good sign that the governor himself is bringing the news. If the Persian king has ruled against us, Tattenai probably came in person to gloat and to force us to comply."

"He can't stop us, Saba. The Almighty One assured us that Zerubbabel himself will complete the temple."

"We need to go to the palace and hear the news. Dinah will have to wait a little longer for us."

"I agree. But no matter what happens, Saba, we can't let the news spoil Hodaya's wedding."

"I know, I know." They turned up the street to walk the short distance to the governor's residence, meeting other priests and city leaders along the way. News of the caravan had traveled quickly, and Zerubbabel didn't need to call for a meeting as the chief priests and elders stopped working and streamed to the reception hall. Governor Tattenai hadn't come after all, but had sent his administrator to read the Persian king's letter. Zerubbabel wasted no time on formalities with his Samaritan visitors but called the secretary up to the platform to read the letter aloud. The hall quieted. Iddo held his breath, gripping Zaki's arm.

"In response to Governor Tattenai's letter," the secretary read, "King Darius ordered that the archives stored in the treasury in Babylon be searched. In them, a scroll was found from the first year of King Cyrus concerning the temple of God in Jerusalem. King Cyrus' proclamation said: 'Let the temple be rebuilt as a place to present sacrifices—'"

Iddo exhaled and leaned against his grandson. "So. They found the original decree after all."

"'It is to be ninety feet high and ninety feet wide, with three courses of large stones and one of timbers. The costs are to be paid by the royal treasury. Also, the gold and silver articles carried to Babylon by King Nebuchadnezzar are to be returned.'

"After finding the original proclamation," the secretary continued, "King Darius then took the matter under consideration and sent this letter to Governor Tattenai, stating the Persian king's decision: 'Now then, Tattenai, governor of Trans-Euphrates, you and your fellow provincial officers, stay away from there. Do not interfere with the work on God's temple.'"

A great shout went up from the assembled men, drowning out his words. Iddo couldn't stop his tears. They could continue to build! The Persian king himself had said so. Eventually the hall quieted again when they saw that the secretary was waiting to read more:

> "'Let the governor of the Jews and the Jewish elders rebuild this house of God on its site. Moreover, I hereby decree that the expenses of these men are to be fully paid out of the royal treasury, from the revenues of Trans-Euphrates, so that the work will not stop. Whatever is needed for their offerings to the God of heaven must be given them daily, without fail, so they may offer sacrifices and pray for the well-being of the king and his sons.'"

Another cry of joy filled the hall. Some men hugged each other, others shook their heads in disbelief. "Did you hear that, Saba?" Zechariah asked above the noise. "Not only does Tattenai have to let us build, he has to help us pay for it with tax revenue!" Again, the clapping and cheering quieted when they saw that the secretary still wasn't finished:

> "'Furthermore, I decree that if anyone changes this edict, a beam is to be pulled from his house and he is to be impaled on it. And for this crime, his house is to be made a pile of rubble. May God, who has caused his Name to dwell in Jerusalem, overthrow any king or people who lifts a hand to change this decree or to destroy this temple in Jerusalem. I Darius have decreed it. Let it be carried out with diligence.'"

Deafening cheers rang in Iddo's ears. This final portion of King Darius' decree meant that the work could proceed without fear of reprisals or terrorist acts from their enemies. "This is more than I dared to hope for," Iddo murmured as Zechariah hugged him tightly. "God is with us . . . He is with us."

"Yes! And since Governor Tattenai has to share his tax revenue with us, you can hire more laborers, Saba. The work will go faster."

"Spread the news!" Prince Zerubbabel shouted. "Tell everyone in the city and in all the villages and towns. We must celebrate this good news!"

"We need to go back up to the temple, Zaki. I need to tell all my workers that—" But Zechariah didn't seem to be listening as he released Iddo again. Without a word, he pushed his way to the front of the hall, weaving between the cheering men before leaping onto the platform beside the prince.

"This is what the Lord Almighty says," he shouted, and the hall quickly grew quiet. "'I am burning with jealousy for Jerusalem! I will return to her and dwell in Jerusalem, and the mountain of the Lord will be called the Holy Mountain. Once again men and women of ripe old age will sit in the streets of Jerusalem, each with a cane in hand because of his age. The city streets will be filled with boys and girls playing there. I will save my people from the countries of the east and west and bring them back here to live; they will be my people, and I will be faithful and righteous to them as their God.'"

He paused, and Iddo could see tears on Zechariah's face as he took another deep breath to continue. "'You who were there when the foundation was laid for the house of God, let your hands be strong so that the temple may be built,' declares the Lord Almighty. 'Before that time, no one could go about his business safely because of his enemy, for I had turned every man against his neighbor. But now I will not deal with the remnant of this people as I did in the past. The seed will grow well, the vine will yield its fruit, the ground will produce its crops, and the heavens will drop their dew. I will give these things as an inheritance to the remnant of this people. As you have been an object of cursing among the nations, O Judah and Israel, so will I save you, and you will be a blessing. Do not be afraid, but let your hands be strong.'"

Iddo's joy and pride welled up as he watched the prince and the other leaders come forward to embrace Zechariah, talking with him, rejoicing together. At last Zechariah stepped down from the platform and made his way back through the crowd to where Iddo waited.

"Come with me to the temple mount," Iddo said again. "I need to tell—"

"The wedding!" Zechariah interrupted. "We forgot all about Hodaya's wedding! Safta must be wondering where we are!"

"I know, I know, but let's go up to the temple first—"

"Not on your life," Zaki said, laughing. "I'd rather face a den of hungry lions than Safta when she's mad at me."

Iddo felt as though he was floating as they made their way home. Dinah not only forgave them when she heard why they were late, she wept with joy on Iddo's shoulder. Then she quickly dried her eyes again and gave Iddo a list of things to do to prepare for the wedding. "I should put you in charge of rebuilding the temple," he told Dinah. "It would be finished in no time."

Hodaya looked radiant as she sat in her flower-adorned chair later that evening, waiting for her groom. They could hear the shofars, flutes, cymbals, and drums of the groom's procession long before it arrived at the house, making its way up the ramp to the city, winding through the lanes and streets. The music swelled as Iddo's friends and neighbors and fellow priests joined in the parade to his home, singing of brides and unquenchable love. The feast would be held in Iddo's courtyard since Hodaya wasn't able to walk in a procession all the way to Aaron's home in Bethlehem. And what a feast it was! Dinah and Yael and the other women had outdone themselves, loading the tables with food and wine.

Iddo watched Aaron lift Hodaya's veil and claim his beautiful bride, and saw a picture of the Holy One's love for His people, His bride. Aaron didn't care about Hodaya's twisted foot or the fact that she was adopted from the Samaritans. He loved her and accepted her and took her to himself, so they would become one. And even though the Holy One had punished Iddo and His people with exile for a season, they were still His beloved, betrothed to Him once again.

Late into the night, Iddo danced with joy beneath a canopy of stars too innumerable to count.

Chapter 45

Three years later

Zechariah lay in the darkness beside Yael, staring up at the ceiling beams. The temple was finished. Complete. Rebuilt from the ashes seventy years after the Babylonians destroyed it. He thought back to all of the events that had led to this day and could scarcely believe that more than twenty years had passed since King Cyrus allowed him and the other Jews to return to Jerusalem. They'd made such a promising start before the work stalled for sixteen years. Zechariah remembered his long search for God's presence, and how their lives had become as dry and barren as the drought-scorched earth. Then the Almighty One sent Haggai to them like a cloud bursting with rain, bringing renewed life and purpose. The construction had resumed in spite of danger and threats, and now the temple was finished. They would celebrate its dedication today.

Today the golden lampstand would be lit in the Holy Place for the first time and left to burn continually before God. Today the priests would light the incense on the altar and the fragrance would ascend to heaven along with the prayers of the people. The bread of God's Presence, one loaf for each tribe, would be set on the table in the Holy Place today, replenished each week for as long as this temple endured. Zechariah would play the shofar as the priests offered sacrifices and prayers. Joy and anticipation made it impossible for him to sleep.

He rolled over to climb out of bed, trying not to awaken Yael or their newest son, Johanan, born eighteen months after Joshua. But Yael stirred and opened her eyes. "Where are you going?"

"I've been lying here thinking of everything I need to do and worrying that I've forgotten something, so I figured I may as well get up."

"I'm so excited for you, Zaki. And for Saba. You longed for an adventure when we were young, remember? Is this adventure grand enough for you?"

"I could never have imagined a thrill greater than this." He bent to kiss her and said, "Go back to sleep, love. You don't need to get up yet."

He dressed in the dark and felt his way out to the courtyard, shivering in the chill of early springtime. He wasn't surprised to see that his grandfather was awake, as well, gazing at the dark outline of the mountain to the east as if willing the sun to rise from behind it so the day could begin. "Hard to sleep, isn't it, Saba?"

"I've been standing here praising God that I've lived to see this day."

"I know." Zechariah stood beside Saba in the silent darkness, wondering what it was like for his grandfather to have come full circle. To have seen Jerusalem and the temple destroyed, their people slaughtered in an outpouring of God's judgment—and then to feel the cleansing of His grace, to see the city and temple rebuilt, his family reborn. Even as they watched, the sky gradually grew lighter, the familiar outlines of their courtyard became clearer.

"Well, there's no sense in standing around here," Saba said. "We may as well go up to the temple and get an early start."

"Not without something to eat, you won't." Zechariah turned at the sound of Safta's voice, surprised to see that she was awake and dressed, too. She yawned as she bent to rekindle the fire. "Just give me a moment."

"Safta, you don't have to cook—"

"Of course I do! Do you think I would let you leave home on such an important day without food in your stomachs?" She frowned as if to say the question was too absurd to deserve an answer.

Zechariah crouched beside her. "You've played a part in rebuilding the temple, too, you know. All the meals you faithfully provided day after day were just as important as the work of shaping stones and lowering them into place."

She brushed away his praise with a wave of her hand. "I've done nothing at all compared to you and Iddo."

Zechariah was grateful for the simple meal she prepared, and by the time they finished eating, it was light enough to make their way up to the temple mount. When they reached the top of the stairs and saw the enormous structure in front of them, Saba paused. "Look at that," he breathed. "It's beautiful, isn't it?"

"It truly is." Tears sprang to Zechariah's eyes. The dawning sun had turned the temple's creamy-beige stones into gold and filled its courtyards with light.

"God's house could never be built anywhere else but Jerusalem, on this mountain where Abraham offered his son," Saba said.

Compared to the temples Zechariah had seen in Babylon, this one wasn't lavish. They had built it in half the time it took to build Solomon's temple and with a fraction of the laborers. But it stood in the same place and was the same size as his, constructed from the same local limestone and Lebanese cedar. "But no gold," Zechariah said aloud. "King Solomon used thousands of shekels of gold to adorn his temple."

"Never mind," Saba said. "Don't even try to compare the two. Besides, the Holy One wants our devotion, not our gold."

As they walked across the courtyard together to the priests' robing room, Zechariah heard the distant bleating and lowing of the sacrificial animals as they stirred in their pens outside the Sheep Gate. Today the priests would offer up one hundred bulls, two hundred rams, four hundred male lambs, and then twelve male goats for a sin offering, one animal for each of the tribes of Israel. The number of sacrifices was small compared with the thousands of animals offered at the dedication of Solomon's temple. But the remnant of God's people would gather here today in the newly cleared courtyards and feast on the fellowship offerings after the service. They would celebrate their restored communion with God.

God with us.

The thought continued to astound Zechariah.

"I see we aren't the only early risers," Saba said as they crowded into the robing room. Dozens of priests were already preparing for the day's work as the Levite choir and musicians warmed up on their instruments.

"This is a once-in-a-lifetime event, Iddo," the high priest said. "How can anyone remain asleep?" He looked resplendent in his ephod, breastplate, and embroidered robe, the white turban and golden headband on his head.

With so much to do, the two hours it took for Zechariah and the other priests to prepare passed quickly. He was grateful that he'd gotten an early start. Outside, he and Saba washed in the bronze lavers filled with living water. People were already assembling in the courtyards, and Zechariah could feel the excitement building, his heartbeat accelerating. He hoped that Safta, Yael, and the children arrived early enough to find a good place to stand. He searched for them in the crowd as he made his way to the musicians' platform but didn't see them.

He quickly reviewed the order of service for the celebration with the other musicians. It was nearly time for Prince Zerubbabel's procession to arrive, announced by a fanfare of shofars. As Zechariah crowded onto the platform and prepared to play, he overheard one of the Levite musicans say, "It isn't right that our prince can't be properly acknowledged as royalty. He's our king, from the royal line of King David."

"You're right," another man said. "He should be escorted here in splendor the way the Babylonian kings always were. Remember their processions?"

Zechariah remembered. He had once climbed to the top of Babylon's walls with his father to watch a royal procession. The king had traveled in a golden chariot pulled by white horses, and his entourage included soldiers on horseback, noblemen in chariots, and Babylon's glittering idols pulled on golden carts. The people lining the street had bowed down in homage, but Abba said he would never bow to pagan kings or gods, only to the Almighty One.

A few minutes later, Zechariah saw Prince Zerubbabel and his noblemen entering the temple courtyard. He drew a breath and sounded a fanfare on the shofar as the assembled people cheered. Someday, a descendant of David would reign on his throne and the whole world would bow before him. Zechariah closed his eyes as the future peeled open before him and God's word resounded in his heart like a trumpet blast:

> *Rejoice greatly, O Daughter of Zion! Shout, Daughter of Jerusalem! See, your king comes to you, righteous and having salvation, gentle and riding on a donkey, on a colt, the foal of a donkey. He will proclaim peace to the nations, and His rule will extend from sea to sea and from the River to the ends of the earth. . . . On that day a fountain will be opened to the house of David and the inhabitants of Jerusalem, to cleanse them from*

sin and impurity. . . . The Lord will be king over the whole earth. There will be one Lord, and his name the only name.

When Zechariah lowered the ram's horn and opened his eyes he was in Jerusalem again. This celebration was a mere foretaste of that day when the whole earth would proclaim the Messiah as its king—a descendant of King David and of Prince Zerubbabel. Now the prince stood with lifted hands before the waiting crowd.

"Praise be to the Lord, the God of Israel," Zerubbabel shouted, "who with His hands has fulfilled what He promised! As we gather here today to worship Him, He is with us! He is with us! And our ancient enemies are no more. The might of the Assyrians and Babylonians and Egyptians is broken. And yet we have survived. We, the sons of Abraham, are still a people blessed by Him as He has promised. We will continue to live and to serve Him as long as day and night endure, as numerous as the stars in the heavens. Praise His holy name!"

Zechariah sounded the shofar again and the people gave a great shout that echoed off the surrounding hills and resounded in the valley below. When the praise finally died away, the high priest began to pray. Zechariah recognized his words as King Solomon's prayer for the first temple's dedication.

"'O Lord, God of Israel, there is no God like you in heaven above or on earth below—you who keep your covenant of love with your servants who continue wholeheartedly in your way. . . . But will God really dwell on earth? The heavens, even the highest heavens, cannot contain you. How much less this temple we have built! Yet give attention to your servant's prayer and his plea for mercy, O Lord my God. Hear the cry and the prayer that your servant is praying in your presence. May your eyes be open toward this temple day and night, this place of which you said you would put your Name. . . . Hear from heaven, your dwelling place, and when you hear, forgive.'"

The priests began offering the sacrifices, sprinkling the blood around the altar and laying the portions on the altar grate. Smoke and fire ascended into the sky. All the while, antiphonal choirs of Levites sang the psalms of David accompanied by trumpets, cymbals, harps, and lyres. The people knelt on the ground, bowing in reverent worship as the deep voices of the Levites praised the Holy One.

When the sacrifices ended, another great shout of joy went up. Then all of the assembled people joined the choir in anthems of praise: *"Give thanks to the Lord for He is good. His love endures forever!"* The glorious sound surrounded Zechariah, enveloping him, until it seemed as though the heavens had opened and the angelic hosts had joined them in worship. The Almighty One, Creator of the universe, was worthy to be praised! His mercy and grace would never end! And that was the true source of Zechariah's joy, and of all true joy—knowing the love of God.

The sun gleamed from the high priest's headband and golden ephod as he stood before the people and lifted his hands to give the priestly blessing. "'The Lord bless you and keep you; the Lord make His face shine upon you and be gracious to you; the Lord turn His face toward you and give you peace.'"

Zechariah closed his eyes as the Holy One's face shone on him, filling him, consuming him. The temple courtyards fell silent as a sweet breeze rustled about them along with God's overwhelming presence and peace. Then the word of the Lord began swelling inside Zechariah, and he stepped forward to speak it with joy: "'Shout and be glad, O Daughter of Zion. For I am coming, and I will live among you,' declares the Lord. 'Many nations will be joined with the Lord in that day and will become my people. I will live among you, and you will know that the Lord Almighty has sent me to you. . . .' Be still before the Lord, all mankind, because He has roused himself from His holy dwelling."

The dedication ceremony had ended. The great feast of celebration would begin. But Zechariah knew that this wasn't the end.

It was only the beginning.

Glossary

Abba—Father, Daddy.

Aron Ha Kodesh—The sacred ark in the Jewish house of worship where the Torah and other sacred scrolls are kept.

Bar Mitzvah—Son of the commandments—The ceremony at age twelve or thirteen at which a Jewish boy is considered a man and can read Scripture in the synagogue.

Beit Knesset—House of Assembly, later called a synagogue in Greek.

Bimah—The raised platform in a Jewish house of worship where Scripture is read.

Gan Eden—the Garden of Eden.

Haroset—A mixture of chopped apples, nuts, etc., eaten at Passover to remember the mortar used by slaves when building in Egypt.

Kippah—A small headcovering worn by Jewish men.

Levite—A descendant of the tribe of Levi, one of Jacob's twelve sons, who later became temple assistants.

Mikveh / Mikvoth (pl)—A bath used for ritual cleansing and purity.

Mishneh—The "second quarter" of Jerusalem, built during King Hezekiah's time.

Negev—The South, referring to the southern region of Israel.

Phylacteries—Small boxes containing Scripture that Jewish men attach to their foreheads and arms while praying. (See Deuteronomy 6:8).

Rebbe—Rabbi, teacher.

Saba—Grandfather.

Safta—Grandmother.

Seder—The Passover meal and celebration.

Shabbat—The Sabbath, a Jewish day of rest. It begins at sundown on Friday and lasts until sundown on Saturday.

Shalom—Peace. A greeting that can mean hello or good-bye.

Shalom bayit—Peace in the home.

Shofar—A musical instrument made from a ram's horn.

Simchat Torah—A holiday celebrating God's gift of the Torah at Mount Sinai.

Sotah—An adulteress.

Teshuvah—Repentance, turning from evil, changing directions in life.

Torah—The first five books of the Bible, which contain God's Law.

Yeshiva—A Jewish school where Scripture is studied.

Ziggurat—A stepped pyramid used for worshiping pagan gods, like the Tower of Babel.

A Note to the Reader

Careful study of Scripture and commentaries support the fictionalization of this story. To create authentic speech, the author has paraphrased the words of biblical figures such as Zechariah and Haggai. However, the New International Version has been directly quoted when characters are reading, singing, or reciting Scripture passages.

Interested readers are encouraged to research the full accounts of these events in the Bible as they enjoy the RESTORATION CHRONICLES.

Scripture references for *Return to Me:*

2 Kings 17:24–40
2 Kings 25:1–21
Ezra 1–6
Haggai 1–2
Zechariah 1–14
Daniel 5, 9

More From Bestselling Author Lynn Austin

To learn more about Lynn and her books, visit lynnaustin.org.

For the first time, beloved author Lynn Austin offers a glimpse into her private life as she shares the inspiring, deeply personal story of her search for spiritual renewal in the Holy Land. With gripping honesty, Lynn seamlessly weaves personal events with insights from Scripture as she finds hope, renewed faith, and a new sense of direction in her journey throughout Israel.

Pilgrimage

Experience the history and promises of the Old Testament in these dramatic stories of struggle and triumph. When invading armies, idol worship, and infidelity plague the life and legacy of King Hezekiah, can his faith survive the ultimate test?

CHRONICLES OF THE KINGS
Gods and Kings, Song of Redemption, The Strength of His Hand, Faith of My Fathers, Among the Gods